The Cup of Ghosts

ALSO BY PAUL DOHERTY
FROM CLIPPER LARGE PRINT

The Anubis Slayings
The Horus Killings
Murder Imperial
The Song of the Gladiator

The Cup of Ghosts

Paul Doherty

W F HOWES LTD

This large print edition published in 2006 by
W F Howes Ltd
Unit 4, Rearsby Business Park, Gaddesby Lane,
Rearsby, Leicester LE7 4YH

1 3 5 7 9 10 8 6 4 2

First published in 2005
by Headline Book Publishing

A CIP catalogue record for this book is available
from the British Library

ISBN 1 84505 927 1

Typeset by Palimpsest Book Production Limited,
Polmont, Stirlingshire
Printed and bound in Great Britain
by Antony Rowe Ltd, Chippenham, Wilts.

This book is dedicated to an awe-inspiring mother
Vivien Rose Self
Lost too early in life
From her loving family

PROLOGUE

Tolle Lege, Tolle Lege.
(Pick up and read, pick up and read.)

St Augustine of Hippo, *Confessions* VIII

'Bless me, Father, for I have sinned. It is many years since . . .' I sat back on my heels and gazed at the white, waxen face of the corpse stretched out on the low bier before me. Father Guardian, at least eighty-five summers old, stitched in his shroud, ready for the good brothers to carry him to the church to lie ringed by purple candles before the sanctuary, a hallowed place where angels hover so that the hordes of demons who prowl, hunting the souls of the dead, cannot trespass. Later those same brothers, the Poor Men of Grey Friars, which nestles under the shadow of St Paul's, would chant their requiem mass, and afterwards bury Father Guardian in God's Acre, to shelter beneath some battered cross until the elements melt and Christ comes again.

I describe Father Guardian as past his eighty-fifth

1

summer; I'm not much younger. For months I had prepared myself to be shrived by him. To the rest of the community I am a simple anchorite from her lonely cell, more concerned about cleaning the garden paths or scrubbing the kitchen flagstones. Father Guardian, however, suspected my secret. Often, when the other brothers were busy, he'd search me out in the apple orchard or the sunken garden where I'd be weeding the fringes of the carp pond. He'd touch me gently on the shoulder or pluck at the sleeve of my gown, and invite me to some shady arbour or lonely garden nook where we could sit and talk about the old days. I never told him much, though he knew who I was. How I'd served the Queen Mother, Isabella of France. How I had been with her from the time she descended into hell until she rose in glory, only to fall again. How I'd sheltered long in the shadow of the She-Wolf, been a disciple of 'that New Jezebel' (a clever play on her name). Oh yes, like a visored knight, I'd been in the heart of that bloody, tangled mêlée when the great ones toppled from gibbet ladders or knelt, as Edmund of Kent did, like a chained dog by a gate until a drunken felon severed their heads. I trusted Father Guardian. I dropped hints and told tales, sometimes referring to the great lords, all gone before God's judgement seat. I described my dreams, about corpses rotting on scaffolds or men, cowled and daggered, stealing through courtyards at the dead of night. Of shadowy meetings in ill-lit chambers, the tramp of armies, the neigh of war-horses; of great feasts and banquets where the wines of Bordeaux and Spain flowed like water from a broken cask, of sweetmeats, gorgeous tapestries and exquisitely decorated chambers; of silent, soft-footed murder in all its hideous forms, of my pursuits of the sons and daughters of that old assassin Cain.

I have seen the days and Father Guardian recognised that. Sometimes, rarely, I would talk of Isabella, she of the lustrous skin and fiery blue eyes, her hair like spun gold and a body even a friar would lust after. Isabella 'La Belle', the Beautiful, of France, who tore her husband from his throne. She locked him in Berkeley Castle, sealing him up like some rabid animal until, so the chronicles report, killers slipped in and, turning him over on his face, thrust a red-hot poker up to burn his bowels and so leave no mark upon the corpse. Of Mortimer, proud as an antlered stag, a king in his own right, a Welsh prince with his secret dreams of power. Of Hugh Despenser, his hair and beard the colour of a weasel, with darting green eyes, fingers itching and heart bubbling with lust to possess Isabella. Edward himself, the golden-haired, blue-eyed king, great of body and small of brain, followed by all the others in their silks and satins and high-heeled pointed boots; lords of the soil who had their day before being murderously dispatched into eternal night.

I closed my eyes then opened them, gazing

round Father Guardian's austere chamber, its limewashed walls, the floor bone-hard and dusty. Only the candles and a small chafing dish sprinkled with incense fended off the cold and the foul stench of death. I studied the corpse's white, pointed face, the eyes half closed, the lips slightly parted. Father Guardian had prayed for me, he'd told me that. Even as he leaned over the chalice to murmur the words of consecration or took the bread to turn it into Christ's blessed body, he always prayed the same petition: that one day I would kneel before him, make my confession and my peace with God, and so prepare my soul for its long journey to join the rest.

'Mathilde.' Father Prior would clasp my hands between his cold, thin fingers and nip the skin gently, those watery brown eyes staring at me compassionately. 'I feel it, Mathilde, your soul is heavy with sin. Your mind, memories and dreams are haunted, they reek of sour evil.'

Shrewd and cunning was Father Guardian. One of the few men I've met who could read a person's soul. Of course, I demurred. I told him that I would keep my secrets and argue my case before God's tribunal like any malefactor would before the King's Bench in Westminster Hall. Father Guardian would only sigh and let my hand go.

Last summer, around the Feast of the Birth of John the Baptist, I began to reflect. I felt as if I had a belly brimming with soured wine. I wanted to vomit, to purge, to clean the evil from my soul, so

I went and talked to her, Isabella, Queen of England, where she lies beneath her chest tomb just to the right of the high altar in Grey Friars. Ah, yes, that was where she asked to be buried, not in a shroud but in her wedding dress, even though she was well past her sixtieth year. As she died, coughing up her life blood, Isabella asked for my hand, begging me with her eyes.

'Mathilde, *ma doucette*!'

Her cheeks were sunken, her hair was grey, yet I could still glimpse the lustrous beauty of former days.

'Bury me,' she whispered, 'in my wedding dress, my husband's heart clasped between my hands but next to Mortimer, like a bride beside her lover! Promise me.'

I kept my promise. I begged to see her eagle-eyed son, Edward the Great Conqueror, Lord of England, Ireland, Scotland and France and any other lands he can seize. I crouched on my knees before him in the Jerusalem Chamber at Westminster Abbey. I whispered out his mother's last wish. The king, of course, cursed me, beat me about the shoulders, though at last he agreed. He ordered his sheriffs, marshals, bailiffs and beadles to clear the highway along Mile End, round past the Tower, so his mother's corpse could be processed in great honour and pomp, with trumpet, fife and drum, amidst gusts of fragrant incense, to be buried, after solemn requiem mass, beneath the flagstones of Grey Friars.

Later, months after his mother's death, the king sent his stonemasons and carpenters to erect a beautiful chest tomb for his 'beloved mother'. You can view it, with its crouching golden leopards and silver fleur-de-lis, its crowns and coronets, its pious inscriptions, all the macabre beauty of the grave. Edward did this as an act of reparation. Isabella had never forgiven him, not for what he'd done to her 'Gentle Mortimer', and that was what brought me to Grey Friars. I came to look after her tomb. The king ordered me here screaming, his foam-flecked lips curling like those of a snarling dog.

'You were with her in life,' he shouted. 'Stay with her in death.'

I joined the Poor Men of St Francis, the Grey Friars, accepting the Bishop of London's licence to be an anchorite in a cell in their grounds. Only Father Guardian knew from the start why I was really there. I was given menial tasks, the lowest of the low. On one matter, however, Father Guardian would brook no opposition.

'If Sister Mathilde wishes to pray by the old queen's tomb,' he declared at a chapter meeting, 'then she must be allowed to pray.'

I did so every day, round about three o'clock in the afternoon, when the church was empty and the good brothers never assembled to sing God's praises. I'd crouch like a dog and press my cheek against the cold stone, running my hand over the carved sculpting. In my mind I went back to some lush garden or splendid chamber with lozenge-shaped floor tiles, decorated cloths on the wall, a fire roaring under the mantled hearth, and everywhere the cloying perfume of my mistress. I spoke to her dead as I did to her alive. She used to call me her Lady of Hell. I was the keeper of her dark secrets.

Anyway, I digress. Last summer I went to her tomb on the eve of the Feast of the Birth of John the Baptist. I recall gazing at a painting on the wall of the Good Thief at Golgotha, his bloody, tattered corpse hanging from the cross, his face twisted in agony, turning to speak to the Saviour, to beg for salvation. Beneath the cross stood the tormentors of Christ with the faces of apes and monkeys, an appropriate scene. I often felt like that Good Thief, but there again, sometimes I allow self-pity to consume me as fire does dry kindling.

On that summer afternoon I closed my eyes, trying to ignore the painting, those ape-like faces, the grimacing monkey mouths, the hanging body laced with blood.

'I've seen so many corpses,' I whispered. I cannot seal the door to the past. The distraction sprang out of the dark heart of a nightmare, a memory of Hereford, and Despenser hanging from the seventy-foot-high gallows; Isabella and Mortimer watching his final torments, eating and drinking, toasting each other with their looted goblets. Despenser's corpse dangling like a doll, feet kicking the air; the executioner scaling the ladder to drag the half-dead man down to slit his stomach and rip off his testicles. Blood lapping out like water from a split cask as Despenser's screams rang across the market square.

'So much,' I whispered. 'So much.' Then I heard her voice, as she used to talk, standing behind me, whispering as if we were lovers.

'Cleanse yourself, Mathilde! Have your sins shriven, know some peace.'

I told Father Guardian this. He just laughed. He claimed the dead were too busy to bother with us. I should look into my own soul. He was talking to me near a fountain, its water splashing up. For some reason I lost my temper, the first time for years, certainly since coming to Grey Friars. I acted like a prisoner locked in a dark dungeon, throwing herself against the door, beating at the iron grille, desperate to get out. I sprang to my feet, striding up and down. Father Guardian grew perplexed.

'What's the matter, Mathilde?'

I crouched at his feet, grasping his bony knee, and stared fiercely at him, a look he'd never seen before. He'd forgotten I was once a player in Fortune's Great Game. I have seen hot blood spurt! I have fought all my life in the press of the court or against furtive, silent assassins. He sketched a cross above my head.

'What is the matter, Mathilde?'

'What is the matter, Father Guardian?' I replied hoarsely. 'I shall tell you about her life, I shall confess my sins.'

Those old eyes brightened. I half rose and, pressing my lips against his ear, began my confession. The faint colour in that old face quickly drained; he drew away, gazing at me horrorstruck.

'I would have to see the bishop,' he murmured. 'Such sins!'

'Such sins, Father Guardian?' I retorted. 'What does scripture say? "If your sins be red like scarlet, I shall wash them white as wool"? Well, Father Guardian, my sins are many, of the deepest scarlet, like the sky on a summer's evening or the red banners of war. I am steeped in villainy, Father Guardian. I am the Lady of Hell. I lived in the shadow of Isabella "La Belle", the Jezebel, the She-Wolf, the Virago Ferrea.'

'You must prepare yourself to receive the sacrament, examine your conscience,' he retorted. 'Be honest with yourself so you will be honest with God.'

By then I had recovered. I realised what I had said: that old man, on a cold stone seat near a fountain, had learnt more in those few precious moments than Edward, the king, would ever learn. Oh, others have tried. I have been offered bribes, lands, manors, even the marriage of some young man, a royal ward. I have always refused. I have met and loved the great love of my life. Moreover, I took an oath of secrecy to Isabella but, on reflection, I believe that oath has now been lifted; I am released from my obligation. On that day near the fountain I shuffled my sandalled feet and apologised for my temper. I promised Father Guardian how, as soon as Advent began, I would kneel in the shriving pew and confess all my sins. I joked how it would take a long time. Father Guardian glanced at me warily, shaking his head.

'Sister Mathilde, honesty is short and brief. Confess who you are rather than what you did.'

During the subsequent weeks I often reflected on his words. The more I searched my soul, the more I realised he had not spoken the full truth. To understand what I have done, to realise who I truly was, or who I am, I would have to describe who Isabella was: the princess from some romance of Arthur who arrived in England at the age of thirteen to marry Edward of Caernarvon and unite England and France in an alliance of peace which would stretch to eternity. Oh, the folly of princes! Father Guardian allowed me the use of the scriptorium and the library. I began to write in a cipher, which could only be translated by me, a legacy from my days as a healer. The weeks turned into months. Summer went, autumn arrived in gorgeous profusion. The paths and gardens of Grey Friars became carpeted with leaves which gleamed like copper before the rains fell and turned them into a dirty mush which I had to clear, stack, dry and burn. I promised Father Guardian that once Advent came and the church was cleaned in preparation for the coming of the Christ Child, I would make my confession.

However, the Lord Satan had not forgotten me. On the Feast of St Luke, suddenly like a thief in the night, death caught Father Guardian. He was found in his bed, sprawled slightly to one side, mouth gaping, eyes hard, his soul long gone to God.

I asked Father Bruno, the keeper of the scriptorium, a gentle, scholarly man with a stooped back and a face like that of a puzzled sparrow, if I could pay my own final respects. He agreed, so I knelt before Father Guardian's corpse. I crossed myself and gabbled a prayer I'd learnt as a child, then closed my eyes. I made a promise, a vow to Father Guardian: I would still make my confession, but not to some priest I didn't know, or one of the brothers, who would only recoil in horror. Father Guardian could sit on the other side of life's veil and hear me out.

On that occasion, after watching his corpse, I rose and noticed a scrap of parchment lying on the writing carrel where Father Guardian used to sit and meditate over some book of hours. I listened intently. The lay brothers on guard outside were gossiping amongst themselves. I crossed swiftly to the desk and picked up the parchment. I immediately recognised Boethius, an extract from his *Consolation of Philosophy*: 'My very strength, Fortune declares, this is my unchanging sport. I turn my wheel which spins the circle. I delight to make the lowest turn to the top, the highest to the bottom. Carry me to the top if you want but, on this condition, that you think it's no unfairness, to sink when the rule of the game demands it.' I smiled. Father Guardian had left this message just for me. I have been on Fortune's fickle wheel, at bottom, top and around again. I have known the glories of victory and the bitter ashes of defeat.

Now Father Guardian had always been good to

11

me, giving me pennies or a silver piece. I had carefully hidden these away. A serving boy I trusted, for a bribe, went to the scribblers and parchment sellers in Cheapside. He brought back rolls of vellum, ink, sharpened quills, a pumice stone, and sand to dry the ink, everything a clerk of the chancery or scribe in a muniment room would need. I will keep my vow in the dark hours of the night. I will buy more candles and light them to write my story and that of Isabella, who controlled the Wheel of Fortune and sent it spinning so that kings and princes, lords and ladies, the mighty and the great crashed to earth whilst others were lifted high in exaltation. I will write about the other great love of my life, the study of physic. Father Guardian knew of my art and skill, but I refused to practise it even though he showed me the friary library. I have done with study. I have read the books, be it those of Islam such as Haly Abbas' *Complete Book of the Medical Art,* those of the ancients such as Dioscorides' *Herbarium.* Galen's *Therapeutics,* Caelius' *De Medicina,* or the texts from Salerno and Montpellier. I can mix moss and stale milk to create a powder which can scour and heal the filthiest wound. I can tell you if a man has taken his own life, died from a rebellion of the humours or suffered a death other than his natural end. Oh yes, murder in all its guises! Like the first I studied – Sir Hugh Pourte, sprawled in a courtyard, his skull cracked like a walnut with the blood and brains spilling out. The first time I went through that dark door to the House of Mysterious Death. Yes, I'll begin there, but first, how did I arrive there?

So many years ago! So many lifetimes! Yet no one can contradict me. No one can stop me hurrying down the ill-lit passage of time to those autumn days of October 1307 when I sheltered in Paris, enjoying the sweet life of youth, my heart brimming with ambition to be a physician. I'd hoped for that. I'd prayed for it. I'd spent every waking hour thinking about it, ever since I had left the village of Bretigny to work for my uncle in Paris, where I had proven myself to be the most ardent scholar, avid for the horn book. I could write all my letters correctly, use the calculus, and had learnt the Norman French of the court. I became most skilled in learning. My mother's only child, she lavished on me all the love and care she used to lavish on her husband. My father had been an apothecary from a family of healers. Ever since I was knee-high to a buttercup, he talked to me about his art, be it in the fields and woods, where he would instruct me in the use of herbs, or in that dark treasure chamber of our own little house with its manuscripts and leech books, its jars and coffers crammed with healing potions and deadly black powders. Learning? I took to learning as a bird would to the wing. My father died; my mother could do little for me. She would often gaze at me sad-eyed.

'Mathilde,' she would murmur, 'with your hair as black as night, your dark eyes and pale skin,' she'd smile, 'you might catch the eye of a merchant widower. You are slender and tall . . .' She would break off as I pulled an ugly face, and laugh. 'Or you could go to your uncle in Paris.'

I made my choice, so she dispatched me into the great city, to the one man I grew to admire above all others: my uncle, Sir Reginald de Deyncourt, Senior Preceptor in the House of the Temple, a physician-general, a man dedicated to serving God and his order, as well as those who needed his skill, until Philip of France, that silver-headed demon, decided to intervene.

CHAPTER 1

Charity is wounded, Love is sick.

'*A Song of the Times*', 1272–1307

'*Oh dies irae, dies illa.*' So the sequence from the mass for the dead proclaims: 'Oh day of wrath, day of mourning.' I shall never forget my day of wrath, my day of mourning: Thursday 12 October 1307. I was about twenty years of age, apprenticed to Uncle Reginald. I'd journeyed from our small farm near Bretigny to Paris with fervent aspirations of becoming a physician and an apothecary. My uncle, a gruff old soldier, one of the two men I've ever loved, the father who replaced the one who disappeared when I was a child, took me into his care. He lavished upon me all the love and affection Tobit did on Sarah. A true gentlemen, a perfect knight in every way, Uncle Reginald was a man of deep prayer and piety. He fasted three times a week and always went to Notre Dame, late on Friday evenings, to place a pure wax candle before the Statue of the Virgin. He would kneel on the paving stones and stare up at the face of the lady he called his *Chatelaine*. Uncle Reginald was a man of few words, of moderate temper and sober dress. He was a saint in a world of sinners. He always thought I'd be the same. However, my early time with him was only an introduction to a life steeped in every type of villainy cooked in hell.

You must remember, before I narrate, what has happened, how the world has changed since my youth. War now rages from the Middle Sea all through France and the northern states. The Great Pestilence has made itself felt; a towering yellow skeleton, armed with a sharp scythe, has culled the flower of our people. Asmodeus, the foulest of demons, the Lord of Disease, has arrived amongst us. Cities lie empty, their streets strewn with the rotting, putrid dead. The symptoms are always the same: the curse of the bubo beneath the armpit, the body on fire as the stomach vomits black and yellow bile. The smouldering funeral pyres have become symbols of our age. The sky is blackened by smoke, whilst the sweet fertile earth is polluted, yawning to receive our myriad dead.

In my youth, the faculty of medicine at the University of Paris was like a dog, hair all raised, teeth bared, jaws snarling against women who practised medicine, but it had yet to bite. Later it did, at the time of the great killing in England, the Year of Our Lord 1322, when it prosecuted Jacqueline Felicie for practising as a physician without medical training. Felicie declared, supported by evidence and witnesses, that she had cured people where licensed graduates had failed. She also maintained (and I have read her defence) how women preferred to be treated by one of their own kind. 'It is better and more appropriate,' Felicie argued, 'that a wise and sagacious woman, skilled in the practice of physic, should visit another woman to examine her and to investigate the hidden secrets of her being, rather than a man.' Poor Felicie, her defence did not hold. In my youth it was different. I was protected. Uncle Reginald was a high-ranking Templar. He was also a skilled surgeon and physician who had practised his art in Outremer, the Holy Land of Palestine. He had been at the siege of Acre and campaigned in the hot lands around the Middle Sea. He had also experienced the healing arts of the Moors, Saracens and other followers of Mahomet. Oh, the Queen of Heaven and Raphael the Great Archangel Healer be my witnesses, Uncle Reginald was a physician *sans pareil*, skilled and cunning, a true magister – a master of his art.

Do not be misled by the legends of the Temple, the allegations of sodomy and sacred rites. True, the Templars had their secrets, they possessed the likeness of the face of our Saviour as well as his burial shroud, but they truly were men of this earthly city: bankers, warriors, and above all, physicians. They venerated the Virgin Mother Mary and extolled women more than other men did. Uncle Reginald was much influenced by the followers of

St Francis, especially the Liberian Anthony of Padua, who praised our sex and would say no ill word against us.

Uncle Reginald was a Physician-general, a supervisor of the Temple hospitals in Paris, and that was where my education began. 'You want to drink at the fountain of knowledge,' he thundered, 'then so ye shall!' My studies were highly disciplined. Uncle Reginald would make me translate a passage from Latin into the common patois then into Norman French before rendering it back into Latin. He'd give me a list of herbs, their proper names, powers and effects, then take the list away and test me rigorously. He taught me the gift of tongues and how to imitate the correct meaning. Above all, he taught me medicine. I became his apprentice as he moved from hospital to hospital, from one sick chamber to another. I'd stare, watch, observe, remember and recite: these were his axioms. 'Mathilde,' he would wave his finger, staring at me with lowered brows above piercing eyes, 'we physicians cannot heal; we can only try to prevent as well as offer some relief. Remember what you see. Observe, always observe, study carefully, define the problem and propose, if you can, a solution.'

Uncle Reginald was critical of the claims of other physicians. He bitterly attacked Lanfranc of Milan's *Science of Surgery* and openly mocked physicians' obsessions with urine, faecal matter and purgation. He was appreciative of the Arab commentators Averroes and Avicenna, deeply interested in Galen and, above all, in the writings of Bernard de Gordon of Montpellier, whose *Regimen Sanitatis* he would swear by. Uncle Reginald was fascinated by the beat of the blood in the wrist or throat, the odour of his patients, their eyes, tongue and the texture of their skin. 'Observe,' he would bark, 'examine, then reflect.' He was pessimistic on what he could achieve and was always downcast if he felt tumours or lumps within the body. On herbs and potions, however, he was most skilled, arguing that that was one field of knowledge where he could both sow and reap the harvest. I became equally proficient in the mixture and effects of different plants: what proportion should be given, what results expected.

'We must be humble,' Uncle Reginald argued, 'and recognise our limitations. Herbs are our weapons, the arrows in our quiver, the one thing we can control; that, and the cleanliness of what we do. Mathilde,' he would lecture as he walked up and down some chamber, 'the cause of infection I do not know, but its effects are all around us. So wash your hands, clean a wound, apply a pure poultice, and always remember that dirt and death walk hand in hand.'

For eight years that was my life, my being, my very soul; from its first blossoming to the full ripening. Uncle Reginald! Whether I trotted beside him down a row of beds or was sent like some herald into the city to buy this or that. Other young women married, but my life was Uncle Reginald. God rest him. God knows, I have spent most my life, at least in physic, obeying him.

My life, at least with Uncle Reginald, ended as I have said on Thursday 12 October 1307, when Philip of France, Philip 'Le Bel', he of the light blue eyes and silver hair, struck like a hawk and destroyed the Temple. My uncle and I had been visiting a farm the Temple owned just outside Paris, the fields around it being rich in herbs. We unexpectedly returned to the city. My uncle decided to stay in a small tavern close to the Porte de St Denis. From its cobbled yard I could see the soaring gallows of Montfaucon and the red-tiled roof of the Filles de Dieu, the Good Sisters, who always gave the condemned criminals, hustled up to be hanged from the great gibbet above its deep pit, a final cup of wine. On that heinous day my uncle acted like a man condemned to those gallows. He was troubled, agitated and ordered me to keep close in my chamber just beneath the eaves of the old tavern.

I, of course, was desperate to return to Paris: a farmer's daughter, I had become bored with the beauties of nature, its open fields, lonely meadows, brooding granges, rat-infested barns and silent, twisting track-ways. I was only too pleased to forsake them all and plunge into the city of Paris, as eagerly as any miser would a horde of silver coins. I'd grown to love the city, with its various markets: the Place Mordare for bread, the Grand Châtelet for meat, Saint Germain for sausages, the Petit Pont for flour and eggs, the great herb market on the quayside of the Ile de Cité, or Le Marché aux Innocents where you could buy anything you wanted. Noise and gaiety were my constant companions. People shoving and pushing, whispering and shouting:

'Dieu vous garde!'

'Je vous salue!'

I'd been my uncle's messenger to this place or that, coursing like a hare through the city. By my twentieth summer I was still fascinated by the chestnut-sellers from Normandy, the cheese-hawkers, the plump apple-sellers with cheeks as red as the fruit they sold. My uncle had taught me all about the tricks of the market. Innkeepers and wine merchants who mixed water with wine, or bad wine with good. Women who thinned their milk and, to make their cheeses look richer and heavier, soaked them in broth. Drapers who laid their cloths out on the night grass so in the morning they weighed heavier. Butchers who soaked their meat or fishmongers who used pig's blood to redden the gills of stale and discoloured fish. Clothiers who had one yardstick for selling and another for buying. He also advised me to be wary about those who sold goods in dark streets to deceive the unsuspecting, and made me memorise all I learnt and observed about the city I loved. Each trade had its quarter. Apothecaries in the Cité. Parchment-sellers, scribes, laminators and book-sellers in the Latin Quarter. Money-changers and goldsmiths on the Grand Pont. Bankers near the Rue Saint Martin and mercers in the Rue Saint Denis. The colour and hurly-burly of city life never seemed to die. Richly brocaded burgesses sweeping down to picnic by the Seine. Knights in half-armour riding by on fine palfreys or noble chargers. Lavishly dressed gallants posing with falcons and sparrow-hawks on their wrists. It was like visiting a church and going from one wall painting to the next. So much to see! I took to it with all the vigour and curiosity of youth.

I loved the city! I was well protected. My future ran like a broad, clear thoroughfare before me. When I wasn't at my studies or in the hospital, I'd wander from quarter to quarter, observing the beggars in the church doors or by the bridges; the peasants coming in from the country with their carts and wheelbarrows; the artisans and craftsmen shouting and gesticulating from behind their stalls; the wandering jongleurs, monks and friars in their dark gowns and pointed hoods; the canons of the cathedral with all their pomp and ceremony; the ermine-clad professors of the Sorbonne and their motley retinues of students and scholars. Royal couriers beat their way through the crowd with their white wands of office. Heralds in resplendent tabards, trumpets lifted, shrilled out harsh music to draw the attention of the crowds before a proclamation was read out. Harness jingled like bells as nobles from their great houses rode down past the bridges and gates of the city to hunt in the fields beyond. Ladies lounged in their litters, taking the air. Judges in their bright scarlet, surrounded by royal men-at-arms, processed down to the law courts. Pilgrims off to Saint Geneviéve or Notre Dame chanted their prayers or sang sweet hymns. Prisoners, manacles held fast, were driven under the whip to the Grand Châtelet. Clerks and scribes scurried along to the great palace and castle of the Ile where Philip ruled France as a hawk does its field, ever-watchful, ever-menacing.

I was impatient to visit these city sights again. I couldn't understand my uncle's harshness. He towered over me in the tap room of that tavern, grasping me by the shoulder, pushing me towards the stairs.

'Go up to your chamber, girl!'

He very rarely called me that. It was always 'Mathilde', or '*ma fille*'. Uncle Reginald's face looked strained, a haunted look in his eyes, he kept glancing over his shoulder towards the door.

'What's the matter, sir?' I demanded.

'Nothing,' he whispered, then he quoted a line from the Gospels: '*Tenebrae facta*. Darkness fell.' I recognise that phrase now, the description given to the night Judas left to betray Christ. Again, I tried to reason. I was hoping to go into the city, perhaps visit one of the taverns near the hospital, mix with the scholars, dance a jig or indulge in some other revelry. My uncle lifted his hand and glared at me.

'I have never struck you. I will if you do not obey my order. Go to your chamber, small as it is, rat-eaten and mouse-gnawed, it's the safest place for you. Stay there until I come.'

I hurried up the stairs, my feet drumming on the wooden steps. I pulled aside the battered door and flung myself into the chamber, blinking furiously, trying to quell the tears of fury stinging my eyes. The chamber was narrow and dirty though the bed was comfortable, its sheets clean – my uncle would insist on that – whilst the servant who brought my food up had covered it with a wooden bowl against the mice which scurried in the corners. Cobwebs hung like sheets from the rafters. I moved to the window, a small wooden casement door filled with horn, and pushed it open. At least I could look out over the city. The sky was a dullish grey, a cold wind had risen. It was that dying time as autumn fades and winter with icy touch makes its presence felt. The room was cold. I closed the window and noticed the wine just within the door, a battered pewter pot next to a small bowl. I filled the bowl to the brim and drank quickly, then went across and lay on the bed.

When my uncle shook me awake, it was dark. He was leaning over me, face close to mine.

'Get up,' he urged. 'Get up now.'

I was almost dragged to my feet. My uncle had brought my cloak and belt with a dagger in its wooden scabbard. He made me wrap the belt about me. I protested. I said I needed to visit the latrine. He laughed strangely and pushed me out of the chamber down the stairs. By the time I reached the bottom, I'd clasped the cloak securely. The cold night air woke me roughly. My uncle thrust a piece of parchment and a bag of coins into my hands, then gestured frantically towards the narrow gate leading to the alleyway beyond. A cresset torch lashed to a pole, thrust into the soft mud between the cobbles, provided some light for the ostlers and grooms flitting like ghosts across the yard. I turned. Uncle stood concealed half in the shadows. At last, in the flickering flame of that torch, I glimpsed his terror. He'd aged, his face was drawn and haggard, his eyes red-rimmed. He kept muttering to himself, wary of a door closing, a dog barking or strangers slipping through the darkness. He took my hand and pressed it against the bag of jingling coins.

'You are to go now, Mathilde.'

'Why, Uncle?'

'Don't ask.' He moved his face closer. 'For the love of God, Mathilde, don't ask, just go. Take what I have given you. The gate of Saint Denis is still open. You are to enter the city. Make your way to the house of Simon de Vitry near the Grand Pont. You know him; I've sent you on errands to his house. He's a cloth merchant, a banker and a man I trust. Do exactly what he tells you.' He pushed me towards the gate, thrusting me into the alleyway.

'Go, go,' he hissed through the darkness. 'Go now, Mathilde, before they come.'

Something about his tone, those words . . . I caught his terror. He flapped his hands, a gesture

I had never seen him make, indicating that I must run. I wanted to stay, discover who 'they' were. Something about him, just standing there in the poor light, the torch spluttering behind him, the way his shoulders hunched, his hands flapping like the wings of a pinioned bird . . . I turned and slipped into the shadows.

Eternity has passed since that hideous night but I remember it well. I ran blindly through the streets, tears stinging my eyes. On the one hand, like any young woman, I had a grievance against my uncle; my resentment festered. Yet I'd caught the smell of terror, the rank odour of fear, and I wondered what was to happen. I recall stopping on the corner of a square. Above me a statue of the patron saint of that quarter gazed blindly down in the light of the candle burning beneath it. I stared back and tried to recall what had happened that day. We'd arrived at the tavern early that morning. Uncle had left me, gone into the city and returned a stranger; that's right, his manner had changed, distracted, agitated, bribing the landlord for this or that. One thing I did notice: he'd removed his Templar ring and any other sign that he belonged to that order.

I heard a sound and glanced around. Archers dressed in the blue and gold royal livery, gleaming sallets on their heads, were gathering across the square, spilling out of the side streets. Knights in half-armour made their way out on snorting destriers, preceded by footmen carrying flambeaux.

The air filled with the clatter of rasping hooves, the creak of leather, the jingle of harness. Beneath all this the ominous clatter of weapons, swords being unsheathed, shields being slung, orders rapped out. Dull, threatening sounds seeping through the smoky air like a foul mist. Across the square beggars had torched a bonfire of rubbish in front of a church. The leaping flames revealed the tympanum above the doorway; a vivid depiction of Christ coming on the Last Day, escorted by angels with fiery swords to repel the demon lords of the air. Christ the Judge seemed to be coming for me!

I ran like a whippet through the undergrowth, down lanes and runnels, the half-timbered houses leaning over as if conspiring to conceal the starlit sky. I slipped on a mound of dirt, drove away yapping mongrels, whining beggars and screeching cats. Jesus Miserere! I was innocent! I was a maid hurrying through the hideous runnels of Paris! A thousand nightmares lurked in the shadows, but knowledge inspires fear. I had no real experience, not then, of how vulnerable a woman truly is when protection is withdrawn. The sons of men are also the sons of Cain: '*In hominum mundo, lupus homini lupus* – in the world of men, man is wolf to man;' but to women he is a ravening beast! True, some hearts sing a noble hymn, but it is often hidden beneath the raucous howling of the pack. On that night I was an innocent, fleeing miraculously through the pens of countless savage predators. Perhaps an unseen angel flew before me with a face of fire and a flaming sword. I was also young and I was armed. The dark shadows slipping out of doorways slunk back. An unnamed terror drove me on, lacing my face with sweat, soaking my body in its icy coldness.

Thank God I knew Paris! Twisting, turning like a hare, I reached La Rue des Moines leading down to the Grand Pont and the great stone-built house of Simon de Vitry, the mercer. It stood in its own grounds. The postern gate was open. I flung myself through, knocking aside the sleepy-eyed, ancient night porter. Across the grass I flew like a speeding arrow; the kitchen door was bolted. I ran around the side of the house, gasping and cursing, up the main steps, grasped the iron chain and pulled until the bell tolled like a tocsin through the house. The patter of running feet echoed faintly. In a window to my right a light flared as a candle-lantern was lit. Chains were dropped, bolts drawn, and the door swung open. I recognised Monsieur Simon. He gazed at me in surprise, then beckoned me in. I slipped through the door and gave way to my exhaustion, slumping down to the ground, fighting for breath. The merchant, a kindly man with the face of a genial monk, crouched next to me, pulling his winter robe close about. His breath smelt of wine, his fingers were cold, his eyes anxious.

'What is the matter, Mathilde?' he asked. 'Are you in trouble? Were you attacked?'

I handed over the parchment my uncle had given me, but even as Monsieur Simon took it, I cursed my own stupidity. I wished I'd stopped and read it. The merchant walked across the hallway to where a solitary candle flared on a table beneath a picture of St Anthony exorcising demons. In the shifting light these fiends of hell sprang to life. Monsieur Simon picked the candle up and, turning his back on me, walked into his chancery. I glanced at the doorway, the light beneath it strengthened as more candles were lit. A short while later the merchant came back as agitated as I was, fingers fluttering, wetting his lips. He knelt down beside me.

'Mathilde, *ma petite*, you must come, you must come.' He half dragged me to my feet and pushed me across into the chancery. The piece of parchment was gone. Logs crackled in the sullen red heat of the fire. Whatever Uncle had written this merchant had destroyed. He sat me down in a chair and brought a jug of ale tasting musty and tangy, then roused his household, two servants and a maid, whilst the chancery clerk, his trusted steward, was brought into the room. I was asked to stay outside on a bench. The chancery door was locked and bolted. I heard whispers, raised voices, cupboards, coffers and chests being opened as if the merchant had abruptly decided to make a full tally of what he was owed. The clerk was dispatched into the night. Only then did Monsieur Simon, at least an hour after I had arrived, join me on the bench. He gazed at me strangely, as if weighing my worth.

'You'd best come with me.'

The house was opulent, with a fine built-in staircase. He took me up past two furnished galleries to a fetid garret, very similar to the one at the tavern. He ushered me in and sat for a while on a stool staring sorrowfully at me.

'What is the matter, monsieur?' I asked.

'What is your name?' he replied.

'Why, monsieur, you know my name. I am Mathilde, my uncle is—'

De Vitry sprang up and poked me in the shoulder.

'You are no longer Mathilde de Ferrers,' he said, 'but Mathilde de Clairebon. You are my distant cousin. You come from Poitiers. You have some knowledge of books and physic. Your mother died recently so you came to work in my house, isn't that correct?'

'Monsieur Simon,' I gasped, 'what is this about? Why is my name being changed?'

He gestured vaguely towards the window.

'Sit down, sit down, Mathilde.' He went across, pulled the door firmly close and secured the bolts. He then brought his stool nearer, first placing a candle between us. He studied me with a mixture of anger and sadness, as if he wanted to help, yet resented my presence.

'Mathilde, I will be like a bowman,' he whispered. 'I will fire the arrow as close as I can to the mark. There have been rumours for days, how King Philip of France wishes to move against the Order of the Temple—'

'Impossible!' I interrupted.

'Listen, Mathilde.' He tapped me gently on the cheek. 'What your uncle discovered today is that tomorrow morning, every Templar in the Kingdom of France will be arrested on charges of practising sorcery, black magic, sodomy and God knows what else.'

'Lies!' I blustered back.

'What the king wishes is what the king wants,' Monsieur Simon replied. 'There has been chatter amongst the bankers and the merchants for many a year about Philip's treasuries being empty. He lusts after the gold and silver, the wealth, the lands, the granges, the barns, the pastures and the meadows of the Templars. He believes the order is a coven of witches and sorcerers, warlocks and wizards. He has petitioned Pope Clement V to suppress it, arrest its leaders, every knight, your uncle amongst them—'

I would have jumped to my feet but Monsieur Simon pushed me back.

'No. Listen, Mathilde, to what I say. If this is true, if Philip of France has decided to destroy the Temple, your uncle and his companions, anyone who has anything to do with the Temple and wears its insignia, be they knight, serjeant, page, squire or maid, is under suspicion. You cannot help your uncle. By tomorrow nightfall he will be arrested. He may try to flee but he'll be captured. The charges the Templars face are hideous.'

'Why?' I asked.

'Greed,' Monsieur Simon replied. 'Pure greed,

the desire of a powerful king to plunder a rich order. Mathilde, about seven years ago, Philip of France wished to join the Temple order himself; he wished to become its Grand Master on the death of his wife.' He lowered his voice. 'They say Philip actually murdered his wife, Jeanne de Navarre, in order to secure this, to become a bachelor, a celibate, but the Templars refused him. Philip never forgives an injury or an insult. He also needs money. He doesn't care how he obtains that money, or what lies he fashions.'

'But the Pope?' I gasped.

'The Pope,' Monsieur Simon grimaced, 'the Pope, Bertrand De Got, Clement V, is Philip's friend, sheltering in exile at Avignon! What do you think Clement V will say, especially when Philip offers him some of the plunder?'

'But the other princes?' I stammered. I knew a little of Templar affairs and recalled my uncle's description of how the order owned houses from the wilds of Ireland to the borders of the icy lands in the East.

Monsieur Simon hunched his shoulders.

'There is nothing like treasure, Mathilde, to turn a man's heart!'

'And me?' I asked.

'If you go out into that street, if you are recognised for what you are,' he wagged a bony finger in my face, 'you will be arrested. You are no longer Mathilde de Ferrers but Mathilde de Clairebon from the town of Poitiers, my distant poor kinswoman come to act as a maid in my house. Don't betray me, Mathilde. Don't put me and mine in danger, otherwise I will turn you over to the royal serjeants. They'll manacle you, load you with chains and drag you to the Grand Châtelet or some other dungeon where you risk either being buried alive, or facing a mockery of a trial before being taken out to be hanged or burned.' He chewed on his tongue. 'I could still do that. There will be a reward, money offered to those who betray Templars or their kin, not many will escape Philip's net.'

My hand dropped to the dagger in my belt.

'Don't threaten me!' Monsieur Simon scoffed. 'Your threats mean nothing to me. I have retainers. I have only,' he fished under his robe and brought out a silver whistle on a gold chain, 'to blow on this and your life will be over, as simple as snuffing out a candle. But I owe your uncle a favour. Many years ago he saved my life; since then he has always treated me honourably. I'm doing this for him, not for you. You are my prisoner. This chamber will become your world until I tell you the time of change has arrived.'

'And my uncle?'

'Believe me,' Monsieur Simon replied, squinting his eyes, 'if I could help your uncle I would. There is nothing I can do. Shall I tell you what I will do, Mathilde? What all the merchants and bankers of Paris will be doing tomorrow? They'll be opening their ledgers and household books. They'll be poring over their calculus. How much does the Temple order owe them? How much do they owe the Temple? They'll find, like me, that they owed more than they were owed. So we'll all keep silent. The king has removed a problem; if that's what the king wants, then the king shall have it. The Templars have no friends! You have one friend, me. Now, Mathilde de Clairebon from Poitiers, do you understand? Do you understand?' he repeated. 'If you fail me, I shall betray you, as simply,' he snapped his fingers, 'as that!'

I was too terrified, too anxious, too surprised to object. I nodded dumbly and moved across to the bed, I lay down, turning my back to him, and I crossed my arms and drew my legs up as I did when I was a child, when the shadows on the far side of my bedchamber were really phantasms of the night waiting to pollute me. I heard him leave.

The next morning when I woke up, my door was locked and bolted. I couldn't leave so I became Monsieur Simon's prisoner. The chamber must have been used as a cell before. It boasted a small cubicle built into the outside wall with its own latrine, a jakes pot over a narrow gully. After two days the stench grew so offensive the steward brought up pails of rainwater to clean it.

Monsieur Simon also brought me food, some clothes and a psalter, as well as a copy of Joinville's *Chronicle of the Crusades*. He refused to tell me what was happening in Paris.

Weeks passed. Looking out of the window, an arrow slit aperture, I watched the frost harden, the trees shed their leaves. One night Monsieur Simon came to see me. He asked how I was, said my imprisonment would soon be over and that tomorrow morning he would take me out. I was roused before dawn. The room was freezing cold, the small charcoal brazier had long smoked itself to ash and the candles had guttered to blackened wicks.

'Quick, quick.' Monsieur Simon gestured. 'Quick, quick, come!'

I dressed swiftly. The merchant gave me a heavy robe with a deep cowled hood.

'Wear that,' he ordered.

We went down the stairs and broke our fast in the scullery on a bowl of steaming oatmeal and some watered ale served by the sleepy-eyed maid. We left the house, slipping into the alleyway. I recalled the night I fled here. Now the streets were fairly deserted. I glimpsed certain images as we hurried along. A cowled Capuchin priest, preceded by little boys swinging a lantern and ringing a bell, carried the viaticum in a pyx to someone at death's door. Beggars cried for alms. Cripples slouched on the icy steps of churches, clacking-dishes out, pale, pinched faces pleading for mercy. A group of roisterers staggered by, bellies full of ale, mouths spitting curses. A prostitute in a tawny gown, an orange wig on her balding head, shouted abuse from a doorway. Monsieur Simon, grasping my arm, hurried me on. Every so often he would pause to ensure the hood and cowl were pulled close over my head. We entered the main thoroughfare. Doors were opening, stalls being laid out. The stench was rich, a mixture of saltpetre strewn to cover the odours from emptied cesspots, and piles of rotting vegetables heaped in corners.

'Monsieur Simon,' I murmured, 'where are we going?'

'Shut up,' he urged. 'Keep your face hidden.'

We turned and twisted. Eventually I recognised the thoroughfare leading down to Montfaucon, the execution place, the slaughteryard of Paris. Crowds were already thronging. Monsieur Simon approached the men-at-arms guarding the path. He whispered to a serjeant, coins changed hands, and we were allowed a place close to the road. I could see the entrance to the Maison des Filles de Dieu. The good nuns were already clustered on the steps, goblets of wine in their hands. Somewhere close, a beggar boy chanted a death carol, 'La mort de vie', his dirge deepening my sombre mood.

The crowds grew quickly, more people spilling out on to the thoroughfare, eager to catch a glimpse of what was going to happen. The blast of a trumpet cut through the morning air, followed by the dull beat of the tambours. I strained my neck, peering over the guards. The heralds came first in their blue and silver tabards, trumpets blowing, drums rattling; behind them lines of men-at-arms, steel helmets glistening. A company of royal archers followed, leading the execution carts, the hangman and his assistants dressed in black leather tunics, red masks concealing their faces. The tumbril they sat in was full of their torture implements as well as the ladders, ropes, and chains used to hang their victims. This was followed by another cart. Six grey figures huddled there. I found it difficult to breathe, my heart racing, stomach lurching. I wanted to be sick. I knew who was in that cart! It approached slowly, wheels creaking, the oxen pulling it being guided by a red-masked executioner who kept cutting the air with his whip. The cart drew alongside. I slipped through the guards and, like others, grabbed the side of the tumbril as if I enjoyed studying the faces of men about to die. They all looked the same, dressed in soiled robes, feet bare, their faces masks of injuries, bruises, welts and cuts, beards and hair a tangled mess. They reeked of the prison, the filth and mud they had squatted in for weeks.

'Monsieur,' I gasped. A man inside the cart lifted his face and I gazed into Uncle Reginald's eyes. They were dulled; his nose was strangely twisted and swollen; a bruise on his right cheek had blossomed purple and ripe.

'Uncle,' I whispered.

He shook his head. 'Vengeance is mine, said the Lord,' he hissed. 'Remember that, Mathilde, vengeance is His.' I caught the foul stench of his body then, with surprising strength, he pushed me away as if I was a tormentor. I staggered back. Monsieur Simon caught me by the arm and pulled me away. I stood and watched the execution carts reach the gibbet of Montfaucon soaring above the deep pit beneath. The executioners scrambled like monkeys up the ladders. The ropes were fixed, the nooses hung. Once ready, the prisoners were hustled from the cart and up the ladders. These were taken away and the bodies danced in the air, as the victims, strangling in their nooses, fought for breath. I felt ice cold, as if all my blood, all my humours had frozen. I can't remember how Uncle died. All I saw were six men perform that *danse macabre,* before falling silent, heads down, feet slightly swinging, as death gave them blessed relief.

Monsieur Simon dragged me away, pushing me ahead of him back down the streets to his house. When we reached it, he took me into his comfortable solar. Tapestries and paintings adorned the walls, its floorboards, polished to gleaming, were covered with thick Turkey rugs, whilst a fire roared in the mantled hearth. He led me to a stool, brought me a cup of posset and sat next to me, shaking his head, whispering under his breath. I allowed my body to thaw even as I tried to curb the rage boiling within me.

'Why?' I asked.

'I have told you why. Philip of France lusts after the wealth of the Templars. The knights themselves he does not need. They all face charges of sorcery, wizardry, sodomy, idolatry, as well as crimes I've never even heard of!'

He let me stay near the fire most of that morning. I remember studying the triptych on the wall which celebrated the martyrdom and glory of St Agnes. Strange, isn't it, how God works His secret purposes? I would see that painting again in a place I least expected. For the rest I warmed myself and wept. I wept for what I had seen and for what I had lost. I wept for my uncle and raged at Philip of France. My anger didn't subside; I just grew weary. Monsieur Simon called his steward and maid. They brought up a chair and the good merchant moved me, like a mother would her child, to huddle there, shrouding me in a woollen robe. Afterwards he crouched beside me, whispering his warnings. How I was to keep my name changed and do exactly what he said.

'And what is that?' I asked sleepily, wearily. I recognised the goodness of this man; hard-headed, sharp and acquisitive, nevertheless Monsieur Simon had kept his promise to my uncle.

'The best place to hide you,' the mercer's face creased into a smile, 'is where no one will look: the royal household! I have friends. I have, how can I put it, people who owe me money. In return for a favour, such debts will be cancelled.' He paused. 'You must leave France, Mathilde, and never return. It's best for both of us.'

'But how?' I stirred in my chair, my sleepiness forgotten, the pain of seeing my uncle hang now dulled by the drugged wine this merchant had given me. 'How can I leave France, where do I go? My life is here. My mother is little more than a peasant woman.' I laughed. 'What help can she provide? What assistance can you give, Monsieur Simon?'

'Listen now.' He brought the stool closer. 'As I said, the best place for you to hide is the one place they will never look, the royal household. No, no, listen.' He lifted a hand. 'I know members of the retinue of Charles de Valois, the king's brother. I will discharge their debts in return for a favour. You know Edward of England?'

I shrugged. 'A warrior king,' I replied. 'My uncle talked of his wars against the Welsh somewhere to the west and against the Scots in the north.'

'A warrior king,' Monsieur Simon agreed. 'I have met Edward of England on many an occasion as I have . . .' He paused, as if checking himself. 'Anyway, many years ago, during the reign of Pope Boniface VIII, Edward of England was trapped by Philip of France. Gascony, the great wine fields around Bordeaux, still belonged to the English. Philip, through trickery, occupied it. Edward, busy in his own wars, had to swear to Pope Boniface that his eldest son, also named Edward, would marry Philip's infant daughter Isabella. At the same time Edward of England, a widower, agreed to marry Philip's whey-faced, pale-skinned sister Margaret; that marriage went ahead, a treaty was sealed and Gascony was restored to the English. Edward of England, however, did not wish to marry what he calls his Prince of Wales, his heir apparent, to a French princess. Do you know why?'

I shook my head.

'Philip of France dreams other dreams,' Monsieur Simon whispered. 'That one day he will become the new Charlemagne of Europe. He has three sons, Louis, Philippe and Charles. He has married them, or he intends to marry them, to the heiresses of Burgundy so as to take that rich land back within the fiefdom of the crown of France. The same is true of Gascony. In the marriage treaty Philip has stipulated that one grandson will sit on the throne of the Confessor at Westminster; another will become Duke of Gascony. You see the plan, sooner or later, preferably sooner rather than later: Gascony will be brought under Philip's rule, while he will control his grandson the English heir, first through the marriage of Isabella and secondly because any fruit of that union will be his kinsman.' Monsieur Simon spread his hands. 'Peter Dubois, Philip's own lawyer, has seen France's future, a kingdom with natural borders: the sea in the west, mountains to the south, the Rhine to the east.'

'And the northern principalities?' I asked. 'Flanders, Brabant, Hainault?'

'Weak,' Monsieur Simon retorted. 'To be taken by conquest. Only Philip found to his cost that it is not as easy as he thinks.'

I nodded in agreement. Five years earlier, France's finest armies, its massed chivalry, had been humiliatingly defeated by Flemish pikemen at Courtrai.

'But Philip still dreams on.' Monsieur Simon was talking as if to himself. 'Edward of England died last July near the Scottish border, still determined to bring that kingdom under his rule. His heir apparent, the Prince of Wales, Edward of Caernarvon, is not of the same mould as his father; he's a courtier, a poet. He broke off the war with Scotland and hastened south to the fleshpots of London and the loving embraces of his close friend Peter Gaveston, a Gascon, the son of a witch or so they say. Whatever the truth, young Edward loves Gaveston more than anyone in the world.'

'Yet he is to be married to Isabella?'

'Two problems have flourished like weeds.' Monsieur Simon winked at me. 'Edward of Caernarvon refuses to believe the allegations against the Templars.'

My heart warmed to this prince I'd never met.

'That came as a surprise to Philip,' Monsieur Simon whispered. 'But the second was an even greater insult. Edward of Caernarvon seems, how can I put it, most unwilling to fulfil the obligations of the treaty and marry Philip's daughter Isabella.'

'And what has that to do with me?'

'Oh, everything.' Monsieur Simon stared down at the floor, lost in his own thoughts. 'I know that,' he whispered. 'Truly I do, the machinations of princes. In the end,' he lifted his head, 'Edward of Caernarvon is a weakling. He is playing games. Sooner or later he will succumb to Philip's demands. The Templars of England will be arrested, the order destroyed. More importantly, Edward of Caernarvon will do what Philip of

France says. He will marry Isabella, either in France or in England, but that marriage will take place. Now I've been to that mist-strewn island with its rough-tongued people. Philip of France wishes to organise a household for his young daughter, to accompany her to England. In many ways it will mean exile for life. As you can imagine, Mathilde, very few are eager to join her.'

'And I am to go with her?'

The merchant tapped me gently on the cheek.

'It's the safest place for you. The persecution of the Templars will continue. Philip will ask for lists to be drawn up. It's only a matter of time before some sharp-eyed lawyer, scrutinising such lists, wonders where your uncle's niece Mathilde de Ferrers disappeared to. They will want you. You've just reached your twentieth year; more import-antly, you're associated with the Temple, however lowly your status might be. Marigny and other royal ministers will interrogate you. Do you hold any of its wealth? Do you know where any is hidden? Do you know the whereabouts of other Templars? Did you carry any messages? Do you have any information? Mathilde, your uncle was a high-ranking officer; you are valuable. You could be used, tortured to provide false evidence. Oh, don't worry, searches will be made, but by then, God willing, you'll be gone.'

'To England?' I gasped. 'With the Princess Isabella?' I pulled myself up in my chair and, try as I might, I couldn't stop the shivering, as if suffering from a sudden attack of the ague. The logs crackled, flames burst out, sparks rose, black dust floated up. The voices in the house sounded hollow. I was standing at a crossroads. I could, if I wanted, get up from that chair, step out from that house and return to my mother's farm. Yet I would only bring the terror with me. When the royal serjeants came, they wouldn't care about a solitary woman and her daughter too stupid enough not to flee.

Monsieur Simon seized my wrist; surprisingly strong, he squeezed tightly.

'That is all I can do for you, Mathilde. To stay here is dangerous. To return to your mother even more of a hazard. You've seen enough of Paris, Mathilde! Do you want to become a beggar, join the Coquillards roaming the Latin Quarter? Waiting for the day when you'll be arrested for a brawl, some crime or felony? You too will take the cart to Montfaucon. Or will some pimp seize you as his whore? I must have your decision, yes or no?'

I'd rolled the dice. I'd made my choice. 'I have to go,' I whispered. 'And the only way is what you describe.'

'Good.' Monsieur Simon heaved a sigh of relief. 'Tomorrow morning you leave.' Then he added in a mysterious whisper, 'Before my next guest arrives.'

I was roused before dawn. Servants clattered up the stairs with pails of hot water, followed by others carrying Monsieur Simon's heavy tub. I was told to strip, to wash carefully and dress in the sombre clothes Monsieur Simon had brought: blue hose, soft leather boots from Spain, linen undergarments, a dark blue gown with a waist-band which had a concealed fold for a dagger and a ring for my hand.

'A gift,' Monsieur Simon explained.

Finally a heavy dark-brown cloak fastened round the neck with a silver clasp. Monsieur Simon also provided a money belt with little pouches sewn along the edge, each crammed with silver coins.

'I would like to say this is also a gift from me.' He shook his head. 'The wealth was your uncle's. You have it now. I can give you nothing else. Remember, you are Mathilde de Clairebon, distant kinsman of Monsieur Simon de Vitry. Look,' he urged, coming up close and peering up at me, 'I've studied you, Mathilde. You have a ready ear and a quick tongue!' He smiled. 'Your knowledge of physic, herbs and potions is truly remarkable. Your uncle also told me you know Italian, you can speak the Norman French of the court; it's only a matter of time before you study English, learn their customs, adopt their ways.'

'What will I be?'

'What the Princess Isabella decides. You will be introduced as a *demoiselle de chambre*.'

CHAPTER 2

Perfidy reigns and Malice is engendered.

'*A Song of the Times*', 1272–1307

I breakfasted, the last time I ate in that house,
and left. Monsieur de Vitry carried the panniers containing all I possessed. Advent was
approaching; sprigs of green festooned doorposts
close to where the lantern horns glowed on their
hooks. Horses dragging huge logs plodded along
the streets. A water-seller, a gaunt figure, shouted
briskly at the top of his voice, about how he sold
the purest water from the clearest spring. A man on
the corner cooked hot pies on the stove he'd set up
well away from the watchful eye of beadles and
market bailiffs. Glimpses of life I'd never forget. We
hurried down cobbled streets, shop signs creaking
in the bitterly cold breeze. We passed a church; on
its steps a choir of young scholars were singing lustily
about the Virgin giving birth to a royal child. I still
felt sleepy, as if walking through a dream.

We crossed bridges and on to the causeway leading

to the royal palace close by the church of La Sainte Chapelle. Men-at-arms milled about; a group of mailed knights clattered by. Under the yawning, gaped-mouth gatehouse, Brabantine mercenaries, the nose guards of their helmets almost hiding their faces, stopped us. Passes were produced and we continued on, up cobbled track-ways, through another gateway and into the maze of tunnels and passages which connected one palace building to another; a dizzyingly changing place, soaring turrets, crenellated walls, steps which seemed to lead no-where. Mist swirled like smoke from a cauldron, cloaking the servants hurrying by. The smell of the stables, dung and wet straw, mingled with the sweet odours from the kitchens and butteries. We crossed rutted yards and baileys where the palace folk thronged around steaming pots. Butchers hacked at carcasses, their tables flowing with blood which drove the roaming dogs frenetic with excitement. Smiths, armourers, carpenters and masons filled the air with the clamour of their workplaces. Women washed laundry, ostlers exercised horses. A mad-man, locked by his feet in the stocks, pretended to be a priest celebrating mass. So witless; the fellow ignored the three corpses dangling from a nearby gibbet pole. I glanced away as hideous memories blossomed. A great hangman, King Philip! I later learnt how his favourite punishment was to hang court malefactors from the branches of the apples trees in his orchard.

We went inside, along dark passages. Meagre

candles glowed, lanterns hanging on chains glimmered like beacon lights. Guards stood everywhere, lances poised. The deeper we went into the palace, the more luxurious the surroundings became: tiled floors, whitewashed walls decorated with paintings, elaborate crucifixes, cloths of gold and resplendent tapestries. The sweet smell of perfumed sandalwood and costly incense became more noticeable. The guards here weren't mercenaries but knight bannerets wearing the blue and gold livery of the royal household. They stood at the entrance to doorways or at the foot of polished staircases, swords drawn. Time and again they stopped us. Time and again Monsieur Simon produced his letters and warrants. Eventually we reached the royal quarters, where a chamberlain greeted us in the hallway. The floor was of black and white tiles, the walls covered in tapestries depicting glorious white swans on silver lakes where the rushes sprouted a vivid green. I studied these as Monsieur Simon explained our presence. The chamberlain looked askance at me, tapping his white wand of office against his shoulder as if he was inspecting a bundle of cloth. He pulled a face.

'Lady Isabella,' he sighed, 'will not be in her chamber but where she always is, the fountain courtyard.'

We left the hall, down a wooden-panelled passageway, and went back into the cold air. This was no cobbled bailey but a spacious courtyard with buildings of eye-catching honey-coloured stone surrounding it. The paving stones were of the same hue; in the centre a fountain splashed, the leaping water creating the impression of summer though the ice in the basin proved it was still winter. Pots of crackling charcoal sprinkled with a herbal perfume provided some warmth. In a corner two knight bannerets, cloaks pulled close, stood out of the biting wind talking quietly between themselves. The chamberlain gestured. A figure, almost shrouded in a gold-edged blue robe, sat with her back to us, staring at the ice in the fountain bowl.

'I can't announce you.' The chamberlain seemed strangely frightened. 'The Lady Isabella has a temper. She does not wish to be disturbed when she is talking to Marie.'

'Marie?' Monsieur Simon whispered. 'Who is Marie, is it a pet fish or bird?'

I kept staring at that still figure, motionless, as if carved out of stone. The chamberlain whispered to my companion. Monsieur Simon clasped my hand, then left hurriedly. I never saw him alive again. A short while later he and his entire household were murdered, but, God assoil them, I shall come to that.

At the time I stood until I became aware of the cold, how my thighs and legs ached. I walked across, round the bench, and gazed down at the small figure. She'd hidden her hands beneath the cloak; now these came out, fingers so delicate, and her head came up, the hood pushed back, and I looked on Isabella for the first time. She had lustrous golden hair, parted along the middle, and falling down to her shoulders. A lively, rather thin face with an elfin look, the nose pert, the lips flamered, but those strange blue eyes with their Moorish slant were truly beautiful, a legacy I later learnt from her mother, Jeanne of Navarre. She peered up at me, swinging her feet in their hard-soled sandals.

'Who are you?' She cocked her head to one side and looked me up and down. 'Just who are you? Why are you here?'

'Madame,' I stammered, 'madame, I am Mathilde de Clairebon. I am to join your household as a *demoiselle de chambre.*'

'Come here, Mathilde.' She smiled. I stepped closer. She abruptly swung her leg back and kicked me viciously in the shin. I yelped in pain, lifting my foot to nurse my ankle. She noticed my anger, my clenched fist. The knights in the corner became alerted by the altercation. I heard their raised voices, the sound of a drawn sword. Isabella's face grew serious.

'Don't do anything,' she whispered. 'Fall to your knees.'

She gestured with her hands, indicating at the knights to stand back, then leaned closer, her faint herbal fragrance, rosewater and something else, tickling my nostrils. Her skin was pure and clean, her teeth white, not a mark; the nose didn't look quite so pert but rather sharp, whilst those eyes were a brilliant blue, so clear yet so striking, and her skin glowed as if dusted with gold. She raised a hand, pushing a few hairs from her forehead, and felt her throat.

'They say I have a swan neck,' she murmured. 'One day I will be truly beautiful. What do you think, Mathilde?'

'Madame,' I retorted, 'you are as beautiful as any jewel. Any painting I have seen of an angel would compare with you.'

She lifted her foot and pressed it against my groin.

'Are you virgo intacta?'

I was so shocked by the question from one so young, I just gaped back.

'Who are you, Mathilde, really? You're frightened, aren't you? Why are you frightened of me? No one is frightened of me. Yet,' she turned quickly as if someone was sitting beside her before glancing back at me, 'Marie doesn't like you.'

'Madame,' I demanded, 'who is Marie? I can't see anyone.'

'Of course, you can't.' She laughed; not a girlish giggle, but a deep, throaty laugh as if she was truly amused by my reaction.

'You can't see Marie. No one can see her except me. I've seen her for years. She always comes with me. She's my lady-in-waiting. She died, you know, some years ago, or so she told me, of the sweating sickness. Now she comes back and talks to me. She sits on my bed while I sew a piece of tapestry or try to read the book of hours Father gave me. You've met my father?'

I shook my head, the ice was soaking through my knees. I was aware of how cold the air had become. The knights ignored us as if they were used to such scenes. I turned my head slightly to see what they were doing and received a stinging slap on my face.

'I am the Princess of France.' Isabella smiled at me. She touched me gently where she'd struck me. 'I didn't mean to hurt. I have talked to Marie about you. I'm afraid she truly doesn't like you. Now, what answer do you make to that, Mathilde?'

'I don't like her either, madame,' I replied.

'Now isn't that strange?' Again the laugh. Isabella watched me curiously. 'Here I am, Isabella of France, the only daughter of the great Philip, soon to be the wife of the King of England, mother of his heir. Every time I mention Marie they humour me, Mathilde. Some people even claim they can see her. So I ask them to describe her and they always describe me. If you really could see her, you'd know that she has black hair, black as a raven's wing and very dark eyes. She looks like one of the moon people, the road wanderers. Anyway,' she continued, hands resting in her lap, swinging her feet like any little girl, 'anyway, I've asked Marie why she doesn't like you. She won't reply. You say you don't like her, which will be interesting.' She leaned nearer. 'We're leaving soon, you know that? I am to go to England, to become queen of that fairy isle, to sit on the throne at Westminster to be crowned, and to share the bed of Edward. Do you know Edward, the young king?'

I shook my head.

'They say he is very handsome,' she continued. 'He looks a little like me, a distant kinsman; Father explained how we are related. They say he too has golden hair, blue eyes and a lovely beard and moustache. They also say other things: how he prefers to dig a ditch, thatch a cottage or be taken along the river in a barge and joke with varlets, labourers and other servants of the meaner sort. He has a pet lion and a camel in his great fortress, the Tower of London. Do you want to know something else?' She looked around. 'I've discussed this with Marie: they say he likes other men. I've heard of that; brother Louis told me what they do to each other: they put their thing,' she pressed her sandalled foot against my groin, again, 'not into a woman's place, because a man doesn't have that, but elsewhere.' She turned slightly and patted her own rump. 'Do you know what they mean, Mathilde?'

I did, but I shook my head, only to receive another slap, this time softer, on my face.

'You're not a very good liar, Mathilde. You will be, if you serve me and live in my household. You do know what I am talking about?'

She turned, cocking her head slightly as if listening to her invisible companion. She glanced at me out of the corner of her eye.

'Shall I tell you something, Mathilde? Marie has

changed her mind. She thinks she likes you, and so do I.' She began to sing softly under her breath, a Goliard hymn, a wandering scholar's filthy song. I wondered who could have taught her that.

'Can I trust you, Mathilde?'

'With your life?'

'Don't be stupid.' She pouted. 'Can I trust you?'

'Of course, madame, I am your servant.'

'Of course you are,' she mimicked, eyes dancing with merriment. 'I told a lie. They *are* frightened of me! They want me to leave and I want to go. Mathilde, have you heard the stories? How my father may have poisoned my mother? That's what the gossips claim. Father heard a servant girl repeat it; she was burned and her lover was hanged in Father's apple orchard. He claimed they were guilty of treason, but why should he burn a girl and hang a boy because of rumour and malicious gossip? Anyway,' she continued, 'they'll be glad to see me leave here. They're frightened, you know.'

'What of?' I asked.

'Ah, you'll see. Virgo intacta,' she murmured. 'I am supposed to go to Edward virgo intacta.'

'Of course you are, your grace,' I hastily replied, just wishing I could get up from my knees.

'You may sit beside me now.' The order came so swiftly, I wondered if she knew exactly what I was thinking and who I really was. I sat down beside her. She edged closer, pressing her body against me. I felt her warmth and realised she must have a jar of heated coals beneath her cloak to fend off the cold.

'You see, Mathilde, no one really wants to come with me to England. Father has chosen the ladies for my retinue as well as the servants for my household. Most of them will be his spies and dutifully report back. I told him that I wanted servants I could trust, people not from the court. Father, of course, has had his way, so he's become too bored, or too busy, to deal with it. Uncle Charles said he would do what he could. He mentioned you. Anyway, you are a change!'

Again she turned away to talk to the invisible Marie, chattering away in a language I couldn't understand. She glanced back at me.

'You're wondering what tongue I'm using. Well, I will tell you, it's a language only Marie and I understand.'

'How long has Marie been with you?'

'Oh, as long as I remember. I was telling you why they are frightened, my brothers and my father? Well, for the last two years my brothers have come into my bedchamber. Oh yes they do.' She nudged me playfully. 'They slide between the sheets and fondle my body; even Father, when he wishes to embrace me, puts his hands where he should not. I know that, Mathilde, because of Ursula; she was an old lady-in-waiting, one of my mother's people, dark of skin, with a sour disposition but a keen eye and an even sharper tongue.'

'And what happened to Ursula?'

'She protested. She objected to what she had seen and became angry with my brother Louis.

55

Anyway,' she shrugged, 'a week later Ursula fell down some steps and broke her neck. They buried her in the poor man's plot in the cemetery, the one the soldiers use, as no one claimed her body. She had no relatives here.'

The two knights remained huddled in the corner, lost in their own conversation, no longer bothered about me or the princess they were supposed to be guarding.

'Yes, they are frightened,' Isabella repeated. 'They don't want me to tell Edward what has happened. Can you imagine, Mathilde, if the new King of England, that lusty warrior, discovered I had shared my bed with my own brothers, where we'd played tumble games? He'd object. He'd write to the Holy Father in Avignon. I have sworn an oath to my father and my brothers to keep silent on that matter, provided I have my way in certain things; one of them is you, Mathilde. You will sleep at the door of my chamber.' She rose to her feet and thrust the small heated pot she brought from beneath her cloak into my hands.

'Warm yourself and come, follow me.'

We entered the palace, and climbed a wooden staircase. The princess's chambers stood along a small gallery, three rooms in all: a main chamber, flanked by a waiting room and another for stores. The gallery was of polished wood, panelling along one wall and against the outer one deep window seats overlooking the fountain courtyard. Ladies-in-waiting were sitting there muffled against the cold, warming themselves over chafing dishes, pretending to be busy with embroidery; of course they had been watching us all the time. They rose as the princess approached. One hastened forward and grasped her by the hand, exclaiming loudly how cold her mistress felt. The princess shrugged this off and dismissed them. She swept into her own chamber. I followed.

'Close the door,' the princess called out over her shoulder. I put down the warming pot and hastened to obey.

'Pull the bolts at top and bottom,' she continued. 'So no one can disturb us.'

I did so. Isabella turned, unfastened her cloak and let it fall. She was dressed in a blood-red woollen gown edged with ermine, fastened at the neck by a silver cord. Before I could protest, she undid this, easing the gown over her shoulders to fall at her feet. She then removed her kirtle, and her undergarments, until she stood naked before me, a young woman's body, breasts already sprouting, hips widening. She turned, spreading out her hands.

'Demoiselle Mathilde, this is what I will take to Edward of England. Now it's time for something warmer.'

She redressed in woollen undergarments, quickly putting on a blue and silver gown, taking a pelisse from a peg on the wall to wrap about her shoulders. I was so embarrassed at her actions I glanced round the chamber, at the bed drapes, the Turkey rugs, the glorious coloured arras and tapestries resting against the pink-painted plaster. Above me hung a wooden chandelier; it carried six candles and could be lowered by a rope to shed greater light. Across the room stood a small writing desk and high-backed chair. The desk was covered with pieces of parchment and quills. Around the chamber ranged chests, some sealed and locked, others, with their lids thrown back, from which spilled precious cloth, brocaded clothing, belts, books, all the possessions of a rich, spoilt, pampered girl. Well, that was my first impression. I was yet to realise how Isabella could have performed in any mummers' play, shifting from mood to mood, sometimes a child, at others a young woman. Now and again she'd act the innocent until her face assumed a cunning look as if she was calculating everything, weighing all she saw and heard in the balance. Whatever Marie had told her, Isabella had seemed to greet me as if I was a long-lost servant, as if we had known each other for years. Now she walked across and sat on the high-backed chair before the writing desk. She snapped her fingers, gesturing at a quilted stool in the corner.

'Bring that over here, Mathilde, sit next to me.'

I did so, and Isabella rubbed her hands. 'I'm cold.' She pointed to the wheeled brazier just inside the door, the charcoal spluttering, small tendrils of smoke escaping, mingling with the perfume of sweet powders sprinkled on top. 'Bring that across, Mathilde'. I hurried to do so. Once I had taken my seat, she gestured at another table where there was a jug of fruit juice and two goblets.

'Fill both, one for you and one for me.' So the game continued as she sent me hither and thither around the room, for this or that. Eventually she tired and turned to face me, once again swinging her legs, as if wondering whether to kick me or not.

'Well, Mathilde, what are we to do?' She steepled her fingers, pressing her hands hard. 'We should be in England now.' She smiled. 'But Edward refuses to arrest the Templars! Now he is saying he doesn't want to marry me.' She threw her head back and laughed. 'Father's rage is to be seen to be believed. Spots of anger appear,' she tapped her own cheek, 'on either side, red splotches like those on a jester, and here,' she pulled her lower lip down, 'a white froth bubbles. They say my father has a heart of ice; I know different. He throbs with fury at the English king's insults. So, Mathilde, we might spend a long time together before we take the road and cross the Narrow Seas to that mysterious island!' She pushed her face closer, as if I was a child. 'The mysterious island.' She grimaced. 'Nothing mysterious about it; only wet, dark and green, with elves and goblins living in the forest. They do say London is a magnificent city, like Paris, with a great thoroughfare and stalls which sell everything, and I,' she tapped her chest, 'will be queen of it all, but only if Edward stops baiting Father. Now, this is what I want you to do,

Mathilde. I want you to listen to me.' She wagged her finger. 'No, don't object.' She blinked. 'Looking at you, Mathilde, I suspect you are a keeper of secrets. If I told my father about that, he would have you investigated. Why do I know that? Well, you are the only person who really wants to go to England, so what are you hiding? Why do you want to flee?'

I kept my face impassive and held her gaze.

'The more I look at you, Mathilde,' she gossiped on, 'the more I like you.' She smiled. 'You're wondering why I am telling you all these secrets? Quite simple!' She clapped her hands. 'If you told other people they wouldn't believe you, whilst if my father or brothers realised you now know, they'd certainly kill you! Oh, Mathilde,' she breathed, 'it is so good to talk to flesh and blood!'

She got up to confront me squarely, staring at my face as if seeing me for the first time. 'I wonder who you really are,' she repeated. She screwed her eyes up, no longer a young lady, more a mere chit of a child, yet there was something highly dangerous about her. Isabella was quick-witted, her moods ever changing; she had yet to learn how to school her expressions, she was still young and innocent enough to let her mask slip. She was weighing me carefully in the balance. She touched my face. 'Olive skin and smooth,' she murmured. 'Thick eyebrows over green eyes, black hair, like Marie's, cut into a bob. They say you're trained as a leech, an apothecary.' She laughed. 'You're a woman and too young to be an expert, a *peritus*, but you can stare and watch. I believe you'll be the sharpest arrow in my quiver. Stretch out your hands.'

I did so. She gently eased back the sleeves of my gown and scrutinised my wrists and hands. 'Soft but used.' She held up the callused finger of my right hand. 'And a quill? Do you play hazard, Mathilde?'

'At times, my lady.'

'Good, I like to play. I have my own dice. They are made out of ivory. What my brothers don't know is that they are cogged; I always win.' She laughed behind her fingers. 'Now, Mathilde,' she rapped me again on the ankles, this time more gently, 'you will hold office in my household. You will be my *dame de la chambre*: where I go, you follow. If I ride, you will either accompany me on horse or run beside me. You are my messenger and my taster. Oh yes, I want you to make sure that if wine and food are brought to my chamber, they remain pure and untainted.' Again the low laugh behind splayed fingers; all the time those keen blue eyes scrutinised me carefully.

'Above all I need someone to confide in. I am getting bored with Marie. I am not too sure if I should take her to England. Now listen.' She grasped my hand, and pulled me to my feet as if I was her dearest friend, linking her arm through mine. We walked to the casement window and stared down at the fountain; the water in its bowl was frozen hard, the carved stonework, representing a sea monster, had a gaping mouth and staring eyes. 'If we do go to England, we have to cross the Narrow Seas,' she murmured. 'That's dangerous. Now, Mathilde, give me your promise.' She nipped my arm. 'One day, when we trust each other, you will tell me who you really are. Until then,' she patted my hand, 'I'll keep you safe.'

We left her quarters to walk through the palace. For a while Isabella simply strolled around the galleries and hallways. She showed me the archives, the scriptorium, the library with its precious manuscripts, bound in leather and edged with gold, chained to their stands. All the time she chattered like a squirrel on a branch. I still could not decide whether she was artless or very cunning, a court lady or a girl whose wits had turned. We entered the grand hall. For a while we watched actors, tumblers, conjurors and animal trainers rehearse their tricks whilst being inspected by a chamberlain who was to decide on which revelry to choose for some feast. A bell tolled, so we went to the buttery, where Isabella sat like any serving wench, tapping the table, gossiping with the maids, whilst demanding that we be given freshly baked bread with honey and jugs of light ale. Afterwards we returned to Isabella's chamber. Once there she ordered more food, this time a tray of spiced meats and a flagon of the richest Bordeaux. I was surprised, bearing in mind her tender age; nevertheless she filled both cups to the brim and swallowed a little of hers, before pushing it into my hands, her face all angry.

'You're a bitch!' She pouted. 'You're lazy! You should have tasted it first.'

I sipped from both cups and held them out for her to choose, and she snatched one from my hand. That was how the dance began. Where Princess Isabella went, I followed. Sometimes she would sit in the window seat, jabbing a needle at a piece of embroidery like any soldier would his sword at a straw man in the exercise yard. When she grew bored with this, she asked for musicians and skilfully accompanied them on the rebec, flute or harp. One thing was constant: Isabella's love of books. I thank God for my own studies. Sometimes she would read the tales; other times I did whilst she acted certain parts. I was correct: Isabella was a mummer's girl. She could slip from one role to another and mimic people as easily as a mirror reflects light. She was deeply intrigued by my knowledge of physic and herbs. Her courses had already begun and she suffered from the cramps. At first she refused my ministrations, but then agreed. She wanted me to examine her urine, but I quoted from the tract of Isaac Judaeus: 'All urine is a filter of the blood and properly indicates two things, either an infection of the liver and veins, or an infection of the intestines and viscera. Of other things, it gives only indirect indications.'

Isabella stared gape-mouthed, then burst out

laughing. I thought she would strike me; instead she caressed my cheek.

'You recite better than my father's physicians.'

I remained silent.

'So, physician?' She clutched her stomach in mock pain.

'Southerwood,' I replied, quoting from Abbot Strabo. 'Its tops, flowers or seeds boiled is the correct remedy for cramp. Pliny recommends sage with wormwood.'

'And you?'

'Mugwort and camomile will help.'

Apparently it did. Isabella's interest in herbs and medicine quickened. She declared as much when she borrowed books from her father's library. In truth, they were for me. I was grateful and, for the first time, read a fresh treatise of Bernard de Gordon, the physician from Montpellier, his *De ingeniis curandorum Morborum.* At the same time Isabella kept me well away from the other servants; if anyone came close, she would imperiously intervene and dismiss them. I was given my own chamber beside hers. A comfortable room with a soft bed, a brazier, sticks of furniture and a lavarium; there was even a coloured cloth tied to the wall and a black crucifix with an ivory figure of Christ writhing against it. The window was shuttered against the cold and beneath it was a quilted bench. I thought I would sleep apart from her, but on my first night, Isabella made it very clear that I was to lie on a palliasse, especially ordered from the stores, just inside her room.

Two days after I joined her service I met her three brothers. They sloped up the stairs like hunting dogs, padding along the gallery in their quilted jerkins and tight-fitting hose, feet pushed into pointed slippers, small jewelled cloaks clasped about their shoulders. I understood why the princess was so wary of them. All three were silver-haired demons. Louis was small, with the sharp, pointed features of a grey-hound, ever-darting eyes and nervous gestures, particularly with the jewelled girdle around his waist. He looked at me only to dismiss me as you would a mongrel. Philippe was much taller, broader, with a nervous tic in his face and hooded eyes above a sharp nose and prim mouth. A man of violent temper and hot humours, a man I judged not to be crossed. Charles was stout, with a fat red face, his paunch already proclaiming his love of wine; every time I met him he was never far from a cup. They lounged in their sister's room, legs stretched out like a pack of lurchers playing with some quarry before they killed it. They had high-pitched voices, arrogant and abrasive; gabbling like nasty geese. They seemed fascinated by their sister. They had their own ladies, their own separate households, yet they were constant visitors to Isabella's quarters. They brought gifts, sweetmeats, a triptych depicting the martyrdom of St Denis, baubles and toys; even a ferret, though that was later killed by Charles's pet greyhound.

A sinister trio, dangerous men who tapped their dagger scabbards as they talked; they despised the servants and were cruel to their own retinues. All three swaggered into Isabella's chamber like suitors for her hand, eager to see her yet rivals to each other. Isabella always received them elegantly but coldly. She would sit like a little snow queen from a romance, hands on her knees, face fixed in the same twisted smile. On one occasion Louis tried to grab her by the waist and pull her close. Isabella lunged like a spitting cat; even I was surprised at how swiftly the needle-thin stiletto appeared in her hand. She pressed this against her brother's cheek. They continued their argument in whispers. Louis, nursing the slight prick on his face, stepped away. He muttered something to his brothers, and they all left laughing; only then did Philippe glance towards me, a sly smile on his angry face. They slammed the door behind them and began to tease and flirt with the ladies outside. Isabella sat down abruptly. Her mood changed, she was no long imperious, but pallid-faced, tears trickling down her cheeks. I hastened over to kneel before her, but she patted the settle beside her. I never touched her. I never spoke. I simply sat while she put her head down, shoulders shaking, not raising her face until the tears had stopped.

'Is it always like this, Mathilde?' she murmured. 'In every family? Do the brothers put their hands up their sisters' gowns, clasp their necks and pinch their breasts? Do they, at the dead of night, steal between their sisters' sheets?' She blinked and bit her lip.

'I just pray I'll be gone, be away from here and never return!' She patted my hand. 'You'll come with me.' She smiled tearfully. 'Mathilde the silent, though.' Her smile disappeared. 'As your heart grows older, it will come to sights much colder.' She slipped a costly ring from her finger and pressed it into my hand. 'Remember me! Remember my words!'

In time I met Philip, the king, himself, booted and spurred from the hunt, striding up the stairs amongst his henchmen, Enguerrand de Marigny (ah, my red-haired enemy!), de Plaisans and Nogaret, those sly lawyers who had scandalised Christendom by ordering their servants to attack the previous pope, Boniface VIII, in the town of Anagni. They, too, scarcely gave me a second glance. They would later wish they had! I was summoned across and made to kneel at the king's feet. He pushed his jewelled fingers hard against my mouth, then put his hand beneath my chin, forcing me to look up. I have heard many tales about Philip Le Bel. They're all true! Philip's face was like ivory, his hair silver; at a swift glance you'd think he was an albino. His eyes were clear blue, his touch icy, his manner cold. He stared at me without any change of expression, patted me on the head as if I were a dog and pushed me away.

At first I remained very nervous; worries about my mother (I dared not write to her), nightmares about Uncle Reginald and fears about my own safety plagued my sleep, but as the days passed, I began to relax. My chamber was comfortable. The princess never mentioned Marie. Instead she talked to me about everything. She knew all the chatter and gossip of the court. Which lady was unfaithful to her husband, who was in favour and who was out, all the time watching me, studying me carefully. One afternoon, shortly after I arrived, the princess sent me on an errand to the other side of the palace; I was to enquire about a stool she'd sent to the royal carpenters. I was on my way back when a young lady stepped out of the shadows just within a doorway.

'Demoiselle Mathilde?' My sleeve was plucked. I glanced at her. She had beautiful red hair framing an impudent face; her gown cut low, she moved closer in a fragrant gust of perfume.

'Madame?'

'I am from Monsieur Louis, the princess's brother.'

'I know who he is,' I replied. She grasped my hand. I felt the small sack of coins.

'Monsieur Louis would consider it a great favour if you could keep him informed about his sister's moods.'

I snatched my hand away; the purse fell to the floor.

'If the princess's brother wishes to know about his sister's temperament, he should ask her directly. I bid you good day.'

I was so immersed in what had happened, I became lost in the maze of galleries and passageways, so it took some time before I returned to the princess's quarters. When I entered the chamber, I was surprised to see her seated in the high-backed chair before the fire, with the young lady I'd met on a stool beside her. As soon as I appeared, Isabella flicked her fingers. The lady rose, curtsied, grinned at me and swept out of the room.

'Come, Mathilde.' Isabella's fingers fluttered. 'Come here.'

I sat on the footstool; she gently patted my hair.

'You passed scrutiny, you can't be bought! No, no, now listen, this is what I want you to do. You know the university quarter, how the different students from each kingdom are divided into nations? I want you to go to the English quarter. I want you to move amongst the students and the scholars, especially the clerks from the retinues of the English envoys. You are to discover all you can about my future husband, Edward of England!' She paused. 'All I know about him is what I've been told!' She imitated the portentous tone of an envoy. 'How courtly! How handsome.' She winked. 'I've yet to meet a man I can trust. Anyway, will you do that for me?'

'Of course, my lady.'

'Good, Mathilde. I am aware, from what you've told me, that you know the city well, though how and why I've yet to learn. So . . .' Isabella thrust a purse into my hand. 'You refused that once,' she smiled, 'this time it's yours! Buy them wine, Mathilde, let their tongues chatter. When you've finished, come back and tell me all you've learnt.'

Strange, isn't it? How we judge children? We betray our arrogance – small bodies must house small minds. It's not true. Isabella was thirteen years of age but she had all the wisdom and cunning of a woman of threescore years and ten.

I packed a set of panniers and left the palace the following day. It was good to be back in the city. Especially the Latin Quarter with its taverns, cook-shops, narrow streets, some cobbled, others not, the air rich with different fragrances and odours, the crowds colourful and jostling. I entered the quarter where the English nation lodged. Students in ragged gowns who lodged in narrow chambers were only too willing to escape to the great tap rooms and eating halls of the taverns. A noisy, colourful throng, young men full of the lust for life, quoting poetry, carrying a pet weasel or squirrel, arguing, fighting, dicing, chasing each other, constantly looking for a penny to profit or a woman to seduce. They rubbed shoulders with the tight-waisted, square-bodiced ladies of the town and ignored the moral warnings of the rope-girdled Franciscan in his earth-coloured robe who stood on a corner preaching against the lechery of the world. They played the rebec and the flute, sang songs of nonsense, crowned a dog as King of Revels and made a beggar with his clack dish lead him up and down the half-cobbled street. I had met a few English before; now I immersed myself in the company of these tail-wearers with their sardonic humour and harsh tongue. I became accepted and so closed with my quarry.

English envoys had arrived in Paris to negotiate with Philip. Of course their clerks and scribes, after the long day's business was done, were eager for mischief amongst the English nation. I began to frequent a tavern, the Oriflamme, with a spacious tap room, not too clean; the rushes on the floor often squelched under my boots whilst some of the odours were definitely unsavoury. Nevertheless, this was where the English clerks congregated. At first they were sly-eyed and tight-lipped, but it's wonderful what a flask of wine, a game of dice, joyful banter and a shared song can change. True, they were full of their own importance. They gave away no secrets; after all, these were clerks of the chancery, trained at their universities of Oxford or Cambridge in all fields of law and duplicity. What I wanted was not their secrets, only the chatter of the court, and they were most willing to share it. I rented a narrow garret with no window except a hole dug through the wall covered by a piece of hardened cloth. With Isabella's silver it was easy to pose as the daughter of a French lawyer waiting for her father to join her from Dijon. If you pretend to act the mummer's part, and retain the mask, the world, in the main, will believe you. Once they'd downed their cups and filled their bellies, the clerks regaled me (acting very much the innocent lady) with stories about the English court, especially the rise of Monsieur Gaveston, the king's favourite, to the earldom of Cornwall.

'Oh yes.' One of them winked at me, tapping the side of his nose. 'Earl of Cornwall Gaveston now is, bosom friend of the king, who calls him his dear brother.'

'And the other great lords accept this?' I asked.

'Of course.'

They chattered on, explaining how Edward of England had no desire to arrest the Templars in his kingdom, whilst he had little inclination for travelling to France, marrying the French king's daughter or fulfilling the treaty's obligations.

'If he doesn't,' one narrow-faced clerk muttered, 'there'll be war and no more journeys to Paris. At least,' he smiled in a fine display of cracked teeth, 'until a new peace treaty is signed.' He put his cup down.

'And there's the secret . . .'

CHAPTER 3

The fraud of Rulers prevails, Peace is trodden underfoot.

'A Song of the Times', 1272–1307

Narrow Face, all pimpled and sweaty, stared at me, his half-open mouth slobbering food. He was trying to look cunning, but like all such men he was stupid. He looked me up and down as if I was some mare at Smithfield Market, wiping his mouth on the back of his hand. His companions had turned away; some were already arguing about whose dice they should use in the cracked cup, the others were distracted by one of those travelling players who'd appeared in the tavern doorway dressed in black, with the white outline of a skeleton gaudily painted over. He brought his own stool, stood on it and began to intone one of those tearful dirges about death:

> When my eyes mist,
> And my hair hisses,

And my nose grows cold,
And my tongue does fold,
And my strength slacken,
And my lips blacken.
And my mouth gaping . . .

The students took up the refrain of this travelling English mountebank, probably some scholar
from the English quarter trying to earn a crust. I
was about to turn back when I glimpsed that face
which was to haunt me all my life, serene and
smooth under grey-dashed hair. It was the eyes
which drew me, with their far-seeing gaze. The man
was studying me intently. Someone moved between
us, and when he passed, the man with the far-seeing
gaze had disappeared. I felt the sharp edge of the
table press against me. Narrow Face had lurched
to his feet, leaning drunkenly across, grinning in a
sickening display of yellow teeth.

'Would you like to know the secret, *ma jolie*?'

'Of course' I simpered and, a short while later, I
found myself strolling arm in arm with Narrow
Face through the nearby cemetery of L'Eglise des
Innocents. It was a macabre place, overlooked by
the gleaming casements of large merchant houses
and entered through a huge porch in a double
gateway. Just inside the cemetery was a shrine to St
Valery, patron of cures for ailments of the groin.
Narrow Face sniggered and pointed out the crude
wax penises hanging alongside the shrine. That clerk
of the red wax, a member of the King of England's

privy chamber, as I later found out, preened himself showing off his knowledge, pointing out the different stalls and booths selling tawdry trinkets, ribbons and disused clothes. He bowed mockingly at a brace of *filles de joie* who went tottering past on their stiffened pattens, faces gaudy, hair all dyed, hitching up their skirts to display well-turned ankles.

We stopped beneath a tree where the coffin of an excommunicate hung dripping with dirt from the branches. Narrow Face explained how this was the closest such a wretch could come to consecrated ground. I listened as if attentive to every word, though the noise around us was deafening. Red-faced traders shouted and bawled, trying to be heard over a blacksmith, face all blotched and burnt, who'd set up his forge just within the gate and was banging on his anvil as if beating the devil. A Crutched Friar, face hidden deep in his cowl, was standing on a tomb chest, warning anyone interested how in hell usurers boiled in molten gold, gluttons feasted on toads and scorpions, whilst the proud would be hooked to an ever-turning burning wheel. Beneath the makeshift pulpit a madman, festooned with shells, did a dance, whilst a group of children chased a bell-capped monkey who'd escaped from its owner.

I leaned hard on Narrow Face's arm and picked my way around the clots of mud and other rubbish strewn across the paved path which wound itself through that place of death. *Kyrie eleison, Christe eleison* – Lord have mercy, Christ have mercy. Sweet

Jesus Lord, have mercy on me! I remember that day so well! The first time I killed a man! *Initium homicidum* – the beginning of the murders! All I meant to do was kiss Narrow Face, whisper sweet words and promise him another assignment. After all, I did as much to those apprentices I flirted with when I worked for Uncle Reginald. All I wanted to learn was what he knew. We reached the charnel house, the arms of the Guild of the Pin and Needle Workers displayed on the wall in shiny blue and red. I glanced across at the tracery grille on the tomb of a young woman with serene marble face and folded marble hands; for a brief moment I wondered where I would lie and what death I would face. Uncle Reginald's fate was still very much in my thoughts. We went round the building. I was teasing Narrow Face, asking him about the great secret. We stood in a narrow, darkened alleyway which separated the charnel house from a line of elms fringing the high curtain wall of the cemetery.

'The secret?' I whispered, leaning back against the harsh brickwork.

'Oh, very important.' Narrow Face pressed his body against mine. He had a faint sour smell. He glanced sideways as if about to reveal some great mystery.

'The King of England,' he whispered, 'will not marry Princess Isabella; he is resolute on that. He will defy her father.'

'But that's no secret . . .'

Narrow Face stepped hastily back. I had

betrayed myself. I still had not learnt the trick of keeping the mask firmly on.

'How do you know that?' Narrow Face's hand slid to the wicked-looking poignard pushed through a ring on his belt. 'How can a wench no better than a tavern slut be party to such knowledge?'

I kept still, cursing my own stupidity.

'Are you one of the Secreti?' Narrow Face stepped forward; the dagger point came up, pricking under my chin. The clerk watched me closely. 'I am,' he hissed, 'a scholar of the halls and schools of Oxford. Do you know what that means?' He pressed the dagger point deeper. 'Do you truly think I am stupid, *putaine*?' He drew back his head, hawked and spat in my face. I kept still. He grasped my hand and felt the skin of my palm.

'Soft,' he whispered hoarsely, 'like your flesh beneath.' He pressed his groin against me. I flinched at his fetid breath. 'You *are* one of the Secreti!' he accused. 'One of the gargoyles, one of King Philip's legion of spies. Well, I'll have my pleasure first.' He pressed the tip of the dagger harder as he pushed up my skirt.

'Please, please!' I begged, trying to distract him.

He laughed, lost in his own intended pleasure. I drew the Italian dagger from my own waistband, and as he pressed against me, one hand scrabbling at the points of his hose, I thrust deep, hard, into his left side up towards the heart. The shock and the pain sent him staggering back at a half-crouch, mouth open, coughing up his life blood.

He lurched towards me. I moved quickly along the charnel house wall, which he hit, striking his head, before collapsing to the ground.

I fled the cemetery of the Innocents out on to the busy cobbled streets. Strange sights and sounds confused me, bells clanged, faces under wimples gaped in surprise, beggars scowled shrouded in their hoods, a pig nosed at the bloated corpse of a cat, a blind child clattered with his stick, a mastiff howled, hair raised, teeth snarling. I fled down an alleyway. An apothecary sign creaking in the breeze caught my glance. I remembered Uncle, his kindly eyes and gentle, soothing voice. I crouched in the narrow doorway of the shop, fighting for breath, wiping away the sweat. Narrow Face's death was one thing, but the chatter he brought also frightened me. If it was no longer a rumour, if Isabella did not travel to England, what hope for me?

I calmed myself. I had to return to Simon de Vitry; he would know what to do. I approached the merchant's house avoiding the postern gate, I went up to the main door; it was off the latch. I opened it, stepped into the vestibule and was greeted by the horrors. A few paces away the manservant lay in a pool of his own blood, a crossbow quarrel firmly dug into his back; the clerk lay half out of the small chamber the merchant had first taken me to. At the bottom of the stairs the maid sprawled face down. She had taken a bolt in the chest, and the blood billowed out in a pool beneath her. I distinctly remember the balustrade was blood-free but I noticed a blur of blood high on the white plastered wall. I was so shocked by the horror of it all, I simply stared around this place of sudden death. I went back to the front door, pulling across the bolt, and gazed at the three corpses, all taken by surprise. Death had swept them into his net, suddenly, abruptly. I went across, gingerly edging round the pools of blood, and felt the skin of each corpse. They were not yet cold, the blood still congealing. I climbed the staircase, past the maid's corpse, trying not to look at her staring eyes, shocked in death. I studied the bloodstain on the plaster and shook my head in surprise, then looked back at the servant girl's corpse. She lay sprawled at the bottom of the stairs, slightly turned over; the crossbow bolt must have thudded into her and she had fallen forward, the blood splattering down her front on to the stairs. So how had the plaster been stained? Unless the assassin had moved the corpse then tried to climb the stairs, but he would have followed the same route as me, holding on to the balustrade, which was blood-free. I continued up.

Monsieur Simon de Vitry lay on the small gallery just beneath a diptych showing Lazarus summoned from his tomb. The merchant was still wearing his nightgown, his flesh not yet cold. I reasoned that the assassin must have struck shortly before I came, then fled. I stepped over de Vitry's corpse and entered his small bedchamber; its chests and coffers had been wrenched opened, papers and parchments tossed about. I examined the ground carefully, looking at the stains. How many assassins had there been? All I could find was one bootprint. I looked back down the stairs; the windows were unshuttered, probably the last act by the servant girl before she was surprised by this devil's ambush.

I know nothing of the humours of the mind. Narrow Face's death may have unsettled me, but now I felt cold, detached and determined, my blood beat steady, my breath calm. I felt as if I was watching some village masque or a miracle play on the green. I was to observe what the actors said, listen to their chants, but not be part of their drama. I was in great danger in that house, but I wanted to know why Monsieur de Vitry, who had helped me so much, had been slaughtered. If the hue and cry were raised, '*Au secours!*' or '*Aidez moi*' were shouted, I could end my days being buried in the air, swinging off the platform at Montfaucon. However, only one thought remained. Uncle Reginald had helped me and he was dead; this man had helped me, now he was murdered.

I went back into the bedchamber, where coins were spilt out on the floor. Precious items, statues and silver candle-holders had not been stolen, the pretence of robbery had not even been invoked as the reason. One killer, one assassin, callous and arrogant, had struck as sure as a cock on a dung-hill. He must have felt protected. I recalled Narrow Face's words about the Secreti, the agents of Marigny, Philip's dark shadow. Philippe, Isabella's brother, turning to stare at me with that twisted smile on his face. Had Simon de Vitry been murdered because of me?

I returned to the vestibule, increasingly aware of the harsh, brooding silence. I glimpsed a picture of the crucified Christ, his eyes staring out of a haggard face at this scene of reeking, hell-spawned malice and evil. I murmured the 'Benedicite' and looked down at the servant, the crossbow bolt embedded so deep into his back. He must have known his murderer. He must have opened the door, inviting him in before turning to lead him up to the merchant's bed-chamber. Was it someone important? Someone dispatched by Philip or Marigny? Certainly a person this household trusted. I walked across to the clerk's corpse. The quarrel which had killed him was different from that used against the servant. Yet I could only detect one bootprint, not two. How could the assassin have acted so quickly? I closed my eyes, imagining a man carrying a sack containing arbalests, small crossbows neatly primed, taking one out then another, dropping the sack as he walked quickly across the hall. The maid tripping down the stairs, another quarrel loosed, but why that bloodstain so high on the wall?

Sounds from the streets outside echoed eerily. The chanting dirge from a funeral procession, a hired poet interspersing each verse with a poem about death. I recall a line: 'I lie wounded in the shroud'; it aptly described what was happening to me. The stink of the charnel house and cemetery appeared to have followed me here. I glanced round once more, crossed myself and slipped into the street. I returned hastily to the palace. Strange how life changes! I now carried a royal seal. The guards and serjeants-at-arms scarcely gave me a second glance. I entered the royal quarters and found the princess in the fountain courtyard. She sat head bowed, golden hair tumbling about her. She was dressed simply in a tawny gown and cloak, muttering quietly to herself. I walked across and went to kneel. She glanced over her shoulder.

'Mathilde, come here.'

I joined her on the bench. She looked up, blue eyes enlarged in her ivory-pale face. She had a linen parcel folded in her lap which she now covered with her hands.

'They have arrived,' she whispered, 'the envoys from England, Sir Hugh Pourte and Sir John Casales. They are here about the marriage. They say it will not proceed.' She freed one hand and clasped mine.

'I must escape, Mathilde! What shall we do?'

I clutched her fingers, cold as a sliver of ice. She did not resist as I undid the linen parcel I took from her lap. Inside lay four wax figures smeared with blood and dung. Each wore a tiny paper crown, all four were pierced by a vicious-looking bodkin.

'My lady.' I took the parcel from her and, walking across to the large brazier, thrust the parcel deep into its fiery coals.

'I hate them!' The words rasped the air like a sword

being taken from its scabbard. I glanced at the knights sheltering around the other brazier, talking quietly amongst themselves. I walked swiftly back, sat by the princess, clutched her hand and confirmed what she already knew about the intended marriage. She heard me out, nodding wordlessly.

'Be strong, be cunning!' I whispered. 'Whatever happens, retain your mask.' I half smiled at the way I had panicked and been so stupid with Narrow Face. I would not tell the princess that, not yet.

I took her by the arm and raised her, and we walked slowly back into the palace, the knights hurrying behind. I pinched the princess's arm and pointed to a fresco on the wall displaying plump children playing joyfully in a wine press. I traced the coloured ivy which snaked through the painting and began to describe the properties of ground ivy, called ale-tooth. How vital it was for the brewing of ale and how Galen recommended it to treat inflammation of the eyes. We strolled down galleries and passageways. I gossiped like a jay; beside me the Princess eased her breathing and forced a smile. We wandered into a small chapel, its walls decorated with gleaming strips of oak. At the far end stood a simple altar on a sanctuary dais, to the right of that a shrine to the Virgin dressed as a queen holding the Divine Child on her knee. I made the princess kneel on the cushioned prie-dieu; candles flickered on their stands before her. I opened a nearby box, took out a fresh candle, lit it and watched the flame dance as I thrust it on to the pointed spigot. I stared up at the severe face of the Virgin. I found it difficult to pray. I recall saying the same words time and again, '*Ave Maria, Gratia plena, Dominus tecum . . .*' but after that I kept thinking of Narrow Face staggering away from me, blood splashing through his lips. Yet I felt no regret, no contrition, no desire to have my sins shrived. I glanced away. There was a painting of a corpse in its shroud on the side wall of the Lady Chapel, a memento mori: 'Take heed of my fate and see how sometimes I was fresh and merry, now turned to worms, remember that.' I read the scrolled words and thought of Uncle Reginald and Monsieur de Vitry. I vowed to remember them, and him, the man whom I'd glimpsed in the Oriflamme tavern, those beautiful eyes with their far-seeing gaze. I had to pinch myself. Had I truly seen him? Or was he part of a dream? Fable or truth, I vowed I'd never forget him.

Once we'd returned to the princess's private quarters, Isabella abruptly grew tired, which I recognised as a symptom of deep anxiety, a fever of the mind. I poured her some apple juice mixed with a heavy infusion of camomile and made her drink. She lay down on her bed, bringing up her knees, curling like a child as I pulled the cloak over her. Later in the afternoon a finely caparisoned herald came knocking on the door. He announced that His Grace the King would, just after vespers, entertain the English envoys in the White Chamber of the palace; the princess must attend.

Isabella woke up refreshed. I informed her about the royal summons and her mood abruptly changed. She chattered about what she would wear and spent the rest of the afternoon preparing herself, servants and valets being summoned up with jugs and tubs of boiling water. Isabella stripped and washed herself. She perfumed and anointed her body, allowing me to dress her in linen under-garments, purple hose and a beautiful silver dress, high at the neck, with an ornamental veil set on her head bound by a gold braid and studded with gems. She opened her jewellery casket, slipping on rings, silver bracelets and an exquisite pectoral set with rubies and sapphires. She preened herself in front of the sheet of polished metal which served as a mirror, looking at me from the corner of her eye and laughing.

'Now you, Mathilde.' Isabella was generous. She never referred to her earlier symptoms, before she'd fallen asleep, as she made me wash, helping me to anoint and perfume myself, choosing clothes for me to wear. A page was dispatched to her father saying that Mathilde, Isabella's *dame de chambre*, would be accompanying her to the banquet. As the bells of St Chapelle tolled for vespers we made our way down to the White Chamber: a small gleaming hall, with pure white-painted walls covered with hangings, its windows of thick glass decorated with the heraldic devices and armorial insignia of the Capets, the royal house of France. The polished floor reflected the light of sconce-torches and that of a myriad of candles spiked on a wheel which had been lowered to provide even more light. A fire leapt merrily in a cavernous mantled hearth. Part of the hall had been cordoned off with huge screens decorated with sumptuous tapestries in blue, red and gold depicting the romance of the Knights of the Swan and their assault on the Castle of Love. Other cloths bore beautiful roundels in vigorous colours showing the Six Labours of the Year.

The king, his ministers and three sons stood before the huge hearth; on each pillar of this an elaborately carved woodwose glared into the screened-off area as if resenting the wealth on display along the three tables. Isabella swept forward to be greeted. I was ignored. The king and his entourage moved around her. They all looked magnificent in their blue and white velvet suits; brooches, rings and chains of office sparkling in the light. I stood at the corner of the screen. Prince Philippe was glowering, lips moving wordlessly as he half listened to the sottish Charles. I did not wish to catch their eye, so I studied the three strangers. The nearest was dressed in the dark robes of a royal clerk; he had a smooth olive-skinned face under night-black hair swept back and tied in a queue. The other two were English, clearly having some difficulty in understanding the swift conversation in courtly Norman French. One was slightly hidden; the other was a lean beanpole of a man with sour face and sour eyes: Sir Hugh Pourte, merchant prince of London. His companion moved into the circle of light and I froze: Sir John Casales, a handsome, vigorous man with the face of a born soldier, harsh and lean, keen-eyed, firm-mouthed, his greying hair cropped close. He was dressed simply but elegantly in a dark green cote-hardie over a black velvet jerkin and hose of the same colour; his Spanish riding boots, their soft leather gleaming in the firelight, gave more than a hint of the military man.

I stood, watched and remembered. Sir John Casales, his right hand cut off by the Scots at the Battle of Falkirk. He had visited my uncle, but that had been years ago. I quietly prayed to the Virgin that he would not recognise me. Casales' eyes, sharp as a fox, shifted towards me then looked away. It had been years since we met, and even then I'd been standing in my uncle's shadow. I comforted myself with the thought that to a man like Casales, I was nothing more than another servant.

The conversation around the hearth was muted. Sir Hugh Pourte seemed distinctly sour; Casales acted more agitated: the courtier-knight shuffled his booted feet and stared around the hall; apparently what he was listening to was most unfavourable. King Philip himself had grown slightly red-faced, and eventually he turned away and signalled to his retainers; heralds in their gorgeous tabards lifted trumpets and shrilled a blast, the sign that the feasting was to begin.

We dined magnificently on venison and boar, roasted and basted with juices. The king announced, from where he sat in the centre of the middle table, that the meat was fresh straight from the forest of Fontainebleau, brought down by himself. Philip's love of hunting, be it of beast or man, was famous. The main course was followed by a cockatrice of chicken and pork, apricots and oranges from Valence, all served on tables covered in glistening white samite cloths and decorated with plates, jugs, cups and goblets of silver and gold embroidered with gems and stamped with the royal arms. Philip sat enthroned like a silver lion, aware of his power; on either side of him ranged the English envoys. I sat at the end on one of the side tables, Isabella to my left. She'd acted the part, moving amongst the men like some well-trained nun, her lovely face framed by a shimmering veil over that beautiful golden hair. She kept her face impassive even as she sat down, then her eyes changed and I caught the glint of mischief. She leaned over as if to move a cup. 'Mathilde,' she whispered, 'this will be most amusing.'

For the first part of the meal the royal musicians in the nearby gallery, decorated with banners and pennants displaying the Capetian arms, played soft music. A young chorister sang a blood-tingling song: 'I fled to the forest and I have loved its secret places.' The wine jugs were passed round, the hum of conversation grew, Philip, like a skilled lawyer, guiding his guests to what he really wanted to discuss. He made a flourish with his hands at the serjeant-at-arms commanding the heralds beyond the screens; three trumpet blasts shrilled, the sign for the hall to be cleared of all servants and retainers, even the musicians from the gallery and the guards near the door. I watched this royal tableau develop. Philip remained impassive as a statue, silver hair falling to his shoulders, blue eyes crinkled in a false smile, his smooth-shaven face glowing like alabaster. Further down the table sat his minions. Marigny, slender, red-haired and sharp-faced, with hooded eyes and a sharp pointed nose. Nogaret the lawyer, an ever-smiling bag of fat, blond hair shorn close to his head, a cynical face with eyes which regarded the world with contempt. Des Plaisans, Nogaret's alter ego, a lawyer with the ugly face of a mastiff, jutting jaw, thick-lipped, eyes ever darting. These men had killed my uncle, yet I was not ready, skilled enough, to retaliate.

I'd seen enough death that day: Narrow Face slumped against the wall, de Vitry and his household soaking in their own blood. I wondered then if I was petrified, turned to stone like a child who survives a massacre and cannot comprehend what has happened. Looking back, I know different. I have fought in battles, in bloody mêlées. I have also talked to soldiers. I understand what they mean by the phrase 'ice in the blood': a mysterious determination to remain calm, a belief that the death of one enemy does not mean you are safe from the others. In that White Chamber so many, many years ago, God assoil me, I was like that. My time had not yet come. I was still on the edge of the crowd, watching events move slowly to their climax.

Whilst the hall was cleared, the king sat, hands to his face, now and again glancing to his right and left at the English envoys. Pourte sat slouched; the wine had not improved his sour disposition. Casales was leaning forward, holding his goblet above the table.

'My lords,' Marigny must have caught his master's glance, 'we must return to the vexed matter of the Templars, heretics, sodomites—'

'Not proved,' Pourte barked back, 'not proved, sir. That is a matter for our sovereign lord and the justices of the king's Bench at Westminster.'

'But they are criminals!' Marigny retorted in a high-pitched voice.

I sat and listened as that demon incarnate spewed out his filth. How 134 out of the 138 Templars arrested in Paris, including the Grand Master Jacques de Molay, Geoffrey de Charney, the Preceptor of Normandy, and Jean de la Tour, Treasurer of the Paris Temple, not to mention the ploughmen, shepherds, blacksmiths, carpenters and stewards to the number of 1,500 had been dis-patched to stinking dungeons and torture halls. In the main, they'd all confessed. I also heard the names of the traitors, former Templars expelled from the order, men Uncle Reginald had men-tioned over a goblet of wine: Esquin de Floriens, prior of Montfaucon, and Bernard Pelet, names that will always live with the infamy of their accusations, the spilled-out vomit of evil souls. How the Templars were devoted to the devil. How they proclaimed that Christ was a false prophet, justly punished for his sins. How initiates of the Temple were commanded to spit, trample, even urinate on the crucified Christ. They also had to kiss the Templar who received them into the order on the mouth, navel, buttocks . . . even the penis. Marigny described how the Templars were devoted to Baphomet, the demon who appeared in the form of a cat, or skull or head with three faces.

Casales and Pourte shook their heads in disbelief. Casales glanced quickly at me but showed no recognition. I did not care; I seethed with rage. I knew the Temple. I recognised these allegations for what they truly were: the horrid spilling of nasty, narrow souls. Satan and all his lords of the air had swept up to dine in that ghostly chamber with its tapestries and statues, silver pots and golden goblets, and his banners and pennants had been unfurled as the Templars, God's good men, were hunted to their deaths. Pourte objected and referred to stories about Templars being tortured with the strappado or their feet being basted with animal fat and placed in front of a roaring fire until their bones fell out.

'Such men,' he commented, 'would confess to anything.'

I drank noisily from my goblet and glanced away. Isabella was watching me curiously, a faint smile on her lips. She knew! I placed the goblet down. Marigny was moving the conversation towards the intended nuptials of the princess. All eyes turned to her. Again Pourte began to voice objections. How he and Casales believed the marriage was in the best interests of the English crown but his seigneur, the king, did not. Marigny silkily pointed out that French troops were massing on the borders of English-held Gascony, whilst wasn't Edward of England facing war in Scotland against the redoubtable Robert de Bruce? At this moment Bruce was the French king's enemy, but there again, matters might change. Casales intervened; the negotiations flowed back and forth like water in a millpond; the rest of us were ignored.

The king's sons had drunk deeply and were glancing hot-eyed at their sister. Isabella sensed this, signalled to me and rose, bowing to her father, who flicked his fingers as a sign she might retire. Everyone else either rose or staggered to their feet. Isabella curtsied to them all and, followed by me, swept out of the hall up to our own chambers. She remained silent and severe even when we were alone with a serjeant-at-arms on guard outside. I lit more candles and tapers and helped her to undress. She kept on her shift, covering that with a fleur-de-lis cloak, and sat on a high-backed chair, turning to look through the window casement.

'Mathilde,' she whispered, 'lock the door.' I hastened to obey, but when I tried to turn the heavy key it would not move, whilst the bolts at top and bottom seemed rusted hard.

'My lady,' I gasped.

'Look out of the door,' she ordered. I did so. The gallery outside was deserted. No serjeant-at-arms; only shadows dancing in the lantern light, silent except for the creak of wood and the scurrying of mice. I stood listening to the faint sounds of the palace.

'They will come.' Isabella's voice grew vibrant. 'They will come tonight, Mathilde!'

I stared down the gallery, wondering what to do.

'We can't flee.' Isabella spoke my thoughts. 'There is nowhere to go.'

I stood indecisive until I recalled Simon de Vitry's house; pushing open the door, the sprawled corpses, those crossbow bolts embedded deep in their flesh. I flew down the gallery.

'Mathilde!' I heard Isabella cry out; she must have thought I was fleeing. At the end of the gallery stood an unlocked aumbry containing arms: bows and arrows, poles and spears, and what I was looking for, a small arbalest. Even as I grasped it and the quiver of quarrels, I wondered if the assassin who'd slipped into de Vitry's house had had something similar: small crossbows, perhaps two or three already primed in a sack. I ran back down the gallery, throwing myself through the half-opened door, then slammed it shut and leaned against it. Sweat soaked me. Isabella, still seated on the chair, watched me intently. I pointed at the narrow cot bed I slept in, then primed the arbalest, sliding a quarrel in, winching back the cord.

'You've done that before, Mathilde?' Isabella murmured.

'My uncle.' I paused. 'Yes.' I smiled bleakly. 'I used to go hunting, as I will tonight.'

Isabella rose from her chair and climbed into bed.

I went round the chamber, extinguishing the candles, then lay down on the cot. I listened to the noise of the palace and heard a creak along the gallery outside. The door opened, and two figures slipped in. They ignored me and raced across the chamber. The light was poor but I could make out the shapes; Louis and Philippe had come to abuse their sister. No guard stood outside; no attempt was made to stop them. Louis threw himself onto the bed. I heard Isabella's stifled screams as his hand went across her mouth. I slid from the cot bed; Philippe turned. I brought up the arbalest, aimed and loosed, immediately putting another quarrel in the slot and winding back the cord. The first bolt smacked into the wall beside the princess's bed almost hitting the window.

'Get out!' I screamed. I even lapsed into the soldier's patois my uncle had taught me. The princess leapt out of one side of the bed. She wrapped her cloak about her and moved towards me. Both intruders were drunk, swaying on their feet; I could smell their wine-drenched breath even from where I stood.

'Who are you?' Louis lurched forward, lower lip protruding, eyes bleary. Philippe was so drunk he slumped down on the end of the bed.

'I am Mathilde de Clairebon,' I replied, '*dame de chambre* for your sister, appointed solely to look after her. My lords, she does not want you here. You must go!'

'And what if . . .' Louis made to take another step. I raised the arbalest, 'what if . . .' he stood back, swaying, 'we do not wish to leave?'

'Then, my lord, like any knight, I would do what my duty to your sister, to the king and to God requires. Perhaps the king's court will decide whether I did wrong or not.' I'd plotted this as I lay in the dark, waiting for them to come.

Philippe lurched to his feet, wiping his mouth on the cuff of his sleeve.

'I want to get out.' He hurried past me into the gallery to retch and vomit.

Louis stood, hands on hips.

'And if we return?'

'If you return, my lord, I assure you of this: I will write certain letters and lodge them with people I trust in Paris. Should this happen again, copies of those letters will go to His Holiness in Avignon, not to mention the King of England! I leave it to you what your father would think of that.'

Louis shook his head, lust burning like fire in his eyes. For a few heartbeats he considered attacking me. I took a step back, allowing him to leave. He sighed noisily, brushed past me but turned at the door.

'Mathilde de Clairebon,' he pointed a finger at me, 'I shall not forget you.'

'My lord, I thank you for the compliment. Rest assured, I shall always remember you!'

Louis left, slamming the door behind him. I could hear his hoarse whisperings to Philippe out in the gallery, then their footsteps faded. I immediately took a chair, brought it across and pushed it against the door.

'Why didn't you do that immediately?' Isabella walked over to me, her face white as snow, her eyes no longer blue but dark pools. She was on the verge of tears, lower lip quivering.

'My lady, every battle has to be fought; you simply choose your field. Tonight we fought and we won! I do not think they will return.'

Isabella came close, grasping me by the shoulder; being slightly shorter than me, she stood on tiptoe and kissed me softly on the lips, then on each cheek.

'Come with me, Mathilde.'

She led me out of the chamber. I hastily slung a cloak around me, keeping the arbalest and quiver of quarrels beneath. We went along the gallery and down the stairs. I realised we were returning to the chapel which we'd visited on my return from the city. The door was off the latch, and Isabella led me into the sweetened darkness, where the faint candles, now capped, still glowed before the statue. She hastily pulled the bolts across, then walked to where the sacred host hung in its silver pyx box from its chain on a wall bracket; next to it the red sanctuary light glowed. Isabella acted as fervently as any priest. She took the pyx down and laid it on the altar. She then beckoned me forward and made me put my hand over the pyx, placing hers on top.

'I swear,' her eyes held mine, 'I swear by the body and blood of Christ, of our seigneur Lord Jesus, I'm your friend in peace or war until death.'

'And my lady,' I placed my hand on top of hers, 'I am yours!'

Isabella blinked back the tears, picked up the pyx and replaced it on its hook. She led me by the hand to sit on the edge of the dais. The chapel was cold but our cloaks were thick and furred. Isabella tapped me on the knee.

'Mathilde, tell me now who you really are; your secret will be safe with me.'

So I did. My life as a child, my father, the farm at Bretigny, my journey to Paris, Uncle Reginald, my years as his apprentice, his arrest and execution. I did not pause. I told the truth. I was safe with Isabella, she would not betray me. I also told her about Narrow Face's death, the massacre at de Vitry's house. She listened carefully, nodding all the time. When I finished, she again grasped my hand as if trying to draw its warmth for herself.

'They've always come,' she began. 'They always have, as long as I can remember. I hate them, Mathilde, they see me as a toy, a whore; their own sister, a princess of France! I too have the Capet blood in me. I too am a direct descendant of the sacred Louis.' She gestured at a fresco on the far wall celebrating that holy French king of whom

Philip was so proud. 'They come whenever they please. If my mother had lived she could have saved me. She died, you know, a strange sickness. Some whisper my father killed her! So desirous was he of entering the Templar order, of living the life of a so-called celibate. In truth all he wanted was their wealth, their houses, their farms, their granges, their fields, their livestock. He'll do anything, Mathilde, to get his own way. What he wants has all the force of God's law.'

'They will not return,' I said, 'your brothers; I don't think they will!'

Isabella nodded. 'It is becoming too dangerous,' she agreed. 'If their games cost my father, they would feel the full fury of his wrath.' She narrowed her eyes. 'Our father would not be pleased.'

'Have you ever thought of appealing to him?'

Isabella laughed, a strange strangled sound at the back of her throat.

'As the root, so the branches, Mathilde. He too is not free of all guilt in such matters. He is not really my father, not here.' She tapped her chest. 'In my heart, in my soul he is not my father, and one day I shall have my revenge. Come, Mathilde.'

CHAPTER 4

Faith, fettered in prison, is very desolate.

'A Song of the Times', 1272–1307

We rose and had reached the door of the chapel when the alarm was raised; a hunter's horn wailed, a funereal sound, proclaiming chilling news. Other horns took up the call. Along the gallery outside pinpricks of light appeared, and the crash of doors being flung open shattered the silence. A royal serjeant-at-arms came running in through a postern door leading from one of the courtyards. He'd lost his helmet, the chainmail coif pulled close around his head, dark red cloak trailing. He stopped when he saw us and, staring wide-eyed, raised the horn to give another blast. Isabella told him to be quiet as the entire palace was now aroused. She curtly demanded the cause of the disturbance. The soldier, breathless, simply pointed, then led us back into the court-yard, now ablaze with lantern flame. Retainers and soldiers gathered in a pool of torchlight around a body sprawled in an ugly, crooked fashion on the paving stones. I forced my way through, Isabella shouting orders that others stand aside, and I crouched before the corpse of Sir Hugh Pourte. The merchant prince was clothed only in a night-gown, now pulled high over white bony knees; his eyes were open and glazed in death, and his nose, mouth and ears were blood-splattered. He'd twisted his neck, which hung eerily loose like that of a dead chicken. His flesh was still warm, the muscles supple – death had been most recent.

'Regardez.' The harsh Navarrene accent of one of the soldiers caught my attention. I looked up at the palace wall: on the third tier, about nine yards above us, the great window casement had been opened.

'Et là, et là!'

I followed his direction. Under the window was ranged a series of rusty iron brackets driven into the grey ragstone wall to secure ladders placed there so masons, carpenters and glaziers could carry out repairs. From one of these, glinting in the torch-light, hung a thick gold chain last seen around Pourte's neck at the banquet the night before. Had Pourte dropped this, tried to retrieve it and fallen?

'Mathilde! Mathilde!' Isabella's voice stilled the clamour. I too heard the dull thuds and faint shouts from within the palace. Isabella had retreated into a circle of men-at-arms; she was gesturing with her hand that I investigate the noise.

I hastened back into the palace. By then I knew my way. Pages were now lighting more torches. The galleries were full of spluttering lights and moving shadows; shouts echoed to the clatter of arms and the sound of running feet. I went up the stairs to the third gallery. It was long and narrow, with doors on either side; soldiers and servants thronged, some still rubbing the sleep from their eyes. Soldiers clustered round one of the doors. I recognised Casales and the olive-skinned clerk Rossaleti amongst the black shapes in the torchlight; they were forcing a door which, as I hastened down, snapped back on its hinges. Now I was Isabella's *dame de la chambre*, but to those men clustering in that room I was simply a serving wench, of no more importance than the rodents which ran screeching and squealing from their presence.

Pourte's chamber was large. I could make out a four-poster bed with its curtains pulled closed; the rest was dark, as the cold night air pouring through the open casement window had snuffed out the candles. Casales and the others, chattering in English, lit some candles and immediately checked certain sealed caskets, ignoring those chests with their lids thrown back. Casales sifted through parchments on the table; from the tone of his voice he believed Pourte's death was an accident. None of the caskets or baskets from the secret chancery of England had been tampered with. Nothing was missing. They then clustered round the window; from their cries and shouts I gathered they'd glimpsed the golden chain. Marigny and others now stood in the doorway, reluctant to trespass into the chamber of an English envoy. Rossaleti invited them in and, in Norman French, quickly explained how it must have been an accident. Had they been roused by Pourte's fall? Marigny asked. Rossaleti explained how he, Casales and Nogaret had been deep in conversation in des Plaisans' chancery office when the alarm had been raised. They'd hurried up and forced the door. It had been locked and bolted, the key still inside; when they broke it down, this was what they had found. Rossaleti pointed to the window and the small stool beneath it. He explained how Pourte must have gone to the window to take the night air, dropped his chain, leaned over to recover it and fallen to his death. Nods of approval and grunts of assent greeted this. Rossaleti then turned abruptly, as if aware of my presence, and glared fiercely at me. I bowed quickly and left.

By now, the princess had returned to her own chamber. Servants, roused by the commotion, were cleaning the gallery where Philippe had vomited. The sullen-faced serjeant had returned to his post, the red welt on his cheek and his hostile glare clear testimony of Isabella's fury at his earlier desertion.

'You're late!' the princess snapped as I closed the chamber door.

'My lady, I am tired.' I snuffed the candles and lay down on my own bed, pulling up the coverlet to hide my face. I felt sick and tired, hot with a clammy sweat; so much had happened, such a nightmare of a day.

'Mathilde,' Isabella's voice was soft, 'Mathilde, I missed you, I was frightened!'

'My lady, let us go to sleep.'

'What happened to the Englishman?' Isabella mocked. 'Did he try to fly?'

'No, my lady, they claim he went to the window to take the air, dropped a golden chain, tried to recover it and fell to his death.'

'But you don't believe that, Mathilde, not you with those sharp eyes of yours. You remind me of a cat I used to have. It always knew where the mice holes were. It never approached, it simply sat far off and watched.'

'My lady,' I struggled up and leaned against the feather-filled bolsters, 'I find it difficult to understand why Sir Hugh Pourte, who was in his nightshift, should be carrying a gold chain to a window. The man had drunk deeply, he was tired. The night air was bitterly cold. Why should he open the window so far? Why should he be clutching a gold chain? Moreover, and I will have to reflect on this, but if he stood on a stool and leaned out he still could not have retrieved it. Why didn't he take a hook or a sword, something to loop back the chain?'

'So he didn't fly and he didn't fall. Are you saying he was pushed?'

'Perhaps, my lady.' I closed my eyes and recalled that corpse lying so crookedly in the courtyard; the bruises on the side of the head, the broken neck, the blood seeping out from the skull like yolk from a cracked egg.

'And yet you say the door was locked and bolted from within.'

'My lady, who is Ralph Rossaleti?'

'Ah . . .'The princess giggled. 'He is our watchdog, Mathilde, one of Father's senior clerks. He is going to carry my secret seal in England; what I write, he will know. He will be our adviser.'

'A spy, my lady? Your father's spy?'

'We'll see.' Again Isabella's voice had a lilting tone. 'We are to meet him tomorrow, he and Sir John Casales. Perhaps you could ask your questions then. Mathilde?'

'Yes, my lady?'

'Do you ever pray?'

'I try to.'

'I do! I pray. I prayed to be delivered from my brothers. You're an angel, Mathilde, an answer to my prayer.'

I lay back down again, pulled the coverlet up and drifted into a sleep full of nightmares: of dark figures dancing on the end of scaffold ropes, of faces staring at me from a haunted cart rumbling across a cobbled yard. When I woke, just before dawn, I was sweat-soaked and thick-headed. The princess was asleep, deeply so, perhaps relieved about the dangers she had been rescued from. I opened the chamber door; the serjeant had been replaced by two more. I went back inside and splashed water over my face from the lavarium. Drying my hands, I quickly dressed and went out into the palace, up the staircase and back to Hugh Pourte's chamber.

The broken door now leaned against the wall. The chamber had been stripped of all its possessions. I crossed to the bed and pulled back the curtains; the bed had not been slept in. I looked around. Pourte had filled a goblet full of wine. I picked this up, sniffed and tasted: nothing but the best from Bordeaux. I walked to the window, stood on the stool, opened the casement and leaned out. I recalled Pourte's height; even he could never have reached that chain, so why had he tried? Was he inebriated? If he had been killed beforehand, how did his assassin enter and leave his chamber when the door was locked and bolted from the inside? I went down on my knees like a dog examining the floor between the edge of a Turkey rug and the stool near the window. I used my fingers and found a rusty-red stain, scraping at it I picked it up, and sniffed it; it wasn't wine, but blood. I crawled nearer to the window and found other drops, but nothing on the sill or ledge. This blood could have been the result of anything; was it even Pourte's? Had he been assassinated and killed in his chamber by a blow to the back of his head, his neck broken, the casement opened and his corpse tossed out? If so, how had the killer escaped? I went back to the window, stood on the stool and looked over the sill. The assassin could have climbed up from outside but the window would have been closed as the night was bitterly cold. He ran the risk of being noticed, whilst it would have been both difficult and dangerous for anyone to climb up by themselves on a dark freezing night.

I left the chamber and went down to the palace death house which stood at the end of a long path leading to one of the orchards. I opened the door and walked in. The death house contained a long row of wooden tables, some empty, others covered with dirty sheets. A rusting brazier, glowing with ash and strewn with herbs, did little to hide the reeking odour of death and decay. Along the white-washed wall was a crude picture which brought alive Ezekiel's vision of the Valley of Dry Bones: stark depictions of skeletons thrusting up through the iron-grey soil. The brooding silence and those lumps of flesh under their dirty sheets provoked a deep unease. I pulled back one covering; an old man lay sprawled beneath. On the next table was Pourte. He'd been washed and smeared with some herbal oil. I examined his body; it was scarred and bruised, though nothing recent, except the purple-red bruise on the side of his face, the skull cracked like a shell and his neck as loose as a piece of slack rope. I scrutinised the corpse carefully and wondered again what had really happened. Why should Pourte be killed here, and by whom? Did his death concern me or Isabella, my mistress?

I walked out of the death house. The light was still murky, the wind shifting the mist into swirling wisps as if an army of ghosts was milling about. I was so absorbed with myself, I tripped over the halberd deliberately placed across the threshold. As

I tumbled forward, a piece of coarse sacking, reeking of tar, was thrown over my head, and an arm, tight as a noose, went round my throat. The voice was slurred, nothing more than a hoarse whisper:

'Mathilde, Mathilde, tell your mistress not to pry! Keep to your chambers and your embroidery!'

The grip tightened. I began to choke, then I was released and pushed violently forward. The grip had been so vice-like, the sacking wound so carefully around me, that by the time I had recovered and torn off the blindfold, my assailant had gone, and there was nothing but the mist, the smells of that open wasteland and the muted sounds of the palace coming to life. I picked myself up.

When I returned, Isabella was at her prie-dieu, dressed and gowned, demure as any convent novice. For a while I just stood leaning against the door, wondering who had attacked me and why. My throat and neck felt sore, my cheeks burned hot, my body was drenched in a clammy sweat. I took a deep breath, came up behind her and peered at the small, beautifully scripted book of hours she was reading from. The capital A of the prayer *Adjutorium nostrum in nomine Domini* – Our help is in the name of the Lord – was exquisitely painted, though the miniature itself made me smile: the painting showed a collection of ravens, bedecked like princes, being preached at by a cat garbed in the mitre and cope of a bishop.

Isabella turned sharply, eyes bright with mischief.

'Master Rossaleti painted that. He's a trained

scribbler as well as a clerk. He was once a Benedictine monk.' She chattered on. 'Well, he was married once but his wife was crushed by a cart, so he became a clerk.'

'So you know Rossaleti well, my lady?'

'Of course; he was my tutor. He knows all the stories about Arthur and his knights.'

'But you said he was a spy.'

'It's logical,' Isabella laughed, getting to her feet. 'Everyone in my household, apart from you, is a spy! The Secreti, the Secret Ones, Marigny's coven, hover everywhere. Anyway, we have to meet Rossaleti and Casales just after noon.' Her smile faded as she noticed the scuff marks on my face and neck, and her hand went out. 'Oh Mathilde, what is wrong?' She touched my chin gently, her blue eyes troubled. 'Mathilde, what happened?'

I told her about my visit to the death house and the assault that ensued. Isabella sat down and listened, tapping her foot against a stool. When I'd finished, she picked at a thread on her cuff.

'I do not know,' she murmured, 'why someone should attack you. Was it because of last night? Your visit to Pourte's chamber or the death house?' She shrugged. 'Anyone could be responsible: Louis, one of the Secreti?'

She turned to the table and closed the book of hours. 'Listen to the palace, Mathilde! We sit and hear the sounds. We see people go here and there but we don't know the truth behind what is really happening. The same is true about you, about me . . .'

I stared at this young woman, in many ways a mere cipher in her father's plans, a child amongst adults, a dove amongst the hawks. Or was she? At times she betrayed a cunning and astuteness of which her father should have been proud.

'The Templars, the massacre at de Vitry's house, the death of the Englishman Pourte have one thing in common.' She smiled. 'Me!' She pulled a face as I stared in puzzlement. 'My father has to pay a huge dowry to the English, but his treasury is empty. The plunder of the Temple will fill it. De Vitry was one of his bankers. He negotiated on behalf of the Temple and other merchants, such as the Black and White Frescobaldi of Italy. De Vitry's death,' she nodded, 'might be a blow to him!'

'And Pourte?'

'Ah, the Englishman. Edward chose well. Both he and Casales are of the English royal council. I understand they speak for my marriage.'

I remembered the banquet the night before. Pourte and Casales did not really believe the message they had brought; that was why they had been chosen, to give as little offence to the French as possible. Both men had clearly been discomfited, having to argue a policy they did not believe in.

'Webs within webs,' I replied. 'So why were de Vitry and Pourte murdered? Was it because of you, because of me?' I did not wait for an answer. 'Of course,' I whispered, 'there may be other reasons, whilst I was warned simply because I was caught prying.'

'And there's something else.'

Isabella rose and took a key from a chain around her neck. Kneeling down, she removed the Turkey rug and, using a thin knife, prised loose a block in the wooden floor. Stretching down she took out a small coffer, which she opened. She grinned mischievously at me.

'Only Maria knew where this was hidden.'

'And where is Maria now?'

'Gone away.' Isabella laughed. 'She'll never come back. Here, this is for you.' She handed across a small scroll, its seal broken. I immediately recognised the script of de Vitry, the distinctive sweep of the quill. I'd seen enough in his chancery office to recognise it. I unrolled the scroll. The date at the top was inscribed a day before he was murdered. It was written in the cipher de Vitry and I had learnt from Uncle Reginald, in which the Greek alphabet is transposed by a series of even numbers and the last letter, omega, is translated into French as A.

'You were gone.' Isabella answered my stare. 'I too, Mathilde, protect myself. All letters to my household are delivered directly to me, remember that.'

She leaned forward excitedly. 'What does it say?'

'My assailant,' I replied hotly, 'told you to stay in your chambers with your embroidery.'

She stamped her foot and made a rude sound with her lips.

'What does it say, Mathilde?'

I hid my annoyance at her intervention and walked across to the small chancery desk; with Isabella standing over me, I translated the message.

'La Rue des Ecrivains – above the sign of Ananias. Trust him if you have to! If he is gone, if God's will for you is manifest, you will find him above the Palfrey in Seething Lane off Paternoster Row in the city of London.'

'What does this mean?' Isabella asked.

'It means, my lady,' I turned and looked at her, 'that de Vitry reflected and wondered if I was safe here. I suspect he felt guilty. He was a good man. He sent me this as further help, whilst all the time it was he who needed assistance.'

Isabella leaned over, her lips brushing my ear as if we were lovers. 'We don't need him, Mathilde, always remember that. We are, as your assailant said, here in our chambers with what he calls our embroidery. God willing, Mathilde, you and I will weave something which people, including my father, will always remember. Never forget that!' She spoke with such passion; spots of anger appeared high in her cheeks, and her blue eyes glared furiously. I'd never seen her like that before; I had still failed to realise the deep well of resentment in that young woman. Ignored and abused, she was weaving her own web of revenge, eager to carry it out. That is what I want to tell you. I must describe it as I would emerging symptoms or the converging of the planets to move logically in sequence; I must depict truthfully what we felt, what we saw, what we did at a particular time. I am determined not to appear arrogant, as if I could predict what was to happen. Hindsight makes wise men of us all and only a fool, or a liar, ascribes to such wisdom.

We spent the rest of the morning preparing for Casales and Rossaleti. The princess was now being treated as a person in her own right, and when we moved down to her father's council chamber, only a royal scribe, a pallid-faced old man, joined us. Isabella sat at the top of the table in a high-backed chair, I on her left, Casales and Rossaleti to her right. The scribe perched at the end of the table, pen poised above the ink pot, ready to take memoranda, to report back to his masters everything that was said. I stared round the council chamber. A plain, stark room, its plaster a dull white with paintings on the wall showing scenes from the life of Christ. At the far end hung a huge crucifix; at the other was a dais and a row of writing carrels where royal scribes could sit and be summoned by their masters if they needed them. The ceiling was beamed like a barn. The more I sat there, the more I wondered if it was pretence. Was this some sort of tableau, a court masque for Philip, Marigny or one of the Secreti to observe? Isabella, dressed ever so demurely, certainly behaved herself.

'You've asked to see me, sirs?' The princess, following court protocol, began the discussions. The scribe waited, pen poised. Rossaleti replied with the usual pleasantries. I studied both men. Casales was a tough professional soldier, a knight who'd journeyed far and fought in many battles. His hair was cropped short, his lean shaven face showing the scars of his years on campaign. He kept his severed wrist in its sheath of leather hidden beneath the table. He had the look of an ascetic: deep-set eyes under thick brows, a pointed nose, thin lips. The only relief in such a hard face was the dimple on his chin. In many ways Casales reminded me of some of the Templars. He was dressed simply in a green cote-hardie over a black jerkin and hose. He wore no jewellery except for a silver chain round his neck, a gift, so he told me later, from his long-dead mother. He was a professional fighter, so he found it difficult to stay still, his left hand constantly tapping the table. Only once did he glance at me, but again he betrayed no sign of recognition and I breathed an Ave in relief. Casales spoke courtly French and I gathered he was a close confidant and a leading henchman of the English favourite Lord Peter Gaveston, Earl of Cornwall. Casales explained he was half Gascon himself and had served Lord Peter both in Gascony and in England. He and Rossaleti had spent months in Westminster, meeting over the intended marriage and a firm friendship had developed between the two envoys.

Rossaleti nodded understandingly while Casales spoke. Sitting opposite, I could see that Rossaleti, garbed in black like a Benedictine monk, was not as young as I had thought. He looked to be from

Italy or the sun-rich provinces of the south, a hand-some, almost girlish face with dark eyes and olive skin, but this was offset by the deep furrows in his cheeks. He was a man always on the verge of smiling with ever-shifting eyes which stared curiously at you as if weighing your secret worth. Rossaleti was King Philip's man body and soul, and yet, at the time, I took to him. I tried to ignore the heavy gold ring emblazoned with the Capetian arms on the middle finger of his right hand which constantly moved, touching the Ave beads around his neck. Rossaleti, soft spoken, would intervene every so often to guide the conversation to its true purpose. How the marriage between Isabella and Edward of England might be a matter of dispute, yet the English king's love and personal regard for his betrothed was unsullied. In other words, both men were proclaiming that Isabella was not to be offended; the hostile stance adopted by the English king was only a matter of politic.

Isabella listened attentively to their courtly speeches and replied in kind. Down the table the scribe's pen scratched the parchment. I recall jumping at a harsh sound from one of the windows behind me. I glanced round and glimpsed the shape of a raven pecking at the hardened glass. Isabella smiled at this and brought her speech to a close, trailing her pretty white fingers across her forehead. My mistress then expressed her deep condolences at the death of Sir Hugh Pourte. Casales nodded.

'Our visit,' he smiled crookedly, 'has been much

marred by tragedy. One of my clerks, Matthew of Crokendon, was found stabbed in the Cemetery of the Innocents, no one knows by whom. He was last seen leaving a tavern with a wench, a whore, but no one can recall her.'

I set my face like flint as Casales proceeded to discuss the removal of Sir Hugh Pourte's corpse back to England. Isabella, her features schooled, listened attentively and offered her help. Only when Master Crokendon was mentioned again did those angelically innocent blue eyes shift quickly to me, a look of mock sorrow on her face.

At the end of the meeting the scribe asked if the white wine and doucettes should be served. Isabella shook her head and rose quickly. I followed. My mind seethed like a bubbling cauldron with images of Narrow Face spitting blood, falling against the charnel house wall, and my uncle being thrust up the gallows ladder to the waiting noose. In truth I was frightened, but Isabella touched me comfortingly, a swift caress across the wrist as I followed her to the door.

'My lady?'

Isabella turned.

'My lady,' Casales scraped a bow, 'I understand from your father that you are leaving on a visit to the city.'

'Why yes,' Isabella replied. 'I have several purchases to make. I need to visit the markets. I must write to my betrothed. I need certain parchments.' She gestured at the scribe hastily collecting his pens and papers. 'I need to go to the Rue des Ecrivains.'

'In which case, my lady,' Casales scraped another elegant bow, 'may we accompany you? My lord has asked me to describe to you what I can about England, London and Westminster.' His voice took a teasing turn, and Isabella replied in kind. Casales again expressed a wish to join us, explaining that the sudden death of his colleague Sir Hugh Pourte must be mourned but that the tasks assigned to him by the King of England had to be carried through.

Isabella could not refuse such pleasantry. She came back to the table gesturing at both men to sit, and asked the scribe to serve the wine and the plate of doucettes. Isabella was a mistress at that, skilled and adept in dealing with people. She soon drew Casales and Rossaleti into conversation about themselves, asking questions about Casales' service in Scotland and other places. Afterwards she turned to Rossaleti, expressing her deep regret for the tragedies which had occurred in his life. Although she was only thirteen, Isabella was definitely her father's daughter. She could, when she wished, be charming, kind, understanding, listening attentively, nodding at the appropriate places. Both men, experienced and skilled in their own affairs, chattered like children, but then, at the time, we were no different. Both my mistress and I had a great deal to learn. Only when the wine and sweet cakes were finished did Isabella point at the window, murmuring how the day was drawing and that we must leave soon. She welcomed them joining us, and a short while later we all left the palace.

It felt so strange, leaving the royal precinct, crossing the bridge into the city. Isabella and I, swathed in cloaks, rode palfreys, Casales and Rossaleti beside us. Our entire party was circled by a troop of mounted Genoese crossbowmen in their red and green livery, steel morions on their heads, their heavy arbalests strapped to their backs or hanging from saddle hooks. Heralds and trumpeters carrying their gleaming silver instruments and the blue and gold banners of the royal household went before us in their splendid tabards to keep back the crowds. The smells and the sounds of the city greeted me like a strengthening breeze, recalling all the memories of my long youth with Uncle Reginald. I tried not to reflect, even as I murmured the Requiem for him and Monsieur de Vitry. I owed both of them my life, so my deep debt to them would last for ever. Reflecting on Marigny's speech at the banquet, I realised how both Uncle Reginald and de Vitry had surmised correctly. Anyone associated with the Templars, be he knight or hireling, had been swept up by Philip's edict. If my uncle had not been so careful, and Monsieur de Vitry so generous, I would now be in a dungeon at the Chatelêt or, perhaps, a corpse swinging on some rope from the public gallows. Such thoughts chilled me. I again vowed to act the part assigned to me: to pretend to the present, be fiercely loyal to the past and, if necessary, seize what opportunities the future offered to take justice and revenge.

I hitched my cloak closer about me, comforting myself with such thoughts, reins in one hand, the other gripping the high saddle horn. I stared out across the sea of faces: women in their veils and wimples, florid-cheeked merchants, the apple-sweet faces of children held up to see the spectacle of royalty passing, the lean white faces of cowled friars, the bleary eyes of the poor, all gathering to gape as the great ones processed into the city. Isabella whispered something to the serjeant-at-arms, the leader of our escort. The man looked surprised but shouted an order and our cavalcade swung off the main thoroughfare and down busy side streets. Houses loomed over us, their upper storeys leaning so close to each other they blocked out the sunlight. We passed darkened doorways which housed their own silent watchers, white-eyed beggars, garish whores, women with their children. Signs creaked eerily, the clatter and hubbub of the small work-shops dying away as the craftsmen hurried to stare at our gorgeous procession. Only once did we stop, to allow passage to a shabby funeral procession preceded by boys swinging censers and a ragged friar holding a cross. The filth and stench of the runnels forced Isabella to use a spikenard, yet such smells, rank though they were, brought back memories of my joyful days as Uncle Reginald's messenger in the city.

We debouched into a square where ointment- and

perfume-sellers had their stalls, the sweetness of their produce doing something to mask the pungent odours of the gutters full of dirt and refuse. Across the square rose the sombre Church of the Forgotten Souls, surmounted by a dramatically carved tympanum of Christ harrowing hell. Casales and Rossaleti expressed surprise, but Isabella declared she wished to arrange masses for the soul of the dead Hugh Pourte. We entered the walled enclosure around the church. Casales said such charity wasn't necessary but Isabella was already calling for a page to help her dismount. Escorted by two of the Genoese, we pushed open the iron-studded door and stepped into the candlelit darkness. Before us a long, ghostly nave swept up to a raised sanctuary where the high altar stood at the top of steep steps, a place of worship, of moving darkness with the sanctuary lamp gleaming like a beacon. Taper lights fluttered beneath shadow-wrapped statues. From the oratories on either side of the nave came the chanting of the requiem masses, their ghostly refrains drifting on the incense-laden air:

'I John saw a new heaven and a new earth . . .'

'Eternal rest grant to them, O Lord and let perpetual light shine upon them . . .'

Isabella swept down the nave towards the mercy seat, where a monk sat like the Angel of Doom behind a high table. The Genoese bowmen wandered off to view a painting near the gallery porch. Isabella paused, plucking at my cuff.

'I come here,' she whispered, 'to have masses said

for my murdered mother. I shall now pay for one for Hugh Pourte.' She opened her hand to show three silver coins, 'and one for your uncle.' Isabella crossed herself and continued on to the mercy seat, a cushioned bench with a high back. We sat down. The monk opposite, his face half hidden by a deep hood, picked up his pen and opened the casket ledger before him. On either side of this two candles poured pools of light. The monk did not greet us, but immediately consulted the calendar of saints and inscribed the three masses for the names Isabella whispered. She was careful about my uncle, only whispering, 'Lord Reginald.' The monk murmured in reply, arranging the masses for certain days, and indicating in which of the oratories they would be celebrated. Isabella took little note of this; we would never be able to attend them. In a whisper that monk of death, the Recorder of Forgotten Souls, provided other details, talking softly to us as if he was delivering absolution for our sins.

I became distracted by the arras hung over the screen behind the monk, its scenes brought to life by the glowing candles. The arras proclaimed a vision of purgatory, with souls in every posture of physical torture, suspended by meat hooks driven through their jaws, tongues and groins frozen hard in ice or boiling in bubbling vats of liquid metal like fish in hot oil. A clever device! It must have forced all visitors to this church to concentrate on the Last Four Things, their own meeting with death and what secret sins they were guilty of. The painting showed how the promiscuous had fire burning between their legs whilst drunkards were forced to drink scalding vermin. It did make me wonder about the love of Jesus and the fate of Uncle Reginald. Such a man, surely, had suffered all his purgatory in the dungeons of the Chatelêt. And, if Christ was good and God was compassionate, Lord Reginald would be welcomed into paradise without suffering such pains.

Abruptly the murmured conversation between Isabella and the monk changed. Isabella was leaning over the table, speaking in Navarrese, a tongue she'd learnt from her mother and one she lapsed into whenever she was troubled or agitated. She was pushing across a second purse. The monk swiftly took this and handed over small pouches which disappeared into the voluminous pockets of Isabella's robe. Again the monk spoke, this time not in whispered French but harsh Navarrese. Isabella replied just as quickly. I caught the phrase 'Frater Marco'. The monk sketched a blessing. Isabella rose, bowed to the high altar and left.

We were halfway down the nave when Isabella paused. She pointed up to the hammer-beamed roof where the artist had fixed roundels depicting the serene faces of angels. She acted as if she was describing them to me.

'Brother Marco is a Crutched Friar,' she murmured. 'He was once a member of my mother's household. He too knows the God-given truth about the past. He is also a herbalist, a skilled one; he gives me certain powders.'

I caught my breath as Isabella's strange blue eyes glanced sideways at me. 'Poor Mother was tended to by three of my father's physicians. Mathilde, I know the truth.' Her voice grew fierce. 'In the last two years all three have died with the cramps, a seizure or,' she pulled a face, 'something else?' She hastily made the sign of the cross. 'No one,' she hissed, 'will pray for their souls.'

'And the fresh powders?'

'Mathilde, Mathilde, we may not go to England. If not,' she glared at me, 'what protection do I have?' She left the words hanging like a threat. She called out to the Genoese, and we left the church. Casales and Rossaleti helped us mount and we rode out of the enclosure. The Rue des Ecrivains was close by, a broad alleyway where the sellers of unscrubbed and untreated vellum, ink powders, pumice stones, leather bindings, seals and wax had their stalls and shops. A cluster of colourfully scrolled signs proclaimed the different merchandise available. A noisy, merry place thronged by scholars from the halls garbed in all kinds of tawdry finery, short cote-hardies, ragged cloaks, with cheap jewellery glittering on their fingers and wrists. The scholars jostled busily with apprentices in their sombre fustian. Street-walkers and whores lurked at the corners of alleyways and in doorways, waiting sly-eyed for custom.

Isabella's arrival caused the entire street to be cleared. We stabled our horses in the courtyard of a spacious tavern, and Isabella busied herself as I slipped further down the street on the pretence of doing some errand. I found the sign of Ananias, hurried down the runnel beside it and up the rickety outside staircase, and knocked at the door at the top. Footsteps sounded, followed by the noise of chains being released and bolts being drawn. The door swung open, and a dwarf, garbed in dark brown, glared up at me, his small villainous face shrouded by a close-fitting hood. He reminded me of some malignant goblin.

'Your business?' his voice squeaked. He forced a smile at the coin I held up and waved me in. The chamber was strange, almost ghostly. It had been stripped of everything except a few items: a stool, a table and a bed with a straw mattress beneath a crucifix. It was clean and sweetly smelling. I brushed by the dwarf and walked into the centre of the room. Despite the grey chill outside, the chamber was warm and welcoming. I felt something strange even then, a presence pleasing to me. I walked over to the table and stared down at the circled imprints on the two sides and the one in the middle. Had this served as an altar? Was the man sheltering here a priest? But why celebrate the mass in a garret when there were churches on every corner? I wondered who he could be. I recalled the man I'd glimpsed in the Oriflamme, the one with the far-seeing gaze. He had been studying me but had then disappeared. A coincidence? A figment of my fevered mind? One of the Secreti following me through Paris? But why had be been looking at me so sadly? And why disappear?

'He's gone!'

I turned. The dwarf was staring greedily at the coin, one hand on the rough handle of the knife pushed into the shabby leather belt about his waist.

'I mean no harm,' I replied, walking back to stand over him. 'I have men outside.' The hand fell away, and I crouched down. 'Who was here?'

'A stranger, hair all shorn,' the dwarf gabbled. 'Solitary, close-faced, he hired this from the master, he came then he went, perhaps a scholar?' He spread his hands. 'He paid his rent and, three days ago, packed his panniers.' He pointed to the wooden spigots driven into the wall. 'Then he left.' He shook his head. 'I don't know who he was, why he left or where he's gone.'

I handed the coin over and rejoined the princess' party reassembling in the tavern courtyard. Isabella summoned me over to show a quiver of pens and some costly parchments she had purchased. As I examined these, I murmured what had happened. Isabella looked surprised, but shrugged and moved away to converse with Rossaleti. A short while later we left the city streets as the church bells rang for afternoon prayer. The bright, cold sunlight was quickly fading and the freezing air made us move briskly through the noisy streets. We crossed the river bridge, making our way through the mist-strewn parkland which surrounded the palace. Casales and Rossaleti, who had been describing to us the glories of Westminster, now moved to the front gossiping together, letting their horses find their way.

I glimpsed the black shapes flittering between the trees and bushes alongside the track-way just before the crossbow bolts tore through the air. One of the heralds screamed as a quarrel bit into his arm. Another volley clattered before we recovered and the black-garbed figures, swords drawn, swirled out of the trees. Their intended quarry seemed to be Casales, whose horse reared in fright, but that one-handed knight was a killer born and bred. He drew his sword in a flash of silver, turning his horse to meet his opponents, striking skilfully to the left and to the right. Our startled escorts recovered their wits and hastened to help, as did Rossaleti, driving his horse forward to protect Casales' back. Our attackers faded away as quickly as they'd arrived, black figures fleeing like demons at the appearance of the Holy Rood. The serjeants-at-arms shouted for order, forbidding any pursuit, which would have been fruitless amongst close-packed trees with the mist thickening and the daylight fading. Casales and Rossaleti dismounted and turned over the corpses of four of their attackers. I urged my horse forward as Casales removed the hood and mask of one of the surviving assailants, who had received an ugly sword wound to the side of his neck. He was young, his unshaven face a tapestry of bruises and scars; some footpad from the slums. Rossaleti questioned him, but the man's lips only bubbled blood, so the clerk, losing patience, drew his dagger and cut his throat.

He and Casales remounted. I remember Casales' apparent fury at how such an attack, so close to the royal palace, had been aimed at him. No one dared to protest. Instead the Genoese lashed the feet of the dead attackers and dragged them behind us as we continued into the palace. The alarm was raised, and even the king and his coven of ministers hastened down to the courtyard. Casales kept his voice low, but from his face and the way Marigny and Nogaret were nodding their heads, he was developing his tale that Pourte's death might also have been caused by the coven which had attacked us. King Philip himself examined the corpses before ordering them to be stripped, disfigured and gibbeted on the great gallows outside the palace gates.

CHAPTER 5

The Care of this wicked race is blind.

'A Song of the Times', 1272–1307

Isabella and I had little time to reflect or discuss
what had happened. In preparation for her
possible departure for England, the princess's
household had expanded to include more servants.
Many of these I simply cannot remember. Reflecting
on the past is like standing at the mouth of an
alleyway eagerly waiting for someone, or something,
to appear. You are aware of many others but your
soul, your heart, your eyes search only for what you
want. So it was with the people about the princess,
porters, maids, soldiers, retainers. Moreover, I
always avoided them, remembering the power of the
Secreti as well as the popular adage that Judas always
has a smiling face and kissing lips. I could trust no
one.

On that same evening of our return from the
city, both Isabella and I were summoned to the
tribunal chamber where King Philip sat enthroned

behind an oval oaken table. The king was dressed in a blue robe or coat emblazoned with golden lilies, a relic of St Louis hanging on a chain around his neck, fingers brilliantly decorated with precious rings. On either side sat Marigny and Nogaret, garbed in black like crows. Behind the king hung an exquisitely embroidered arras demonstrating how his great ancestor St Louis approached the port of Damietta, a vigorous, striking picture of armoured knights on snorting destriers beneath gorgeous banners. In the background was a pure blue sea, and guiding it all, the Holy Spirit in the form of a snow-white dove with eyes of amethyst and wings edged with gold. The Holy Spirit, however, did not hover close in that council chamber. King Philip was seething with anger (though he could dissemble with the best) after his confrontation with Casales, his icy-blue eyes hard as glass. He kept tapping the table, head slightly cocked as if listening to the crackling from the braziers. Knight bannerets stood around dressed in royal livery, their hands resting on their swords. One, however, his sword-belt between his feet, sat on a stool to Marigny's right, a handsome-faced man with oiled black hair, neat beard and moustache. In looks he reminded me of Rossaleti. He sat slightly forward, smiling at the princess. The more I stared, the more certain I became that I had met him before.

Marigny spoke for the king, describing the marriage negotiations, expressing his royal master's deep frustration at Edward of England. At last King Philip held up his hand for silence, eyes fixed on his daughter. Oh, I remember that arrogant gaze! Now steeped in years, I still wonder why I didn't spring to my feet and accuse him of the truth, pour out the horrid litany of his hideous sins against Uncle Reginald, his own daughter, me and all the others. The answer, I suppose, was that, is that, I was young, I wanted to live, yet there was more. In the Tower of London and elsewhere I have looked upon fabulous beasts such as Edward of England's favourite leopard, a ferocious animal which would have torn me to pieces, yet I could only stare and watch. King Philip was the same. On that particular evening, as he talked about the death of Pourte, the attack on Casales and the dangers threatening the princess, he acted the leopard, dangerous, cunning, twisting and turning. I glanced around. Isabella's brothers were not present. I could have taken pride at driving them away, but in truth I only played a part. Louis and Philippe, now sober, were keeping their distance because they were not arrogant fools. The presence of Casales, the possible imminence of their sister's nuptials, not to mention the brooding wrath of their father, had cooled their wicked ardour.

On that freezing December evening, in the season of expectant souls, King Philip was certainly intent on his daughter's welfare. He dramatically described the danger which had threatened her during the attack. He never once glanced at me, but Marigny's sallow face, with those unblinking eyes, dark pools of ambition and power, studied me as if seeing me for the first time. I learnt a lesson then that I've never forgotten. *In mundo hominum* – in the world of men – women are like children and the old; they are not ignored, they are not even noticed, they don't even exist, until it matters. My heart warmed to Monsieur de Vitry. He had recognised that truth, acted upon it and so kept me safe. Casales had not recognised me, nor did the knight sitting on the stool whom Philip now introduced as Sir Bernard Pelet, loyal subject, former member of the accursed Templar order, who, according to the king, had done so much to bring God's justice, and the crown's, to the full. Philip proudly announced how Pelet was to be Isabella's master-at-arms, *custos hospicii*, keeper of her household both here and in England. Pelet, God curse him, basked in such praise like a cat before a fire.

Isabella must have sensed my mood; she answered quickly and prettily, whilst I could only stare in silent horror. I had met Pelet before, but again I'd been in the shadows. Uncle Reginald had once talked warmly of him as a good knight at the Temple treasury, when in fact he had been the traitor at the feast. I'd heard enough of the chatter and the gossip to learn that Pelet had been most ferocious in bringing accusations against his former comrades and, possibly, had had a hand in my own uncle's downfall. I could not even look at him, and I was greatly relieved when the meeting ended.

Once alone, Isabella cleared her inner chamber except for a page who was instructed to sit by the door and play a gentle tune on the viol.

'Something soft,' the princess whispered, 'to soothe the soul.' She didn't talk, but sat in her throne-like chair and, picking up a household roll, began to read it as if fascinated by the expenses of her buttery. Never once did she glance up at me. I wanted to be alone. I went across to the writing carrel fixed against the wall beneath a painting celebrating the Finding of the Child Jesus in the Temple. Isabella often sat there studying her horn book, inspecting her accounts or writing out some letter for a clerk. I sat down, my back to her, aware of the viol's melody rising and falling, the distant sounds of the palace, Isabella gently humming under her breath. For a while I could only fight the emotions which boiled in my heart and sent my blood coursing so that the humours in my belly turned sour. Pelet was to join us! An assassin, a Judas! I rose and took down the leech book, to study an infusion to soothe my anger, but found myself turning the pages to study the elements of deadly nightshade, foxglove and other powerful poisons. I was already thinking of revenge.

Lost in my studies, I was startled when Isabella put her hands on my shoulders, kissing me gently on the back of my head. I turned round. The viol-playing had ceased, the chamber was empty. Isabella was dressed in her nightshift, her hair loosed. She pressed a goblet of hot mulled wine into my hand and stared down at the page I was studying.

'Listen, Mathilde no, no, no!' She shook her head. 'Not that way! Come, come.' She made me prepare for sleep. After we had drunk the wine, she insisted I share her bed. I doused the candles and lay beside her in the dark. In the faint light I could glimpse the golden sheen of her hair. She leaned over and touched my cheek. 'I used to creep in and lie beside my mother.' She edged closer, staring at me through the darkness. 'She would tell me stories about Spain, about Rodrigo Diaz, known as El Cid, or she'd describe Santiago, the great mountain shrine to St James. I used to feel so close.' She paused. 'Do you know any stories, Mathilde?' She was trying to distract me, so I told her one from Bretigny about a hobgoblin who ate proud princesses. Isabella laughed and seized my hand. 'Soon,' she stifled a giggle, 'I will lie with Edward of England. Have you ever lain with a man, Mathilde?'

'Only in my dreams, my lady.'

Isabella laughed again. 'Mathilde, swear, swear that you will do nothing to hurt Pelet.'

I remained silent.

'Swear,' she breathed, 'and you shall have my sacred oath that I will take care of that devil! Mathilde, I promise you.'

I swallowed my pride and hot words and promised.

'Good.' Isabella rolled over on her back.

'So much mystery,' she breathed. 'The attack on the Templars: the massacre at Monsieur de Vitry's: Pourte's death; the assault on Casales.' She rolled over on to her side again. 'Casales even maintains the clerk murdered near the charnel house of the Innocents shows how dangerous it is for him to be here. They say the clerk, Matthew of Crokendon, was with a young woman. He was seen walking with her in the cemetery.' Again she touched me lightly on the cheek. 'Be careful, Mathilde, that you are not recognised.'

I closed my eyes and I listened to Isabella's soft breathing. I pushed my hot hand between the smooth cold sheet and the feather-filled bolster.

'And your father?' I asked. 'What does he say?'

'He believes . . .' Isabella paused. 'He believes there are those in England bitterly opposed to my marriage. They would like nothing more than to create mayhem in these negotiations. De Vitry was used by my father in the collection of my dowry, Pourte was a confidant of the English king and Lord Gaveston, as is Casales; they both supported the marriage. There are those in the English council chamber who'll be quick to point out that not even English envoys are safe in France.'

'Who leads these?' I asked.

'The English king's uncle, Henry Lacey, Earl of Lincoln, and Edward's powerful cousin, Thomas,

133

Earl of Lancaster.' She paused as if listening into the dark. 'Marigny has even hinted, God forbid, that danger threatens me, hence Pelet.'

'And you?' I asked.

'Soon I will reach my fourteenth summer, Mathilde, yet sometimes I feel like an old crone steeped in the frenetic turbulence of intrigue. My marriage is a matter of papal arbitration; Clement V of Avignon is my father's creature. The English are also bound by solemn treaty, yet, Mathilde, to answer your question, we are figures in some dark, devious and wicked game waiting to be played out. So, be careful, especially over Pelet. You promised?'

'And I promise again.'

'Deo Gratias, Mathilde.' She laughed abruptly. 'Let's go back to hobgoblins. Shall we call Louis one?'

Such were the days as we waited, one following another. Casales dispatched letters and messengers back to his masters in England. Advent prepared to give way to Christmas. Boughs of evergreen appeared in the chapel. The priests wore vestments of purple and gold and empty cribs were set up in the royal cloister as the palace prepared itself for the feast of Christmas. The huntsmen thundered out, verderers and hawkers driven by their passion for the chase and the kill. The royal larders become stocked to overflowing with venison, boar, rabbit, plover, quail and duck. The palace galleries and chambers echoed with music as the choirs rehearsed the 'O' antiphons of Advent as well as the hymns for Christmas, haunting melodious tunes, bittersweet, about a Virgin maid bringing forth the God child in the bleak heart of winter.

The days were short and dark, bitterly cold, so we kept to our chambers. Every day was purgatory, with Pelet trying to act the perfect, gentle knight towards both of us. Never once did such a fair face hide such a foul heart; a traitor, a coward, a Judas incarnate. Isabella, however, openly favoured him, and as the days passed, I wondered if she'd remembered her vow. Casales and Rossaleti now became constant visitors to the princess's chambers, yet as the negotiations flagged, their courtesies sounded more hollow. Isabella, who discussed the matter secretly with me, seized her opportunity when the two men shared wine in her chamber just before vespers on Laetare Sunday in Advent.

'My lord,' Isabella, cloaked in furs before the fire, stretched out a delicate hand towards the flames, 'tell me plainly about your king. He protests great love for me, yet—'

'My lady,' Casales intervened, 'Edward of England—'

'I know,' Isabella merrily interrupted, 'is a stark, fair bachelor standing over six feet, well proportioned, of goodly features. His hair is golden, his eyes are blue, his face comely to the eye. A skilled horseman, a warrior bloodied in the wars of Scotland, a true knight. He loves his friends and is much given to hunting.' Isabella parodied the nasal twang of a nun breathlessly reciting a well-known litany. 'But if he loves me, why does he delay? Is not our marriage a matter of papal decree, of solemn treaty between our countries, so why this tarrying? What is the real reason? What manner of man is my future husband?'

Rossaleti nervously cleaned his mouth with his tongue and glanced away, the consummate courtier, the skilled scribe. Casales was much different: a solitary, brooding man, very conscious of his injury, quick-tempered, nevertheless astute enough to understand Isabella's impatience. He smiled, coughed and opened his mouth to reply. Isabella, sitting to his right, leaned over and touched him gently on the arm.

'Please,' she begged, 'no more fanciful phrases or courtly courtesies.'

Casales sighed and stretched in his chair. He was dressed in a loose shirt and hose under a thick military cloak; on the floor beside him lay his war-belt. Being an accredited envoy, he was one of the few allowed to carry arms in the royal presence.

'My seigneur the king,' he began carefully, 'well, I have known him as long as I have the Lord Gaveston.' He glanced at Rossaleti and brought a finger to his lips, a sign that he was speaking *in secreto, sub sigillo silentii* – in secret, under the seal of silence.

'As the father, so the son,' Casales continued wearily, 'or sometimes the opposite. *Mon seigneur* was only a child when his beloved mother Eleanor of Castile died. The present king's father loved her passionately. After her death, when her corpse was brought south to London for burial at Westminster, the old king built a splendid cross at every place the cortège rested.' He glanced quickly at Isabella. 'I tell this to show Edward's abiding passion for his first wife. When Eleanor was alive, the English court was filled with music. After she died,' he grimaced, 'the music stopped. The only time I remember the old king asking for minstrels was to distract his mood when his physicians had to let blood.'

'He loved her so much?' Isabella whispered.

'Oh yes,' Casales agreed. 'Edward the First was a man of iron, of fiery temper; he almost killed a servant who hurt a favourite falcon. The royal birds were the only things he loved after his wife died. When they fell ill, he even sent wax replicas of them to the shrine of the Blessed Thomas of Canterbury to seek a cure. It's a pity, my lady, he didn't love his heir half as much. Prince Edward was raised by himself in a palace at King's Langley in Hertfordshire. A lonely boy, he was left to his own pursuits, his pet camel and leopard, or sailing along the river with his bargemaster Abscalom. Friendships with the sons of servants flourished; the prince often became involved in their rustic pursuits, ignoring the code of arms or the discipline of the horn book. He grew like some neglected plant. By the time the king, his father, realised this, it was too late; the child begets the man. Prince

Edward was lonely. He entertained strange fancies and created a mythical brother.' Casales ignored Isabella's sharp gasp.

'My lord,' I asked, 'he has brothers?'

'Half-brothers.' Casales smiled at me. 'The issue of the old king's second wife, Margaret of France, my lady's aunt; they are still mere babes. No, the prince wanted a brother, a companion. Forsaken by all, he grew to resent his father, and all this took flesh in Lord Peter Gaveston, who joined the royal household in Gascony. My lady, Gaveston was the brother the prince hungered for, his blood companion, playing Jonathan to Prince Edward's David.' He spread his hands. 'As the scriptures say, "David's love for Jonathan surpassed all others."' Casales drew a deep breath. 'Prince Edward's attachment to Gaveston deepened, they became one soul. The old king objected, but the prince was adamant. His father tried to punish and humiliate him but it made no difference. Prince Edward even asked his father to create Gaveston Earl of Cornwall. The old king, notorious for his furious rages, made even worse by an ulcerated leg, physically attacked his son, hitting and kicking him, screaming that he was a knave and that he heartily wished he could leave his crown to another. Gaveston was immediately exiled.' Casales rubbed his face. 'Once the old king died last July, Gaveston was recalled and ennobled, made Earl of Cornwall and married to the king's niece, Margaret de Clare. The earls of Lincoln and Lancaster opposed such advancement of a commoner, a Gascon whose mother, allegedly, was a witch. But *mon seigneur* was obdurate. It is not just a matter of Gaveston, but of opposing the will of his dead father, be it Scotland, the oppression of his ministers—'

'Or my marriage?' Isabella interjected.

'Yes, my lady,' Casales confessed. 'And now you have the truth of it. Whatever his father wanted Edward our king wishes to overturn, desperate to kick against the goad, so only God knows where it will lead.' Casales turned to me, glancing narrow-eyed. 'Have you ever been lonely, Mathilde? Do you know what it is to be by yourself?'

Of course I could have told the truth, but to these two men I was what I pretended to be, a lady-in-waiting, *dame de chambre*, a commoner much favoured by the princess. I realised what Casales was implying. He'd made his decision about me: I was a favourite of the princess and, therefore, must understand the importance of Gaveston. I hastily agreed, though I should have reflected more carefully on what he'd asked. Casales moved on, committed to telling the truth. He explained how Edward of England was lashing out against any who had opposed him during his youth. He specifically mentioned Walter Langton, Bishop of Coventry and Lichfield, former treasurer of the old king, who had tried to curb the prince's expenditure. He had now been stripped of office and arrested.

'And what do you think will happen?' Isabella asked.

Casales raised his good hand.

'*Mon seigneur* the king is a greyhound lithe and fast, he twists and turns. In refusing your marriage he taunts his father and yours, God forgive him. In this he is supported by Lord Gaveston, but in the end,' Casales nodded at the casement window, 'day dawns and dies, night falls, the passing of the hours cannot be stopped.'

'Is that how you view my wedding?' Isabella teased.

Casales sipped from his wine cup. He ignored my mistress's question and made an admission, a startling one; I remember it well.

'The old king,' he said as if speaking to himself, 'was a cold, freezing frost upon all our souls, hard of heart and iron of will.' Casales raised his maimed wrist. 'I was a member of his battle group at Falkirk when we defeated Wallace. My lady, forget the tales of gentle knights. In battle the soul becomes ferocious. At Falkirk I was surrounded by a party of Scots and dragged off my horse. I fought for my life and I lost my hand. A barber surgeon cleaned the stump, pouring boiling tar on the torn flesh. The old king passed me by; he paused, stared down and said I was fortunate. "Better men have lost more": that was the old Edward of England; he could chill to the very marrow.'

Casales' honesty, though refreshing, did not lighten our mood. Isabella wondered if Edward of England would face war rather than submit to the wishes of his father and hers. She said we would send a personal letter and a brooch from her jewellery box. Casales and Rossaleti were planning to spend Christmas at Westminster and were already preparing to leave for Wissant. Rossaleti, I remember, was greatly disquieted. He confided to both the princess and myself that he had a deep fear of rivers and seas, so for him a winter crossing of the Narrow Seas was one of the horrors of hell. Perhaps he had a premonition of his own death, which was more than Pelet did.

Two days after the meeting with Casales and Rossaleti, I began to suffer nausea and cramps in the belly, as did the princess. Her stomach, like mine, was strong, so I first thought this might be due to the malevolence of the princes, Louis and Philippe. That precious pair delighted in perpetrating malicious tricks such as putting a dead rat on a chair, leaving the dung of one of the palace lurchers outside our chambers or knocking a servant as he brought us food and drink. They were men with the narrow souls of spiteful boys. On the second day our symptoms increased, with heavy sweats and vomiting. By the morning of the third day, however, the infection began to diminish. Pelet was not so fortunate. He too was seized with violent cramps, shuddering under a ferocious chill. Isabella herself administered to him, as did a gaggle of royal physicians. I tried to intervene, but the princess brusquely ordered me away.

In the end the good doctors were unable to help.

They recommended poultices and potions to drain the malignance from the humours, but Pelet continued to weaken. He eventually lost consciousness and died within seven days of the onset of the infection. By then I was fully recovered. I felt no compassion for Pelet, especially when he ranted about shadows clustering around his bed. He lapsed into his native tongue of Langue d'Oc, screaming at the crucifix for mercy. 'He who sows the tempest reaps the whirlwind', or so Scripture would have us believe. Pelet was an assassin many times over. God wanted his soul for judgement. I could only stand and watch the effects of arsenic poisoning run their natural course. I thought it most fitting. After all, Uncle Reginald with his manuscripts was as much an authority on poisons and noxious potions as the Scriptures are on theology. A little arsenic may help the stomach, but too much and a powerful fever seizes its victim. That was Pelet's fate. I recognised the symptoms, the good physicians didn't. On reflection Isabella must have served us both something to sicken our humours, perhaps a little stone-crop or pepper mixed with heavy vinegar to create an illusion. The royal physicians, as is their custom, could only grasp their manuals and urine jars, shake their heads and moan about the fevers and agues of the day and congratulate Isabella and myself on our miraculous recovery.

Isabella acted the professional mourner. She placed the coins on Pelet's eyes and lighted a taper before the rood screen in La Sainte Chapelle. Of course, Philip and his coterie may have suspected, but at the time arsenic was rare, whilst mine and Isabella's sickness pointed to a sudden infection which Pelet couldn't fight, a twist of fate, mere mischance. Isabella's subterfuge was deception enough. She never uttered a word to me, and when I tried to speak, pressed her fingers against my lips.

'Gone to God, Mathilde,' she whispered, 'to answer the cries of vengeance for spilling innocent blood.'

I couldn't think of a more fitting epitaph. By then Casales and Rossaleti had left for England, but two days before Christmas, the very evening Pelet's corpse was dispatched into the city for burial, a mud-spattered messenger thundered into the palace courtyard. The news he brought soon spread through the palace: Casales and Rossaleti were returning! On their way to Boulogne, near Montreuil, they had met three new English envoys, Sir Ralph Sandewic, constable of the Tower of London; Lord Walter Wenlok, Abbot of Westminster; and Sir John Baquelle, knight. These three had braved the freezing Narrow Seas to bring startling news. Edward of England had acceded to all the French demands. The marriage to Isabella would go ahead. The English king even named the place: the Cathedral of Notre Dame at Boulogne, in the county of Ponthieu, a strip of Normandy still under the rule of the English crown. The marriage would take place in the New Year, and certainly no later than the Feast of the Conversion of St Paul, 25 January. The messenger carried a letter sealed by both Casales and Rossaleti summarising their news; this was proclaimed throughout the royal residence and again by Marigny at a splendid banquet hastily convened in the Fleur-de-lis Chamber at the centre of the palace.

The joy of Philip and his ministers was evident. No cost was spared. Musicians with rebec, tambour and viol played merry tunes, whilst jugglers, tumblers, clowns and jesters entertained the royal household. We all feasted on succulent venison and the juiciest flesh of fish fresh from the royal stew ponds, followed by beef and pork served in a wine-based sauce, thickened with capon meat and almonds and seasoned with cloves and sugar. A minstrel disguised as the Angel Gabriel sang a robust song dedicated to Isabella:

> She stands in her satin gown,
> If anyone touches her,
> The gown rustles,
> Eia –
> She stands in her golden gown,
> Her face like a rose and her mouth like a
>   flower,
> Eia.

The object of all this merriment and rejoicing remained ivory-faced, blue eyes staring. She hardly drank at all but sat, lips moving wordlessly. Once the banquet was over and the king's favourite lurchers had been allowed into the chamber, Isabella withdrew, gesturing at me to follow. She ordered the pages who carried the flambeaux to escort her to the small chapel she was accustomed to visit. Once inside she dismissed them, telling me to lock and bolt the door. The chapel was freezing cold, its brazier nothing more than a pile of ash and cinders. Isabella, ignoring my protests, took off her gown and robes. Dressed in nothing but her shift, she walked barefoot up to the sanctuary and prostrated herself about two yards before the rood screen. Stretched out on the ice-cold flagstones, she crept forward like a penitent crawling to kiss the cross on Good Friday and lay beneath the rood screen, arms extended, face down. I tried to cover her with my cloak, but she shrugged it off. I squatted at the foot of a pillar, the cold creeping up my own legs, the muscles of my back cramping in discomfort. Palace bells marked the passing hour, but still the princess lay as if asleep. Eventually she rose, dressed and smiled at me, pinching my cheek.

'Mathilde, I have given thanks for my deliverance from hell. Now come,' she teased, 'tonight we pray, tomorrow we act all merry.'

Casales, Rossaleti and the other three English envoys arrived early on Christmas Eve bearing gifts and letters from Philip's 'sweet cousin' the King of England. Isabella was ordered to meet them in the royal council chamber shortly after the Angelus. Casales and Rossaleti, however, still unshaven and ill-kempt after their hasty return, first attended her in her chamber to explain the status, power and purpose of the other three envoys. Both sat close to the hearth, muttering about the freezing weather and how it chilled their very bones, before describing the men Isabella would meet. Sandewic was an old soldier, Keeper of the Tower and Justice of Gaol-delivery at Newgate, the most foul prison in London and the last resting place of many outlaws. 'He's hanged more felons than I've drunk cups of wine,' Casales exclaimed. 'A royal bully-boy, an intimate friend of the old king, he loves that grim fortress the Tower of London; he regards it as his own personal fief. He even pays for the upkeep of its small chapel, St Peter Ad Vincula, from his own pocket. Sandewic is fierce,' Casales continued, 'the English crown's man, body and soul! He once arrested a papal tax collector who'd vexed the old king; he took the tax collector's money and told the fellow to be out of the kingdom within three days or he'd hang him from the Tower walls.'

'Oh dear!' Isabella pretended to be frightened. 'And is Sir John Baquelle a greater beast?'

'Ah, Baquelle is a London merchant, a friend of Pourte's, rich and powerful. A justice of the city. Whereas the citizens of London are terrified of Sandewic, Baquelle they hate because he's a royal appointment.'

'And Lord Walter Wenlok?'

'Abbot of Westminster,' Rossaleti scoffed, 'and very much aware of it.' He coughed, recollecting himself. 'He's been abbot for over twenty years, a close friend of the old king and a special confidant of the new. He is much liked by my Lord Gaveston.'

'And the death of Pourte and the attack on you?' Isabella asked. 'What are your thoughts now?'

'Suspicion is not evidence,' Casales replied, chewing his lip. 'Of course *mon seigneur* the king knows of it and has protested.' He raised his eyes to the ceiling. 'But that is just straw in the wind.'

'And my betrothed's abrupt change of mind?'

'Only God knows!' Casales murmured. 'My lady,' he smiled, 'soon to be your grace. Perhaps the change is just hard politic, the inevitable.'

My lady glanced sharply at Rossaleti, who nodded.

'My lady,' Casales repeated, 'this is not some speech from a romance, but please remember, *Mon Seigneur* the King of England has undiminished love for you.'

'And the Lord Gaveston?' Isabella's ambiguous question startled Casales, who glanced quickly at Rossaleti. The clerk just smiled serenely back as if that answer was not his to give.

'*Mon Seigneur* the king,' Casales hastily declared, 'loves his lady, whilst his love for Lord Gaveston is that for a dear brother. These new envoys will assure you of this.'

'In which case, monsieur,' Isabella rose, smoothing

down the folds of her gown, 'it is time we met our visitors.'

We went down to the council chamber. Everything was prepared as if for a mass, candles glowing along the polished table, the fire fiercely crackling the scented pine logs, the braziers sparkling, the tapestry-covered walls hidden in the shadows, pierced no doubt by peep-holes and confessional gaps where Marigny and his Secreti could lurk. The three envoys were grouped at the far end of the table. Sandewic was what he looked, a veteran soldier, an old knight, who'd kept his fealty to God and his king. I took to him immediately; my heart warmed to his blunt goodness. He reminded me so much of Uncle Reginald. Looking back, I realise, in truth, that some men possess an innate decency, a richness of the soul. Sandewic was one of these. He had a falcon-like face, a beaked nose, a hard mouth and glaring eyes beneath bushy brows. He was dressed in the old fashion, no fripperies, simply a long, sleeveless dark-green gown over a jerkin of rich murrey, a sword-belt wrapped round his waist, a silver chain of office hanging about his neck. Sandewic's steel-grey hair straggled down to his shoulders though his white moustache and beard were neatly clipped. He knelt when Isabella approached, kissed her hands then, most movingly, turned to me and did the same, clasping my fingers. My soul kissed his, my life touched his. *Jesu miserere mei*; his brutal death struck deep and hard with me.

Baquelle was different, small, fat and pompous,

a radiant, jolly face under a mop of black hair. He was dressed in the finest jagged coat, particoloured hose and blood-red Cordovan riding boots. Baquelle didn't know whether to bluster or fawn, whilst his so-called courtly speech was clumsy enough to make Rossaleti hide his smile. A true merchant prince full of his own importance, he was very much the royal envoy and gave my mistress the sketchiest of bows.

Lord Walter Wenlok, Abbot of Westminster, was garbed in the black robes of a Benedictine but they were of the purest wool and edged with ermine, whilst his stiffened hood, pulled elegantly back, was lined with costly purple samite. Wenlok was proud in both manner and appearance. The tonsure on his head neatly cut, his smooth-shaven patrician face composed in a mask of sanctimonious serenity. A thin-lipped, arrogant-eyed man who, in the circumstances, should have looked into his soul and the coming call for its reckoning rather than emphasising his power. He stretched out a claw-like hand so we could kiss his thick abbatial ring. Isabella did so quickly, I followed suit, then we settled down to exchange pleasantries. Courteous questions provoked courteous answers. Old Sandewic, however, broke from this.

'My lady,' he leaned against the table, 'you shall certainly be called Isabella La Belle. You will win the hearts of all loyal subjects with your beauty and grace.'

My mistress blushed slightly and bowed her head in thanks.

'*Mon Seigneur*,' Sandewic continued, ignoring a vexed glance from Wenlok, 'is greatly desirous of meeting you. All is prepared. You have apartments at the Tower; clean, swept and hung with the most beautiful tapestries. Every luxury will be yours. At Westminster, after the recent fire, your chambers have been completely refurbished. Outside the gardens are newly turfed and trellised, their stew ponds drained and cleaned. You even have your own quayside at Queen's Bridge, repaired as of new.' The old knight beamed around at his companions, but his hand kept going to his ear; I could tell that his nose and throat were inflamed with the rheums. Such ailments did not diminish his enthusiasm and deep admiration for Isabella's beauty. I recalled the legendary love between Edward I and his Queen Eleanor of Castile; perhaps Sandewic hoped that this might happen again.

'At Dover,' Sandewic continued brusquely, '*Mon Seigneur* has prepared the royal ship *The Margaret of Westminster*, named after your noble aunt. Both it and its escort of boats and barges have been completely refurbished. The royal ship contains new wardrobes and butteries fitted for your comfort.'

Isabella caught Sandewic's enthusiasm. The atmosphere became most relaxed, wine was served, sweetmeats offered. Baquelle and Wenlok now followed Sandewic's lead. The merchant described the eagerness of Londoners to see their new queen, whilst Wenlok extolled the beauties of Westminster Abbey where she would be crowned. Isabella thanked them prettily, excused herself and withdrew to revel in what had so unexpectedly happened.

King Philip now emerged in all his glory. He had Edward at his feet; his daughter would be Queen of England and his grandson would sit at Westminster and wear the Confessor's crown. The joyfulness and merriment of the French Christmas court became a heavy perfume. The Angels' Mass was celebrated at midnight followed by the Dawn Mass then the Shepherds' Mass, glorious liturgical ceremonies, the priests vested in the gold and white robes of the great feast. The royal chapel rang with hymns: *'Hodie ego Genui te'* – 'This day I have begotten you'; and *'Puer natus nobis'* – 'A child is born'. The air became rich with incense, as if some perfumed mist had come down from heaven and God's glory joined with ours in all the receptions, carols, dances, mummers' plays and festivals. It was hard to decide whether King Philip was celebrating the birth of the Christ child or the future birth of his grandson.

On Christmas evening, in the Fleur-de-Lis Chamber, Philip staged a great banquet: four tables in a square cordoned off by screens draped with gorgeous tapestries depicting the Glories of the Lilies and the exploits of the Capets. On the high table Philip, Marigny and Nogaret sat with Wenlok

151

and Baquelle. On the second his three sons entertained Casales and Rossaleti; I noticed Louis glaring at me spitefully. On the third table sat important clerics, diplomats and officials. On the fourth, opposite her father, Isabella attended by me, entertained Sandewic and the leading clerks of the English embassy. A truly splendid feast, with soup of ground capon thickened with almond milk and served with pomegranates and red comfits. Roast dishes, kid cooked in cream, ducks and chicken, crayfish set in jelly, followed by frumentary. Musicians played lustily and choirs of silver-voiced boys carolled sweetly.

Oh, I remember that evening well. Murder also joined us. I was sitting next to Sandewic and quickly realised that he was not only present as an envoy; in the eyes of the English king, at least, he was to replace Pelet as *Custos*, keeper or protector of the princess's household once it left for Boulogne. Sandewic first apologised for not giving me a gift, then handed me his dagger with its beautiful curved blade and ivory handle. I thought he was deep in his cups, but he pressed this gift on me, pushing the gold and red sheath into my hands, his eyes brimming with tears.

'I had a daughter once,' he murmured. 'You have her eyes and ways.' He then turned away to talk to one of the clerks. I could see he was melancholic. I had already exchanged gifts with my mistress; she had given me a copy of Hildegard of Bremen's sayings with its most famous edged in gold: *Oh man look to man, for man has the heavens and earth and all other created things lie within him. He is one with them and all things are hidden within him.* In return I'd given the princess a ring, a gift from my Uncle Reginald which she much admired. At the feast I sipped my wine and watched Philip toast the taciturn Wenlok of Westminster, wondering what I could give Sandewic, who reminded me so much of my uncle with his stern looks and gentle ways. I touched him on the shoulder; he turned back all eager-eyed.

'Gold and silver have I none,' I retorted brightly, echoing the words of St Peter in Acts, 'but what I have, I give thee freely.'

'Which is, mademoiselle?'

'Sir, you suffer from the rheums, your limbs ache and your head is heavy and dulled.'

'A wise woman, Mathilde!'

'Wise enough, sir, to know that warm oil, salted water and a potion of vervain would help you.'

Sandewic thought I was teasing him, but once assured, he accepted my help, apologising as old men do for his obvious discomfort. Nevertheless, he was cunning and astute. He drank sparsely of the different wines and was describing his beloved Tower with its great four-walled donjon, girdling walls and yawning gateways when we were abruptly distracted by a commotion at the king's table. Lord Abbot Wenlok seemed in difficulties. He had slumped back in his chair, gripping the table as if experiencing a severe giddiness.

Servants and retainers clustered about. Sandewic rose from his chair, the English clerks following. Isabella glanced sharply at me, indicating I follow. At first I thought the Benedictine lord had drunk too much. They had taken him into a small chancery room and made him comfortable on the floor, pushing brocaded cushions under his head. Wenlok, however, seemed unaware of what was happening; he twitched and convulsed, muttering about the cold stoniness in his feet and legs.

A physician was hastily summoned, but Lord Wenlok's distress increased, his words becoming garbled; he retched but could not even spit into the maplewood bowl thrust under his mouth. He lay back, croaking hoarsely. More cushions were pushed under him. The death rattle echoed in his throat. Sandewic knelt beside him and tried to comfort him, but the Lord Abbot, head going from side to side, eyes stark in distress, mouth gaping for breath, was unable to respond. A priest was called. He muttered the words of absolution above the dying man's hideous sounds. Wenlok shook violently, gave a loud gasp then lay still, head falling to one side.

I crouched beside Sandewic, pretending to offer solace even as I pressed my fingers against the abbot's leg, stomach and hand. I felt the hardness of the muscles, as if rigor mortis had already set in. I knew more than those physicians. I had studied the properties of every type of hemlock, be it poisoned parsnip or any other variety. I recognised its singular symptoms, recalling Plato's descriptions of Socrates' death amongst the Ancients: the stiffening of the limbs, the creeping loss of feeling, the strangulated breath followed by the final convulsions. Abbot Wenlok had been poisoned, hemlock mixed with wine, but why, how and by whom?

CHAPTER 6

The Sons of Iniquity crush those who
resist.

'A Song of the Times', 1272–1307

Wenlok's death cast a shadow over the
Christmas celebrations. Philip and his
ministers ostensibly grieved deeply but
the truth was that the French court regarded
Wenlok as an old man who'd been sent on an
arduous journey in the depths of winter; he'd
simply suffered a seizure and died. His corpse was
washed and embalmed, his walnut coffin crammed
with tablets of perfume and sacks of herbs then
sealed for dispatch as swiftly as possible back to
Westminster.

Once again I journeyed down to the death house,
where two grimy-faced retainers were preparing
the abbot's body whilst a member of Wenlok's
retinue, a young chaplain called Robert of Reading,
recited the office of the dead. He'd reached the
words 'Ah, good Jesu – leave me not reprobation,

think my soul caused thy Incarnation', the sombre phrases rolling out made all the more solemn by the Latin. I stood swathed in a cloak; the death house was bitterly cold. I watched intently whilst slipping Ave beads through my fingers. I had placed at the head of the corpse the winter flowers the princess had sent, together with an evergreen spray. Now I scrutinised the cadaver carefully. Rigor mortis had of course, by St Stephens Day, turned the dead flesh marble hard, but I also noticed the faint purple-red rash on the hairy stomach; the same had appeared on the dead man's cheeks, whilst his tongue and lips were purpled as if with wine. Philip's physicians might have entertained suspicions, but who dared to voice them? Or again, they might have been ignorant of hemlock in all its forms, be it garden or water hemlock. Death always occurs quickly, from commencement to finish, perhaps in no more than three hours, whilst the effects would have been hastened depending on whether the poison was distilled from the fruit of the hemlock, its leaves or, more deadly still, a root over a year old. Wenlok's age and weariness, not to mention the wine, might have enhanced its malignant effects.

The door of the death house opened and Sandewic came in carrying a requiem candle. He placed this on the corpse table, crossed himself and abruptly left. He was waiting for me outside, blowing on his mittened fingers and stamping his feet. The ground was slippery with ice so he offered me his arm. I could see he was in discomfort with a soreness in the ear and throat.

'Come,' I invited him, 'the princess would like to see you and I can practise my skills.'

He grinned mischievously and patted my hand.

'Truly fortunate I am. I never thought a damsel so fair and young would show such affection.'

We lapsed into teasing, so reminiscent of my days with Uncle Reginald that tears burnt my eyes, which I quickly put down to the cold. Sandewic stopped halfway across the yard and stared out over the wasteland. Servants were pulling Yule logs to the cavernous kitchen doorway, escorted by maids, their arms full of evergreen holly, its blood-red berries full and rich. Others carried tendrils of ivy, all to decorate the kitchen, butteries and servants' chambers, for St Stephen's was their day of celebration.

'He was murdered, wasn't he, my lord Wenlok?'

I stared coolly back.

'As was Pourte, as Casales nearly was? As I might be?' Sandewic hawked and spat.

'Why?' I asked. 'Why do you say that?'

He was about to reply when Casales and Rossaleti came through the doorway carrying funeral candles, capped against the breeze, which they wanted to place on the corpse table. They paused to greet us. Casales looked anxious and drawn.

'My lord.' Casales came as close as he could, talking quietly in the English tongue. 'My lord, the sooner we are gone from here—'

'Ay,' Sandewic interrupted, 'but we must await the will of princes.'

We exchanged pleasantries with them, then continued into the palace, where I made Sandewic comfortable in the princess's quarters. I examined his ears and throat carefully, then I prepared a solution of warm water, heavily salted, and told him to breathe it in through his nose. He did so, choking and spluttering, coughing up the infected phlegm. After he'd finished I poured warmed oil, specially distilled, into his ears to loosen the hard wax. I gave him vervain for his throat and dressed a small ulcer on his leg with a herbal poultice.

Isabella, busy with certain lists from her father, wandered across to watch. She always had a firm stomach, my mistress, despite all her exquisite courtly ways. She was particularly fascinated by the final potion I mixed for Sandewic, taken from the kitchens and apothecary stores: finely ground dry moss, soaked in an astringent and mixed with the powdered cream of very stale milk. I informed both that I did not know how it acted but it was a sure cure for many internal infections when the body's humours turned hot and the patient felt as if he was on fire. Sandewic was definitely feverish. He slowly relaxed, drinking the cup of posset Isabella prepared at the hearth. He informed me how he distrusted all physicians and then questioned me closely on my skill and where I had studied. I told the tale I had so carefully prepared and rehearsed like a scholar does a syllogism. Sandewic believed me, or I think he did. In turn I questioned him on the deaths of Wenlok and Pourte, but he was on his guard, although he grudgingly conceded that he was suspicious about both their deaths.

'The night Pourte died,' he declared, 'Casales and Rossaleti were closeted with des Plaisans and Nogaret. Apparently Pourte declared he was too tired to attend; he had to sleep. Consequently he was alone. It's possible that the real murderer or murderer's hired assassins, the same who later attacked Casales.' The old knight continued as if talking to himself. 'But last night, how could Lord Wenlok be poisoned except by someone at his own table?'

'Or before,' I interrupted. 'Hemlock is a creeping poison.'

'True,' Sandewic agreed. 'I have spoken to Marigny. Liar though he may be, he claims Lord Wenlok was very quiet, tense, as if unwell from the very beginning of the banquet. He drank and ate very little.' Sandewic stretched out his infected leg on the footstool and sighed in relief. 'I feel better!' he murmured. 'It's good to sit, to be warm. I pity poor Wenlok. Sir John Baquelle,' he added as an after-thought, 'is a good man, but he has dismissed the Abbot's death as an act of God. Baquelle is more interested in the present business.'

'Which is?'

'My lady, your marriage, of course!'

'And Edward of England?' Isabella snapped her

fingers, eager to return to a question which constantly vexed her. 'He changed his mind just like that!'

'An arrow is loosed!' Sandewic growled. 'It may fly, it may rise, but eventually it has to fall.' He tapped the arm of the chair. 'Your marriage, my lady, is set as if in stone. There is no other way.' He yawned. 'As for Templars? Well, the head of that order is France, and if that's cut off, what use the arm or leg? *Mon seigneur* the king knows that. He will not imprison or torture the Templars, but he is eager to seize their wealth.'

'My lord,' I asked, still fascinated by what he'd said about the murders, 'do you know of a Monsieur de Vitry?'

'I've heard the name. Marigny mentioned something about a massacre. Wasn't he a merchant who played an important role in the collection of your mistress's dowry?' He looked at me. I never answered, so he stared into the fire.

'Do Pourte, Casales, Wenlok, Baquelle and you,' I asked, 'have anything in common?'

The old knight, growing tired and dreamy-eyed, thinking perhaps of other Yuletides as the ancients do when dozing before a fire, simply shrugged. Now I am old, I recognise that feeling of surrender, of preparing for the final rest, to sleep forever. Sandewic shut us off. Then he abruptly straightened in his chair, still ignoring my question, put on his boots, gathered his cloak, thanked the princess and left. I was sad when he was gone.

161

It was as if the fire had dulled or the candle wicks dimmed. I sat on the footstool warming my hands. Isabella came behind me, pressing her hands on my shoulders.

'There's a hidden tension,' she whispered, 'ghosts so fierce they gather in the gloom around us and look on. Abbot Wenlok's death is dismissed as an unfortunate accident, but Casales and Rossaleti, so I hear, as well as Sandewic, are apprehensive and fearful. Oh Mathilde, what shall we do?' She leaned her face against the back of my head. 'We are,' she whispered, 'in the presence of terrors. I must tell you. Father watches me like a basilisk does its victim. Pelet's death has gone unmentioned but not forgotten. Marigny's men have been here. You are summoned to the Chambre Ardente at the hour of vespers. You must go alone.'

I whirled round. Isabella looked frightened. 'There is nothing I can do, as yet,' she pleaded.

'What do they want?'

'To question you.'

'About what?

'Perhaps who you really are . . .' The princess's voice trailed off.

I spent the remainder of that day feverishly preparing myself. Isabella tried to help, distracting me with chatter about our intended departure. Casales and Rossaleti came, eager to explain how the English king felt secure in Boulogne, a port on the Narrow Seas well within the county of Ponthieu, an enclave of Normandy still under English influence. They openly confessed that Edward entertained great suspicion towards his 'sweet cousin of France', especially after the deaths of Pourte and Wenlok, not to mention the attack on Casales. Surprisingly, neither betrayed any suspicions about Wenlok's death but repeated how, on his journey to the Ile de France, the abbot complained frequently of feeling unwell, which they thought was due to a hard sea crossing in the depth of winter. They also talked about Isabella's journey, reassuring us both that the royal ship, *The Margaret of Westminster*, would provide a safe and secure passage. Rossaleti was desperately anxious about that; he pleaded with the princess to join her, as the *Margaret* was much safer than the other cogs available. Isabella laughingly agreed. The two men left, and as the bells of Sainte Chapelle tolled the call for vespers, two knight bannerets, accompanied by a Dominican friar, presented themselves and asked me to accompany them.

They were brusque and severe. I collected my cloak, squeezed Isabella's hand and joined them. We went down the stairs, threading our way through the passageways and galleries, all lit by candles, and across ice-cold courtyards to the Chambre Ardente, which was housed in the base of a soaring tower. The Chambre Ardente was, in theory, the royal household court, similar to that held by the marshal in England. In practice, however, the Chambre was an inquisitorial court with all the powers of oyer and terminer, to listen and decide on indictments; it could, if it wished, impose the death penalty. The chamber itself was cavernous. Torches provided light as well as cast shadows over what had to be hidden. Its red-brick walls were covered in thick embroidered tapestries, depicting all forms of judgement. On one, Christ, ghostlike, swathed in swirling drapery, presided. Below the divine throne all kinds of demons prowled, waiting for judgement to be passed. A veritable gallery of hideous figures, bearded and winged, with scaly skin and manes of fire, readied to grab the hapless sinners to rip out their bowels and crunch their hearts. In the corner, specially illuminated by a fiery brazier, St Michael weighed souls in a set of scales as a devil reached to grab one for his supper. The purpose of this tableau, springing to life in the shifting light, was to instil terror and fan the flames of fear. I vowed I would show no weakness.

Around the chamber stood royal guards, whilst scribes crouched busily over writing tables. At the far end, on a dais, sat Marigny behind a high oaken table, his red hair gleaming in the torchlight. His two minions, Nogaret and des Plaisans, sat on either side, with hooded clerks perched like ravens at each end, pens poised. Marigny beckoned me forward on to the dais, gesturing at a stool before the table. I approached and sat down.

'Mathilde, welcome.'

'Seigneur, why am I here?'

Marigny, surprised, leaned across, hunter's eyes

staring from that pallid face, mouth puckered in disbelief at such insolence.

'This is the court of the royal household. You are a member of that household. You are to be summoned here as we wish.'

'Seigneur, why?'

'Mathilde, are you in God's grace?' des Plaisans asked.

'If I am, sir, I beg God to keep me there, and if I am not, I humbly ask Him to return me there. Why do you ask?'

'You act the wise woman,' Nogaret simpered, 'or something else. You know a great deal about simples and potions.'

'So do the royal physicians. What are you hinting at, that I'm a witch?'

'No.' Des Plaisans sat back in the shadows.

'Mathilde, Mathilde,' Nogaret took up the attack, 'you're not being tried.'

'So why am I here?'

'You have won the princess's favour so quickly . . .' He paused.

'I cannot answer for my mistress; you must ask her yourself.'

'Mathilde,' Marigny's face wrinkled in amusement, 'do not be afraid.'

'Who claims I am?'

Marigny leaned his elbows on the table, rocking backwards and forwards as if considering my reply. I steeled myself. I hated these men, so why should I be afraid of their questions? I had been in the household of Uncle Reginald, the hardest task-master. He had acted like a magister from the schools as he questioned me on what I'd observed and studied even after some errand into the city. He would loose questions like a master bowman would arrows. I was prepared, I was skilled. I thought of him then. I thanked God for his iron discipline. Marigny fluttered his fingers, gesturing at the others to keep quiet. He picked up a scrap of parchment.

'Mathilde, you were recommended by Monsieur de Vitry.'

'I was.'

'He was recently murdered.'

'God rest him, and may the cross of Christ bring his assassins to speedy justice.'

'Of course, of course,' Marigny murmured. 'Did you attend the funeral of this great friend?'

'I never said he was a great friend. I lit a taper and paid for a requiem mass to be sung.'

'Very good.' The reply came in a hiss. 'And you are from Poitiers, Mathilde de Clairebon?'

'Of course. My mother was a widow, my father an apothecary, hence my knowledge of potions.' I knew by rote what Monsieur de Vitry had taught me.

'You seemed very interested in the deaths of Lord Pourte and Abbot Wenlok.'

'No, sir, I wasn't; but my mistress was. After all, they were English envoys dispatched to her. I went where she told me. I lit corpse candles when she told me.'

'Where is the cathedral at Poitiers?'

'On the Rue de la Chaine.'

'Its name?'

'Notre Dame la Grande, but there is another cathedral,' I chattered on, 'that of St Pierre. However, the place I loved to pray at was the Baptistry of St Jean with its very old font, an eight-sided pool dug into the ground. Did you know?' I leaned forward as if excited. 'It has a fresco from ancient times, of the Emperor Constantine. I—'

'What is this? Why the delay? Mathilde, I have been waiting.'

I'd heard the door to the chamber open, and when I turned, Isabella, shrouded in her robe, golden hair hanging all loose, stood in the door-way, a polished mirror in one hand, a jewelled comb in the other. Everyone in the chamber, including the three fiends behind the table, sprang to their feet.

'What is this?' Isabella repeated, sweeping into the chamber. 'I thought you had summoned my servant because of my imminent departure, but this?' Her voice thrilled with anger. 'Is this a court? What are the accusations? Who is the plaintiff? My lord,' her voice assumed a more strident, pet-ulant tone, 'I am the Princess Royal, soon to be Queen of England. In a brief while I must leave my father's house. I need Mathilde, there is so much to do, so little time to do it, so why is she here?'

'My lady.' Marigny came round the table, hands

extended. 'Mathilde can return to you. We are simply questioning her to make sure that she is a fit companion for you—'

'I will be the best judge of that!' Isabella snapped, staring into the darkness behind Marigny. 'And tell my beloved father so!'

I, too, gazed into the shadows behind the table. Philip undoubtedly lurked there, closely watching these proceedings.

'Mathilde,' Isabella snapped her fingers, 'come, we have things to do. My lords.' She made the most courteous of bows and, beckoning to me, swept out of the chamber.

Once we'd left, the princess hurried like a woman possessed along the galleries, eager to place as much distance as possible between herself and those she had left. We walked through the royal cloisters, an eerie experience. Frost whitened the grass of the garth. A cloying mist curled, its tendrils sweeping in as if seeking the gargoyles squatting at the tops of pillars or hidden in corners. Demons carved in stone glared balefully down at us. I gazed up at the sky and heaved a sigh of relief: the moon was at half-quarter. I'd always been haunted by a childhood tale of terror which claimed that during the time of the full moon, gargoyles and other strange demons sprang to life and went prowling through the darkness, seeking whom they could devour. On such a black night, hurrying from the Chambre Ardente with its own devils of flesh and blood, I could well believe such a tale.

Once back in her own chamber Isabella dismissed the sleepy pages and maids and took me into the window enclosure, sitting me down beside her. She opened the latched door and stared out, oblivious to the cold breeze pouring in.

'Strange,' she murmured, 'when I was a child I heard a sermon by a Franciscan preacher about the devil. He described Satan as having a face blackened by soot, his hair and beard falling down to his feet. His eyes were of glowing iron, sparks sprang from his mouth and evil-smelling smoke billowed out of his mouth and nostrils. He had feathered wings sharp as thorns, his hands bound by manacles.' Isabella grasped my arm and drew me closer, resting her lovely head on my shoulder. 'Then Mother died. I rose one night, came here and opened this latch window. It was a beautiful summer's night. In the cloisters below my father was strolling with his coven in the cloisters. They wore their capuchons and deep-sleeved robes; bats were squeaking, rooks calling. On that night I changed my mind about the devil. The true demons were out there and the bats and crows, their servants, came flying out of the sleeves of the robes of my father and his minions. On that same night I dreamed an owl flew into my mouth, sat down on my heart and embraced it with its taloned claws. In my nightmare I went hunting with my father in the woods of Fontainebleau; they say it's haunted by the devil, riding a dog, scouring the woods with a troop of demons dressed in black. Anyway, I felt as if I was condemned to ride those woods for ever.' She lifted her head. 'Dreams, physician, how can you explain them, eh? A trick of the digestion or humours out of harmony, fanciful theories?' Isabella closed the window. 'Mathilde, I always remember that evening. What I thought, what I saw, what I felt when I dreamed: I thought I was trapped in hell, but now I am to be freed. You must come with me. I need you.'

'My lady, I am grateful.'

'Don't.' Isabella drew a deep breath and rose to her feet. 'Don't be grateful.' She picked up a set of Ave beads, lacing them through her fingers. 'Just be careful, Mathilde! The demons may know who you are and they may try, just once more.'

Warnings are like birds; they come and go, quickly forgotten, especially in that busy Christmas season. The feasting and revelry over the twelve days of the holy feast culminated in the ceremonies of the boy bishop and other jester antics of the Epiphany. During this season the English envoys were constant visitors to Isabella, dancing attendance on her, Baquelle in particular eager to describe London and its importance. On reflection Baquelle was a busy-body, full of his own importance. Lord Wenlok's death hardly concerned him, even though it was he who was charged with arranging the dispatch of the abbot's embalmed corpse back to his brethren at Westminster, a task he accomplished as if sending a basket of wheat or a tun of wine. Sandewic grew more taciturn, studying me closely as if trying to reach a decision. Casales and Rossaleti worked closely together; through them I learnt the news of the two courts. How the confrontation between the English king and his leading earls had intensified, whilst in Scotland the war leader Bruce was threatening England's northern marches. In Paris the passion of the Templars continued with denouncings, torture, mock trials and false convictions, followed by bloody execution. I prayed on my knees for those unfortunates. I lit tapers for their souls. I gazed into the night and vowed vengeance, but my time had not yet come.

After Marigny's questioning I also reflected on de Vitry and his household, slaughtered by that mysterious assassin. Had he been lurking there when I entered? Who could it have been? Even Sandewic, a seasoned warrior, could not annihilate an entire household so quickly. And Sir Hugh Pourte falling like a stone from that window? Was the outside wall scaled by black-garbed assassins? And Lord Wenlok ending his pompous life writhing on the floor like a wounded dog? Why had they all been killed? Murder or a series of accidents? All a mystery, but those were my green days of youth before I'd passed through the Valley of Deadly Nightshade and walked the Meadows of Bloody Murder. Moreover, I was distracted. The French court were now preparing to leave, one busy day following another. The list of Isabella's possessions grew as her father insisted that she be a resplendent bride, a royal Capetian princess, soon to be Queen of England and the mother of a long line of kings.

New household officials gathered. Isabella's retinue became swollen with the appointees in every department: the kitchen, the buttery, the chancery, hanaper and chapel. Of course, many of these were Secreti, placemen appointed by Marigny. Others were chosen by Isabella herself, men and women such as her nurse Joanna, who'd served her as a child. A few were complete strangers; one in particular had significance for the future, a Gascon, Jean de Clauvelin, from a small village, or so he claimed, outside Bordeaux, now working in Soissons. He was a notary who had acted as attorney for the Abbey of St Jean des Vignes; a dry-eyed, scrawny-headed, dusty-faced man with a nervous tic in his right cheek, ink-stained fingers and constantly dripping nose. Despite his appearance Jean was most skilled in chancery work; even so Isabella was surprised at his appointment and petitioned her father for the reason. King Philip's reply was curt: de Clauvelin was an accomplished man who would be acceptable to the English court. Isabella pulled a face when she heard this but did not demur. On one thing, however, she was determined, reminding me of our mutual oath. In public she would act her part, but never, in the company of her household, must she and I discuss what she termed *res secretae* or *les affaires secrètes* – secret matters, a promise both of us kept. True, God knows, our secret circle increased, but that was the way of it,

I swear on the Gospels, on my soul. Isabella was queen, later ruler of England for over twenty years, but she never broke that oath until Mortimer. Ah yes, Mortimer, but he was a new world of fresh beginnings. I strike my breast – *mea culpa, mea culpa* – but I digress.

Isabella's wardrobe became filled to overflowing, crammed with precious goods. Two crowns ornamented with gems, gold and silver drinking vessels, precious spoons, fifty silver porringers, twelve great silver dishes and twelve small ones, dresses of gold, silver, velvet, satin and shot taffeta, gowns of green cloth from Douai, six beautifully marbled and six of rose scarlet. Costly furs, hundreds of yards of linen, night cloths, shifts and cloaks were provided together with splendid tapestries emblazoned with lozenges of gold depicting the arms of France, England and Navarre. Throughout these preparations, however, she remained highly anxious, more about me than herself. She asked me time and again what had happened in the Chambre Ardente. Every time I answered she would nod and concede that her father's minions dare not do anything against me because of her, at least nothing direct. Nevertheless I was to be careful. She made a practice of publicly sharing whatever I ate, whilst I accompanied her everywhere. Murder, however, creeps soft and sly.

On occasions I had to perform errands to the city for my mistress. I loved such outings, especially expeditions to the left bank of the Seine. Nothing was more refreshing than crossing the bridge, past the Petite Chatêlet and into the narrow winding lanes with their tall gabled houses rising up from the cobbles, leaning towards each other, one storey stacked above the other. The lower ones were decorated with incredible carvings of fantastical beasts and creatures. I loved to dally and stare at these as I did the forest of scrolled, painted signs of the shops and stalls offering a wide range of goods. It was good to stand at stone fountains or pause under the arched shrines at every corner with torches burning in constant prayer beneath. The shifting sea of colour and smells, the ordinary chatter of the day soothed the soul; the constant braying of horses and pack animals answered by the yip of dogs or drowned by the strident shouting of journeymen above the clanging of bells. Despite Isabella's strictures I needed such visits, an escape from the oppressive atmosphere of the court. Usually I would cross the bridge accompanied by two Genoese bowmen, cheerful rogues specially chosen by the princess, brothers Giacomo and Lorenzo, small and squat, with tough, scarred faces. They were twins, two friendly gargoyles; the only way I could tell the difference between them was that Giacomo had a slight cast in one eye.

Now, once the festivities of Christmas were finished, sometime after the Feast of the Relatio Pueri Jesu de Aegypto on 7 January, the crowds on the bridge were too pressing. Giacomo declared we would take a boat from the royal wharf to the

Quai des Augustins on the far bank. The Princess was sending back to a parchmenter a bulky parcel of certain goods found wanting. I remember that morning so well. Casales, Rossaleti, Sandewic and Baquelle were in Isabella's chambers. The English envoys, increasingly concerned about the amount of goods being stockpiled, were engaged in teasing banter with Isabella's officials. I wanted to escape and instructed Giacomo that we would go before noon. We left the palace, and the crowds milling along the bridge confirmed our decision to take a royal boat across the fog-bound river. We hurried down to the wharf, where our craft had been prepared. I sat in the stern, grasping a hunter's horn; Giacomo asked me to blow it every so often so as to alert other boats on the river, whilst he lit the lantern hanging from a hook on the prow. The two brothers grasped the oars, grinning wickedly at me. I always filled the mouth of the horn with spittle, which made them guffaw with laughter. They bent over the oars, giggling and chattering to each other. To humour them I blew a long braying blast; through the mist other horns answered whilst flaring lanterns winked warningly. Our boat surged forward to be caught by the river to twist and shudder on its current.

Death is surely like a shaft loosed out of the darkness. We had hardly gone far when I heard a sound to my right, the mist shifted and the huge sharp prow of a large war barge was almost upon us, bearing down with hawk-like speed. It crashed into us, dead in the centre. The two Genoese simply went under. I slipped down into the swirling dark water, the cold numbing me until I panicked, gulping mouthfuls as I sank into the gloomy-green bubble-strewn depths. Giacomo and Lorenzo were already drifting corpses weighted down by their cuirasses and war-belts. I didn't know if they could swim. I could; after all, the rushing streams and weed-strewn ponds and lakes of Bretigny nourish many plants, so I'd learnt to swim as I had to walk. The real danger was my heavy boots and cloak. I kicked and shrugged these off and broke to the surface. All was silent and deserted except for the distant noise of horns and the mist-shrouded glow of lamps. I lunged out, hoping I was swimming back towards the royal quayside, and screamed as a boat pulled alongside. Torches flared, rough hands grasped my shoulders. I kicked and screamed until a hard voice shouted:

'*Taisez vous, taisez vous, nous vous aidons!*' Be quiet, be quiet, we are helping you'.

I was dragged aboard, glimpsing dusty, seamed faces; one of these bent over me, chattering like a sparrow. I became aware of the stench of raw fish and struggled to sit up, coughing and retching. I was safe amongst these poor fishermen. They gathered around me asking questions. I begged them to search for my escort. They did so but it was fruitless. The raw cold gave me a fit of the shivers. The fishermen said they had to leave, they could do no more, comforting me with goblets of raw wine, declaring that such accidents on the river were common, especially when the sea mist rolled in. Nevertheless, I could see even they were suspicious. The war-barge which had hit us had quickly disappeared. I'd glimpsed no lantern light on its prow, heard no horn to betray its presence. No alarm had been raised. All I could remember was its shooting speed, like that of a lunging snake.

The fishermen wrapped me in coarse blankets, sat me in the stern and brought me back to the Maison du Roi at the centre of the palace. The captain of the guard, realising what had happened, sent a message before us. Isabella, accompanied by Casales, Rossaleti and Sandewic, hastened down to the courtyard to meet me. She thanked the fishermen lavishly, instructing Casales to take their names for future rewards, while Rossaleti was sent back for a small cup of silver which Isabella pushed into their hands. Casales and Rossaleti were full of questions; Sandewic remained tight-lipped, staring at me intently, his falcon-like eyes cold and hard, shaking his head as if talking to himself. Isabella asked where Baquelle was; Sandewic gestured with his head towards the gatehouse.

'Gone to the city.'

'I hope he is safe,' Isabella whispered.

All three of the English envoys decided to search for Baquelle, whilst Isabella took me into the kitchens. I stripped and wrapped myself in a thick robe, soft slippers on my feet, then squatted in front of the great roaring fire and drank mulled wine until I drifted into sleep. When I woke I was in Isabella's chamber, none the worse for such an ordeal, though frightened and fearful. I wanted to scream at the princess that we should leave. She just sat on the edge of the bed grasping my hand, stroking it carefully, questioning me closely. She agreed it was no accident. I, too, was certain of that, but as for why and who was responsible . . . Isabella explained that when I'd left she'd been talking with the English envoys. The appearance of her brothers, smiling maliciously, had provoked her unease; they'd come up pretending they wanted to talk to the English but then sauntered off. I asked if she thought they were responsible. Isabella shook her head. She said she didn't know, but confided that all three, together with Marigny and Nogaret, would escort us to England after the coronation. She ordered food from the kitchens and fed me herself. Now and again she'd pause, patting me on the arm, muttering in Navarrese, a sign of her own deep agitation.

After that I never left the palace. I remained haunted by those chilling images, the sharp curved prow, the boat bearing down on us, the Genoese bowmen, arms and legs splayed, floating down into the green darkness, the icy waters wrapping around me. Who had planned it, why? Were they waiting for us? I'd made a mistake. Our preparations that morning had been loudly proclaimed,

Giacomo and Lorenzo going down to the royal wharf searching for a boat. Such anxieties vexed my mind and gnawed at my heart. Of course the attack was meant to look like an accident, but what was its sinister root? The malice of the princes, Isabella's brothers? Marigny's suspicions? King Philip's resentment at my closeness to his daughter? Or was it something else?

Uncle Reginald had instructed me always to study cause and effect, to gather evidence, yet in my heart, I was convinced the attack had something to do with the massacre at the de Vitry mansion. Marigny had specifically questioned me on that, but why? Had the lonely assassin been hiding there all the time, watching me closely? Had I seen something the importance of which I did not recognise at the time?

Sandewic came to visit me. He brought me a present, a copy of Trotula's writings which he'd bought in the Latin Quarter. The rough old soldier pushed this at me, saying that he was grateful I had survived, adding that he was even more grateful that his rheums and fever had disappeared whilst the ulcer on his leg had healed beautifully. He was clumsy and off-hand. He wished to talk with me but he was still suspicious and wary, so after a short while he again mumbled his thanks and left. As for the rest, my mishap was viewed as an unfortunate incident; courtesies were offered, polite messages sent, but it was a mere speck on the court preparations. By the Feast of St Hilary these were completed and the heralds proclaimed the day and hour of departure.

A long line of carts, carriages and pack animals crossed the Seine bridges, skirting the city, heading north-east into the barren, frozen countryside towards Boulogne. An uncomfortable, jolting journey. The great power of France, banners and pennants fluttering, moved slowly through the bleak countryside, levying purveyance as it went, resting at royal manor houses, palaces, priories and monasteries. Isabella and I journeyed in a carriage stiffened with cushions but still jarringly uncomfortable; we would often change and risk the bracing air by riding soft-eyed palfreys. At night we ate, drank and warmed ourselves, then slept the sleep of exhaustion. It was a hard, coarse winter. The countryside never seemed to change, just rutted track-ways winding past ice-bound fields, meadows and pasturelands, all shrouded by those soaring hedgerows and deep ditches so common in Normandy. The peasants, learning of our approach, gathered their goods and stock and fled, but the seigneurs, priors and abbots had no choice but to smile falsely and welcome our arrival as a great privilege.

Isabella and I kept to ourselves. Now and again we tried to distinguish and name the different plants we noticed or speculate about what would happen in Boulogne. The English envoys were often in attendance but they too became numbed with the sheer grind of the passing days. At last we approached the coast, the countryside giving way to sand-strewn hills and wastelands. A salty, bitter sea wind cut at our faces yet we all rejoiced as the spires and turrets of Boulogne came into sight.

CHAPTER 7

The peace of the Church perishes and
the arrogant reign.

'*A Song of the Times*', 1272–1307

How can I describe it? All of Europe had converged on that port. Philip's allies from Lorraine, across the Rhine, Spain and elsewhere had gathered to witness a marriage which was to proclaim a lasting peace between England and France. Only one thing marred the enjoyment. Edward of England had not arrived. Despite his promises, there was no news of the English king. Casales, Rossaleti and the rest became highly anxious. We moved into Boulogne; the rest of the court were left to look after themselves, but the royal party lodged in a manor house close to the cathedral of Notre Dame, high in the city within its inner ring of walls. I hated the place, cold and austere, despite the best attempts of the citizens to festoon their streets and alleyways with banners, painted cloths and gaily coloured ribbons. All I truly wanted was for Edward of England to arrive, for the marriage to take place and for us to leave France for ever. A time of remembrance. I'd come so far, yet I was so young. My dreams in the chamber I shared with Isabella were often marred by nightmares, and phantasms, especially about Uncle Reginald seated in that cart, pushed up the ladder at Montfaucon, the noose being put around his neck. I became so agitated I fell ill, and used my own skill at physic to calm my humours.

Philip's anger at the delay was obvious, royal messengers being sent out almost by the hour to seek out the English party. At last the news arrived. Edward of England had been delayed but he had left Dover, he had arrived at Wissant and was hastening with all speed towards Boulogne. The bells of the city rang out to greet him as Isabella and I went up on to the walls to watch his approach. A mass of brilliant banners announced his arrival. I glimpsed the golden leopards of England against a scarlet background, a swirl of riders, cloaks flying, soldiers and knights dressed in the royal livery all clustered round a horseman resplendent in scarlet and silver, his golden hair clear for all to see. Edward of England had arrived! A forest of pavilions grew up round the town, every available chamber and garret was taken, even the porches and gateways of churches and taverns as the great ones assembled with their retinues. The English had wisely camped in and around the town of Montreuil. From there Edward led a delegation into Boulogne to treat with his future father-in-law over Gascony and other vexed questions. There was no formal meeting with Isabella; protocol and etiquette demanded that Edward keep his distance from his intended bride.

Casales, Sandewic and Baquelle provided juicy morsels of gossip about the proceedings. Relations between the two kings remained as frosty as the weather. Edward had agreed to suppress the Templars, being more vexed by the demands of his own leading earls regarding Gaveston. These he had ignored, even appointing Gaveston, fully invested as the Earl of Cornwall, as regent during the royal absence. Of course, we weren't satisfied until we'd studied the English king when he visited Philip. Isabella and I seized secret vantage points to achieve this. Edward II was over six foot tall, broad-shouldered, slim-waisted with the long legs of a born horseman and the wiry arms of a swordsman. He was handsome-faced, slightly olive-skinned, a strong contrast to his golden hair and neatly clipped fair beard and moustache. He had heavy-lidded blue eyes, the right one slightly drooping as if he distrusted the world, an impression heightened by the wry grimace of his mouth. He walked quickly, hands swinging, carrying himself arrogantly, yet when he relaxed he appeared to be courteous in the extreme. A weathercock of a man! I watched him closely; even from those few glimpses at the start of my life, I gathered Edward was changeable. He'd pat a servant on the back but, if the mood took him, lash out with fist or foot and hurl a litany of abuse. He had a carrying voice and a commanding presence. A man of nervous energy who shouted at his grooms to take care of the horses, gazing round as if expecting some French bowman or assassin to be lurking nearby.

Edward was apparently eager to finish the wedding celebrations and leave. He did little honour to Philip or the French king's feelings, complaining bitterly about the cold, the loneliness of Boulogne and the need to return to England to deal with pressing business at Westminster. According to Sandewic, Edward advanced the argument that he'd come to France, he'd marry Isabella, do homage for Gascony, suppress the Temple, so what else did Philip want? Of course, the source of his distress was the growing crisis in London between Gaveston and the earls, led by the king's cousin Thomas of Lancaster. This group of barons, who would come to dominate all our lives, were also hostile to a French marriage. They openly demanded their king ignore all such revelry, summon a new army and march north to deal with the Scots, who were launching raids across the northern march. On one thing all the earls agreed: Gaveston was to be exiled. According to Casales he was no more than a Gascon squire who'd been created a premier earl, and now the great earls had to gnaw their knuckles as Gaveston reigned supreme.

All these observations and news swirled around us as Isabella prepared for her wedding at the cathedral of Notre Dame in Boulogne, where the

Archbishop of Narbonne, together with other leading ecclesiastics, would celebrate her betrothal and nuptial mass. On the Feast of the Conversion of St Paul, 25 January 1308, Isabella, resplendent in a silver gown of pure silk, a white gauze veil held in place on her head by a circlet of finest gold, met her royal bridegroom, garbed in robes of blue, scarlet and gold, at the door of Notre Dame to exchange vows. The princess looked and acted the part of the *Grande Dame* from the romances she so avidly read. I was not allowed near her, being herded into the cathedral porch with other retainers, whilst the princess was escorted up the church by leading ladies from the courts of Europe. The nuptial mass was celebrated, the powerful voices of the cathedral canons singing the melodious plainchant refrains whilst Isabella and Edward knelt on splendid prie-dieus before the high altar, half-hidden by the clouds of incense streaming out of the many censers. Once the Archbishop of Narbonne had sung the 'Ite Missa Est', king and royal bride walked hand in hand down past the choir and into the nave to receive the applause of the aristocratic congregation. Afterwards they proceeded out on to the steps to be acclaimed by the crowds, whilst fresh choirs carolled 'Laus Honour et Gloria Vobis' followed by a hymn to 'Isabella Regina Anglorum', even though she had yet to be crowned.

Later in the afternoon, as darkness drew in, the feasting and banqueting took place in the royal mansion hastily refurbished for the occasion. I did not attend. Court protocol and etiquette demanded that during her first marriage days, Isabella could only be waited upon by women of the royal blood who had witnessed the nuptials and the consequent royal bedding. I kept to my lodgings in the nearby old bishop's palace, accepting, like my companions, the remains of the feasts: scraps of venison, pork, beef, fish, half-eaten manchet loaves, bruised fruit and jugs of wine of every variety.

Isabella did not ignore me. She sent a small purse filled with English silver and a piece of parchment on which a forget-me-not flower was carefully inscribed. More importantly, Sandewic came into his own. He was now *Custos*, knight-keeper of the princess's household. She was the centre of the English court so her retinue was embraced by the English king's peace. During the wedding days Sandewic used the opportunity to bring in an escort of Welsh archers, little wiry, dark-faced men who spoke a tongue I could not understand. They were clothed in Sandewic's livery, a white lion rampant on a green background, they carried longbows of yew with wicked-looking stabbing knives dangling from rings on their belts and quivers of yard-long shafts strapped to their backs. These archers guarded and patrolled the bishop's palace, cheerful men who loved to drink and sing the haunting songs of their country. They were most vigilant and careful, demanding that the servants who brought my food first taste it before they allowed them through. Oh yes, those days marked a sharp shift in the seasons! I too was now in the power of England.

Casales and Rossaleti also recognised their tasks were changing. Rossaleti prepared himself to carry Isabella's secret and privy seals though she quietly vowed that only she and I would seal what she and I should only know. A distance grew up between Casales and Rossaleti; they were no longer envoys but members of different households. Baquelle came into his own, being specially charged with organising the English departure from Boulogne to the nearby port of Wissant. Of course Sandewic gave me the news about the banquets and feasts hosted by the various courtiers with their flowery speeches and empty promises. He also took me out through the dreary mizzle of a Norman winter to view the sights.

Boulogne was a town transformed; banners, streamers, brightly coloured ribbons flapped everywhere alongside the fleur-de-lis of France and the leopards of England. Bishops, nobles, haughty ladies, high-ranking clerics, swaggering mice-eyed retainers tricked out in their glorious attire of ermine, brocade, satin silks, linen from the looms of Flanders and goldwork from Cologne. Sleek horses of every type, sumpters, destriers, palfreys and cobs, clattered across the frost-glazed cobbles. In the fields outside town the war-pennants fluttered and glowed in the bursts of weak sunshine.

The might of Europe, garbed in the armour of Liege and Limoges, Damascus, Milan, London and Toledo, had come to do mock battle in the lists, those great tournaments and tourneys organised in Isabella's honour. The frozen meadows outside the town walls were transformed by a host of standards all displaying their exotic insignia: wolves, wyverns, leopards, dragons, fire-breathing salamanders, suns and moons, wheat sheaves, fabulous birds, charging boars, rampant lions, crouching dogs, all parted per pale or per fesse, per cross or bend sinister. All these emblems were painted in the colours of heraldry, azure, gules, sable, vert, purple and argent. In the centre of this city of silken pavilions stood the lists, where knights in plate armour, helmets carved in terrifying shapes and surmounted by brilliantly coloured plumes, charged, lances splintering, shields buckling. As one joust finished another began to the blast of trumpet and horn, the air riven with the clash of steel, the thunder of hooves and the heralds shouting, *'Lessez les aler, lessez les aler, les bons chevaliers!'* Pages and squires clustered round the heroes who'd survived the battling of the last few days, all intent on winning the golden crown. I quoted the lines of a troubadour:

Speech does not comfort me,
I am in harmony with war,
Nor do I hold or believe any other religion.

Casales, who accompanied Sandewic and myself, seethed with humiliation at not being able to participate. He laughingly mocked my criticisms but Sandewic looped his arm through mine and nodded.

'I've seen enough of battle!' he remarked as we walked away, gesturing with his head. 'It is nothing like that.'

By then it was the end of January, and the feasting and revelry were beginning to pall whilst the tournaments and tourneys had already led to the deaths of four young knights killed in a furious mêlée, a supposedly friendly joust between the courts of England and France.

'It is time we were gone,' Sandewic growled as we took off our cloaks in the buttery, warming our hands before the fire after our icy walk back from the tourney field. 'The pot is beginning to bubble and the scum rises to coat it all,' he added. 'We should go before any real mischief is done.'

'Nonsense,' Casales objected, gesturing at Rossaleti, who was busy at the table transcribing household lists. 'We have enough provisions whilst never again will the courts of England and France meet.'

'I don't like weddings or nuptials. They harvest bitter memories for me,' Rossaleti intoned mournfully. Without any invitation the clerk threw down the quill pen and began to describe his own early days as a Benedictine novice and how he realised that he was not fit to take solemn vows. He talked about his marriage and the tragic death of his beloved wife, speaking so wistfully that he stirred the memories of others. Casales described his wedding day and the death of his wife in childbirth, and the long arduous years since. Sandewic nodded sympathetically but lightened the mood by describing his own marriage of many years, its humour and companionship, though he grew sad with sorrow over his wife's death and his frequent quarrels with his children. I sensed the deep sadness of these men who, in the words of Sandewic, had become 'priests of politic', giving up their own lives in the service of their king.

Our mood was lightened by Baquelle's arrival. Sandewic winked at me and put a finger to his lips, for Sir John needed little encouragement to sermonise us on his all-important marriage to the sister, as he kept telling us, of the most powerful wool merchant in England. The little knight, cheery-faced from the cold, was full of what he'd seen and who he'd talked to, determined on delivering a lengthy sermon about the different courts which had assembled. Sandewic ordered a cask of Bordeaux to be broached and cut Baquelle off in full flow by declaring that we were sitting as if visited by the Three Summoners of Doom: Sickness, Old Age and Death. He filled our cups with the heady claret, ordered Rossaleti to fetch his dulcimer and told us not to be *faux et semblant* at such a joyous time but to revel and carol with the best. Rossaleti brought his dulcimer in and Sandewic broke into a bawdy song about a knight, his lady and a cuckolding friar whose testicles the knight vowed he would enshrine in a hog's turd. Sandewic had a powerful voice, as did Casales, and both roared out the filthy but very comic song as Rossaleti tried to pluck music on the dulcimer. Sandewic taught me the words and made me join in the singing till tears of laughter bubbled in my eyes. A warm, amicable afternoon to spite the hailing sleet and numbing drizzle outside, yet it is curious, isn't it, looking back, how every torchlight creates its own host of shadows?

On 2 February we celebrated the Feast of the Circumcision of the Christ Child. I crowded into the great cathedral of Notre Dame, standing between the baptismal font and the devil's door through which Satan left every time a child was baptised. By craning my neck I could glimpse the great ones gathered in the choir stalls, but because of the heavy rood screen all I caught were flashes of colour. I composed myself to watch the ceremonial entry into the church of a young mother and her child seated on an ass in commemoration of the Virgin and Child coming out of Egypt. A choir carolled the well-known hymn 'Orientis Partibus Advenitavit Asinus, Pulcher et Fortis': 'From the Eastern lands comes the donkey, beautiful and brave, well-fitted to bear his burden. Up donkey and sing.' The subsequent mass, a vibrant, noisy assembly, marked the end of all the celebrations. During this the congregation imitated the braying of a donkey at the usual liturgical responses, as if both court and crowd were eager to seize this opportunity to offset the pompous, solemn liturgies of the previous days. Afterwards the great ones dined in the hall of the Maison du Roi.

In the evening, as darkness fell, Isabella returned to our lodgings escorted by a retinue of squires and pages with flaring torches and surrounded by a gaggle of leading noblewomen. These gathered in the courtyard as the princess dismounted from her palfrey. They crowded round her, wishing her well, leading her into the hallway. Isabella, pale with tiredness, stood with a false smile. When they had all departed, she grasped my hand and allowed me to lead her up to the bedchamber. She had the door bolted and locked, kicked off the heavy brocade slippers, loosened the ties and bows of her gowns, and left them lying on the floor. Then she picked up a coverlet from the bed, wrapped it round herself and crouched like a scullery wench before the brazier, warming her fingers. I gave her warm ale mixed with hops to soothe her and she grasped the goblet, drinking greedily before turning to me.

'You will ask?'

'You need not answer.'

'Edward of England is kind and gentle, a courteous, chivalric knight.' Isabella laughed. 'He says he loves me and asked to see me naked. He showed me what he called bed wrestling and the troubadours prettify as lovemaking. Afterwards he entered me and hurt me; sometimes he liked to mount me as a stallion does a mare. Then he held me in his arms and kissed me.' She spoke in a dry, flat tone, not hurt or wounded; the physical aspects of her first nuptials Isabella dismissed with a mere shrug.

'Edward has moods, Mathilde. He never forgets an injury. He can be as attentive as a lovelorn squire but then he'll sit staring into nothing, lips moving as if talking to himself. Mathilde,' Isabella moved to face me fully, 'I wonder if my husband Edward of England is slightly fey.' She blinked, licked her lips and smiled brilliantly. 'He hates my father. He detests the very sight of him, claiming that his own father and Philip of France richly deserved each other. When I told him I felt no different, Edward roared with laughter and hugged me tight. I told him about you, Mathilde.' She put her goblet down and grasped my hand. 'But not all about you. He said you are most welcome, his house will be yours, adding that we shall all plot against Philip. He loves that, Mathilde, to mock, to turn the world on its head. During the mass this morning he led the braying, laughing out loud like a schoolboy released from his horn book.'

'And the Lord Gaveston?'

Isabella wound together a few loose threads on the coverlet.

'They are as one, Mathilde! Edward says Gaveston is his brother, his father, his sister and his mother.'

'And his lover?'

Isabella shook her head, not denying it, more bemused and bewildered.

'We shall see,' she breathed. 'We shall see.'

'And the deaths of Pourte and Wenlok?'

'Edward remained tight-lipped about those.' She pulled the coverlet closer. 'He did not seem pleased about either man, muttering that both had supported his marriage to me or, rather, the French marriage,' she smiled, 'as well as the arrest of the Templars, but opposed the advancement of Lord Gaveston. Did you know, Mathilde, Casales, Sandewic and Baquelle have the same mind on these matters? Edward still trusts them but does not like their views.' Isabella stared into the fiery coals. 'In the end Edward of England,' she whispered, 'could be a goat, a donkey, even a pig and I'd still dance on my back for him!' She glared fiercely at me. 'I am free, Mathilde, we are leaving! Now is our winter; soon the spring will come and I'll sow the seeds for the future. We'll watch them grow in summer and rejoice at harvest time!

Isabella retired, crawling between the linen sheets, pulling the blankets over her head, while I drew the curtains of the bed about her. I sat for a while before the brazier, warming myself, half sleeping, as I reflected on what Isabella had said. One fact was emerging: Pourte, Wenlok, Casales, Sandewic and Baquelle were confidants of the king, and had all advised him not to advance Gaveston. I remembered what Isabella had said about her new husband. Could Edward be responsible for those two deaths? For dispatching those assassins? There again, I'd learnt that others in England were opposed to the French marriage; perhaps they had

had a hand in the mischief? I realised I could make little sense of it. I recalled my visit to the Rue des Ecrivains, that strange empty chamber and the man who'd been sheltering there. He'd disappeared so quickly and was apparently waiting for me in England. Was he the same man I'd glimpsed in the Oriflamme tavern? Was he involved in these mysteries?

I was about to retire when Sandewic and Casales arrived. I didn't have the heart to dismiss them so I entertained them downstairs in the small parlour. One of the Welsh bowmen had built up the fire and served us some scraps from the buttery. Both men brought news. Tomorrow the English would leave Boulogne for Wissant. We were to be up before dawn. Outside I could already hear the porters and carters bringing out the wagons, checking the sumpter ponies.

'It's finished!' Sandewic sighed in relief, stretching back his head as if to relieve the tension in his neck. 'And now back to England.'

'And Gaveston?' Casales interjected.

'Mais oui!' I smiled. 'And Gaveston.'

'Mathilde, your mistress may have her part to play,' Sandewic declared. 'The problem with Edward of England is that he is bereft of good counsel. Most of the leading earls of his kingdom are as young as he: Guy of Warwick, Thomas of Lancaster. They are also hot-tempered and fiery-natured; they see themselves as the king's natural councillors, his advisers by birth.'

'So they naturally resent Gaveston.'

'They hate him!'

'But surely,' I declared, 'the old king's councillors still play their part?'

'Gone,' Sandewic replied wearily. 'Robert of Winchelsea, Archbishop of Canterbury, is old and still in exile. Robert Baldock, Bishop of London, the former chancellor, is in disgrace because he too opposed Gaveston and the king, as did Walter Langton, former treasurer, Bishop of Coventry and Lichfield. Both bishops have been stripped of their offices and possessions and now remain under house arrest. Others are old or frail. The council chamber is empty, Gaveston alone has the king's ear, and that,' Sandewic pointed a finger at me, 'is dangerous!' He paused, collecting his thoughts, and stared up at the ceiling. 'What is even more perilous,' he added almost in a whisper, 'is what Philip of France intends. What does he plot in that subtle teeming mind?' He glanced out of the corner of his eye at me. 'Oh, he can exchange the kiss of peace and call Edward his "fair son", but Philip of France dreams his dreams. He is ready to summon up the ghosts of the past!'

When I questioned Sandewic on that, be became taciturn and withdrawn. A pity; the old constable's remark was a key to these mysteries.

We left for Wissant the following morning, Edward processing out of Boulogne with very little ceremony, a studied insult to Philip. Isabella acted likewise, dispatching a mere messenger to make her farewells, saying she was concerned that she take everything with her. The long line of English carts, carriages and sumpter ponies poured out of Boulogne with standards flying. On either side of the column trudged Welsh bowmen in their steel morions and leather jerkins, whilst further out, light horsemen scouted the way before us. Isabella could have ridden in a litter; instead she bestrode a palfrey, often galloping up and down the long column of soldiery offering sweetmeats and smiles of encouragement. She did this unabashed, golden hair falling down, gown hitched up to display the froth of skirt and pretty ankles beneath. The troops loved it and cheered her loudly. Edward, riding at the head of the column, sent back his thanks to his *charmante* but kept to the fore, setting the speed of our march.

It proved an uneventful but uncomfortable journey. Nothing singular occurred except for Sandewic and Casales detaching themselves from the column, riding out with a small escort of mounted archers to explore the countryside. At first I wondered if they suspected an ambush. On their return at night they came and sat beside the roaring fire, muttering among themselves. I questioned them closely. Sandewic's reply was off-hand. I snapped at both of them that I could understand any danger, especially in France. Sandewic almost leaned into the fire, so chilled was he after his arduous ride.

'Did you notice?' he whispered, and glanced

around, but there was no one; Isabella had returned to her pavilion.

'Did I notice what?' I retorted.

'For the love of heaven, the roads!' Sandewic exclaimed. 'They are repaired, hedges cut back, streams forded with fresh bridges, peasants hurrying away at our approach . . .'

'And?' I insisted.

'Philip himself is preparing to come here,' Sandewic declared. 'We found outposts manned; a line of beacons runs along the coast. Villagers talk of troops being dispatched to ports further to the east, of boats and barges being collected.'

'Preparations for the royal wedding?' I asked.

'Possible,' Sandewic grumbled, gesturing into the dark. 'I've informed the king, but all he's interested in is Wissant.'

Edward's desire to reach the port was understandable. The countryside between Boulogne and the coast was desolate, frozen wasteland offering little protection against the biting sea winds. We reached the port the following day and gazed down at *The Margaret of Westminster* and its escort riding at anchor. The royal ship was magnificent, a great masted cog with high stern and jutting prow. It was my first encounter with the sea and I soon understood the sailor's prayer, 'From perilous seas Lord deliver us'. The journey out by barge to the warcog was the beginning of the terrors. The powerful, swift swell of the heavy grey water, the salting spray, the blasting wind, the dangerous climb up the side on to the ever-moving deck cannot easily be forgotten. Our embarkation was hasty and rough. The king was resolute on an evening departure. He was first aboard, striding the deck, his cloak thrown back, strong booted legs spread against the sway of the ship. I passed him, the closest I'd been, as the princess hurried to her cabin beneath the stern. He winked at me boyishly. An open, very handsome face with a straight nose, full lips, the golden hair matted by sea spray; his blue eyes, however, were cold and angry as if the soul behind seethed in fury.

Once Isabella was settled, I went and stood beneath the canopy near the steps leading up to the stern. Edward was still pacing up and down, roaring at the captain, dragging the latecomers, including a bedraggled, terrified Rossaleti, over the side, almost throwing him on to the deck. Sailors and servants were sent staggering as the king shoved and pushed, bellowing orders at the captain, who retorted with a stream of curses, gesturing at the sky and the shore. Edward shook his fist at him. The captain hurried down from the poop, screaming invective and waving his hands. Edward shoved the man up against the mast, talking to him fiercely, the crew pattering by them, all unconcerned, bare feet slapping the soaking deck. The captain replied just as furiously. Edward turned away, hands on hips, swaying with the motion of the ship. Then he turned back roaring with laughing, grabbed the captain by the jerkin, dragged him forward and thrust a handful of coins at him. The captain had won the argument. We waited until our escort ships were fully ready before the *Margaret* turned, dipped its sails three times in honour of the Trinity and made its way out into the open sea.

Visions of hell! I have witnessed many, but that first journey across the swollen, tempest-tossed Narrow Seas was a true descent into Hades. Gusty gales, crashing waves, the ship rising and falling as it fought the seething sea. Salt water gushed everywhere, stinging cold, flying spray sharp as a razor; the giddiness, the nausea, the sheer terror of being imprisoned within wooden walls against the brute passion of nature. I retched and vomited, no longer caring. Nevertheless, one memory survives. The king came down and knelt beside me, his smiling face coaxing me to drink pure water; he stroked my hair, telling me not to be afraid, calling me by my name, saying I shouldn't worry. Later he helped me up on to the deck. I became aware of whirling, starlit skies, the surge of the wild sea and the blasting force of the wind. The king held me very close, telling me to breathe the fresh air, not to think but to rejoice! I was leaving France; I was free of the malignant power of Philip. He then took me back down, wrapped me in a cloak and knelt by Isabella shivering in her cot-bed, rubbing her hands, talking quickly in English which I could not understand.

I fell asleep. When I awoke, dawn had broken. Screams from the deck above sent me hurrying out. The *Margaret* had sighted land but the crew had assembled to watch their king flay a man who had fallen asleep during his night watch. The unfortunate had been guilty of nothing but exhaustion yet, clad only in a soiled loincloth, he was lashed to the mast, his back criss-crossed with bloody scars from the cane a sweaty-faced Edward held in his hand. The king stood, chest heaving, teeth bared, eyes staring. The flogging ceased as I reached the top step. I grasped a rope to steady myself against the swell. The king lifted the cane, glimpsed me then threw it to the deck, shouting that the man should be released. The sailor was unbound and collapsed on to the deck. Edward took a pail of salt water and poured it over the man's scarred back; the sailor screamed. Edward knelt beside him, turned him over and, shouting for the captain, took the proffered cup of wine, forcing it between the man's lips. He then rose, dug into his purse, forced a gold coin into the man's clenched fist, kicked him gently in the ribs and hurried on to the poop to stand by the pilot.

The *Margaret* made its way in under the brooding cliffs of Dover and the soaring castle which dominated them. We disembarked on barges and boats. Isabella was quite ill and had to be carried ashore. I staggered behind, so absorbed with being back on land, I hardly noticed the retinue awaiting us. Isabella was carefully housed in her litter, and I was about to join her when the shrill blast of trumpets echoed through the mist. We were on the quayside, which was dank, wet and reeking of salty fish.

The mist shifted and a wall of brilliant colour advanced through the murk. I was aware of a tall, slender, dark-haired man dressed brightly as the sun walking towards Edward, who stood a little ahead of us ringed by Sandewic, Casales and others of the royal retinue. I leaned against the litter and stared as if I was seeing a vision. Behind the sun-dressed man trooped a cohort of what appeared to be gaudily dressed children, jumping and leaping, the bells on their costumes tinkling out. Beside these strode standard-bearers carrying banners embla-zoned with the insignia of a scarlet eagle, its wings outstretched; and following hastily on, a group of noblemen and women dressed in the finery of the court. Gaveston in all his glory had arrived! Edward did not wait but ran towards him, arms outstretched. They met and embraced, hugging and kissing, ignoring the protests and exclamations of the lords and ladies who had accompanied Gaveston as well as those coming up the steps from the barges and boats.

At the time these were simply shapes, hot-eyed, choleric-faced individuals, cloaked and furred, fingers, wrists and throats glittering with jewellery; men and women who, at first, were mere shadows, though in time they would touch my life with their ambition, greed, vindictiveness, vices and virtues, talents and weaknesses. I could not immediately give them names, but their titles were already known. Guy Beauchamp, the dark-browed Earl of Warwick; Aymer de Valence, slender as a snake with the pious face of a priest; Thomas of Lancaster, tall and angular, with pallid features, a hooked nose and arrogant grey eyes; Bohun of Hereford, squat and burly; and, of course, Mortimer of Wigmore. On that day, however, it was Gaveston and Gaveston alone. The king dragged him by the arm back to the litter, pulling aside its curtains. Both men squatted down. Gaveston moved on to his knees; grasping the princess's hands, he kissed them both on the palms and the backs, offering her undying fealty.

Isabella, exhausted after the sea voyage, struggled to sit up against the cushions. She replied in a strong voice how pleased she was to finally meet her 'sweet cousin'. Once again Gaveston bowed, head going down in deep obeisance before, one hand on the king's shoulder, he forced himself up and stood looking down at me.

Gaveston was a truly beautiful man. He was dressed in cloth-of-gold jerkin, hose and costly cape beneath a pure woollen cloak thrown dramatically back over his shoulders. A brilliant amethyst brooch clasping the collar of his jerkin glowed in the dappled light, long white fingers glittered with precious stones, whilst the perfume from his robes smelt exquisite. He stood as tall as Edward with dark hair and fair, smooth-shaven skin; a girlish face, soft-eyed and full-lipped. At first glance he seemed effeminate, but a closer look revealed a firm chin and a thin, imperious nose whilst those liquid brown eyes mirrored a shifting range of emotions. Even then, in those few heartbeats of our first meeting,

Gaveston changed, eyes and mouth wrinkling in a welcoming smile until he tilted his head back and heard the muttering around him. Immediately his face hardened, lower lip jutting out, eyes narrowing, skin tightening in anger, rendering his high cheek-bones more prominent. He glanced imperiously around, then stared back at me; he smiled, shrugged, grasped my fingers and kissed them, welcoming me in a clear, vibrant voice, his courtly French tinged with a slight accent.

Around us swirled what I had first thought were the cohort of children; they were in fact the king's jesters, the *stulti, mimi et histriones* so beloved of Edward of England. Little men and women dressed garishly in chequered cloth and multicoloured hose, some had their pates shaven in the form of a tonsure and marked with a cross. They rejoiced in names such as Maud Make-Joy and Robert the Fool, Dulcia Wifestof, Griscote (Grey Bread), Visage (The Face) and Magote (the Ape). Some of them were sensible, others clearly made fools by either God or nature. They all danced round the king and Gaveston, made a fuss of Isabella and myself, leaping and cavorting even as the king finally greeted the sullen-faced nobles who'd gathered with their wives to welcome him.

So, so many years ago, yet the memories come hurtling back clear and stark. It was a time of dreams, like the waking time after a deep sleep. The schoolmen talk of distinguishing between what is real and what is not; perhaps they have it wrong.

There are no differences, just varying, conflicting realities. I was free of France, yet in a way I was not. I had been pitched and tossed on the Narrow Seas to be caught up in the murky swirl of the English court. I had been confined within walls of wood but now I was hurried up the steep, winding path to the forbidding fortress of Dover with its yawning great gatehouse. We went in under soaring towers and sombre walls, along narrow galleys and passageways into a broad cobbled bailey, busy as a Paris street. Smiths and tinkers hammered and clattered, horses neighed, fleshers sliced carcasses and hung them on hooks so the blood would drain into the waiting buckets. Dogs barked, ponies reared and whinnied. Children screamed as the womenfolk busied themselves over washing vats. The filthy ground seemed to swell and move. I was giddy and nauseous. People appeared, a moving sea of faces either smiling or forbidding. Greetings were offered, then at last we were alone in a stark but comfortable room at the base of one of the towers: a cavernous chamber with arrow slits for windows, its walls and floors warmed with coloured cloths and rugs. Chafing dishes and braziers were plentiful, whilst a strong fire glowed in the great hearth. A huge four-poster bed dominated the room, its fringed curtains pulled back, the linen sheets warmed with pans of fiery charcoal.

Isabella and I immediately went to sleep whilst porters and servants brought up our baggage and all the other goods being ferried to the quayside. I woke once, sharply aware of the different realities, the ordinary and extraordinary which I'd noticed over the last two days, then I fell asleep again.

Later that day, still confused and tired, we dined in the great hall of the castle, long and cavernous like a tithing barn with brightly emblazoned cloths and drapes hanging from the hammer-beam roof. All the windows and arrow slits had been shuttered against the bitter draughts. The fire in the hearth was a mass of burning logs. We sat on the dais with Casales, Sandewic and Baquelle, together with a group of leading lords and ladies. The only other guests, an open snub to Edward's leading courtiers, the royal dwarves and jesters, were seated at a special table beneath the salt. Edward spent most of the meal teasing these, throwing pieces of stewed meat and chicken at them, lounging back in his throne-like chair, thumb to his mouth, slurping from his wine cup and roaring with laughter at the antics of his 'special guests'. He behaved like an uncouth young man. The royal favourite, magnificently attired in scarlet and gold satin, did not participate in the king's revelry but intently watched Isabella and myself as if weighing our worth, plotting what to do next. On one occasion he leaned over and grasped my hand.

'Mathilde,' he whispered, 'bear with us for a while, nothing is what it appears to be.'

For the rest the conversation was about the imminent arrival of the French party in their ships, the issue of safe conducts to them under the privy seal, the forthcoming journey through Kent to London and the date of the coronation. The meal ended on a sour note with two of the leading earls, Warwick and Hereford I believe, objecting to the clamour of the jesters. Edward replied that if the earls wanted to leave they could, which they did, bowing to the king and Isabella but openly ignoring Gaveston.

Eventually Isabella returned to our room, the king staying in the royal chambers adjoining the hall. He entreated Isabella to visit him but she pleaded exhaustion after a long journey. For a while she sat on the edge of the bed, combing her hair and humming softly to herself. I busied myself with various tasks. I was eager to determine that the books and precious manuscripts Isabella had brought with her, many dealing with physic and the properties of herbs, had not been lost.

'Mathilde,' Isabella called out.

'Your grace?'

The princess smiled and patted the bed beside her. 'Come. I must get used to that title.' She handed the comb to me turning slightly so I could smooth out her hair at the back. 'As I must get used to my husband's determination to avenge all insults and demonstrate he is king.' She looked over her shoulder. 'That is the *radix malorum omnium*, Mathilde, the root of all evils here. Edward is, in many ways, a child younger in years than me. He was snubbed and insulted by his own father and his nobles, and he never forgets.'

'And the Lord Gaveston?' I asked.

'I must accept things for what they are, Mathilde. Gaveston is Edward's soul. He fills an emptiness that I could never hope to; I must learn to accept that.'

'And yourself?' I asked. 'What about your emptiness?'

I thought Isabella was crying; her shoulders shook slightly. When I tried to turn her, she pushed me away.

'I don't know, Mathilde. I don't know where the emptiness is and I am not too sure if it can ever be filled.' She turned to me. 'You do that for me. Can't you see? In the friendship I have for you?' She touched me gently on the shoulder. 'I can understand Edward's love for Gaveston; we mirror each other.'

'He should be more cunning, astute.'

'That, Mathilde,' the princess whispered, 'comes with years. The king is insistent on one thing. Tonight we dined in public, but tomorrow, he, Gaveston, you and I will dine alone in his chambers. He has told us to rest as we shall talk and drink until the early hours. I understand that. Soon,' Isabella pulled a face, 'Marigny and the rest arrive; they will watch us like a cat does a bird.'

CHAPTER 8

All the land of England is moist with
weeping.

'A Song of the Times', 1272–1307

The following evening Isabella and I, both
greatly refreshed, joined the king and
Gaveston in the small dining chamber
in the royal quarters. The room had been specially
prepared, its windows shuttered, Turkey rugs laid
on the floor, a great oval oaken table placed
before the hearth so we could all feel the warmth
from the flames licking the sweetly scented pine
logs. The king and his favourite were dressed
sombrely in dark Lincoln green, boots on their
feet, their only concession to finery being the glittering rings on their fingers. They both looked
purposeful, sober and eager to talk. As the various
courses were served, pheasant and hare cooked
in different sauces, Edward described what would
happen over the next month, advising Isabella
about the coronation and the rituals which would

have to be followed. Only towards the end, after the quince tarts were served with sweet white wine, did he order all the servants to leave, no lesser person than Sandewic being left outside to guard the passageways and doors. Edward pushed back his chair, turning slightly towards the fire.

'I like Dover,' he murmured, 'always on the edge of the kingdom, a place to come if you want to escape.' He turned back to us. 'Ah well.' He sighed. 'And now to business.'

Both king and favourite lounged languidly; no more pretence, no acting, no slurping from cups or bellowing guffaws of laughter. No one else was present, though I wondered why a fifth chair had been placed at the table. Edward, tapping his goblet with his fingernails, chattered about our entry into London then straightened in his chair, playing with the ring on the little finger of his left hand. He described the situation in Scotland, the power of Bruce and his threat to the northern shires. He detailed the problems with the exchequer, his lack of monies, the pressing need to raise taxes from both parliament and the Convocation of Clergy. Gaveston remained quiet throughout. Now and again he'd glance at me, but for the most part he sat, head down, listening intently as Edward listed his problems with the earls. He described how his great-grandfather John, grandfather Henry as well as Edward I had all faced strong opposition from the leading nobles with their private armies and retinues, their deep-rooted determination to control the power of the crown.

'Ask Sandewic,' the king scoffed, gesturing at the door. 'Forty-seven years ago he fought for the rebel Earl of Leicester, Simon de Montfort, against my father and grandfather. He escaped the traitor's block because my dear father admired his integrity. One decision,' Edward added wryly, 'on which both Father and I agreed.'

The more Edward talked, the less certain I became. In all this there was some mystery, a puzzle, an enigma. He was talking fluently and logically. Yet why play the other Edward, the feckless king supporting his favourite, patronising jesters whilst publicly insulting the leading earls, not to mention his powerful father-in-law? Edward of England showed a shrewdness not even Isabella had guessed at. She too appeared disconcerted, mystified, as if the husband she was now meeting was a different man from the one she had married at Boulogne; a king who had the astuteness to realise the true relationship between herself and her family as well as that with me, whom Edward and Gaveston now accepted as Isabella's confidante. I hid my own smile. Casales and Rossaleti had reported faithfully back: both the king and his favourite acted as if they had known us for years. Isabella's puzzlement expressed itself in certain questions about the Templars and about her marriage. Edward dismissed these, repeating what we had already learnt from Sandewic: both matters were of political necessity. Edward conceded that there would be no bloody prosecution of the Templars, only the seizure of their wealth, which he desperately needed. He courteously included me in the conversation, though I realised Isabella had not confided the full truth about me to her husband.

Eventually Gaveston rose and placed logs on the greedy fire, then, taking a taper, lit more candles, replacing those which had burnt low. The light flared, bringing to life the beautiful tapestries decorating the walls. Gaveston secured one of the shutters which had slipped loose, then walked over to the door, opened it and had a brief conversation with Sandewic outside. I heard the name Clauvelin mentioned, the mournful notary from Soissons. Gaveston then closed the door and rejoined us at the table. Edward moodily drank his wine as Gaveston began to question both of us about the deaths of Pourte and Wenlok. He drew me skilfully in until I virtually admitted my suspicions that both men might have been murdered. Gaveston and Edward seemed concerned at this but passed swiftly on, asking Isabella if she had known the merchant Monsieur de Vitry. Isabella glanced at me to remain silent. I don't think the look was lost on Gaveston. He chewed his lip as he accepted Isabella's assurance that, of course, Monsieur de Vitry had been known to her as one of her father's bankers, whilst the bloody murder of him and his household had shocked all of Paris. The wine cups were refilled and both men fell silent, lost in their own thoughts, until Edward leaned across the table and grasped Isabella's hands.

'Two things, *mon coeur*, I will ask. I want the truth. Before I ask, let me assure you, on my solemn oath, that you are my princess and wife, the only woman in my life, never to be supplanted.' He spoke with such fervour, face flushed, eyes gleaming. If ever a prince spoke the truth, on that night Edward of England certainly did. Isabella bowed her head to hide her blushes. Edward pressed his fingertips gently against her lips.

'Now tell me, *ma plaisance*, do you accept the Lord Gaveston? If you don't, say the truth. Do you accept him for what he is, for himself and to me?' The silence which followed was tangible, as if some unseen presence leaned forward, eager to listen to Isabella's reply. Gaveston sat, shoulders hunched, no longer the arrogant popinjay.

'I accept him.' Isabella smiled dazzlingly at Edward's favourite. 'I, the Princess Royal, your wife, your future queen, I am also Isabella, recently escaped from France, from my father's court, which had turned so hateful. You,' she pressed her hand against Edward's chest, 'are King of England. You did not ask to marry me. I did not ask to marry you. The times and seasons were not of our making. We must accept the fate God dispenses, so why should I object? Will Monsieur Gaveston take away what is mine?'

Edward shook his head. Gaveston drew in a deep breath.

'The second thing, *mon seigneur*?' Isabella kept her hand pressed against her husband's chest. He grasped it and kissed her fingers.

'Listen well.' Edward's voice fell almost to a whisper. 'You must not, at any time, show any affection for Peter; indeed the opposite, at least for the moment. You must not appear, in public at least, as Lord Gaveston's friend.'

'Why?' I spoke before I thought.

'Because, Mathilde, that is the way things are. Those who are my enemies will betray themselves to you rather than shield their malice from me.' Edward grinned. 'As they say in the schools, *effectum sequitur causam* – effect follows cause. My relationship with my sweet cousin of France is not cordial and its fruit may have grown even more bitter! It is a matter of politic, of logic: as the father, so the daughter. People would wonder why you did not follow in King Philip's footsteps.'

'That would not be too difficult to understand!' Isabella exclaimed.

'You must act the part,' Gaveston insisted. 'His grace has married a French princess; it is important for the Council of England, and above all for King Philip himself, that the French crown does believe or act as if it has undue influence over his grace simply because of his marriage to you.' He bowed to Isabella. 'I have read the writings of your father's lawyers, men like Pierre Dubois. Philip dreams of that day when a Capetian prince, the issue of your body, wears the crown of the Confessor

215

whilst another becomes Duke of Gascony.' Gaveston raised his hands. 'Let Philip have his dreams, it does not mean we have to be part of them.'

Gaveston's answer was logical, tripping off the tongue so easily it made sense. King Phillip's ambition was well known; his bullying over Isabella's marriage and the question of the Templars had been public. Edward was now forced to oppose him or appear as Philip's minion. Nevertheless, I remained uncomfortable, uneasy.

'What does that mean, my lord?' Isabella asked. 'In practice?'

'According to the marriage treaty I am to furnish you with lands and estates here in England. For the time being I shall not do that, though,' the king added quickly, 'I shall ensure that secretly you lack for nothing.'

'You could do more.' Isabella lifted her wine goblet and toasted him. 'This castle now holds all the marriage goods and gifts from my father, uncles, brothers, Marigny and the rest of the coven.' She spat the words with such hatred she surprised even me. 'Why not give them all to Lord Gaveston?' Isabella drank from the goblet. 'I don't want them. I want nothing from them. I'd sooner be turned out in my shift on the castle track-way. I'd rather dwell in a charcoal-burner's cottage in your dank woods and call it my palace than live on anything they have given me. You have my answer.'

Gaveston and the king looked at her in surprise, clearly startled by the passion of what she'd said.

'*Alea iacta*,' Gaveston murmured. 'So the dice are thrown and the game begins.' He rose to his feet, went into the shadows and brought back a silver-edged box long as an arrow coffer. He placed this on the table, pulled back the clasps and took out two beautiful sables, one dark, the other snow-white. 'These are from the forests around the frozen seas to the north.' Gaveston laid them in Isabella's lap, then took a small leather pouch out of the coffer and shook out the most brilliant ruby set in a golden star. He placed the chain around Isabella's neck and knelt before her. Isabella took his hands between hers and quietly accepted his fealty.

'As for you,' Gaveston pointed at me, getting to his feet, 'I've heard so much about Mathilde the wise woman.' Edward and Isabella laughed, breaking the tension. '*Cavete Gascones*,' Gaveston continued, '*ferentes dona* – beware of Gascons bearing gifts.' He dipped into the chest again and brought out a book edged with scarlet stitching and fastened by gold clasps. He placed this on my lap. Edward and Isabella were whispering together, golden heads close. Despite the gifts and courtesy I felt a brief stab of envy which I quickly dismissed. I undid the clasps and read the carefully inscribed title: Galen's *A Treatise on the Difference of Symptoms*. I thanked Gaveston courteously. He sat down and began to question me closely about my knowledge of simples and potions. He explained how his mother, Agnes, had also been a wise woman in the town of Bearn in Gascony. As soon as he mentioned

217

her name, Edward stiffened and drew away from Isabella. Gaveston's face was no longer smiling; the skin was drawn tight, and tears brimmed in his eyes. He forced a laugh but his eyes frightened me, as if he could see, or was invoking, some heinous memory.

'Let me tell you, Mathilde,' again that high-pitched laugh, 'a story from Bearn about a haunted house. A man called Raoul de Castro Negro thought there was a hidden treasure in his house just within the main gateway at Bearn. He employed two magicians to cast a spell and find this treasure. What exactly they did, and whether they found any treasure, I do not know.' Gaveston blinked. 'But after that, they left. Now Raoul had a servant called Julian Sarnene, who returned to the house. Shortly afterwards Sarnene was found in the town square claiming he was blind and unable to hear. He remained ill and disabled for some weeks, but just before Easter he indicated he wanted to be taken to a local shrine. Some friends helped him to travel there by donkey. They arrived at the shrine on the Wednesday of Holy Week and Julian prayed before the statues of the Blessed Virgin and St Anthony. At the hour of compline his hearing was restored. The next day, after the mass of the Lord's Supper, his sight returned as well. Fully restored, he went back to Bearn. Now, of course, all this was hailed as a miracle and Julian was summoned to the bishop's court, where he told a strange tale. He claimed he had entered his master's house after the magicians had gone and found it full of strange birds and animals, including three horses with horns like goats, emitting fire from their mouths and backsides. On them, facing the tails, sat three fearsome men with clubs. Julian said he was utterly terrified and tried to make the sign of the cross but one of the beasts restrained his hand. He attempted to pray but fled back into the town square where he was found. What do you think of such a story, Mathilde?'

'What happened to Raoul?'

Gaveston pulled a face. 'He fled. The Inquisition were hunting him for consulting magicians. So, what do you think of Julian's story?'

'I don't know,' I confessed.

'I asked a question, wise woman.' Gaveston grasped my shoulders, his grip so hard I winced. Isabella protested and Gaveston released his hand.

'Please,' his voice turned beseeching, 'as a woman who has studied potions and powders.'

'Some would allege it was witchcraft,' I replied. 'Others that the man was healed by God's kind courtesy and boundless mercy, as well as the intervention of the Blessed Virgin and St Anthony.'

'Or?'

The silence in the chamber grew oppressive.

'I'd be more prudent myself,' I conceded. 'There are certain potions, wild fruit, the juice of mushrooms, not to mention the oil from the skin of a toad. These can create magical fantasies, nightmarish dreams; hence the story about witches who claim to fly, or the visions of madmen, or saints,' I added.

'And the physical symptoms?' Gaveston asked. 'The blindness, the deafness?'

'They too would follow.' I picked up my wine goblet. 'It's no different from this.' I swilled the wine around the cup. 'Wine can create illusions and dreams. Its effects on the body are well known. What is true of the fruit of the grape is true of other plants.'

'But what do you believe, Mathilde, magic or scientia?'

'Scientia,' I replied quickly. 'All natural causes must be removed before any others can be put forward as an explanation.'

'Good, good.' Gaveston leaned back on the chair. 'I thought you would say that.'

The sombre atmosphere, however, did not lift. Gaveston rose, studied the hour candle burning on its spigot in the corner and went to the door. From the conversation I gathered Sandewic had been replaced by two of Gaveston's Irish retainers, mercenaries wearing the livery of the scarlet eagle.

'Come in, do come in.' Gaveston welcomed the notary Jean de Clauvelin into the chamber, inviting him over to the fifth chair. He made him sit down, filled a goblet to the brim with rich claret and pulled across a silver trancher so de Clauvelin could eat the leftovers. Isabella looked surprised. Edward sat, chin in hands. De Clauvelin attempted to bow and scrape but the king gestured to the chair, murmuring that this was not the occasion for courtesies. Gaveston sat close to the overwrought notary, picked up a piece of meat, dipped it into a bowl of sauce and thrust it into de Clauvelin's mouth.

'Jean, Jean!' Gaveston declared brusquely. 'I am so glad you are in attendance.'

'Your grace, it was a great honour to be included in my lady's retinue . . .'

'Of course, of course.' Gaveston refilled de Clauvelin's goblet. 'I need words with you, sir, regarding the Abbey of St Jean des Vignes, or rather its abbot, who is indebted to me for certain sums. I need your advice, now . . .'

I watched the tableau with a growing sense of horror. Gaveston reminded me of a powerful cat playing with a mouse. De Clauvelin was overcome by the favourite's chatter and grace, and failed to sense the anger seething in this powerful lord. Just the way Gaveston kept tearing at the meat, filling de Clauvelin's goblet . . . Once the flagon was empty, he went across to the dresser table to refill it. De Clauvelin, flattered, gossiped about the abbey. Gaveston waited for the wine to take full effect, then rose to his feet, stepped behind de Clauvelin, and in the blink of an eye the garrotte string was looped over the notary's head and wrapped fast around his throat. De Clauvelin dropped his goblet, half staggering to his feet, but Gaveston, face bright with angry glee, forced him back.

Isabella went to protest; Edward caught her with a restraining hand. The king sat fascinated, face slightly flushed, head to one side, watching de Clauvelin half choke. Gaveston bent down, pulling at the garrotte.

'Jean de Clauvelin,' he intoned with mock solemnity, 'more rightly known as Julian Sarnene: you, sir, are an assassin, a cunning man from the town of Bearn in Gascony. You drank a potion and saw a vision. You claimed to fall into the hands of the powers of darkness, only to be cured. When the miracle was examined, my mother Agnes de Gaveston was asked by the local bishop for her advice.' Gaveston pulled at the cord, then relaxed it. 'She rejected your claims, mocked them and said it was nothing to do with Satan but depended on what you had eaten or drunk, whether you had taken any potion.' Gaveston loosened the garrotte string a little more. 'Your ploy to gain sympathy and raise money from an alleged miracle proved unsuccessful. Your whole story became suspect, your allegations against your former employer of dabbling in witchcraft not proven. You hoped to acquire his wealth, to be rewarded. Later, when my father, Arnaud de Gaveston, was away soldiering, you secretly denounced my mother as a witch to the Inquisition. There were many, envious and hateful, who were quick to believe you. You provided information about my mother's knowledge of potions and herbs. My mother was truthful. She answered the questions, but in doing so condemned herself by rejecting stories of demons and miraculous cures and insisting that natural causes must be first examined. She was tried and burned. You were given silver and protection. You disappeared, only to resurrect as Jean de Clauvelin, lawyer and notary.'

Gaveston pressed his lips closer to Clauvelin's ear.

'I have hunted you, sir, high and low. *Mirabila dictu* – it is wonderful to say what you can discover as Earl of Cornwall, regent of England, close confidant of its king. Last year, when I was in France, I discovered your true name and hiding place.'

'It's not me, it's not me!' Clauvelin begged.

'The Inquisition, near Carcassonne, says it is.' Gaveston released the garrotte string completely, leaving his victim to sprawl in his chair. 'The Inquisition are men of great detail,' Gaveston continued. 'You have a mole on the right of your neck.' He seized de Clauvelin by his scrawny hair, tugging down the man's high collar and twisting his head for us to see. 'You also have a scar, an inch long, on the inside of your left arm.' He took the notary's arm, ripping back the sleeve of his jerkin, sending clasps and buttons scattering across the table, and turned the arm so we could glimpse the raised welt. Finally, one hand on de Clauvelin's shoulder, Gaveston thrust his hand down the front of the notary's jerkin and dragged up the metal cross on its copper chain. In the candlelight I glimpsed the embossed crucifix of the Inquisition. Gaveston ripped this from his neck and threw it on the table.

'Given to everyone,' he hissed, 'who falls within the protection of the Domini Canes – the Dominicans, the Hounds of God, Sancta Inquisicio, the Holy Inquisition.'

De Clauvelin, pale-faced and drenched with sweat, leaned against the table.

'They would not reveal . . .' he gasped.

'Oh yes they would,' Gaveston scoffed, sitting down next to his victim. 'Oh yes they did! Money and power, Monsieur Notary, are the two keys to any secret. You don't deny it. Well, of course you don't. You do remember, so many years ago, de Clauvelin, what, twenty-two?' He pushed his face closer. 'I was a mere babe. You thought I'd forget.' He picked a crumb from the notary's jerkin, brushing it tenderly. 'I hunted you down, I searched France for you. The Abbot of St Jean des Vignes does owe me money; he did turn on you, didn't he? He began to question you about certain rents which had disappeared, as well as the claims of a young woman about your forced attentions. You were only too willing to receive King Philip's letter of appointment; he, of course, couldn't give a fig about you!'

'*Mon seigneur*,' de Clauvelin bowed his head, hands outstretched towards the king, 'mercy!'

Edward gazed back stony-eyed.

'Soon you will sleep.' Gaveston smiled, glancing across at me. 'Monsieur Sarnene, I laced your wine with poppy juice, and when you awake, after your fall, you'll be in hell!' He picked up his own goblet.

'*In infernum*,' he chanted, satirising the office of the dead, '*diaboli te ducent* – into hell the demons will lead you.'

De Clauvelin, coughing and spluttering, made to rise only to collapse against the table and fall to the floor. Gaveston sprang up.

'So soon, so soon?' He kicked de Clauvelin, who moaned but lay still. Edward also rose and joined him, and both viciously kicked the prostrate man with their booted feet.

'Stop, my lords!' Isabella begged, hands to her face. I sat cold with fear. Isabella shouted again. Both men paused, chests heaving, faces wet with sweat. Gaveston wiped his brow on the back of his hand.

'He sent my mother to a hideous death. She was strapped to a pole in the town square at Bearn, brushwood piled high against her. The flames roared so high, the heat became so intense, the hangman could not get to her to give her the mercy death, to strangle her. They say her flesh bubbled like . . .' His voice faltered and he looked away. Edward moved to comfort him. Gaveston picked up his goblet and threw the dregs of wine over the unconscious man.

'He'll die quickly, not like my mother!' He kicked his victim again and looked beseechingly at me. 'I had to do it now. He thought the world had forgotten, but I am not the world.' He strode across the room and opened the door; his two assassins slipped in. Gaveston kicked the prostrate man.

'There's a narrow postern gate in the curtain wall. It's used for throwing away slops and refuse. You'll find the hinges oiled, take him and throw him out.'

I closed my eyes and thought of de Clauvelin's body falling down that sheer rocky abyss into the freezing, swirling sea.

'Give out that he was walking on the parapet and had drunk too much wine.' Gaveston clicked his tongue. 'Say he slipped; who will question, who will care?'

The two men removed the body. Gaveston started breathing deeply. He appeared self-satisfied, content, rubbing his stomach like a man who'd enjoyed a good meal.

'Justice,' Edward murmured.

Gaveston collected the notary's clasps, buttons and cross and threw them into the fire. He insisted on one final cup of wine. We sat and drank, the mood swiftly changing. De Clauvelin was forgotten, at least by them, and for the first time I wondered if Isabella and I had exchanged one prison for another. The princess made to leave. Both Gaveston and the king, now all courteous, walked us out into the gallery, which was filling with retainers and servants preparing for the king to retire. Gaveston's chamber was further along. We entered it. I clutched the presents he had given us. I was tired, needful of silence, desperate for sleep. The favourite's chamber was like an upturned treasure chest, with costly clothes and precious ornaments flung around. Both he and the king were now talking of their royal progress through Kent to Becket's shrine at Canterbury and the jewel they were to present there. Gaveston wanted to show it to us, excited like a child about a gift he had prepared. I stared at the great bed, its pure linen sheets thrown back. On the floor beside it were hunting boots decorated with gilded spurs; in the far corner a hooded falcon on its perch, jesse bells ringing as it moved restlessly. I glimpsed a triptych hanging rather crookedly from a hook on the wall hastily put there when Gaveston had set up his household. I went across to put it straight and hid my surprise: the painting celebrated the martyrdom and glory of St Agnes; I had last seen it at de Vitry's house. At first I thought it was a copy, but the slightly rusting hinges along the folds of the picture and the dark patches around its glowing edge convinced me it was the same I'd seen in Monsieur Simon's house. So how had Gaveston acquired it? Noting my interest, the favourite sauntered across to describe his deep devotion to the saint who shared his mother's name. Isabella heard this and hastily made a sign that we leave. I joined her; we both bowed to the king and Gaveston and withdrew.

Once alone, Isabella declared she did not want to retire. She studied Gaveston's gifts and wondered about the events of the evening.

'They did the same as your father,' I retorted, 'a fine display of power and terror; which is why de Clauvelin was killed in our presence. They intend,' I added, 'to be the sole masters in their house.'

Isabella pressed one of the sables against her cheek and smiled. 'As do I, Mathilde, as do I!'

We left Dover the next morning, a glorious cavalcade, the might of England. Edward cheerfully announced he had no intention whatsoever of waiting for his French guests and the sooner he returned to Westminster the better. The weather, I remember, had made one of those startling turns, as if nature itself wanted to greet England's new queen: rain-washed, clear blue skies, a bright winter sun, the ground firm underfoot, the air bracing but not cutting. Edward and Gaveston moved to the head of the column with their retinue of dwarves and jesters, eager to hunt with hawk and falcon. They'd often break away from our line of march, cantering across the fields to fly their magnificent birds against herons, plover, anything which dared wing its way under God's own heaven. Time and again I saw these predators loosed, wings beating as they fought the breezes to gain ascendancy, floating like dark angels against the blue before making their breathtaking, magnificent plunge.

Both Isabella and I were ignored, as the great game had truly begun, though we had enough to distract ourselves. We rode palfreys, accompanied and protected by Sandewic, Casales, Rossaleti and Baquelle, who were eager to describe the countryside we were passing through. Despite the severity of winter, the land had a softness unique to itself, so different from the bleak plains of Normandy. The countryside spread out like a carpet on either side, great open fields of iron-hard brown soil awaiting the sowing. Meadows and pastures for the great flocks of sheep, thick dense woods, dark copses with small hamlets nestling in the lee of a hill or some forest clearing. The poor are the same wherever they are, and they are always with us. The roads were busy with those searching for work as well as merchants, friars, tinkers and chapmen with their pack donkeys and sumpter ponies, carts and barrows all of whom had to hastily pull aside as the royal cortège approached. On one occasion we passed a troupe of moon people, perpetual travellers, with their brightly painted wagons, gaudy harness decorating their horses. They clustered together on the side of the road dressed in their garish clothes and cheap jewellery, offering trinkets for sale. Pilgrims going to and from Canterbury, Rochester, or Walsingham further to the north also thronged, Ave beads slung round their necks, pewter medallions pinned to their ragged cloaks. These lifted their hands and, as we all swept by, called down God's blessing on Edward and his queen.

Such sights in the open fresh air were calming after the turbulence of the recent days. Our four companions described the countryside, its crops of wheat and rye as well as the fruits and vegetables, parsley, leek, cabbages and onions, plums, pears and apples, grown by the peasant farmers.

I noticed how, unlike Normandy, there were few hedges, the different holdings being separated from each other by baulks of unploughed turf. These gave the land a strange, striped appearance though increasingly more harvest ground was being turned into pasture for sheep, English wool being in constant demand throughout Europe. As we passed their thatched-roof wattle-and-daub cottages, the peasants came hastening out to gape and cheer. The deeper we journeyed into Kent, however, the more prosperous the small villages became, their stone houses and churches seeming commonplace. These were usually grouped round some magnificent red-brick or honey-coloured stone manor hall with fine tiled roof, stacks to draw off the smoke, heavy oaken doors and windows full of mullioned glass.

We were met at crossroads, parish boundaries and town gates by hosts of important officials, sheriffs, stewards, bailiffs, constables, dignitaries of church and state, all dressed in their grandeur, heavy chains of office slung round their necks. They offered gifts and protestations of loyalty which Isabella accepted, replying in a clear, carrying voice, sometimes lapsing into English, which she had so zealously, though secretly studied. Each place had striven to do its best. Gibbets had been cleared of strangled corpses, stocks emptied, the heads and severed limbs of traitors taken down from the town bars and gates to be replaced with armorial shields or broad coloured cloths. At night we rested in the guest houses of monasteries, priories and nunneries. During the day we would sometimes refresh ourselves at the spacious pilgrim taverns with their ornate welcoming signs and warm tap-rooms. There was very little time to think, let alone converse privately, and the further north we went the busier our cavalcade became. We crossed the gushing waters of the Medway, admired the soaring keep of Rochester Castle and finally lodged at St Augustine's Priory in Canterbury, a mere walk from the cathedral and its spectacular shrine to St Thomas Becket, a mass of gold, silver and precious jewels. We visited the cathedral and prayed at the bottom of the steps; the screen before the shrine was raised so we could make our offerings of flowers, tapers and precious goods.

We also met Isabella's aunt, the Queen Dowager Margaret, widow of Edward I and sister of Philip IV. From the very beginning aunt and niece took an immediate dislike to each other. Queen Margaret was beautiful in a pallid way, sanctimonious and patronising, full of her own goodness and pious acts. A woman who had found religion and lost her heart, totally immersed in her sanctimonious passion to go on pilgrimage. She catalogued the different places Isabella must visit as queen, be it St Swithun's at Worcester, the relics of Glastonbury or the Virgin's House at Walsingham. She gossiped like a fishwife about herself until Isabella, stifling a yawn, thanked her 'sweet aunt'. The queen dowager, however, was not so readily quietened.

Isabella had to force a smile as Margaret perched in a window seat overlooking the cloister garth, describing her recent pilgrimage to view the phial of Christ's Precious Blood at Hailes Abbey. The second woman we met was Margaret de Clare, the king's niece and wife to Gaveston; a whey-faced, rather anxious young woman who kept touching the old-fashioned wimple around her face. She sat like a pious novice, hands in her lap, avidly listening to the queen dowager's monotonous sermons on the different shrines; every so often the younger Margaret would nod in agreement and thrust her needle into a piece of tapestry.

Once Isabella and I were alone in our chambers, the princess sat on the ground with her back to the door and laughed until the tears streamed down her face. She ripped off her head-dress, almost pushing it into her mouth to hide her merriment. At last she composed herself, picked up a napkin, wrapped it around her head and, with the most sanctimonious expression, eyes raised heavenwards, imitated both women, even down to Aunt Margaret's ceaseless nasal homily.

'Oh Mathilde, you must visit Chepstow and the priory there, you know the one, dedicated to the straw in the manger. It holds a turd dropped by the very ox which was there on the first Christmas night, whilst down the road, at the Nunnery of the Blessed Sheep, you can venerate the very fore-skin of the shepherd boy who brought the baby lamb. They even have a leg of the same.' Isabella's eyes moved heavenwards. 'Still with some scraps of meat on because the Holy Family ate the rest.'

She burst out laughing and, getting to her feet, solemnly processed up and down the spacious guest room listing the most extraordinary relics which Aunt Margaret could collect: the Christ Child's first napkin, a splinter from Joseph's work bench, a feather from an angel, a broken thimble belonging to the Virgin Mary. At last she paused, throwing the napkin to the ground.

'Pious bitch!' she muttered. 'So holy she should be dead! Oh, don't be shocked, Mathilde.' Isabella shook her fist at the door. 'Aunt Margaret spies for her brother. If Margaret the Pious has her way, Father will know everything before it happens.' She waved a finger at me. 'I must remember that.' She filled two pewter tankards to the brim with the ale the good brothers had served and sat on a quilted stool staring up at me.

'Well, well, Mathilde, what do you think we are? Two sparrows who have fallen off the ledge into the path of a cat?'

'My lady, your grace, do you love *mon seigneur* your husband?'

Isabella pursed her lips and shrugged. 'Answer my question, Mathilde.'

'Yes!' I replied bluntly. 'We are two sparrows who have fallen into the path of a cat. Edward of England and his favourite are certainly not priests at prayer; we have to walk slowly and very carefully. They have shown their true nature.'

'Which is?'

'They will brook no opposition. Obey them and all will be well. Object or resist the will of the king and anything is possible, which, my lady,' I settled on a bench, 'might include the murders of Sir Hugh Pourte and Lord Wenlok.'

On our journey from Dover I had reflected on that possibility. There was the Council of England and a small inner coven, the Secretum Concilum, the Secret Council, staffed by the likes of Casales, Sandewic and Baquelle as well as those two men so recently killed. Both offered advice which displeased Edward and Gaveston. I shared this conclusion with my mistress, adding that the members of the Secret Council could be under threat, being removed one by one.

'By whom?' Isabella asked.

'Your grace, I cannot answer that.'

CHAPTER 9

All friendship and kindness have
disappeared.

'*A Song of the Times*', 1272–1307

We stayed at the Priory of St Augustine
for some time, waiting to welcome the
French party: Philip's two brothers,
the Counts of Valois and Evreux; Marigny, Nogaret,
des Plaisans and the three royal princes. Two days
after we arrived, these swept into the priory courtyard, a gorgeous cavalcade under their blue and gold
banners, to be greeted by Edward and Gaveston.
The usual banquets and feastings followed in the
priory or the cathedral buildings. Once again
Isabella was surrounded by the ladies of the court
and I was excluded. The princess was certainly at
the behest of 'that green-eyed Reynard', her nick
name for Marigny, who, during mass the morning
after his arrival, stared malevolently at me as he and
the rest processed slowly out of church. I was
relieved to be excluded from all their jostling malice,
whilst Isabella eagerly recounted the details of what

happened. How Edward publicly paid more attention to Gaveston than he did to his 'beloved wife', the royal favourite openly wearing some of the jewels Philip had given to Isabella. The French, of course, objected, and relations between the two courts grew increasingly strained.

I was content to be away from the hurly-burly of meetings, feasts and courtly sessions. Casales, Sandewic, Rossaleti and Baquelle, when they could, joined me in the spacious parlour of the guest house or accompanied me through the priory herbarium, where I discussed the names and properties of the various plants. Sandewic, in particular, showed interest. He was still full of praise for the physic I had given him. He and the rest had no choice but to listen as I explained how the priory possessed a number of gardens: the cloister garden with grass and flowers growing around the holy water stoup in the centre; the cemetery garden with its fruit and blossom trees; the kitchen garden and the infirmary or physic garden to the north of the priory. The latter boasted sixteen parallel beds, well dug and tended, all separated by sanded paths, the herb plots deliberately sited to catch the sun. A pleasant place, even on a winter's day. The fragrance of the plants still sweetened the air despite the small pentile coverings the physic-master, Brother Ambrose, had placed over them as protection against the elements. That old Benedictine was truly a man in love with God's creation, responsible for both the physic garden and the infirmary. He always joined us with a battered copy of Dioscorides' *De Materia Medica* under his arm; little wonder that, after an hour of listening to the infirmarian's lecture on the virtues of feverfew, my companions soon absented themselves.

Oh, I loved that graceful, serene garden, a haven from the hate and intrigue which boiled through the priory like an evil mist and, of course, eventually trapped me. I was leaving the herbarium one afternoon when I glimpsed a monk standing in the shadows of the small cloister, half hidden by a pillar. I had been searching the herb plots and couldn't believe I'd found wormwood growing in one of the beds; I was hastening to speak about it to Brother Ambrose. I left quickly, unexpectedly, and caught my watcher slightly off his guard. He moved swiftly away but stumbled on an uneven pavement, caught the wall and turned in alarm. I was walking swiftly. I glimpsed his face and stopped in shocked surprise. I was certain he was the same man I'd seen in the Oriflamme tavern what now seemed an eternity ago. I would always remember that face, those far-seeing eyes, but surely, I wondered, it couldn't be? In Paris he had dressed as an English clerk, not a Benedictine monk. Was he truly here in England? I was so startled, so fearful, I sat down on a stone sill. Was he a clerk? Had he glimpsed me leave the tavern with Narrow Face? Had he followed us and seen me stab Crokendon behind the charnel house? By the time I recovered, it was too late to pursue him. I was so confused I eventually dismissed it all as a trick of the eyes.

On that same evening, Isabella and her ladies journeyed into Canterbury as the guests of the mayor and the leading citizens of the city, who had arranged a splendid private banquet at the nearby lordly and spacious tavern, The Chequer of Hope. The priory fell silent except for the melodious chanting of the monks at vespers, the Latin phrases drifting across the priory grounds. I dined alone in the small refectory of the guest house. Casales, Sandewic and the rest had joined the king's retinue in Canterbury. I stayed in the refectory for a while, reading in the light of a candle a manuscript Brother Ambrose had loaned me. I was about to adjourn when a lay brother whom the rest of the community called Simon Simplex came bustling in, an old man with tufts of hair sticking out, eyes all milky white, spittle drooling from the corner of his mouth.

'Oh, mistress,' he waved his hands, 'Brother Ambrose needs you in the infirmary.'

I returned to my chamber, collected my cloak and made my way along the lonely cloisters and stone-walled passageways. The bells of the city were clanging out, the monks had begun compline, and a phrase caught my imagination, a quotation, put to verse, from the Letter of St Peter, about Satan being a prowling lion, seeking whom he could devour. I should have heeded the warning.

The infirmary was a two-storey building on the far side of the priory, overlooking the physic garden. The infirmary itself stood at the top of very steep steps. Brother Ambrose had confided to me that the founder of the priory had deliberately made them so in order to force people to reflect on whether they were truly ill before attempting to go up. The steps were so steep, Ambrose himself needed help to climb them, while the injured and sick had to be carried up by burly servants.

By the time I reached the infirmary, darkness had fallen. At the top of the steps cresset torches, fixed either side of the yawning doorway, flared beckoningly in the breeze. From the bushes and trees alongside the building came the final cawing of the crows. The hunting call of a fox yipped through the darkness to be immediately answered by the deep, bell-like baying of the priory dogs. I climbed the steps wondering what Brother Ambrose wanted. Simon had disappeared, so I reasoned it must be pressing business, otherwise Ambrose would have joined his brothers in the choir for compline. I had reached the entrance and was about to go along the narrow gallery, lit only by a single torch and a brazier glowing at the far end just outside the infirmary door, when the sacking, coarse and reeking of the soil, was thrown over my head. I struggled and screamed; a blow to the side of my head sent me staggering. I was tugged and pushed, forced back outside to be thrown down those steep, sharp-edged steps. Images of Pourte falling through the darkness made me fight back, but I was confused. I was losing the struggle, my legs felt weak and my assailant must have pushed me close to the top of the steps when my deliverance came.

'*Au secours! Au secours!*' The voice was strong and ringing; footsteps sounded as if someone was hurrying up towards us. I fought desperately, determined to move away from the direction of that voice and the cruel topple down the steps. Gasping for air, I crashed into the great door, which had been pulled back, and slid to the ground. I freed myself from the sacking, then glanced quickly to the right. Nothing, only the brazier glowing. I crept like a dog on all fours to the top of the steps and peered down. Again nothing. I staggered to my feet and carefully made my way back to the lonely guest house. Reaching it safely, I dragged myself up the stairs, locking and bolting the chamber door behind me.

For a while I just lay on the floor. I needed to vomit and hurried to the garderobe, a narrow recess sealed off by a door. Once my belly settled, I returned and, using the princess's hand mirror, scrutinised the blow to the side of my head. I felt a lump, and tender bruising, but no blood. I changed my gown, treated the bruises on my arms and legs, drank a little watered wine and lay down. A fearsome darkness seem to shroud me, scowling at my soul and hanging like a midnight mist around my heart, chilling my courage, weakening my will. Who would attack me? Why? And my saviour, that clear, strong voice ringing out? I drew some heart comfort from that. The wine seeped in, warming my blood, rousing the humours. I must not, would not, weaken. I recalled Uncle Reginald and the short prayer he had composed:

Christe Jesu who made me out of mud,
And did save me through your blood.
Kyrie eleison, Lord have mercy.

I fell asleep and was roused by the return of Isabella, the princess slamming the door behind her against the gaggle of chattering women. She muttered quiet curses but broke off when she saw me and, grasping my hands, made me repeat what had happened. She examined my head, using my own potions to treat the bruise, and also sent for Brother Ambrose and Simon. Both came up owl-eyed, and knelt just within the doorway as my mistress, despite my protests, hotly questioned them. Brother Ambrose shook his head sorrowfully, claiming he had not sent for me. Did not her grace, he continued, realise that, according to the customary of the priory, women were strictly forbidden to enter the infirmary? Moreover, at the time of the attack he, with Brother Simon, who was wandering in his wits, poor soul, had been in the choir's stalls amongst their brethren. Simon could not help himself but kept muttering 'beautiful, beautiful' as he gazed wonderingly at Isabella. He really could not understand her questions but, with the help of Brother Ambrose, he eventually admitted that one of the brothers had given him the message for me. No, he assured us, he could not remember the face; it was dark and the brother had his cowl up against the cold, but he had blessed him in Latin, quoting St Benedict's greeting. The mysterious monk had claimed he was speaking for Father Prior and Simon had to carry the message to me. I immediately thought of Rossaleti, a former novice in the Benedictine order, and, unlike Casales, Sandewic or Baquelle, fully skilled in Latin. I whispered this to Isabella, then Brother Simon described how this Benedictine had grasped his hands.

'Rough they were,' he muttered, 'like those of a peasant, a breaker of the soil.'

I glanced at Isabella and shrugged. Rossaleti's hands were softer than mine.

Brother Ambrose clambered to his feet saying he must tell all to the prior. Isabella, at my behest, swore both men to silence, placing a silver piece into each of their hands.

After the monks had gone, Isabella stood motionless in the pool of candlelight.

'Mathilde,' she glanced across at me, 'anyone could have attacked you. When we arrived at The Chequer of Hope, people were coming and going. Gaveston chose to ignore my uncles, Marigny and the rest. Anyone, including him, could have travelled the short distance between the tavern and the priory and perpetrated that attack. It would be easy to borrow a Benedictine robe and stand in the shadows, whilst they've all had hours of time to find their way round this priory. Brother Simon is so fey, he would believe anyone or anything.' She leaned down and stroked my hair. 'As you did, Mathilde. You should be more prudent, more careful.'

'Could it have been Gaveston?' I asked.

'Possibly,' Isabella sat down next to me on the bed. 'Like the rest he is a killer.'

I then told my mistress about the St Agnes painting, swearing that I was sure it was the same one I'd seen at Monsieur de Vitry's house.

'It cannot be,' she whispered. 'Gaveston was in England at the time, unless he journeyed to Paris secretly.'

I also told her about the man with the far-sighted gaze whom I had glimpsed in the Paris tavern and again here. Was he the same who appeared when I was attacked at the infirmary? In the end I had to concede we were chasing shadows, so Isabella turned to the doings of the court.

'My husband will not be joining me.' She rose and walked towards the window. 'And I will not be joining him, at least until the French have left. Subtle games, devious ploys, eh, Mathilde, but how, where and when will it all end?'

'In bloody mayhem and death.' The words spilled out before I could stop them.

'Yes, Mathilde, I think you are right.'

We left the priory shortly afterwards, journeying with all speed towards London. Edward, acting as fickle as ever, abruptly announced that the coronation would have to be postponed. This was ill received by the French. Isabella continued to be largely ignored by her husband. Salt was rubbed into the wounded pride of the French by Gaveston openly displaying in his own carts and pavilions the wedding presents given to Isabella by her kinsmen. Sandewic and Baquelle were sent ahead to prepare both the Tower and the city for the royal arrival; Casales and Rossaleti were left to look after us. The dark-faced, liquid-eyed clerk admitted he was in a solemn mood, slightly homesick for France, even though he was kept busy preparing the queen's chancery and other departments of her household. He provided amusement with his constant moans and groans about the cold until Casales had to remind him that the weather in Paris was no different. Once Sandewic had left, Casales grew more relaxed, confessing he found the old Constable of the Tower a difficult companion, with his constant mutterings about the king and Lord Gaveston. Casales attached himself more to me. I would catch him slumped in the saddle, his one good hand holding the reins, his sharp eyes in that severe face under its crop of hair scrutinising me carefully. He noticed the bruising on the side of my head and asked how I came by it. I replied that I had fallen, so he pressed me no further.

Casales repeated the chatter of the court as well as describing the various palaces and the royal manor houses at King's Langley, Woodstock and elsewhere. He was also eager to see London again, describing it to myself and Isabella. 'London is like a rectangle, with six main gates all dating from Roman times,' he explained. 'In the south-east stands the Tower overlooking the Thames, the Conqueror's great fortress, Sandewic's fief. It was built to overawe Londoners with its central donjon. The line of city defence runs north to Aldgate, west to Bishopsgate and Cripplegate then down through Newgate to the Thames. It encloses about a hundred and thirty acres and houses every type of sinner under the sun. What Paris has, London possesses in abundance: ale houses, stews, taverns, inns and brothels, tradesmen, nobles, merchants, clerks and scholars.' He shook his head. 'Everything that crawls or walks under the sun can be found in London. If the devil does brisk business, so does God. There's St Paul's, its steeple packed with relics against lightning, and one hundred and ten other churches, though for every priest there is a prostitute, for every monk a felon, and for every friar a thief. As Sandewic will tell you, the city gallows at the Elms in Smithfield are always busy.'

A few days later we saw London for ourselves. At Blackheath we were met by the mayor, council and leading citizens of the city, hundreds of them dressed in scarlet gowns with fur-tipped hoods. They were ranged like troops in order of their guilds, each under its own colourful standard emblazoned with its particular devices and insignia. These led us north into London and across the long bridge spanning the Thames. Beneath us the river rushed dizzyingly. Barges and boats, all splendidly arrayed, sailed back and forth in an extraordinary display of billowing decorative cloths, blaring trumpets and noisy cheering. On either side of the bridge ranged houses and shops, with gaps in between for the great rubbish heaps, the lay stalls, now cleaned and empty. The pikes jutting up from the rails of the bridge had been cleared of their rotting severed heads and were festooned with coloured streamers dancing wildly in the breeze.

As we left the bridge, the waiting crowds spread everywhere, packed at least twenty deep. The roar of their approval echoed up to the heavens as they greeted their king and his bride. Isabella was garbed in gorgeous robes of scarlet and silver, her golden hair circled by a jewelled coronet, her shoulders warmed by a satin robe edged with costly fur. She rode a milk-white palfrey, accompanied on her right by Edward, clothed in a scarlet and gold surcoat over a snow-white linen shirt, a cape of glory around his shoulders, a jewelled crown on his head. The king rode his father's prancing black destrier Bayard; both it and Isabella's mount were decorated with gleaming red-brown leather harness studded with precious stones. Golden spurs adorned the king's heels, whilst Isabella's stirrups of solid silver, a gift from the city of Canterbury, glittered in the winter sun.

Onlookers later described them as Arthur and Guinevere entering Camelot. In a sense they were correct, for like that tale, Edward and Isabella's story ended in tragedy, but that was for the future, further down the roll of years. On that February morning all of London had turned out to greet their handsome young king and his lovely bride who rode by like a fairy queen, so beautiful, like a mythical lady from high romance. I was all agog for the sights as I'd heard so much about London. On that day I caught the vibrancy of a bustling, teeming city in its springtime vigour, with each of its wards trying to surpass its rivals and so transform London into a great festival ground.

We entered the city proper, the turrets and soaring donjon of the Tower rising to our right, then turned to advance in glory through London's streets to give thanks at Westminster. We passed splendid mansions, the homes of the merchant princes, their black beams and pink plaster hung with cloths of every colour, brilliant banners and glorious standards. Just off the bridge we paused before a symbolically constructed tower. On the top stood a giant holding an axe in his right hand as champion of the city, and in his left, as porter, the keys of the gates. From halberds jutting out from the top of the tower hung mantles displaying the royal arms of England and France. The giant pointed to these and launched into a hymn of praise to his new king and queen.

A short while later we processed up Cornhill to the music of trumpets, horns and clarions, past mock castles built of wood and covered with stiffened cloth painted to look like white marble and green jasper. At the top of the tallest reared a silver lion, exquisitely carved, a shield displaying the royal arms around its neck, in one paw a sceptre, in the other a sword. Splendid pavilions also lined the route, the flaps of their openings pulled back to display images of St George, St Edmund and St Edward the Confessor. In other ceremonial tents boy choirs, dressed like angels in white and gold, sprigs of genet and laurel in their hair, carolled vibrantly, 'Isabella, Regina Anglorum, Gloria Laus et Honor' – to Isabella, Queen of the English, Glory, Praise and Honour.

We journeyed into Cheapside, where the Great Conduit, a spacious building which covered the main watering place of London, had been transformed into a fairy castle, housing maidens dressed in cloth of gold, their hair studded with gems. These sang beautifully, 'Gloriosa Dicta Sunt, Isabella' – Glorious Things Are Said About You, Isabella. And, so it continued as we processed along that great thoroughfare of Cheapside, its magnificent mansions and shops ranging on either side. We went down under the lofty towers and steeple of St Paul's, along the roads bordering the Thames, on to the Royal Way and into the spacious precincts of Westminster. On one side rose the halls and soaring gabled houses of the palace; on the other the glorious, breathtaking vision of stone which was Westminster Abbey, its flamboyant stonework, buttresses, walls, glass-filled windows, lacework carvings and triumphant gateways sparkling in the heavy frost. We entered, processing along its spectacular nave up to the high altar, and Isabella and Edward knelt in the sanctuary to give thanks before visiting the canopied marble shrine of Edward the Confessor.

Afterwards, we journeyed up river to the Tower. We left the King's Steps at Westminster on a magnificent, elaborately decorated royal barge, its boatmen bending over the oars while Edward and Isabella, enthroned under a canopy of cloth of gold, greeted the crowds lining the north bank of the Thames. We passed the famous quaysides of Queenshithe, Dowgate and the rest, and for the first time I experienced the terrors of shooting the waters between the starlings on the arches of London Bridge. A truly awesome experience of thundering, surging water booming like the drums of hell, spray flying like rain, before coming slowly in to moor at the Tower quayside, where Sandewic and Baquelle, dressed in the glowing colours of the royal household, were waiting to greet us.

I shall never forget my first arrival at the Tower, that grim brooding yet in some ways elegant fortress which was to play such a vital role in my mistress's life. Henry III had copied the best of France in the building and renovation of the abbey and palace, but the Tower was a formidable reminder of the old king's warrior ways. No wonder Sandewic was devoted to it. A soldier's place, built for war, its very size and strength sufficient to threaten and subdue the turbulent Londoners, it reared up above the river with its central donjon or keep and girdling walls, deep moats, formidable bastions, dominating towers, cavernous gateways, all defended by crenellations, arrow slits, narrow gulleys and iron-tipped porticullis. We journeyed under the Lion Gate on to the bridge spanning the green-slimed, reeking moat, past the barbican where the King's animals, lions, leopards and other fearsome beasts, prowled and roared. We stopped and listened to these before proceeding on through Middle Tower, under Byward and into the outer bailey, a broad, open expanse stretching between two curtain walls which housed the stables, store houses and living quarters of the soldiers and servants.

We continued on under St Edmunds Tower, through another gateway and into an enclosed courtyard cordoned off by the great four-squared keep as well as the Wakefield and Lanternhorn towers. Royal mansions had been built to connect these towers, magnificent houses of white and pink plaster and jet-black beams on stone foundations with red-tiled roofs. Large glass-filled windows provided both light and air whilst the inside floors were of polished wood. The walls of all the chambers were painted with ashlar, imitation stone, and decorated with eye-catching friezes of animals, plants, flowers, angels, griffins and a whole range of heraldic devices. One of these mansions, which Sandewic called his Castle on the Hoop, was given over to Isabella. An elegant residence, the castle boasted private bedchambers with hangings, chests and counters. On the ground floor was a small hall, exquisitely decorated and hung with vivid tapestries, a polished oaken table ranged along the dais, with trestle boards below for the servants. All the rooms were warmed with braziers whilst fires roared in the ornamental mantled hearths. Each was well furnished with a lavarium, consisting of wash bowls, jugs and pegs for napkins, silver candelabra as well as candle-wheels which could be lowered by pulleys to provide more light. Off the hall were parlours, butteries and kitchens all equipped with every necessity and comfort.

Sandewic was so proud of it all, God rest and assoil his poor soul. He wanted to make us feel safe, secure and comfortable. My heart warmed to his gentle goodness. For a brief while I cried, going off by myself to a deserted parlour because the constable's cordial welcome evoked memories of Uncle Reginald and the warm closeness which he had wrapped around me. Isabella also welcomed the Castle, after the rigours of the royal progress. She doffed her gowns and jewellery, running around the chambers laughing and clapping her hands like the joyous young woman she should have been. It was good to be alone. The king and Gaveston lodged in the nearby Wakefield Tower whilst, God be thanked, the French had stayed at the king's palace of Westminster. Casales and Rossaleti had been given chambers in our mansion whilst Baquelle, full of the glories the Londoners had staged, returned to the great Guildhall in Catte Street to feast and boast with his fellow aldermen.

That February became a time of waiting as preparations were made for the coronation. Isabella had described us as two sparrows. On reflection we were more like sparrow-hawks, still young and tender, whilst the Tower became our safe nesting place. Sandewic, of course, came into his own. He loved his fief, so every morning he would present himself at the Castle on the Hoop with a list of minor ailments which made me smile. I treated blisters with madonna's lily; cat-nip or neo, soaked and roasted, for the rheums and his constant catarrh. He, in turn, was eager to show me the Tower in all its glory. We visited the barbican. Inside stood a long row of specially built cages which contained the savage beasts, gifts for the English king from foreign rulers. One, in particular, fascinated Sandewic: a huge brown bear he called Woden, a fearsome brute who'd rear up, clawing the air. The stench was intense, fetid and foul from the large vats swimming in blood containing the slabs of meat fed to the beasts. Sandewic was particularly pleased with the cages. He had personally supervised their construction so the animals could pace and move. He pointed out how Woden, like himself, suffered pains in the joints. He certainly had a kinship for that great beast, even carrying a basket of fruit into Woden's cage. On such occasions he'd dress in a special cloak fashioned out of boiled leather sheets sewn together; this served as protection against the half-tame bear: Woden would lumber towards him and gently pull at the constable, begging for the food Sandewic eventually placed on the ground.

The constable's great boast, however, was the little Chapel of St Peter ad Vincula situated in a corner of the inner bailey. It had fallen into disrepair and Sandewic had refurbished it out of his own revenues. He was very proud of what he called his *petit bijou* – his little jewel. Inside, the chapel was similar to those built before the Conqueror: a long, barn-like building with beams spanning the narrow nave leading down to a gleaming stone sanctuary with its elaborately carved rood screen and large table-altar standing on a dais. Above this, a spacious oriel window filled with stained glass depicting the liberation of St Peter from his prison in Jerusalem poured in light. The paving stones were smooth and evenly laid, the woodwork gleamed a warm dark brown. Charcoal braziers provided warmth, and to the left of the sanctuary the masons and carpenters had fashioned a small lady chapel with a carving of the Virgin and Child which replicated the famous image at Walsingham. Tablets of incense placed on top on the brazier provided a fragrant perfume whilst the chapel even boasted small benches and prie-dieus. The walls had been sanded, replastered, whitewashed and almost covered by vigorous, vivid paintings describing the history of the Tower.

I remember it all so vividly: a cold morning with

the river mist boiling across the Tower, shrouding walls and turrets, hanging across the ward like a curtain, deadening sound except for the harsh cawing of the ravens. The mist even seeped under the door into the nave of St Peter's. I wondered if the wispy tendrils were the ghosts of those who wander searching for absolution. Sandewic paced up and down the sanctuary describing his work in the chapel. He paused and gestured.

'This, Mathilde, is my Cup of Ghosts!'

I asked him what he meant.

'If only the king would come here!' he continued, ignoring my question. 'If he'd only reflect and pray.' The constable lowered his head, looking at me from under bushy eyebrows. 'This place holds the Cup of Ghosts, just as in Arthur's tale the Chapel Perilous possessed the Holy Grail.' He then swiftly passed on to other matters so I let it rest. 'Soul does speak to soul – *cor loquitur cor* – heart speaks to heart.'

Perhaps even then Sandewic was trying to warn me. A soldier of the old school, he was reluctant to say anything direct yet he tried to be honest and blunt. Once outside the chapel he grasped my hand and took me into a small buttery adjoining a kitchen, one of those outhouses which served the garrison. We sat breaking our fast before the fire. Sandewic could have spoken but servants were milling about. Eventually he grasped my wrist as if he'd had reached a decision and took me out down to the great Watergate; its portcullis was raised, pinpricks of torchlight glowed through the mist and the clatter of men unloading the barges echoed dully. Sandewic pushed me into a recess. He pulled my cloak up about me and thrust a pomander into my hand as some protection against the reeking stench from the waterways. Then he gestured at the torchlight.

'What do you think is happening, Mathilde?'

'They're unloading stores.'

'Weapons,' Sandewic replied. 'Bows, arrows, halberds and shields. I visited the Bowyer Tower yesterday. My lord Gaveston was also there supervising the work; our armouries and smithies are kept very busy.'

'*Mon seigneur* the king is preparing for war against his earls?'

'Yes,' Sandewic agreed. '*Mon seigneur* certainly is.' He turned. We stood as close as lovers. I could smell his ale-rich breath, those watery blue eyes bright with anger. 'Did you notice, Mathilde, when we journeyed here from Dover, how we visited no castles but rested at monasteries and priories?' I nodded. 'Edward was insistent on that,' Sandewic explained. 'He did not wish others to see how those places were preparing for war, garrisoned with troops, full of stores and arms. And in France,' he continued, 'when I went riding out? King Philip was doing the same, preparing.'

'War with France?' I asked.

'Perhaps,' Sandewic replied.

'Is that why the French were told to make their

own way here and kept well away from the Tower?'

We left the recess, going back to the gloomy gateway.

'I've seen war, Mathilde, here in England,' Sandewic declared. 'Brother against brother, father against son. I fought for Earl Simon at Lewes and Evesham. I've seen the dead piled high like blood-soaked sacks, trees rich with corpses, villages burning, their wells crammed with cadavers. I've fought in Scotland and Wales and seen cruelty not even the Lord Satan could imagine: men skinned alive, maimed and tortured then slung in cages over castle walls to rot to death.' He stamped his feet on the cobbles. 'I don't want that to happen again. Tell that to your mistress.'

In the days following I often thought of Sandewic's warnings and discussed them with Isabella. She could do little, being taken up with the coronation, and visited, as she sardonically put it, almost on the hour by Sir John Baquelle. The merchant prince would sweep into her chambers with clothiers, jewellers, goldsmiths, grocers, silversmiths, all eager to offer presents and protestations of loyalty as well as to catch the princess's eye with samples of their goods. In my arrogance I'd always considered Baquelle a pompous nonentity, but that fat, jolly merchant, Lord Pigeon as Isabella secretly dubbed him, was powerful in the city and instrumental in raising the loans for the crown King Edward desperately needed. Baquelle would often be closeted with both king and favourite, as well as with the exchequer officials in the Treasury Tower. I wondered if he too was party to the king's warlike preparations.

Other visitors arrived at the fortress, the great earls with their retinues seeking an audience with the king. Their demands were well known. They wanted a parliament to meet at Westminster as soon as possible to discuss 'certain weighty matters'. Edward fobbed them off with excuses. Marigny and his two familiars, des Plaisans and Nogaret, also arrived to pay their courtesies to both the king and his new bride. Edward met them in the Wakefield Tower. They later shared wine with Isabella, who refused to allow me to attend, claiming Marigny did not wish me well. I was surprised at this, but my mistress was insistent. In the end the meeting did not last long. Isabella announced she felt unwell and returned to her own quarters, where, in the most robust of health, she stormed up and down her chamber cursing Marigny as her father's 'prying eyes'.

'They tried to foist a physician on me!' she exclaimed. 'One of my father's creatures. He became too familiar, he wanted to know . . .' She fought for breath.

'If you have lain with your husband?'

'God's teeth, Mathilde, no! If I might be pregnant with child!' Isabella threw her head back and laughed. 'In such a short time?' she shouted. 'Is he so monkish to know so little, and even if I was, even if I am, he'd be the last to know.' Isabella flounced down on to a bench. 'I informed him I no longer wished to converse.' Isabella bubbled with laughter. 'I clutched my stomach and declared I felt quite sick. I've never seen Marigny smile so much. He even had the impudence to insist, yet again, that I be tended by a French physician.' Isabella blew a kiss at me. 'I told him I was, by you.'

'Was that wise, your grace?'

'Was that wise, your grace?' Isabella mimicked. 'Marigny's face! Oh, Mathilde, you should have seen it, so suffused with rage! He asked if you were another gift I'd given my husband.'

The hairs on the back of my neck curled, a shiver of fear as if some dark presence had brushed me with its feathery wings.

'Mathilde, what is the matter?'

'Madame,' I used the address I always did when I was blunt with her, 'madame, please repeat what you said. Do so slowly.'

Isabella did, then halfway through broke off.

'Of course,' she whispered, 'how could he know?' She rose slowly to her feet. 'How would Marigny know that it was I who recommended Edward give my wedding presents to Gaveston? No one else was present that night. I later spoke to *mon seigneur*, and he swore that the great game was a matter of the utmost secrecy, so who, Mathilde? Sandewic?' she added quickly. 'For a while he was outside the door.'

'Gaveston?' I replied. 'Even the king, despite his protestations?' I thought back to that evening. No one else had been present, and ever since, Isabella had maintained the pretence, even to Casales and Rossaleti, that her wedding gifts had been seized by Edward for Gaveston. I recall the malicious glee of the favourite as he taunted de Clauvelin. Pourte's death, Wenlok thrashing on the floor, the attacks on me. Was Gaveston's hand, even the king's, behind it all? I wanted to sit like a scholar, collect and sift all I knew, but I was unable to. So many matters were pressing in, I was confused. Isabella and I were still pawns in a game we could not even hope to control.

A short while later Casales and Rossaleti joined us. The scribe brought in a sheaf of documents, wax and Isabella's personal seal together with pen-quills and capped pots of dark blue ink. Already the number of petitions to her was growing. Licences to go abroad, pardons for crimes, remission of debts, exemptions from military service as well as pleas for legal assistance, be it against wrongful arrest or vexatious prosecution. Isabella sat at her chancery table sealing the hot wax or writing the phrase *le roi le veut* – the king wishes it – as Edward had conceded that his new wife could respond to petitions, whilst he would confirm whatever she granted. As she busied herself with these clerical tasks, Casales returned to teaching us both English. I had learnt a little with Uncle Reginald; Isabella had schooled herself. Casales now instructed us further at the king's behest, teaching us poems like 'Sumer is-i-cumen', 'The Ancient Rewle' and even some of the bawdy songs so favoured by Londoners. He included the rather difficult words from a song composed, so he claimed, during the reign of the old king 'A Song of the Times', a bitter, stinging attack on corruption. I still remember some of the words:

False and lither is this londe, as each day we
  may see.
Therein is both hate and that ever it will be.

A strange choice, but Casales, who composed his own poems, claimed it caught the spirit of the English tongue.

Both our companions had certainly changed since our arrival in England. Rossaleti was quieter, lost in his own thoughts. He'd look at me, dark eyes full of sorrow, gnawing his lip like a man who wanted to speak but had decided to keep his own counsel. Casales was brusque but more forthcoming. On that particular day he pleaded with Isabella to advise her husband to be more prudent and listen to his councillors. He waited until Rossaleti left and became even more forthright.

'Lord Gaveston,' Casales walked to the door, opened it and quickly glanced into the darkened stairwell, 'Lord Gaveston,' he repeated, closing the door and coming back, 'must be exiled. The French court is grumbling, the great earls have issued writs of arrays summoning out their retainers, the Scottish harass the northern marches, and you've heard the latest news?'

'What?' Isabella turned sharply in the chancery chair.

'The coronation? Tonight the king's council discuss the date but it will undoubtedly be the twenty-fifth of February. According to the Ordo of the Liber Regalis only a premier earl may carry the crown to the high altar, but on this occasion it will be—'

'Gaveston?' I asked.

'Gaveston,' Casales agreed. 'Clad like a king all in purple.'

Later that afternoon Edward and Gaveston, both dressed in loose jerkins, shirts and hose, cloaks wrapped about them against the cold, sauntered across to our mansion. They acted like boys released from the schoolroom, teasing each other over a pet monkey which had stolen one of Gaveston's jewels then bitten one of his lap dogs. When Sandewic joined us they turned the teasing on him and Isabella, and despite the presence of our visitors Edward inveighed bitterly against the leading earls. Gaveston was a born mimic and the king bawled with laughter as his favourite imitated different noblemen, giving them all nicknames. Gaveston even went down on all fours, barking loudly, mocking Guy de Beauchamp, Earl of Warwick, whom he'd dubbed 'The Black Dog of Arden'. Afterwards, as we played dice, Isabella tried to raise the question of the coronation, but Edward deftly turned this aside, drawing his dagger and accusing his favourite of using cogged dice. At dusk both men left, followed by Casales, leaving Sandewic, who sat with a thunderous expression on his face.

'Tonight,' he went towards the door, slapping his gauntlets against his hand, 'we'll meet, we'll talk, but nothing will change.' He paused, wincing at the pain in his thigh.

I insisted he stay and made him confess that the pains from the rheums in his muscles were growing worse. I prescribed some mugwort for a poultice and Abbot Strabo's cure for the pains, the flower of southernwood, quite a precious herb. I had a small portion of it, ground, boiled and strained, and gave him two phials, warning him the taste would be very bitter so he should mix it with wine, to which Sandewic replied that he liked such cures. Once I'd finished I made my own request of him, something I'd determined on during the day, to which Isabella had already agreed. I first swore Sandewic to secrecy, then asked for an escort to accompany me into the city the following day. Sandewic looked surprised but declared it would be best if the escort was one man so we could slip out of the Tower unnoticed. He offered the captain of his own archers, a Welshman I'd met in Paris, a redoubtable, tough-faced character named Owain Ap Ythel, and I accepted.

We left just after dawn the following day, a bitterly frosty morning, the ground slippery underfoot. Ap Ythel came armed except for his helmet. Beneath his hooded cloak he wore a war-belt with sword and dagger and carried an arbalest, the pouch of bolts fastened to his belt. I'd taken a dagger, pushing it into the sheath on my waistband. Sandewic himself let us out from the postern gate and we made our way out of the Tower, through stinking, needle-thin alleyways and on to the broad thoroughfare leading into the city. I was determined to visit Seething Lane and discover who that mysterious person was and if he could help in our present sea of troubles. The Welshman whispered that we could always take a barge from the quayside, but I had not forgotten Paris and did not wish to go swimming again.

CHAPTER 10

Those who were once very powerful now
fall by the sword.

'A Song of the Times', 1272–1307

We made good progress. The frost had hardened the slime and mud on the cobbles whilst the sewer channels, which cut like ribbons down the street, were thickly frozen. The city bells were ringing for prime but the market horns had yet to herald the start of trading so the shops and stalls remained shuttered. Lanterns and candles glowed at windows. The different-coloured signs creaked in the morning breeze. It was so reminiscent of Paris: the smells, that feeling of expectancy before the day begins. The wards' scavengers and rakers were out to clear away the refuse, their great carts moving slowly down the street under banners hung out in preparation for the coronation. Dogs barked and yelped. City bailiffs, in the blue and mustard livery of the corporation, were busy stalking a pig caught wandering from its yard, a strict violation of civic ordinances. Other officials, armed with staves and halberds, were collecting the night-walkers, strumpets, drunkards and other violators of the curfew, marshalling them into line, fettering their hands before herding them up to Cheapside and the great prison cage on top of the conduit. Beggars shivered on corners. Luckless whores called out vainly from darkened doorways or the mouths of runnels. Fritterers, the sellers of second-hand clothing, were already laying out their makeshift stalls, trying to attract the attention of workmen in their shabby cloaks and hures, caps of shaggy fustian, who were making their way noisily across the cobbles in their wooden pattens shod with iron against the slime-strewn ice.

I had told ApYthel where we were going. He knew the city well and advised me to stay on the broad thoroughfares and not become lost in the alleys and runnels, the haunt and hunting ground of rifflers, battlers and other violent felons. We hurried up Cornhill then into Cheapside, which was fairly deserted except for the noisy prison cage. In the stocks a hapless baker sat fastened, shivering despite the pan of charcoal pushed beneath his legs by his anxious family. The placard round his neck warned against such tradesmen putting tablets of iron in their loaves to weigh them more heavily. On one occasion I became breathless and unsteady on my feet, my wits playing tricks on me. I felt, for a heart-beat, that I was not in London but Paris, hurrying through the alleys on some errand for Uncle

Reginald. Ap Ythel noticed this and insisted we stop at a cookshop which had opened early to attract workmen with the sweet smell of its baked bread and tasty pies.

We broke our fast with pots of musty ale. Sitting on a bench outside the shop, I glanced back the way we had come, searching for any sign of pursuit. I could see none, though Ap Ythel had also grown uneasy. He did not question me on what I was doing; Sandewic's word was good enough for him, but he too kept staring back. On one occasion he rose, feet bestriding the frozen sewer channel, gazing narrow-eyed back up Cheapside. He muttered something in Welsh, but when I questioned him he shook his head, drained the ale pot and said we should move on.

We hurried along, past gloomy Newgate and into the alleyways round St Paul's. I stopped to admire its weather-cock, a huge eagle, its outstretched wings carved out of copper, or so Ap Ythel told me. The Welshman, however, insisted that I did not tarry long, explaining that the cemetery around St Paul's was the haunt of outlaws and sanctuary men. We reached Seething Lane, a dark tunnel snaking between shabby, overhanging houses, deserted except for wandering cats, their hideous squalling echoing along the street. As in Paris, the shop, beneath the sign of the Palfrey, was much decayed, a tawdry store house with peeling paint and oiled paper covering the windows. It stood on a corner of an alleyway with outside steps along the side, a place a fugitive could easily flee from. I told Ap Ythel to wait and watch. As I went up the outside steps, they creaked ominously, proclaiming my approach. I reached the top; the door was off the latch and I pushed it open. Inside, a heavy drape billowed out, catching me in its folds. I extricated myself and stepped into the chamber, a twilight place of moving shapes. No candlelight glowed yet the air smelt of wax and incense. I glanced at the bed; its coverlet was neatly pulled up. In the centre of the room stood a table with a white cloth, a silver paten from an altar and two small candlesticks. As I stepped closer, an arm circled my neck, the point of a dagger pricked my cheek.

'*Pax et bonum,*' the voice whispered. 'Who are you?'

'Mathilde de Clairebon.'

'The truth, Mathilde de Ferrers!'

'Mathilde de Ferrers,' I confessed.

'Niece of Sir Reginald de Deyncourt?'

'True.'

'What rank did he hold?'

I replied. The questions continued thick and fast like a hail of arrows. I was not frightened, the grip was not tight and I recognised that same voice, loud and clear, echoing up the gloomy steps of the infirmary of St Augustine's Priory. The man released his arm.

'Tell your escort you are safe.'

I hastened to obey, my belly tingling with excitement. When I returned to the chamber the candles were relit and the stranger, dressed in dark fustian, a stole around his neck, a maniple over his arm, was continuing with the mass he had been celebrating. He stood at the table, head bowed, reading the canon of the mass from the small breviary open on its stand. He held up the unleavened bread, a circular white wafer, and breathed over it the words of consecration, then took the pewter cup and consecrated the wine. I knelt before the table and studied this strange priest. He was a youngish man, slender, about two yards in height. He had a long, rather severe face, slightly sallow; his nose was straight, his lips full, the mouth marked by laughter lines which also creased the most beautiful grey eyes. He had black hair, flecked with grey, parted down the middle. When I first saw him in the Oriflamme tavern in Paris it had been shorter, but now it fell below his ears. High cheekbones gave him that severe, rather ascetic look, yet when he gazed at me, those eyes would crinkle in amusement. He offered me the Eucharist, long, slender fingers holding part of the host, followed by a sip from the chalice, Christ's blood in a pewter cup. After the 'Ite Missa Est', he quickly cleared the altar, placing the sacred vessels in bulging leather panniers. He plucked his cloak from a peg on the door, and also took down a thick, heavy warbelt with its sword and dagger scabbards. He looped this over his shoulder, glanced quickly round the room and came to stand over me.

Ah, sweet Jesu, the memory is as clear as yesterday.

He was dressed in a cote-hardie with dark blue leggings of the same colour; his boots, slightly scuffed, were tight-fitting. He smelt fragrantly of mint and groundnut. He just stared at me. I gazed back. God and all his saints help me, I loved him then. There you have it! After Uncle Reginald, Bertrand Demontaigu was the only man I ever truly loved! You'll dismiss such a tale as the embroidering of troubadours. Do so! I tell the truth. You might, you can, fall in love in a few heartbeats and only later become aware of it. On such occasions the heart doesn't beat faster or the blood surge more strongly. I only experienced a deep peace, a desire to be close to him, to look, to talk, to touch. The schoolmen, when they describe the soul, talk as if it is contained within the flesh. Who says? Why cannot the flesh be contained within the soul and why cannot souls kiss and merge, become one when they meet? The minstrels sing a song, I forget the words, about how our souls are like unfinished mosaics; by themselves they are incomplete, but when they meet the other, they attain a rich fullness all of their own. Bertrand Demontaigu was mine. If he is in hell and I am with him, I shall be in heaven, and my heaven without him would be hell enough. If I close my tired old eyes he is there, serene, calm-faced, with that slightly lopsided smile, and those eyes, full of humour and rich in love, gaze on me. If I sleep he comes; even in the morning, just as I awake, he is always there. I can go through the busy cloisters, I catch a flash of colour. Is that him? On that freezing February morning, so many years ago, he touched my face as he did my soul.

'Mathilde, little one, we must go. Your arrival may bring great danger. The Noctales might have followed you.'

'The who?'

He touched my cheek again. 'Never mind, we must leave.'

'I am have an escort, Ap Ythel, he's—'

'Leave him,' Demontaigu replied, stretching out his hand. 'I am Bertrand Demontaigu, you'll be safe with me.'

I clasped his hand.

'Ap Ythel will be safe too, they're not hunting him. They'll leave him alone once they have this house surrounded.'

'But I saw no one.'

'Of course you didn't, you never do.'

He took me on to the stairwell. I never questioned, I never wondered. I followed him out through a narrow door and down a makeshift ladder into the street. He moved purposefully. We left the foul alley, turned a corner, and a figure, cowled like a monk, slid out of an alcove about two yards ahead of us. Demontaigu pushed me back, dropped the panniers and drew his sword and dagger. His opponent lunged but Demontaigu parried the blow from the long Welsh stabbing dagger. Our attacker, face hidden, crouched in the stance of a street fighter, stabbing dagger in one hand, poinard in the other.

Both men closed and clashed, stamping their feet in a silvery clatter of steel. Demontaigu abruptly broke free but, instead of stepping back, lunged swiftly, driving his sword deep into his opponent's belly. The assassin collapsed, spitting blood.

Footsteps echoed, a horn blew. We fled on down alley-ways and runnels. Demontaigu, hindered by the heavy saddlebags, dragged me by the hand. I stopped, rucked up my skirt and grabbed one of the panniers. Demontaigu, drenched in sweat, clasped my hand and we ran on, a deadly, fierce-some flight through the needle-thin runnels of London, shabby, filthy places, the ground choked with stinking offal and every type of rubbish. Dark shapes clustered like wraiths in doorways and alley mouths. Whores, faces painted chalk-white under dyed red hair, glared at us; beggars, filthy and crippled, waved their clack dishes; thin-ribbed yellow dogs snarled at us; naked children scattered at our approach. Refuse was hurled at us from windows and doorways. We twisted and turned like hares, going deeper into the slums around Whitefriars, London's hell on earth, with its decaying houses and hordes of evil ones. They did not hinder us; they believed we were felons fleeing from the law, whilst Demontaigu's sword-belt warned them off.

Eventually I could run no further. My body was clammy with sweat, pain shot through my side, my legs and feet ached heavy as lead, my eyes were cloudy with tears. We turned down a track-way.

Demontaigu pulled me through a rotting lych-gate into an overgrown cemetery of crumbling crosses and tangled undergrowth. We raced up towards the chapel door. Demontaigu kicked it open and we threw ourselves into the mildewed porch, taking shelter in a recess near the devil's door. We crouched between the baptismal font and the wall, fighting for breath, wiping the sweat from our faces. Demontaigu remained tense, straining like a lurcher for any sign of pursuit. At first he just sat sprawled, legs out, head down. I recovered first, my life-breath slowing. I stared at the crude drawings on the walls, a popular fresco to instruct the faithful about the ladder of salvation to the other world. I remember that so clearly; it suited my own mood after such a furious flight. In the right-hand corner of the picture stood Eden's tree of knowledge with the serpent wound about. Above this a bridge of spikes across which cheating tradesmen were being shepherded by a cohort of demons. Below that a usurer being tortured by fire. In the centre of the picture Jacob's ladder, with souls climbing towards Christ. Some reached the top but the rest were snatched by demons for a grisly array of tortures in hell: a dog gnawed a woman's hand because of her concern for it rather than the poor; a drunken pilgrim was imprisoned in a bottle; demons boiled murderers in a frothy cauldron; a griffin-like creature chewed the feet of lewd dancers. I got up to study it more closely, trying to distract myself. My chest still hurt, my belly pitched. Eventually I ran out into the wasteland to ease myself, the cloying cold chilling my sweat. I washed my hands in a pool of ice and returned to the church.

'What is this place?' I asked.

'The Chapel of Dead Bones,' Demontaigu replied, standing with his back to me staring at the wall painting. 'A great cemetery once covered the entire area. This was built as a chantry chapel where visiting priests could sing the requiem for the dead who throng here.' He turned, beckoning me forward.

I slammed the door behind me. Demontaigu opened one of the saddlebags, took out some bread wrapped in linen, broke it and offered me some.

'Eat,' he urged. 'The bread is dry, it will settle your belly. Eat, wise woman, or I shall quote the old saying, *medice sane teipsum* – physician heal thyself.'

We squatted down, sharing the bread. Demontaigu was now more composed, studying me carefully.

'You're a priest,' I asked, 'yet you killed a man?'

'The right of self-defence,' he replied, 'is enshrined in canon law as well as the rule St Bernard gave our order. The assassin was an enemy of our order. I did not ask him to give up his life.'

'You are a Templar priest?'

'Yes, wanted dead or alive. I come from the preceptory of Amiens.' He continued evenly, 'I am the son of a French knight and an English lady.

When I was a boy,' he bit a mouthful of bread, 'I fell seriously ill. My mother, God rest her soul, made pilgrimage, crawled on her knees up the nave to the statue of Our Lady of Chartres. She vowed that if my life was spared I'd become a priest. My father was a warrior; he was opposed to that, as was I,' Demontaigu laughed softly, 'until I met Jacques de Molay and your uncle Reginald de Deyncourt; good men, noble Templars, they are, they will be, welcomed by *le bon seigneur* as martyrs of the faith.'

'I saw you in the tavern Oriflamme.'

'As I saw you,' Demontaigu pointed back, 'with that English clerk whom you killed. There again, if you hadn't,' he took another mouthful, 'I would have done the same. He too beckoned up his own fate. Death always responds.'

'Why were you there?'

Demontaigu swallowed the bread. 'Listen,' he began quietly, 'and then you will know at least some of the truth. Yes, I was in that tavern. I was also in the priory.'

'Who attacked me?'

'I don't know. Look at you, Mathilde, with your mop of black hair and your clear eyes. Your uncle said you had a comely face. He was wrong. I think you are beautiful, but there again, I'm a knight. I know the courtly ways of troubadours.' His smile faded. 'But no more song. Now, Mathilde, I have vowed on the sacred face to exact God's justice, His vengeance on the destroyers of my order.' He paused. 'Your uncle, Reginald de Deyncourt, was a good friend, a comrade. I fought with him at Acre when the sky turned to fire and the ground swirled in blood, but that was in my youth. I am now in my thirty-sixth year. I returned from Outremer to France to become henchman to Jacques de Molay, Grand Master of our order; when he rose, I rose with him. I know about his dealings with that silver-haired, blue-eyed demon Philip of France.' He chewed on the bread.

'Do you know why he attacked your order?'

'No, not the true reason. I truly don't under-stand it, except for one thing.' Demontaigu waved a finger. 'On one occasion de Molay referred to what he called "The Enterprise of England", but then the sword fell. Templars were arrested all over France. I was fortunate; de Molay often sent me as a messenger to our houses in Aragon and else-where. There was no real description of me. I could hide under my mother's name, be it as a friar or an English clerk. I always keep to the shadows.'

'And Monsieur de Vitry?'

'He was frightened, Mathilde, a good man, honourable and wise; your uncle chose well. Monsieur de Vitry's assistance to you was invaluable. He was correct, the safest place for you was the French court. However,' Demontaigu wiped the sweat from his forehead with his sleeve, 'Monsieur de Vitry felt guilty. He also felt very frightened. God knows what he was doing. He once came to me and asked to be shriven. I agreed and heard his

275

confession. I can't tell you what he said, that is kept under the secret seal, but he was very fearful for the future.'

'Why did he feel guilty?'

'He felt guilty about you. He described you as a dove being left amongst the hawks; he wanted to do something more. I offered my protection, hence his letter.'

'So why was he murdered?'

'Again, I don't know. He asked me to look after you, which I did. I followed you to that tavern, I saw what happened to the English clerk, then you fled.'

'I went to de Vitry's house.'

'And you found him murdered?'

'Yes,' I agreed. 'But I know nothing else.'

'Neither do I.' Demontaigu breathed out. 'I did hear of the massacre. I offered a mass for all their souls.'

'And who was responsible?'

'A sinister mystery!' Demontaigu snapped. 'I became frightened for my own safety. Philip has hired bounty-hunters, the Noctales, the men who walk by night. They hunt other men down for the price on their heads. The Noctales are a guild to be found near the Church of St Sulpice in Paris. They are led by a Portuguese, Alexander of Lisbon.' Demontaigu shrugged. 'I've come across the type before. I've even been one of them, a messenger sent by the Templars to claim unresolved debts.'

'And the Noctales are hunting you here?'

'Of course, as they might be hunting you. Philip is determined to seize all Templars and their associates. Mathilde, Marigny and his demons may know your true identity. If so, they hope you will lead them to other Templars in hiding. The Noctales will follow, as they always do, as night follows day. They swarm like ants yet they know the law. They'll not touch a subject of the English king, but you, me, those who've fled from Aragon, Castile, France or anywhere else are legitimate quarry. They'll try to take me alive, but if not,' he stretched his neck, 'they'll take my head, pickle it in a tun, find some proof for me being a Templar and trot back to Philip and Marigny for their reward. They are also searching for Templar wealth, hidden caskets of jewels, gold and silver.'

'Do they know you?'

Demontaigu turned, as if fascinated by the demons painted on the wall.

'They know me by my father's name, as they do my rank, but as I said, they have no clear description of me.' He laughed abruptly. 'The traitors in our order did not have close sight of me; that's one of the reasons de Molay chose me when Philip struck. I was to go into hiding to exact vengeance, to protect, where I could, our brethren.'

'So I have endangered you?'

'Mathilde,' Demontaigu cupped my cheek, 'they still do not know me.' His hand fell away. 'Don't worry, it would have happened one day, a suspicious innkeeper, an informer.' He leaned back against the wall and sighed. 'I stayed as long as I could in Paris; as I've said, de Vitry felt guilty and asked me for help, so I watched the palace. It was easy enough. I saw you leave. I thought you might be fleeing so I joined you at the tavern. I dressed and acted like an English scholar; I know the tongue. I saw what happened.' He picked at the crumbs on his tunic. 'Then de Vitry was killed. I decided to flee. My brothers had prepared a place in England.' He shrugged. 'I came here to find most of the brethren were in hiding or prison. The power of England has not fully moved against us. William de la Mare, our Grand Master here, lies under house arrest at Canterbury.'

'And you travelled to Dover to watch for me?'

Demontaigu laughed. 'Well, yes and no.'

I felt a deep chill of fear. 'You didn't come for me,' I accused. 'You came for Marigny, didn't you? Des Plaisans and Nogaret?'

'Yes, Mathilde. I came for them. If I can, if God gives me the will, grace and strength, I'll kill them as would other brothers of my order. The Noctales have been released against us for many reasons. If Philip and his henchmen are dangerous to us, we are just as threatening to them. We still have in-fluence, be it with that false priest, Clement of Avignon, or here in England. Above all, we are soldiers, veterans, master bowmen and swordsmen. Life can be so perilous in a street or crossing a square.' He smiled. 'Or even in a palace. I heard about Pelet's death and wondered if you . . . ?'

'No,' I replied. 'That was the princess acting on my behalf.'

'In which case,' Demontaigu replied, 'we are deeply in her debt.'

'And the attack in Canterbury?'

'I was travelling in disguise with false papers. According to them I was Brother Odo from Cluny. The good monks of St Augustine's accepted me; Benedictines are always travelling. I was left to my own devices, given a cell and joined the brothers in their communal celebrations. I watched you. I saw you leave the guest house that night and followed. Mathilde, you acted foolishly in such a deserted place, a hall of shadows. Anyway, I came to the foot of those steps and glimpsed the struggle at the top.' He pulled a face. 'The rest you know.' He patted me on the arm. 'I dared not reveal myself; I returned to London. I would have waited a little longer.' He walked over to the door, opened it, peered outside and slammed it shut. 'And so, Mathilde,' he came over and squatted down before me, 'why were you, a *dame de chambre*, attacked so viciously?'

I told him everything, as if I was a penitent in the mercy seat being shriven by my confessor: all about the deaths of Pourte, Wenlok, the assaults on me and the enmity of Marigny. Demontaigu heard me out, nodded or asked the occasional question. He shook his head after I'd finished.

'Marigny may know who you truly are, but he'd prefer more to use you than kill you.' He paused, listening to the growing sounds from outside, the shouts and cries of traders, the rattle of a cart, the clatter of horses' hooves. 'I certainly agree with you on one matter: de Vitry. Something you saw that day has perhaps placed you in great danger.' He pulled his leather saddlebags closer. 'De Vitry's murder is truly a mystery. He also said something to me, not covered by his confession, about the enterprise of England; that it was really Philip's enterprise but he did not know the details.'

'Could it be an invasion of England, conquest?' I asked.

'Too costly, too dangerous,' Demontaigu replied as if to himself, 'but look, I'm cold and hungry,' he tapped me on the tip of my nose, 'as you must be. The pursuit is cold, the Noctales will withdraw and I'm famished!' He got to his feet. 'I have business at the Tower today, so I will escort you back.'

'What business?' I asked, heart in mouth. 'What business, sir?'

'We have our spies in the French court and in their households.' He walked to the door and paused. 'Today, the Feast of St Callistus, Marigny, des Plaisans and Nogaret are going to the Tower to be received by the king. Last night I met one of my brothers, Gaston de Preux, from the preceptory of Dijon. He is hot-tempered, passionate and tired of being hunted. I tried to restrain him, but on this, he is adamant—'

'Oh no!' I exclaimed.

'He will try to kill Marigny.'

I put my hand against the door and thought furiously about what I could remember. It was true! Isabella had mentioned Marigny's visit, that we would certainly be busying ourselves elsewhere.

'I could send a message to Casales.'

'Ah yes, the one-handed warrior.' Demontaigu smiled. 'The old king much trusted him. He fought hard in Gascony, but no!' Demontaigu tightened his war-belt. 'If Casales or that old lion Sandewic are alerted, Marigny will know. Marigny can die – I want that too. It's Gaston I worry about. I cautioned prudence, but Gaston's heart is like his hair, fiery. If I can, I'll stop him; we should wait for a better day.'

We left that gloomy Chapel of Dead Bones and made our way through the slums of Whitefriars. I felt tired, cold and ill at ease. Demontaigu seemed a warm presence around me, merry and composed. He told me there was nothing to fear. He reminded me that the Noctales did not have his description, adding that we could hide amongst the crowds, whilst I had my head and face carefully hooded. As we pushed our way through the throng, Demontaigu talked softly in French, asking me once again about Pourte and Wenlok's deaths, the assault on Casales, the attacks on me in Paris and Canterbury. I answered and asked him what he would do for the future. His reply was enigmatic: that the safest place for him was near to me. I glanced at him questioningly. He laughed, clapped me on the shoulder and told me to meditate on that as a pious nun would on her psalter.

By then it was mid-morning, the mist had lifted, the sun was strong. The crowds in all their many colours busied about to shop, wander and gape. We left the Shambles, going down past St Mildred's and St Michael's church into Candlewick, then Eastcheap and Pudding Lane. Demontaigu murmured that he was pleased the crowds were even more packed here, people stopping to buy, to argue, to shout, to barter. Two fishwives from Billingsgate were delighting passers-by with a stream of obscenities as they argued over some difference. Portly burgesses tutted and shook their heads, eager to push their plump wives out of earshot of such abuse. A fiddler struck up a tune so that his tamed dog could dance, but the animal caught sight of a cat and set off in hot pursuit to guffaws of laughter. Beggars crawled, whining and importuning, showing their scars in the hope of charity. A Dominican friar, clad in black and white, tried to preach from the steps of a church about the horrors of purgatory. A fop in tight jerkin and hose shouted back that the Dominican should marry and know true pain! This provoked an argument with a group of whores which ended abruptly as the entire crowd scattered to allow through an execution cart with its portable gallows, a dreadful T-shape scaffold with corpses dangling on either end. Demontaigu studied it and turned away as if the sight reminded him of his own danger. He grasped me by the elbow, and we left the thoroughfare and entered the Green Solace tavern opposite St Boltoph's church. The tap room was fairly deserted except for a few traders and chapmen sitting on the barrels around rough-hewn tables. The food was good, I remember that. Demontaigu insisted that we must eat and ordered strips of peppered beef, soft, freshly baked bread and jugs of ale. I broke my fast hungrily, glancing sly-eyed at this Templar priest lost in his own thoughts.

For a while we talked about physic and herbs. Demontaigu said he'd read a treatise on black harrow, or the Christmas rose, and quoted a leech book claiming that 'a purgation of black harrow boar is good for mad and furious persons as well as for melancholy chills and heavy hearts'. I argued back though I secretly realised Demontaigu was only trying to divert me. When we'd finished eating, he leaned close, brushing the hair from my brow.

'Listen, Mathilde, and listen well.'

'Yes, master,' I mocked.

'I will leave you now. I shall go to the Tower by myself. If you are with me you might be recognised, they'll know who I am, they'll note my face, my description. If you wish to contact me, go to a tavern on St Katharine's Wharf, close by the Tower, called the Prospect of Whitby. Tell the taverner that you seek Master Arnaud the bowyer, give the hour then leave. Do you understand?'

'I can hear and I can speak,' I retorted hotly, sad at heart that he was leaving.

'Go now, Mathilde,' Demontaigu murmured. 'The way is clear. You are close to the Tower so no one will harm you. Keep that cowl over your head,' he urged. 'I shall follow.'

Biting back my retort, I went out into the street, following the directions Demontaigu had given me. I walked behind a group of serjeants of the coif returning from the court of common pleas at Westminster and followed these until I reached the alleyways leading down to the river. To all intents and purposes I was a maid dispatched on an errand. I had reached the approaches to the Tower when, close behind me, I heard the rising noise of the crowd. I glanced back; horsemen were making their way through the streets. Marigny! The blue and gold banners of France flapped in the breeze. The French cortège was moving down towards the Tower with all the majesty it could muster. I hurried on and joined the crowds clustering along the approaches to the Lion Gate. I glanced around, looking for Demontaigu, but there was no sign. I searched for the fiery-headed Gaston, but again, I couldn't glimpse anything untoward. I could have walked on and showed myself to Sandewic and Casales waiting outside the main gate, but I wanted to stay. I was anxious for Demontaigu; even a little for Gaston de Preux, whom I'd never met. I also wanted to see what would happen, eager to witness Marigny and the others die. Vengeance, the blood feud, such fires do not start immediately; they are kindled, they rise and fall, they slumber but still they burn. I could watch Marigny be killed. I prayed that he, the arrogant hunter, would become the hunted.

At last they arrived, fleur-de-lis banners slapping the air, sunlight gleaming on armour and precious stones, surrounded by officials and men-at-arms, in all their gorgeous finery. The crowd surged closer. I glanced swiftly about at the chapped faces, the watering eyes, the blousy wantons from the quayside, dust-covered carpenters, ragged children dancing from foot to foot. I searched for the extraordinary: a relic-seller with a string of bones around his neck, his fleshy nose prodding the air like a hunting dog. A jackanapes from some house of fools in his tattered clothes; he had red hair, but he was vacuous-faced and empty-eyed. I glimpsed a young red-haired man pushing his way through the crowds, but he paused to whisper in a young maiden's ear.

The French cavalcade, horses moving slowly, approached the Lion Gate. Casales and Sandewic, in their royal tabards of scarlet and gold with the snarling leopards of England, moved towards them. A friar of the sack, his shaven head gleaming in the sun, broke free of the crowd.

'*Mon seigneur de Marigny, je vous apporte une lettre du roi*' – my lord Marigny, I bring a letter from the king.

Marigny reined in in a clatter of hooves and dust. The friar approached, the piece of parchment held high, then lunged swiftly with his right hand, the dagger snaking up towards Marigny's belly. Sandewic, who'd come forward to grasp the reins, moved even quicker, pushing Marigny's mount towards the assassin. The horse, already startled, clattered sideways, knocking the assassin to the ground. Immediately Marigny's party were surrounded by English men-at-arms. Casales was screaming at others to move forward to form a ring. A horn sounded. Welsh archers poured through the Lion Gate, bows strung. The crowd, startled by this sudden assault, abruptly scattered. I walked forward. A rough serjeant-at-arms seized my shoulder. I shrugged him off and showed him Isabella's personal seal, then hurried on through the gateway. Marigny's party had galloped ahead into the inner ward, which was now in chaos as horses reared, men shouted, gates were hastily shut, portcullis winched stridently down. I kept away from the throng. Marigny wasn't hurt, but was clearly furious. Still mounted, he was shouting in French at Casales. Sandewic was ordering more men forward up on to the battlements. I glimpsed the assassin being led down to a dungeon beneath one of the towers. I slipped through the chaos and went up past the guards to Isabella's chamber. She was standing peering out of a window, its small door-casement opened. She whirled around as I entered and immediately dismissed the pages who were laying lawns of linen on the bed for her to inspect. The princess bolted the door behind them, face flushed, eyes gleaming.

'Mathilde, Mathilde, where have you been? What happened?'

I sat and told her, heads close, whispering against eavesdroppers. She listened intently, though distracted by what was going on outside. When I had finished, she expressed her deep regret at Marigny's narrow escape but said she would act the hypocrite and send him her good wishes. She seemed more concerned with Demontaigu and what he might know, and asked me to repeat what he'd told me to meditate on, 'as a pious nun would on her psalter'.

'He can hide here,' she declared. 'He'll be safe. I'm establishing my household. Whatever he really is can be hidden here. He is knowledgeable in Latin and speaks French and English fluently; he can be my clerk.' She clapped her hands. 'Oh, that would gladden my heart, but Mathilde, the assassin? Find out if he was Gaston, see what can be done. Go to that tavern, the Prospect of Whitby, and find . . .' She paused as Casales knocked and entered. He bowed at Isabella and winked at me.

'My lady, Mathilde must have told you the news. *Mon seigneur* Marigny was attacked; he is unscathed but angry.'

'And the assassin, sir?'

'A madman, your grace. He calls himself Architophel the Archangel, sent by he-who-dwells-in silence to slay the kings of the earth. He believes Marigny is the King of England.'

'Not yet,' Isabella retorted.

'He is in the dungeons, dancing and singing,' Casales continued. 'He is witless but he'll still hang. Mathilde, you have been in the city? You should walk carefully with such fools around. Ah well, we shall all have to . . . Your grace,' he hurried on, 'the coronation is to be proclaimed for the twenty-fifth of February. That's my reason for coming here. *Mon seigneur* the king has ordered me and Rossaleti to ensure everything you need; until then, your grace, as is the custom . . .'

Casales explained how both Isabella and Edward would have to stay within the Tower apartments. I half listened as I wondered about the assassin and who he really might be. Once Casales had left, Isabella told me what I should do, and I returned to the inner ward. Lord Marigny and the great ones had been taken up to see the king, but the courtyard was full of their retainers eating from the victuals the constable had laid out on trestle tables. Eventually Sandewic came stumbling out of a doorway. He caught sight of me and hurried across.

'Mathilde, Ap Ythel returned, he waited, but when he went up the stairs of that house you were gone, so he returned here. I was anxious.' He pulled his beaver hat further down on his head. 'I told no one you'd left but,' he chattered on, 'you've heard the news? Good, good,' he murmured, brushing aside any answer. 'A man touched by the moon, Mathilde, mad and leaping like a March hare. Oh, by the way, I thank you for your potions; they gladden this old frame.' The constable gossiped on, but that's the rub, isn't it? The hidden importance of words. The slip between what the tongue says, the ear hears and the heart understands. Words come back like ghosts to haunt you, but at the time there is little you can do about it. I was all eager to make my request; I was anxious, distracted. Sandewic was of a similar mood, pleased at my safe return yet his mind was elsewhere, so much so I had to repeat my request.

'You want to see the prisoner?' Sandewic glanced at me in disbelief.

'My mistress has demanded it. Her grace wishes to assure herself that this madman is what he acts to be.'

'Could he be any other?'

'Sir Ralph,' I replied, 'that is why I wish to see him.'

The constable bit his thumb, head moving from side to side. 'Oh, follow me,' he grumbled.

We crossed the inner ward, through a doorway of the Wakefield Tower and down the dirt-strewn steps lit by cresset torches. The assassin was confined to a small cell with a grille high in the door. Sandewic opened this and placed a torch in its holder. The prisoner lay crouched in a corner, his brown robe all ragged, his face bruised and filthy, eyes gleaming through the dirt. As soon as Sandewic closed the door behind us, the man leapt to his feet, manacles jangling. He stretched out as far as the chains would allow, then began to dance a fool's jig, leaping up and down, slapping the green-slimed walls before staggering back. He sang some moonstruck song about the fields during the time of bat-flight before sinking to his knees, joining his hands and muttering a garbled version of the Paternoster.

'Insane,' Sandewic growled. 'Moonstruck, out of his wits, but *mon seigneur* the king has judged him. He is to hang tomorrow just before noon on the common gallows at St Katharine's Wharf.'

The madman's head came up; just for a heartbeat I saw the shift in his eyes.

'Mad,' I agreed, 'crazed. I knew a man caught in a similar mood, Gaston de Preux,' I said loudly, 'that was his name. He believed he was a priest. I did all I could for him . . .'

'Pretty lady.' The prisoner stared up at me. I moved so I was between him and Sandewic. The mad look was replaced by a stare of sheer desperation. 'Pretty lady,' the voice mimicked the madness, 'I need the Consolamentum – I need the cross.'

I leaned down, ignoring Sandewic's protest. 'I shall see what I can do.'

Sandewic took down the cresset, unlocked the door and ushered me out.

'Sir Ralph,' I forced a smile, 'let me give the poor wretch some consolation.' I took the Ave beads from my purse and, before Sandewic could object, slipped back into the cell and crouched before the prisoner.

'Gaston?' I whispered. He nodded.

'Tell Bertrand,' he murmured, 'Consolamentum – I look for the cross.'

I dropped the Ave beads into his hands and fled the dungeon. Outside Sandewic stared at me curiously, murmured that I was strange and locked the door. As we left the Tower, Sandewic tugged at my cloak.

'Mathilde,' he drew me close, 'I do not know what you are doing. I keep a still tongue and watch.' He peered up at the grey sky. 'That prisoner, I've met enough madmen, I am beginning to wonder if he is as witless as he pretends.'

I leaned closer and kissed him on the cheek. 'Sir Ralph, what is now in the dark will one day be revealed in the full light of day. I need Owain Ap Ythel again.'

CHAPTER 11

Almost all the nobles spend their time
contriving evil.

'A Song of the Times', 1272–1307

A short while later, with the Welshman full
of questions about what had happened
earlier in the day, we left the Tower and
made our way down to the Prospect of Whitby.
The tavern stood on a corner of an alleyway
looking out on to the quayside and the grim three-
branched scaffold from which hung the corpses of
river pirates. According to placards fastened to
their lifeless hands, the three thieves had robbed
the Church of St Botolph's in Billingsgate of a pyx
and two candlesticks. They'd been hanged at dawn
and swung eerily in the stiff breeze, creaking and
twisting on their oiled ropes. I stared at them,
thinking about Gaston, and walked into the
spacious tap room. It was a pleasant, welcoming
place with a low ceiling, its timber beams blackened with smoke from which hung hams, cheeses

and freshly baked bread in wire cages. A communal trestle-board dominated the room, stretching from the barrels on either side of the counters to the far wall; other small tables stood within the window enclosures. The floor was cleanly swept and strewn with supple green rushes, the air rich and savoury from a leg of pork, basted with juices, roasting above the fire. A tap boy, I have good reason to remember him, tousle-haired and gap-toothed, waved me to a table. ApYthel stood at the doorway, staring curiously in. I ignored the boy and went across to the counter where the tavern-master, a beanpole of a man almost covered by a heavy leather apron, was filling tankards for fishermen who'd just sold their day's catch. I asked about Master Arnaud the bowyer and said I'd return at the hour of vespers. The taverner looked at me and glanced heavenwards.

'Bordeaux!' he exclaimed. 'The best Bordeaux? Of course we have it, mistress, do come and see a tun.' He held a hand up. 'Unbroached, fresh from Gascony, come, come, your lady will be pleased!'

I had no choice but to follow him into the back of the tavern and down the cellar steps. All the time he kept chattering about 'the best of Bordeaux'. He reached the bottom, threw open the cellar door and ushered me in. I waited whilst he lit tallow candles in their lantern horns.

'Smugglers used this,' he explained, moving a mock barrel to reveal the door behind. He knocked, the door opened and Demontaigu stepped out. The

293

tavern-master bowed and left the cellar. The Templar moved into the dim pool of light.

'I knew you'd come,' he murmured. 'I told Master Thomas to bring you down here immediately. Ah well, Gaston is taken, he'd shaven his head so I did not recognise him.' Demontaigu's eyes searched my face. 'We came so close.'

I told him how Gaston was acting frenetic, witless, that he wanted the Consolamentum and would look for the cross when he was hanged at noon the following day.

'He wants to be shriven,' Demontaigu replied, 'God help him. He's acting the fool so as not to be questioned. Look, when you go back,' he urged, 'send him a message, that you'll find him a crucifix. Gaston will understand.'

'And here?' I asked. 'You are safe?'

'The tavern-master's son was a Templar squire in Bordeaux; he is no Judas man.' Demontaigu walked up the cellar and brought back a small cask; the seal on the bung proclaimed it to be Bordeaux, from a vineyard close to St Sardos. 'Give this to your mistress.'

'She knows what you meant,' I replied, taking the cask, 'when you asked me to reflect like a nun: you want to do the same as me, shelter in her household.'

I looked at him so earnestly, Demontaigu laughed and kissed me on the brow.

'I am a priest, Mathilde, yet you look at me . . .' He shook his head. 'Tell your mistress I will be her loyal clerk; I'll be true to her as long as she is true to me.' He kissed my brow again. 'Go, Mathilde, and do not come back here tomorrow.'

Of course I ignored him. I returned to the Tower nervous and agitated. If Demontaigu wanted to be present at the hanging, that might make him vulnerable. Isabella agreed. Demontaigu could enter her household as a clerk, but he would have to survive the dangers of the hanging day. If Marigny and the others suspected the truth, if they, like Sandewic, began to believe the assassin was not the idiot he pretended, the Secreti and the Noctales would swarm like ants.

The next day I left the Tower, again accompanied by the Welsh captain, now accustomed to such duties. He gave me all the gossip. Apparently Isabella had sent the prisoner a crucifix the previous evening. Early that morning a summary court comprising of Sandewic, Casales and Baquelle had been appointed by the king as justices exercising the full powers of Oyer and Terminer. The court had sat in St Peter's ad Vincula but the prisoner had refused to plead; he'd gibbered and moaned before starting his wild dance. He did not deny the attempt on Marigny so he was condemned and handed over to Casales for punishment.

As the Welshman and I left, the execution was already underway. The prisoner had been dragged up from the dungeons, stripped of his ragged brown robe and, wearing only a loincloth, securely fastened to a hurdle attached to a carthorse. The poor man was then dragged on his back across the cobbles of the Tower yard, out through the Lion Gate and into the streets towards St Katharine's Wharf. The executioner led the horse, as his assistant, dressed in black, followed behind. A good crowd gathered, the news of the execution being proclaimed by heralds. Marigny and his coterie were present on a specially erected scaffold draped with cloths. They had come to witness retribution. By the time the prisoner reached the gallows he had already paid in full, his back being cruelly shredded and bloodied by the cobbles. Nevertheless, he was shown no mercy, but released and pushed up the gallows steps, a filthy, bent figure still pretending to be mad.

I scrutinised the crowd. I could not see Demontaigu, but I glimpsed the tap boy from the Prospect, and around him hooded figures. Casales, his injured arm dangling by his side, was supervising the grisly business of the execution, standing at the foot of the scaffold shouting orders up at the executioner now bestriding the gallows' arms. I glanced across at the royal enclosure. Gaveston had joined Marigny and was leaning against the rail watching proceedings intently. The prisoner reached the top of the ladder and half turned to gaze out over the crowd. The hangman fitted the noose around his neck. Casales made a sign, a roll of drums and a blare of trumpets created an expectant silence. This was when the condemned man could shout his last words. Casales bellowed that the prisoner was witless, and was about to give the sign for another drum roll and the removal of the ladder when the prisoner raised his head and, leaning against the scaffold, hands bound behind him, shouted out:

'Good citizens!'

Casales, surprised, stepped back.

'Good citizens,' the prisoner repeated.

I glanced around; a pole with a crucifix lashed to it was being lifted up into the air and a strong voice intoned:

'We adore thee, Oh Christ, and we praise thee.'

The reply from the prisoner was equally lucid:

'Because by thy Holy Cross you have redeemed the world.'

The exchange took the onlookers by surprise.

'Brothers,' the prisoner shouted, 'can I have absolution?' He immediately began to recite an Act of Contrition, whilst from the crowd echoed that clear, strong voice I'd come to know and love, ringing back the words of absolution.

'*Absolvo te a peccatis tuis in nomine Patris, et Filii et Spiritus Sancti*' – I absolve you from your sins in the name of the Father . . .

Casales, now beside himself with curiosity, walked away from the foot of the ladder; a soldier handed him a crossbow, already primed. Marigny and his party, equally startled, were staring out across the sea of faces whose mood, fickle as ever, had turned in a wave of sympathy for the prisoner. Casales recovered himself. I watched the soldiers milling around the scaffold; memories pricked my soul only to swirl away in the excitement and fear brimming in my heart. Gaston was making his final confession, the Consolamentum, whilst absolution was being cried back across the crowd. Casales, God be thanked, at least waited for that to finish. He then made the sign; the executioner's assistant quickly moved the ladder and the prisoner began his macabre dance, twisting and turning on the end of the rope, hideous to watch.

Suddenly the tap boy I'd glimpsed in the tavern came hurtling out of the crowd; the soldiers were facing the other way, and no one stopped him as he leapt on to the prisoner's legs, pulling him down. The soldiers went to drag him off, but the crowd roared: 'Let him be! Let him be!'

The soldiers stepped back, and Casales shouted an order to leave the boy alone. Even from where I stood I heard the final gasps as the prisoner hung motionless whilst the boy raced away to be lost in the crowd. I immediately returned to the Tower and reported all to my mistress.

'He deserved a better death,' she commented and filled two goblets with fresh apple juice. She sipped from hers swaying from side to side as if listening to some distant music. 'Soon, Mathilde, we shall be away from here. I shall be queen and the storm will gather.' She saluted me with her cup. 'My father's secret desires, and my husband's, will reveal themselves in all their sinister colours. Only then, Mathilde, can we join the dance, but for the moment . . .' she sighed and, chewing her lip, stared hard at me, 'we'll act like young ladies all overcome by what is happening.'

We acted that role during those busy days, with clerks and clerics rehearsing the coronation ceremony and describing the 'Ordo' from the *Liber Regalis*. Isabella was also organising her household. Once crowned, she would move to Westminster Palace and assume all the status, duties and honours of Edward's queen even though the future was uncertain, as the rumours seeping in from the city were highly unpleasant. The great earls were now meeting openly at tournaments, reiterating their demands that a parliament be called, Gaveston be exiled and the king 'take true counsel' from those born to give it. The French added to these demands; broadsheets and letters dictated by Marigny, still furious at the assassination attempt, were nailed to church doors and the Great Cross in St Paul's churchyard. These documents proclaimed that anyone who supported Gaveston would be Philip of France's mortal enemy. The leading bishops intervened to mediate and arrange a 'love day' so that Edward and his earls could meet at St Paul's to discuss and resolve their mutual grievances in a sealed pact before the coronation.

Edward rejected all these approaches. He issued writs under the privy seal from his chancery room in the Tower declaring any such meetings hostile to him, treasonable and a threat to his rights; he ordered the great earls to disperse their retinues and not bring them within five miles of the bars and city gates of London. At the same time more royal troops arrived, swelling the garrison at the Tower – so many they had to camp out on the lonely wastelands to the north. Battle barges patrolled the river and cogs fitted with all the armour of war gathered in the mouth of the Thames. Meanwhile Edward and Gaveston feasted in the Tower, or went hunting in the forests and woods around. They openly ignored Isabella, though both men sent her secret messages and tokens of their love on almost a daily basis.

Casales brought us the news. He paced up and down the queen's chamber nursing his mangled wrist, describing the growing crisis with increasing foreboding. Rossaleti, now so quiet and reserved, would sit at the chancery desk nodding in solemn agreement. Isabella remained unperturbed. She reminded me of a cat, watching and listening attentively. She was waiting for that turn of the sea, the opening which would allow her, as she put it, the opportunity to test her claws. I was equally determined, just as resolute.

Old Sandewic continued to watch me carefully. The cold weather and onerous duties weakened his health. I renewed the phials of vervain and other potions to relieve his symptoms, advising caution that he did not take too much. I should have been more prudent about what he actually drank. The constable seemed deeply touched by my care and attention, responding with little gifts. He boasted openly of what he called my prowess in physic. Much to Isabella's amusement, the garrison, its soldiers, servants, wives and families, started to present themselves on a daily basis in the inner ward for help and assistance. Sandewic, God assoil him, opened the stores and provided powders and dried herbs, even dispatching messengers to buy more from the city apothecaries. The ailments were, in the main, mild. I never forgot Uncle Reginald's aphorism, that his patients usually healed themselves despite the best efforts of their physician.

The onset of winter ailments allowed me to observe, treat and learn. I dispensed ver juice for sores in the mouth, ivy juice for inflammation of the nose, pimpernel boiled in wine for the rheums and sweet almonds for earache. There were the usual cuts and scars to clean and treat; fractures to be fixed and contained, poultices applied. I advised on the need to be clean, and when complaints of sickness and looseness of the bowels increased, I examined the meat stores, salted and pickled for the winter, to discover some so soft and putrid they were alive with maggots. Sandewic was furious and the flesher responsible sat in the Tower stocks for a day with the filthy mess he'd sold tied around his neck, the rest being offered to passers-by to throw at him.

More importantly for me, Demontaigu entered Isabella's household, slipping in easily without provoking any suspicions. Petitions had flooded in from many scribes and petty officials, clerks from the halls of Oxford and Cambridge, all seeking placements. Demontaigu was one of these. Armed with false papers, as indeed many applicants must have been, he presented himself before Casales, Sandewic and Rossaleti. He proved himself fluent in English, French, Castilian and Latin. He described himself as a soldier, a scholar who'd studied at Bologna and Ravenna, a Gascon by birth, who had wandered Europe and become proficient in the courtly hand, very skilled in the preparation and sealing of documents, who now wished to seek advancement in the royal service. Since going into hiding Demontaigu had given up using his father's name, hiding behind his mother's so he could mix truth and fable. When he was questioned, he acted respectful and courteous so the recommendation to Isabella to hire him was unreserved, Demontaigu being appointed as a Principal Clerk of the Red Wax in the Office of the Queen's Wardrobe. I felt deeply comforted by his presence. Nevertheless, I acted on Isabella's warning to walk prudently and allow the day-to-day workings of her household to draw him deeper in.

Demontaigu acted the part, being friends to all and allies to none in the petty factions and squabbling for precedence which constantly dominate any great household. When we did meet in some store room to make a tally or supervise the release of goods, we would talk and gossip in whispers. Demontaigu had changed; no longer concerned about his own situation, he seemed more fascinated about what happened to me. *Oh Domine Jesu*

– it was he who prompted me to begin my own journals, written in cipher. I still have these today.

'List,' Demontaigu urged, 'list what happens; they are the symptoms, Mathilde, look for the cause. In the end, all things drain to their logical conclusion; there must be, there will be, a solution to all this.'

I often reflected on that in the days before the coronation. I divided my time between assisting the princess, dispensing medicine and recalling the past. Demontaigu spoke the truth and spurred me into action. The shock and pain of the last few weeks were diminishing. Why should I stand like some pious novice and be attacked, threatened, cowed and bullied by the great ones? I could fight back. Uncle Reginald had been a hard taskmaster; he'd always insisted I keep a book of symptoms.

'Write down,' he'd order, 'everything you observe about an ailment or a herb. Study what you record, reflect, look for a common pattern, and for changes which are not logical. Two things, Mathilde, rule your life: passion and logic. They are not contradictory, they complement each other.' He would stroke my brow. 'I love you, Mathilde, like a daughter, therefore I also want you close. So the first part of my statement is what?'

'Passion, Uncle.'

'Good, and the second?'

'Logic,' I'd smile.

Sweet Mother Mary, even now, years later, the

tears still brim. In that sombre February the ghost of Reginald de Deyncourt came to dominate my soul more and more. Perhaps it was the arrival of Demontaigu, what Isabella called the change in the sea, or perhaps like a swordsman I wanted to step out of the shadows to confront my foes. I returned to my journals, writing down in my cramped cipher everything I could remember: that morning outside the death house, the struggle on the steps in Canterbury and, most importantly, pushing open Monsieur de Vitry's door. I added the petty details of those particular days – what I ate, what I saw – to serve as pricks to my memory. I followed the art of physic, concentrating pre-cisely on what I witnessed, experienced and reflected upon. Time and again I returned to the massacre at de Vitry's mansion. On that day I had killed a man. I was shocked, I had fled, so my soul was agitated. I recalled entering the merchant's house. I fastened on one fact: the main door had been open, off the latch, not bolted. Why? The assassin could have killed and left but, surely, he'd have barred the front door and fled through some window to keep the murders secret as long as possible? Was that it? Did the killer overlook that? Or, and I was growing certain about this, had I forestalled him? Had I entered that house before he could turn the key and draw bolts? Surely a killer would seal the door lest someone come in behind him as I did? In my mind's eye I was standing in the hallway, looking round at the shadowy recesses, the small chambers leading off. Had the assassin been lurking there as I entered? But if so, why had he not attacked me? I asked the same questions of Demontaigu; he too was puzzled.

'Yes, yes,' he'd whisper when we met in some corner of the Castle on the Hoop. 'De Vitry's death lies at the heart of all this mystery. What happened on that day may be the key. So,' he added, 'what would I have done if I'd been the assassin?' He narrowed his eyes. 'I would have locked that door behind me. Yes, Mathilde, that's what I would have done. Why didn't he?'

As it was, I could not meet Demontaigu often. The Tower was a narrow, close place and I did not know whom I could trust. Nevertheless, I was pleased he was a fully indentured clerk of Isabella's household, receiving robes and wages every quarter beginning Easter next. He'd sealed agreements with that plump and vivacious controller, a high-ranking English clerk from the Court of King's Bench, William de Boudon, a man who later played his own important role in the affairs of Isabella, but that is not for now.

De Boudon liked Demontaigu and often used him, so in the Tower I tried to keep my distance. On one thing both Isabella and I had been resolute. Demontaigu was not to strike at Marigny or any of the French party, which would only endanger her and me. Hand on the Gospels, he vowed to obey. Marigny would be left unscathed, though Demontaigu added the ominous phrase 'for as long as he remained in England'.

By the third week of February 1308, the Tower had become the centre of the English court by both day and night, holy days and weekdays, all taken up with the preparations for the coronation. Baquelle scurried backwards and forwards full of his own importance, openly delighted that the king had decided that he and Casales would be Knights of the Sanctuary for the coronation. Both men, clad in full plate armour covered with the royal livery, would stand in especially erected open pavilions at the side of the sanctuary steps during the ceremony. The carpenters, Baquelle assured us excitedly, were already constructing the heavy-beamed pavilions in the transepts of the abbey; these would later be moved and decorated with greenery and winter roses. Baquelle and Casales also acted as Isabella's military escort when Marigny and his coven visited the Tower for formal presentation to the princess. On such occasions, at Isabella's order, I absented myself, as did Demontaigu, though one morning, standing with me on the parapet walk, he pointed out a black-haired, sharp-featured knight in Marigny's retinue.

'Alexander of Lisbon,' he murmured; he turned his back to stare out over the crenellated walls and I gazed down at the Portuguese knight who had become, and would remain, the bane of my beloved's life. Even then, just the way he walked reminded me of a Tower raven, with his jerky, sinister stride, head slightly bent as if searching the ground for something.

Isabella, as usual, received her father's ministers only to quarrel again over the appointment of a physician to her household as well as other sensitive matters.

'He forgets himself,' she declared once Marigny had left. 'This is not the Ile de France. Monsieur de Marigny is beginning to realise the full truth of the phrase "as the father, so the daughter". I heard a curious story,' she continued, 'I've already asked Demontaigu but he cannot help. That Portuguese knight, Alexander of Lisbon? He has licence from my husband to hunt down subjects of the King of France, Templars, hiding in this kingdom. Apparently he has been busy along the south-west coast.'

'And?' I asked.

'Demontaigu said there was a close link between the Templars and the great abbey at Glastonbury, but that none of his brothers would hide there. A Frenchman in those lonely parts, he alleges, would place himself in great danger. So why should Alexander be travelling through such a desolate region in the depth of winter?'

Such remarks had to be ignored with the busy routine of our days. Casales and Baquelle, our constant visitors, brought in cloth of gold and silver, velvets and satins for Isabella to choose from, together with livery, hangings and banners for others in the Tower who would take part in the festivities and ceremonies. At the same time more soldiers arrived, including the Kernia, Irish Kerns, mercenaries loyal to Gaveston whom they worshipped as a great seigneur; these swarmed through the outer wards of the Tower despite Sandewic's strictures. The old constable openly grumbled at their wild ways as well as why the king and his favourite needed such mercenaries. Sandewic's health was certainly failing. I dared not give him further medicines but hoped that once the coronation was past and spring arrived, his health would improve. Sandewic, however, was more concerned about the old bear Woden, who was sickening and refusing his food. Isabella petitioned her husband to have Sandewic released from some of his duties, so a younger man, John de Cromwell, was appointed as lieutenant. The old constable simply became more determined, even spending time supervising the wall paintings in his beloved Chapel of St Peter ad Vincula; he wanted these to be finished before the king left the Tower.

The coronation day approached. Extra seating was erected in Westminster Abbey, triumphal arches in the streets were hung with tapestries and banners whilst the thoroughfares along which the king and queen would pass were cleaned and gravelled. On 23 February, the merchant princes of the city, their barges decked and trimmed with the banners of their mysteries, came up the Thames and joined the king and queen for their coronation rituals in the Chapel of St John the Evangelist. On the morning of the 24th, Edward and Isabella left the fortress for Westminster; a mist-strewn, icicle-hung dawn with lowering leaden clouds and drifting snowflakes. In such bleak weather Isabella glowed like a tongue of flame, dressed in gorgeous robes of gold and silver made from twenty-three yards of precious cloth, all edged and decorated with ermine and overlaid with mother-of-pearl lace. She and I sat in a litter lined with white satin and trimmed with gold damask, drawn by two handsome mules decorated with gleaming harnesses. Above us billowed an exquisitely embroidered canopy of state; alongside marched men-at-arms in livery of scarlet damask.

We left by the Lion Gate and made our ceremonial progress to Westminster. Pageants and displays were staged along the main streets. A tableau of roses and lilies at Gracechurch; near Cornhill a pageant of the virtuous queen; in Cheapside choirs gathered around the beautiful Eleanor Cross to sing Isabella's praises, whilst the city clerk presented her with a purse of a thousand gold marks. Scholars from St Paul's made pretty speeches comparing Isabella to the strong and virtuous women from the Bible. Everywhere the brilliantly coloured crowd gaped and cheered from balconies, windows and doorways, all festooned with cloths, mantles and standards displaying every device and colour.

At Temple Bar the city council formally bade us

farewell. We proceeded along the Royal Way into the precincts of Westminster, a small city in itself with its mansions, stone houses and thatched cottages. Here lived legions of carpenters, coopers, blacksmiths, whitesmiths, jewellers, armourers, bakers and fleshers, as well as those who served in the various departments of the royal household: pantry, buttery, spices, chandlery, wardrobe and kitchen. As in the city, the streets and houses were hung with crimson and scarlet cloth. Along its winding lanes and streets were more staged pageants, allegories and mysteries about fair maidens and giants, angels and devils. Trestle tables groaned with food whilst the conduits splashed out red and white wine. We journeyed into the inner bailey of the palace with its beautiful gabled houses of carved timber, plastered fronts and painted windows, all gleaming with frost and overshadowed by the Great Hall and the soaring glory of St Stephen's Chapel which, at the time, had not yet been finished.

Isabella and I were allocated quarters near the Painted Chamber with its gorgeous fresco telling the story of the Maccabees. Nevertheless, on our arrival that morning, amidst all that swirl of spectacle, trumpets blaring, horns blowing, standards and pennants clustered into a vivid cloud of colour, one memory, almost like a vision, caught my mind. It was as if the dead, the murdered, those souls cast out before their time, congregated about me, whispering at my soul to alert my heart. I was standing in the doorway of the small hall;

across its tiled floor, built against the wall, was a set of stairs, polished to gleaming, stretching up into the darkness. An old porter carrying a coffer on his right shoulder was laboriously climbing up, his left hand holding the wall to keep his balance. Standing in that doorway I felt a shiver of fear, as if the cup of ghosts had spilled out its contents. The scene recalled my entering Monsieur de Vitry's house, its door closing behind me and that servant lying half out of a chamber to my right. The old porter continued up the stairs even as a servant girl hurried down. I glanced around at the alcoves, recesses and corners. I felt as if I was seeing what the assassin had seen in de Vitry's house during those first few heartbeats before he struck, yet I was overlooking something. I became engrossed. Demontaigu pushed by me, hurrying up the stairs with a hanaper of documents. I watched him go.

'Mistress?' Rossaleti, a leather pannier over his shoulders, was staring curiously at me, admiring my gold gown. He lightly touched the veil around my head. 'Mathilde, you look the maiden fair.' I broke from my reverie and thanked him.

Casales came across. We waited for the princess to join us and continued up the stairs where de Boudon and other household officials were waiting to welcome us. A strange candlelit evening followed, with the solemn chanting of vespers and compline by the Black Monk choir at Westminster echoing across the palace grounds; an unsettling evening, of hasty meals and the noise and chatter of excited retainers preparing for the morrow.

The coronation day dawned clear and fair, the bells of the abbey provoking a dramatic response from the nearby belfries of St Stephen's and St Margaret's, all echoing along the fogbound river to be answered by St Paul's and the bells of over a hundred other city churches. We had risen long before dawn, gathering for the solemn vesting in the small hall. Edward, assisted by Gaveston, dressed in scarlet cloth of gold and black leggings but remained shoeless, as did Isabella, clad in her coronation robes beneath a billowing mantle of embroidered silk lined with ermine; on her head a crimson velvet cap adorned with Venetian gold and pearls. To the joyous sound of fife, tambour and dulcimer, Edward and Isabella processed along the coarsely woven blue carpet which stretched from Westminster Hall to the abbey church, walking beneath a brilliant canopy, its staves being borne by Casales, Sandewic (looking grey with exhaustion), Baquelle and one of the barons of the Cinque Ports. I walked behind in sombre dress, keeping to the edge of the carpet along which followed the leading barons of the kingdom: William Marshall bearing the king's gilded spurs; Hereford, the royal sceptre crowned with a cross; Henry of Lancaster, the royal rod surmounted by a dove; and the Earls of Lancaster, Lincoln and Warwick, the three royal swords. Other lords, both spiritual and temporal, followed, then, after a considerable pause,

Gaveston, dressed in gorgeous purple and silver, proud as a peacock, accorded the prestigious honour of being crown-bearer.

At the high altar the king and queen offered a pound of gold in the form of a statue of Edward the Confessor. The choir and sanctuary blazed with the light of hundreds of torches and candles which dazzled in the rich glow of the thickly embroidered tapestries covering walls, pillars, lecterns, chairs and tables. At either side of the steps leading up to the choir and sanctuary stood the great oaken pavilions decorated with embroidered cloths, winter roses and greenery. Casales, his helmet between his feet, stood in the one on the left, Baquelle on the right. They looked out on to an abbey nave packed with visiting dignitaries, the principal ones clustering up the steps to witness the coronation, which was carried through to the blaze of trumpets, heady gusts of incense and the roar of the acclamation 'Fiat, Fiat, Vivat Rex', followed by the antiphon 'Unxerunt Salamonem' – 'They Anointed Solomon'. Bishop Woodlock of Worcester performed the holy unction. The king himself lowered the crowns, first onto his head then on to Isabella's. She acted serenely throughout the proceedings, lips and eyes crinkled in happiness, a faint smile brightening her face, a vision of joy amidst the grim muttering which permeated the coronation. The anger of the earls ran high against the honour and precedence accorded to Gaveston, who not only held the crown

313

but was given the special privilege of fixing one of the royal spurs to the king's buskined foot. Beneath the chanting and the acclamations rose a low chorus of protest from a sea of angry, hot-eyed noblemen whose fingers kept falling to empty scabbards; in other circumstances daggers and swords would have been drawn. Who says the future cannot be predicted by signs and omens? The coronation of Edward II was the herald for the disasters to follow: a day of anger, resentment, jealousy, arrogance and finally murder.

The coronation ended. The royal party and its entourage were processing down the nave when the acclamations and singing were drowned by a violent crash behind us, followed by piercing screams and shouts. The earl marshal signalled us to continue but Isabella caught my eye and indicated that I should go back to investigate the cause of the rising clamour. A great crowd was gathering to the right of the sanctuary steps. Clouds of dust now mingled with the drifting tendrils of candle smoke and incense. Above the crowds I glimpsed a tangle of timbers, twisted greenery and cloths. People were pressing in. A woman, Baquelle's wife, was scream-ing hysterically. Rossaleti summoned men-at-arms to force a way through the dignitaries, black-robed monks and soldiers. Already Casales and Sandewic were pulling at the heavy timbers but there was nothing to be done. The entire wooden pavilion housing Baquelle had splintered and collapsed. Its side-walls had tumbled outwards, and the heavy oaken beams across the top, some two yards above Baquelle's head, had crashed down, crushing the hapless knight in his armour, burying him under their massed weight. Only a hand stuck forlornly out.

Casales, stripped of most of his dress armour, imposed order, telling the men-at-arms to drive away the crowds. He hastily summoned a troop of workmen, who removed the heavy beams. Underneath sprawled Baquelle, his skull crushed, parts of his body armour digging deep into his flesh. The dead knight's head and face were drenched in blood, his finery stained and torn. He was stripped of his armour and laid out on a palliasse brought from the abbey infirmary, a tangled, bruised and bloodied mass of flesh. A priest monk crouched over the corpse, swiftly anointing it, whispering into the dead man's ear the shriving words of absolution. Other brothers tried to console Baquelle's family. The corpse was hastily removed, the abbey emptied. The carpenters and craftsmen, agitated and worried, clustered to discuss what had happened. I glimpsed Demontaigu standing by a pillar, almost hidden in the half-light. He raised a hand and moved away. Rossaleti was asking Casales what had happened, but the knight just shook his head.

'I was standing on guard,' he declared. 'The royal party left the sanctuary. Come!' He included me in his invitation and led us across to his own oak pavilion. In size it was about a yard and half deep, its width was just over two yards and it stood about four yards high. A long rectangle of polished dried oak poles cut in two, it had a narrow cushioned seat at the back, the two sides and back being held most securely by flat wooden slats fastened inside. A master craftsman joined us and explained how the top poles were kept in place by joists reinforced with glue. Casales declared that, once the royal party had passed, Baquelle, exhausted from standing, must have sat down on the seat. He was dressed in plate armour and his weight, leaning against the back, must have caused the top to spring loose and collapse.

Rossaleti had his answer, so he left; Casales was equally impatient to go to seek an audience with the king to inform him of the news. I stayed. I'd glimpsed the suspicion in the master craftsman's eyes as his colleagues had drifted away to whisper in the shadows. I had a few words with the master craftsman then went to pray in the Lady Chapel with its statue of the Virgin Queen holding the Divine Child, beneath that, in a jewelled case, the abbey's great relic, a girdle cord once worn by Christ's mother. I stared at that, half listening to the nave empty. I muttered an Ave but my mind drifted back to Monsieur de Vitry's house. I heard the distant sounds of trumpets from the celebrations in the Great Hall where the feasting had already begun. I ignored them as I recalled that dire day, fleeing from my own killing. My eyes grew heavy.

'Mistress, mistress?' The master craftsman stood in the entrance to the Lady Chapel. I went out to meet him. He handed over a piece of wood. 'An accident,' he muttered. I studied the piece of wood, cut clean from the rest. 'I did that, you see, mistress.' The master craftsman kept out of the light. 'The pavilion was fashioned out of oaken poles split down the middle. The rounded part faced the outside, the smooth and flat for the inside; long poles for the three sides, shorter ones for the top kept in place by joists, sprouting like the protruding fingers of a hand into the prepared spaces.' He explained how the side poles were glued together and reinforced by oaken strips; the ones across the top depended only on the joists and glue as it had been important not to impose too much weight.

'What happened?' I asked.

'Some of the joists at the top must have snapped or slid out. Sir John, God rest him, was a heavy man in plate armour. If he sat down or leaned against the side, that might have weakened the structure. Mistress, those poles across the top are of heavy oak; once loosed, they would drop with all the power of a falling war club.'

'How many joists were there?' I asked. 'Surely there must have been many? What, two on each pole, and there were four or five of those across the top.'

The man just shrugged and looked longingly over his shoulder at his comrades.

'What was the cause?' I asked softly.

'Come and see.' He took me back to the sanctuary steps. I must have been so absorbed with my own thoughts I hadn't heard them lower the second pavilion, the one Casales had used. It now lay face down before the steps. The master craftsman brought a taper.

'They were left over there,' he explained, pointing across to the dark-shrouded transepts, 'until this morning, then carried across here, erected and decorated. We thought it would be safe.'

In the light of the taper I examined the top of the wooden pavilion. Nothing more than half-poles fitted in between the sides and the back. The master craftsman's agitation increased. I grasped the taper, pushing it closer, and gasped in surprise. A gap was evident between the edges of the poles on the two sides as well as the back, wide enough for a knife or thin saw to cut. The glue had also been weakened, some of the joists pulled loose, the gouge marks around the sides clear to see. I whirled round, dropping the taper. The master craftsman glared panic-stricken back.

'We'll say it was an accident,' he mumbled.

'But it wasn't,' I accused. 'When these pavilions were lying down in the transepts someone must have attacked both of them, cutting the glue and sawing through the joist. The light in the transepts is poor. The malefactor must have been working on Casales' when he was disturbed and left, but

Baquelle's was fatally weakened. The joists were cut. After it was raised and decorated, Sir John Baquelle took up his post. He was a large man in heavy armour; he'd move around, lean and sit. The weakened roof eventually snapped and fell in, crushing his skull. Casales was also meant to suffer the same fate.'

'It wasn't us,' the man pleaded. 'It wasn't us! The oak was of the finest, the joist and gaps matching, we cannot be blamed.'

I stared around the gloomy abbey. The candles had guttered; only a few still glowed. The winter's day was drawing in, the darkness gathering; so easy, I reflected, during the days before the coronation, for someone to slip through the gloom with a saw or razor-sharp blade and weaken the roofs of both pavilions. And who would notice? Even when it collapsed, all eyes were on the sanctuary. Both men had apparently been marked down for death. A God-given sign during the king's coronation that all was not well, that the power of heaven did not rest on our prince. Such damage could easily be done in this place of dappled light . . .

'Mathilde, Mathilde!' Casales and Rossaleti, cloaks billowing out, were striding up the nave. Casales described what was happening in the Great Hall; how the coronation banquet had been spoilt by the tragic death of Baquelle, whilst some of the earls had left before the first course had even been served. He stepped into the faint pool of candlelight, Rossaleti like a shadow behind him; both stared down at the wooden pavilion.

'What is the matter, Mathilde?'

I told Casales precisely what I had discovered. The knight examined the pavilion for himself, kicked the side of it and, moving quickly, seized the master craftsman by his jerkin, pulling him close. The man, terrified, spluttered his innocence.

'Let him go,' I declared wearily. 'They did what they were ordered to. They have nothing to do with what killed Baquelle and what could have killed you.'

'I wonder.' Casales released the hapless man, pushing him away. 'I did wonder, just after the king and queen left the sanctuary. I sat down and felt the wood shudder and creak, then I heard the crash as Baquelle's collapsed. How, Mathilde, how?'

'My lord,' the master craftsman was eager to establish his innocence and that of his colleagues, 'we fashioned these pavilions but they were stored in the transepts until this morning. The abbey was open with all the preparations. Look how it is, even now, so dark anyone could have done that damage, for mischief, as an evil jape . . .'

Casales waved him away, staring across at the tangled mess before spinning on his heel and striding back down the nave. He stopped halfway and turned.

'Her grace the queen,' he called, 'says you need not join her. Marigny and the rest are bloated with hate at my lord Gaveston's pre-eminence; she said it's best if you stay . . .'

I did so, returning to our quarters and sleeping fitfully in my clothes until the early hours, when Isabella, accompanied by her ladies, returned heavy-eyed, sick in stomach with muscles aching. I helped her undress. She stood in a shift before the weakening fire, running her hands through her mass of golden hair. I thought she would sleep, but she said her blood was still racing, her mind teeming with the events of the day. She described how the coronation banquet had turned into a mockery, the death of Baquelle hovering like a harbinger from hell over the feast. Matters were worsened by the chaos in the kitchens. Cooks, scullions and servants had been distracted by the disaster so the food had been cold and ill served. The great earls, their pride offended, had glowered and left whilst the French openly complained about the pre-eminence of Gaveston in his purple and silver-buttoned robes, sitting at the king's right in preference to Isabella. Edward had openly cosseted Gaveston, blatantly ignoring Isabella. For the first time I caught her anger and irritation that the great game had gone too far.

As she paced up and down, drinking the watered wine I'd prepared with a heavy mix of camomile, I told her what I had discovered. She agreed that Baquelle's death was no accident, an ominous augury for her coronation. Two more members of Edward's secret council had been threatened and one killed in what could only be described as suspicious circumstances.

Casales had delivered the news to the king and his favourite, leaning over their throne-like chairs, whispering fiercely. Isabella stopped her pacing and, clutching the cup, glared down at me.

'That stopped the revelry, Mathilde. Oh yes, Edward and Gaveston were openly shocked and surprised. Do you know,' she leaned down, 'for the first time I smelt their fear. Think of that, Mathilde, as you dream.'

We slept late that morning. Isabella was preparing to attend another banquet in the Painted Chamber when we were disturbed by furious knocking at the doors and the exclamations and cries of maids and pages in the presence chamber. I hastened out. Demontaigu was pushing his way through, hair and face soaked with the snow which still clung to its cloak.

'Mathilde,' he wiped the wet from his face, 'Mathilde, it's Sandewic, he's ill, he is dying!'

I did not stop for anything but dressed quickly. Shrouding myself in a thick robe and carrying a copy of Isabella's seal, I followed Demontaigu out through the snow-frosted palace grounds to King Steps and the waiting barge flying Sandewic's colours. A clay-cold journey under lowering skies, along a swollen, sullen river with a wintry wind nipping the flesh. I huddled in the stern with the boatmen bending over the oars, sombre figures taking us through the shifting mist. Once we passed under the narrow arches of London Bridge, the waters thundering dully, Demontaigu told me how he'd gone to the Tower to collect and pack certain items. Apparently Sandewic had returned early from the coronation, clearly unwell, and had worsened during the night.

We arrived at the mist-wrapped Tower, hurrying up steps, along gulleys, through gateways dark as a wolf's mouth to the constable's quarters in the central donjon. A small outer chamber led into the inner one, a place of disarray with chests and coffers open, weapons, cloaks, belts and baldrics lying about. Braziers glowed but their scented smell could not disguise the reek of a deadly sickness. Servants milled about. A friar from the Carmelites was already praying by the bed whilst the Tower leech, a balding, grey-faced man, could do nothing except pucker his lips, shake his head and flap his hands.

Sandewic lay on the great bed, head against the bolsters. He already had the look of a dead man. I noticed how the little gifts I had given him over the last few weeks were in places of honour around the small crucifix on the table to the right of his bed. The table on the other side was covered with the small glazed phials and pots I'd used for his medicines. I was immediately surprised at how many there were. Sandewic recognised me, those old eyes still glaring furiously as if he could face down death itself. He spoke slowly, his breath coming haltingly. He talked about great pain, of iced water in his flesh; his facial muscles seemed to be stiffening and he muttered how he could not feel his limbs. From him and the leech I gathered the symptoms had begun shortly after he had retired, a tingling burning of the tongue, throat and face, followed by nausea, vomiting and a strange pricking of the skin. He pointed to a goblet by the bed, the cup was almost drained, the rich claret dregs dry. I sniffed at it and detected the acrid smell of a potion. I hurried to the other side of the bed and picked up the various jars, most of them empty. As I searched, I turned cold with my own numbing fear: there were far too many jars! The nearest one, sealed with a blob of broken wax, was half full. I sniffed it, put it back, sat on the edge of the bed, bowed my head and sobbed quietly, shoulders shaking. Sandewic had been poisoned! Wolfsbane, or monkshood, is noxious, highly deadly, especially its roots and leaves. I recognised both the smell and the symptoms. I had treated similar cases in Paris where peasants had eaten the tuberous roots of the plant believing they were radishes.

Sandewic's fingers scrabbled at my back. I returned to the other side of the bed and gently questioned him. I think he knew that he'd been poisoned through trickery. In gasping whispers he informed me of the stoppered, sealed phials delivered to his quarters which he always believed came from me. He never knew who brought them. He confessed wryly that he'd even shared some of the medicines with old Woden the bear. I could only listen in horror as Sandewic described how, on his return the previous evening, he'd received a fresh small leather sack with a phial. He'd mixed its contents with his wine but fallen asleep; when he awoke he drank deeply. Despite the ravages of the poison now sweeping through his frame, those old, tired eyes smiled at me.

'I am ancient, Mathilde,' he whispered, 'my time has come.' He gestured with his hand. 'Take the goblet as a leaving present; it was a gift from the old king to me, silver and pewter with a horseman carved on the side. See that justice is done. Go and pray for me in my chapel.' He paused, fighting for breath. 'Study my Cup of Ghosts, Mathilde, tell *mon seigneur* the king to study it also, to reflect on the past and not put his trust in other princes. Please . . . ?' He forced one more smile. 'I must make my peace with God and man.'

I kissed him gently on the brow and left him to the Carmelite. I fled that chamber, going to sit at the foot of a pillar in the Chapel of St Peter ad Vincula. Turning my face to the wall, I wept bitterly at the cruel and devious way Sandewic had been trapped. Demontaigu joined me, squatting down in the shadows.

'He's gone,' he whispered, 'shriven and consoled. Mathilde, he was an old man.'

'He was my friend,' I replied through hot, stinging tears. 'He trusted me. Some whoreson bastard saw what I was doing and fed him potions which he thought came from me. That's why he kept thanking me. An old man,' I drew up my knees, 'who trusted me and my skill. He always had aches and pains; the assassin recognised this and used the same clay-coloured phials. It was as easy, and as wicked, as poisoning a child.'

I studied a faded wall painting, a scene from the Apocalypse, the Great Dragon sweeping stars from the sky with his horned tail.

'Since Uncle Reginald was taken,' I murmured, 'and butchered, I have watched and waited without the power to respond.' I pointed to the dragon. 'Yet my opponent is like that, sweeping all he wants out of my life, without any pity, without any mercy.'

'Have you closely studied the symptoms of this malaise?'

'Now is not the time for casuistry, Master Bertrand,' I retorted heatedly.

'No.' Demontaigu edged round to face me. 'You talked of power, use yours. Why have all these men died? Pourte, Wenlok, Baquelle, Sandewic?'

'And nearly Casales,' I added. I told Demontaigu what I'd discovered the previous day.

'And what do they all have in common?' he insisted.

'They are members of Edward's secret council.'
'And?'

'They recommended that Edward marry Isabella, that he move against the Templars, that he keep the peace with Philip of France as well as his great earls.'

'So they were of the peace party; what else?'

'Pourte and Baquelle,' I replied, 'were leading merchant princes. They could rouse London, perhaps even control it.'

'And Wenlok?' Demontaigu asked.

'He controlled the powerful Coronation Abbey of Westminster.'

'And Sandewic?'

'The Tower.' I breathed in, feeling a tingling of excitement. 'Whilst Casales is a leading knight of the royal household.'

'Think!' Demontaigu urged. 'Winchelsea of Canterbury is still in exile, Bishop Langton of Coventry and Lichfield lies under house arrest. The king is bereft of good counsel.'

'But what else?' I retorted. 'What else is there?' I rose and walked to the door.

'Think!' Demontaigu repeated. 'Mathilde, reflect.'

I placed my hand on the latch, blinking back my tears.

'Don't worry, Master Bertrand, if I can, I will think, I will plot.'

When I returned to the keep, Sandewic's household were preparing for the lych-wake, the corpse ritual. They answered my questions. According to them Sandewic had, over the previous weeks, entertained both English and French courtiers and officials whilst a whole host of visitors kept coming and going. I asked for a list; Rossaleti was one of these. In truth, he was no different from the rest except for one thing. I had been Isabella's messenger to Sandewic, so why had Rossaleti, a French clerk, Keeper of the Queen's Seal, often visited the constable's chambers?

CHAPTER 12

Take Vengeance on them, O God of
Vengeance!

'*A Song of the Times*', 1272–1307

Later in the morning, as the bells of St Peter
ad Vincula tolled for the Angelus, Casales
arrived swathed in a heavy cloak. He'd
come on the orders of the king to see the situation for himself. He viewed Sandewic's corpse,
stared gloomily at me and went out on to the steps
overlooking the inner bailey.

'Another death,' he glanced over his shoulder,
'Baquelle, Sandewic.' He came and towered over
me, nursing his maimed arm. 'Was I also meant
to die?'

'Rossaleti,' I demanded, 'have you seen him?'

'Was I too meant to die?' he repeated.

'Sir John,' I shook my head, 'I do not know.'

'Well, to answer your question, I haven't seen
Rossaleti, and there's the mystery, Mathilde.
Westminster still sleeps but a French cog of war has

arrived in the Thames and berthed at Queenshithe. It has come to collect Marigny and his coven. I'll be glad to see the back of those. But as for Rossaleti,' he swaggered down the steps, 'I too am looking for him. I've certain questions I want to ask.'

I watched him go, then visited the Chapel of St Peter ad Vincula. Its door was off the latch as the artist, who introduced himself as the painter of the Great Wonder at St Camillus Hospital on the Canterbury to Maidstone road, was busy finishing the last outlined charcoal sketches on the far wall. He was a veritable squirrel of a man with his popping black eyes and bulging cheeks under a shiny, balding pate. I apologised for not having yet seen the Great Wonder on the Maidstone road but exclaimed with admiration at the wall paintings in St Peter's.

'Poor Sir Ralph.' The author of the Great Wonder shook his head. 'He wanted to see this finished.'

I gently coaxed to him to explain the fresco, executed in an eye-catching red, brown, green and gold. As he did, I understood Sandewic's absorption with this chapel, its stark sanctuary and brooding atmosphere. Sandewic was an old man who had lived during the reigns of King Edward's father and grandfather; a man who must have also heard first hand about the troubles of King John, Edward's great-grandfather. Time and again he had witnessed civil war rage in England between king and earls. More importantly, he knew about the French royal house dabbling their swords in the blood of his country. The frescos in St Peter ad Vincula depicted in great detail the events of 1225, eighty years previous, when Prince Louis of France invaded England in an attempt to usurp the throne of the young King Henry III. Louis had sailed up the Thames and actually occupied the Tower, setting up court and even proclaiming himself 'Louis, by the Grace of God, King of England'. The frescos explained all this, as well as the bitter struggle which ensued. The author of the Great Wonder on the Maidstone road described how Sandewic had learnt all this from the *Flores Historarum* – The Flowers of History – the great chronicle at Westminster.

I studied those paintings carefully. Little wonder St Peter ad Vincula was Sandewic's 'Cup of Ghosts'. It held images not only of the past but also of a possible future. I was still deep in conversation with the author of the Great Wonder when Demontaigu entered the chapel, beckoning me over.

'Rossaleti,' he whispered. 'He's been found dead, his corpse dragged from the Thames. Casales sent a nuncius from Westminster; he believes Rossaleti was trying to reach the French cog of war.'

We left immediately and took a royal barge rowed by master oarsmen; these easily negotiated the rushing terrors between the arches of London Bridge, pulling swiftly through the chilly mist. We berthed at the King's Steps and hurried up across the palace ground, still held fast in a hard hoar frost.

Bells tolled and clanged. Monks flitted like ghosts along paths and corridors. Royal servitors hurried out of doors eager to complete tasks so they could return to the roaring fires within. We learnt that Rossaleti's corpse, because of the celebrations in the palace, had been removed to the death table in the mortuary chapel. Accompanied by Demontaigu, I hurried across the abbey precincts, through the chilly cloisters and down past the chapter house, its statues, carvings and gargoyles glaring stonily down at me. Flambeaux fixed on holders provided light. As I passed the heavy door of the pyx chamber, I noticed what looked like a dirty cloth pinned against it.

'What is that?' I approached and touched the leathery strips.

'Human skin.'

I whirled round. The monk had his face hidden deep in his cowl, the light only catching his sharp nose and bloodless lips.

'I am sorry.' He came forward. 'I'm Brother Stephen, the infirmarian. That,' he pointed to the door, 'is human skin. Richard de Puddlicott's to be precise. He tried to rob the king's treasure,' the infirmarian jabbed a finger at the paving stones, 'held in the crypt below. He was captured, taken out in a wheelbarrow to the gallows in Tothill Lane, hanged and skinned.' He smiled. '*Sic transit gloria mundi* – thus passes the way of the world. Can I help you?'

I explained about Rossaleti. The monk nodded

and took us into the infirmary. Rossaleti's corpse was laid out on a table in the mortuary chapel beyond, a bleak, ill-lit room. The infirmarian lit the purple corpse candles in their black iron spigots around the table and pulled back the sheet. Rossaleti had been stripped naked, washed, oiled and anointed, but the cadaver still reeked of the slime of the river, his soaked black hair fanning out, his olive skin a liverish grey, eyes half open, despite the resurrection coins placed there. I said a prayer for his soul, then examined his corpse.

'There's no mark or bruise,' the monk declared, his voice echoing harshly. 'None whatsoever.'

'Any sign of a potion or philtre?'

'No trace of poison,' the infirmarian replied, 'nothing but the stench of the river and the faint, sweet smell of wine. It appears he took a barge from Westminster.' The monk shrugged. 'He suffered an accident.'

'I am trying to find the boatman.'

I turned round. Casales stood in the doorway. He strode across.

'I've been down to the King's Steps.' He nodded at the corpse. 'A fisherman found him floating in the river, bobbing like a black feather on its surface. Apparently a wherryman is also missing.' Casales widened his redrimmed eyes. 'An accident,' he muttered. 'God knows!'

'But he feared the river.'

'I know,' Casales sighed, 'but not enough to stop

him trying to reach that French cog on a fogbound day.' He rubbed his face.

'Rossaleti was not a member of the secret council?' I asked.

'True, and I know what you're thinking, Mathilde,' Casales glanced narrow-eyed at me, 'but I believe it was an accident.'

'The queen,' I emphasised the word, 'will want to know why he was going there; after all, he was her seal holder.'

'Madam,' Casales made a mock bow, 'I will inform her grace as soon as I discover that myself.'

He left shortly afterwards. Demontaigu murmured that he did not wish to be seen too much with me and followed. I wandered back across the frost-coated grounds into the palace. I returned to the entrance of the small hall where I had stood when I first arrived at Westminster and recalled so vividly my entering de Vitry's house. I opened the door, went in and stood for a while, pretending that this was Monsieur de Vitry's home. I was the assassin, I had a crossbow. A servant walked in front of me, another was coming out from a chamber to my right, a maid was tripping down the stairs. None of them had realised murder had arrived. I pretended to loose one bolt; the servant in front went down. The man to my right was staring; he too was killed, yet that maid coming downstairs? She must have heard, why didn't she turn and run? I recalled her corpse lying at the foot of the stairs. The assassin could not act that fast. I closed my eyes as I realised the hideous mistake I'd made. I'd ignored a rule, repeated to me time and again: Never remove causes, any cause; let them remove themselves. I was so surprised I slid down the wall and crouched, arms crossed staring into the darkness.

Eventually I left and returned to the abbey. Brother Leo, in charge of the library and scriptorium, was intrigued by my request but, having glimpsed Isabella's seal, he quickly agreed. He took me to what he called his holy of holies, the great library of the abbey with its painted windows, gleaming shelves, tables, benches and lecterns. He showed me his store room of precious manuscripts and books, all carefully annotated and shelved, the most precious being chained or locked behind closed grilles. The sweet perfume of ink, pumice stone, parchment, leather and vellum hung like incense in a church; the capped candles and sealed lantern horns burning like tapers in this shrine of scholarship.

Brother Leo ushered me to sit at one table, bringing me a leather writing case with inkwells, pen-quills and parchment. So I began again, writing out a clearly defined list of all that had happened. I worked past vespers and compline, the muffled bells announcing the hours, the plainchant of the monks with their awesome phrases ringing through the air. *You have made the earth quake and torn it open, will you utterly reject us, Oh God? Give us help against our foes.* Such words found a home in my own heart. I prayed to the spirits of the dead who, now summoned, seemed to congregate around me.

Eventually I grew so heavy-eyed Brother Leo had to wake me. I gathered up my parchments and returned to the queen. She was entertaining the young pages at dice; as soon as I entered, she dismissed them. I bolted the heavy door and sat down on a footstool beside her. I was tired but I told her about Rossaleti's death, and as the hour candle burnt another ring, I went back to the beginning. Isabella listened intently, only betraying her own surprise by a sharp hiss of breath or her doubts by questions as precise as from any serjeant of the coif. Afterwards she rose and, leaning on my shoulder, bent down and kissed me on the top of my head. She stood for a while by the window humming softly the tune of the 'Exulte Regina', a hymn chanted during her coronation.

'My husband,' she declared, not moving, 'slept this afternoon. He is now closeted with my lord Gaveston. Come, Mathilde, let's strike at the root of all this.' She smiled, blinking her eyelids in mockery. 'We shall show that Morgana Fey is not just a figment of the troubadours' imagination.'

Isabella and I shared a cup of wine, took our cloaks and arranged for some of the pages to escort us. We left for the king's chamber. We found Edward and Gaveston, dressed in loose attire, belts and boots on the floor, poring over maps on a large chancery table. Edward slouched in a large chair; Gaveston sat facing him. The queen instructed me to follow her in whatever she did, and as soon as she entered the chamber, its door closing behind us, she pushed back her hood and knelt down, bowing her head to the ground. Edward and Gaveston sprang to their feet. The king moved towards her but Isabella stretched out her hands.

'My lords, I beg you, listen to me. Let me take any oath you wish on the pyx holding Christ's blessed body or the sacred book of the Gospels.'

'My lady, what is this?'

'We have reflected on the deaths of Baquelle, Sandewic and Rossaleti.'

Her answer provoked a response. Edward and Gaveston looked agitated and worried.

'Listen, my lords,' Isabella urged. 'Listen well to Mathilde.' She turned and pointed at me. 'Tell them.'

I repeated word for word everything I'd told the queen. I spoke direct. At first both men pulled faces and shook their heads, but my sentences, like arrows, were loosed in a hail. I did not describe the villainy in detail but, having stated my hypothesis, moved ruthlessly to its logical conclusion. Edward, slightly pale-faced, sat back in his chair, gesturing that Isabella too should take her place. The queen, however, shook her head. I continued. Gaveston interrupted me with a spate of questions which I answered. Once I'd finished, Isabella again stretched out her hands.

'*Mon seigneur*, my husband, please listen to me.

I have played your game but now it is ended. I beg you, my lord, to tell me the truth. Tell me you had no hand in the deaths of these men, Pourte and the rest.'

'Of course not!' Edward shouted, banging the table. 'They were, despite their opposition to my lord here, loyal and faithful subjects.' He took a deep breath. 'At first I thought they were mishaps, but Sandewic, Baquelle . . .' He shook his head. 'Secretly in my heart I blamed the great earls.'

'Listen, *mon seigneur*,' Isabella moved swiftly on, 'I beg you. I will take an oath on whatever sacred thing you wish. I speak the truth, I am giving you wise counsel. I may be ignored because of my tender years, my inexperience, but, as *le bon seigneur* is my witness, on one thing I will not be moved.' Isabella's voice grew hard. 'I know my father. Please, I beg you, whatever he has secretly promised on oath, whatever vow he has sworn, whatever hidden design he nurtures, do not, I beg you on my knees, believe him. Tell me, my Lord, as I love you, what he has said to you in hidden corners, in letters dispatched under the secret seal, by word of mouth through Marigny and the other Secreti.' Isabella paused. 'I assure you, my lord, whatever he has promised are lies set to trap you, to bring you and the Lord Gaveston to total destruction.'

'My lord Gaveston,' I turned to the favourite, 'you visited Paris secretly. You met Monsieur de Vitry. You now have his painting of St Agnes.' I paused.

'You travelled around the time the Templars were arrested. Monsieur de Vitry made a reference to a visitor, so, on reflection, it must have been someone important. You, *mon seigneur*, joked about Dover being an ideal place to slip out of our kingdom.'

'Yes, yes.' Gaveston was no longer the popinjay, but hard-eyed, even fearful. 'I visited de Vitry to receive monies disbursed by King Philip; it had to be done that way. I saw the painting. Monsieur de Vitry gave it to me as a gift.'

Edward rose to his feet. He paced up and down, gathering his thoughts.

'For a hundred years,' he began, 'the great earls have fought against my family, our line of honoured kings. My great-grandfather was pursued the length and breadth of the kingdom, losing his treasure in the Wash. My grandfather Henry faced civil war, capture, imprisonment; even my father, the great warrior,' Edward could not keep the sarcasm from his voice, 'was brought to heel with this or that, forced to sign this charter, that charter, making promises, conceding his rights. Parliament and councils, rebellious churchmen and great earls forced him to go cap in hand to beg for money as his treasure chests held nothing but cobwebs.' Edward sat back in his chair. 'Your marriage alliance, my lady, offered another way. Last summer, as you know, my father forced Lord Gaveston into exile. He went to France and was welcomed by King Philip, who pointed out that my illustrious father would not live for ever. Philip promised that if I married you, he would help me crush once and for all any opposition in England. My father died in July last year. Months later, Lord Gaveston returned secretly to France to continue our negotiations. That is when Monsieur de Vitry gave him the painting. Philip offered military assistance; he would finance this with the wealth seized from the Templars.'

I sat back on my heels, nodding in agreement. I recalled de Vitry wishing me to be gone because he expected another guest. Little wonder he was so agitated, torn between me and the machinations of princes.

'The Enterprise of England?' I asked. '*Mon seigneur*,' I held up my hand, 'I do apologise.'

'Don't apologise, Mathilde. Would that change anything? Yes, the Enterprise of England, the true reason why Philip attacked the Templars: he needed their wealth. After Lord Gaveston returned to Paris last December, our secret treaty was confirmed. I would marry Isabella. Our oldest son would be called Louis; our second son would be given Gascony but under complete French suzerainty. Philip would help me crush opposition here and in Scotland. We would make a permanent peace alliance. His enemies would be mine. Above all,' Edward picked up his goblet of wine and drank, 'there would be no opposition here.'

'Of course,' Gaveston intervened, '*mon seigneur* would act differently in public, opposing Philip in everything as long as he could.'

'And me?' Isabella asked.

'Your grace,' Gaveston bowed, 'and I wish you would sit, you are part of the pretence even if you didn't know the true cause. Once spring comes Philip will move.'

'So that's the real reason,' I asked, 'for the great game? You were misleading your earls with a show of insults to your wife, her relatives and the power of France. A cat's-paw,' I continued, 'as you secretly prepared their destruction?'

Gaveston nodded.

'Your enmity to France,' I continued, 'was false. You misled your earls who might make the mistake of conspiring with Philip. You'd learn of their plans as well as collect evidence of their treason.'

Edward and Gaveston smiled like gamblers conceding a game of hazard.

'You asked us to cooperate, thinking we were hurting Philip, but all the time Philip knew the truth, be it about your treatment of his daughter or the giving of her wedding presents to Gaveston.'

'Are you so intent on provoking your great lords?' Isabella asked.

'Of course.' Edward gestured to a chair. 'My lady, please!'

Isabella remained resolute. 'And the deaths of Pourte and the others?' she asked.

'At first,' Edward replied slowly, 'we considered they were mishaps, or even the work of our enemies here in England, but—'

'We thought,' Gaveston interrupted, 'Pourte and Baquelle could deliver London for us, Sandewic the Tower, Wenlok Westminster. So we suspected they were removed by the great earls.'

'My lord, you are correct, but there are other reasons.' Isabella rose and moved to the chair close to her husband, gesturing that I sit next to her. 'My lord, you are now bereft of wise councillors, men of the peace party who might control this and that but might also advise you to pursue a middle way, peace with both Philip and your earls.' She paused. 'That is why my father removed those men. Please, I beg you.' Isabella joined her hands. 'Philip is behind their deaths, as is Marigny. They will invade this country, they are already far gone in their preparations. My father may well destroy your earls, but he will also destroy you once I have given birth to a son. You will die and Philip, in my name, will establish a regency whilst his troops overrun Gascony and any other territory the English crown holds in France. My father's spies are already swarming here. Alexander of Lisbon, leader of the Noctales, hunter of the Templars? He's been busy in the West Country spying out castles, ports, harbours. Once the invasion begins, you will not control it. My father will dictate the terms.'

'*Mon seigneur,*' I spoke up now, certain that we were right, 'you say Philip played the great game, yet we witnessed his fury at being frustrated, even if it was only a matter of pretence. The true cause of such fury was his impatience to destroy your power once and for all.'

342

'He would not . . .' Edward paused at the look on Isabella's face.

'My lord,' she insisted, 'he will! I can bring you proof that Mathilde speaks the truth.'

Edward bowed his head; his favourite leaned across, whispering hoarsely to him. The king nodded, rose and crossed to a side table. He grasped a piece of parchment and a quill pen and wrote a few lines, sealing it with his own signet. He came, stood beside me and laid the document on the table.

'*A littera plenae potestatis.*' The king pressed his mouth against my ear. 'A letter of full power. Mathilde, what you do for the good of the prince has full force of law. Bring me the final proof. You started this hunt; be in at the kill!'

I arrived at the Tower early next morning; the sky was cloud free, the stars glinting like icicles. I didn't travel by barge because of the stiff winter breeze. I was collected secretly from Westminster by Owain Ap Ythel and a troop of mounted archers. The Welshman wanted to talk about Sandewic. I let him chatter as we made our journey through deserted streets, the nightwalkers and rifflers fleeing at our approach, the watch drawing aside to let us pass. An eerie journey, winding our way along runnels; it was like travelling across a city of the dead, the blackness all around us broken by a solitary flaring torch, a winking lantern or the glow of candlelight through mullioned glass or the chink of a shutter. Now and again a dog howled, to be answered by others, or a voice shouted, clear and carrying, followed by the strident cry of a child. I slouched in the saddle of the gentle cob Ap Ythel had brought, reflecting on what had happened the previous evening, what I'd planned for that day. I glanced up to the sky and vowed that before darkness fell again, the assassin would be dead and the power of Philip frustrated.

We arrived at the Tower. I attended morning mass in St Peter ad Vincula. Sandewic's corpse, shrouded and coffined, lay on trestles under a black and gold pall surrounded by six purple funeral candles. The coffin stood just before the entrance to the sanctuary. It would remain there until moved down to Grey Friars for burial opposite Newgate Prison, where Sandewic, as justice, had so often held court. I said goodbye to Sandewic on that cold day so many, many years ago. Now, as I've come to Grey Friars I often visit his tomb in the good brothers' church, but his spirit has long gone. On that February day, however, it was fitting that Sandewic's corpse lie there; the soul does linger on and he could witness judgement pronounced, vengeance for his murder carried out. The priest chanted the refrains of the funeral mass. I listened particularly to the reading from the Book of Job: 'I know that my avenger lives and he, the Last, will take his stand on earth.' I suppose the Angel of Vengeance can appear in many forms, even as a young woman skilled in herbs.

After the mass I broke my fast with Ap Ythel. I

showed him the king's letter and instructed him closely on what was about to happen. He blinked in surprise but agreed. Once my visitors had arrived, the Chapel of St Peter was to be ringed with bowmen, but only at my sign were they to intervene. After I'd eaten, I returned to St Peter's and stood warming my hands over the brazier. The chapel door opened and Demontaigu walked in.

'Mathilde, good morrow, what is this?'

I went down to greet him, even as the Tower bell sounded the hour.

'Do what I ask,' I pleaded. 'You have to trust me, I have the king's authority.' I pointed behind him. 'Stay near the door on the keeper's stool; behind the woollen arras you'll find a crossbow, a pouch of bolts and a war-belt.'

I heard the clatter of the latch and Sir John Casales strode into the church.

'Mathilde, you asked to see me? The hour's so early.'

'Sir John, I have waited for you. Please draw the bolts.'

He did so, took off his cloak, threw it over the keeper's stool, nodded at Demontaigu and followed me up the nave, past Sandewic's coffin and into the sanctuary. Ap Ythel had moved two chairs to face each other. He had also placed Sandewic's cup beside my phials and a jug of claret on the nearby offertory table. Demontaigu locked the door, face tight and poised. He moved Casales' cloak and sat down, fishing behind the arras for the weapons. I gestured at Casales to sit. He did so, his hard lined face impassive though his eyes kept moving to Sandewic's coffin.

'You said it was important?'

'It is, Sir John. This is the day you'll die.'

Casales' good hand went to the war-belt he'd thrown on to the floor beside him.

'Don't!' I warned. 'Demontaigu is a soldier. He has an arbalest, sword and dagger, the door is bolted and outside bowmen wait, arrows notched.'

Casales withdrew his hand.

'Sir John Casales,' I pointed, 'I impeach you as a traitor, an assassin, and a Judas man through and through. You are Philip of France's creature. No, listen please. You killed Simon de Vitry.'

'I . . .'

'You killed him,' I insisted, 'the first day you arrived in Paris. You and your accomplice Rossaleti.'

'This is—'

'Of course, it is the truth. By sheer chance I visited de Vitry's house on that same day, possibly only a short while after the massacre had finished. I made a mistake. I imagined one assassin, with two or three small arbalests and different quarrels, coming through that door; but of course, I was wrong.'

'De Vitry hardly knew me.'

'He knew Rossaleti, a royal French clerk, a member of the Secreti. As I said, I made a mistake. There were two assassins, Rossaleti and you! The Frenchman demanded entrance. The servant who opened the door agreed. He turned and walked ahead of you. Rossaleti killed him with a concealed crossbow, as well as the servant coming out of a chamber to his right. However, a maid appeared at the top of the stairs. You hastened ahead. You may have lost one hand, Casales, but you're proficient enough. You loosed a quarrel, the maid was struck; blood spouting, she staggered. You caught her corpse and lowered it to tumble down the stairs. However, your left hand was splashed with her blood. You continued up, but because of your injury you couldn't grasp the balustrade along such steep steps, so you leaned against the wall and stained the plaster with a dash of blood. I thought that was strange, so high on the wall without any other stains, but, logically, that's how you always climb stairs. I realised that the other day watching a porter, his right hand holding a coffer, making his way up steps holding on to the wall with his left.

'Anyway, you reached the gallery. De Vitry, still dressed in his nightshift, came out of his chamber. He was half asleep and was killed immediately. Despite your maimed wrist, Casales, you're a veteran soldier, cold and severe. You primed both arbalests and proceeded swiftly to other killings. Meanwhile downstairs, Rossaleti, no warrior, stood by the door. He had not locked or bolted it lest someone come, be refused entrance and so raise the hue and cry. You agreed that with him. I entered; Rossaleti hid. I was shocked. I wandered through

347

that hallway and climbed the stairs. You heard me coming and also hid. To you and Rossaleti I was a stranger, a simple maid, but I was also alerted. Rossaleti might not find me easy to kill, nor would you. I might escape, run out of the house, raise the alarm, so you let me leave. All you were concerned about was slipping away as swiftly as possible lest I return with the provost.'

Casales was breathing heavily. He leaned forward, soulless eyes studying me.

'You may have been surprised,' I continued, 'that I didn't raise the alarm. I can only imagine your astonishment when you discovered who I really was, but by then it was too late. I enjoyed Isabella's patronage and protection. You and Rossaleti tried to frighten me off outside the death house after I viewed Pourte's corpse. You dared not kill me. Philip wished to keep his precious daughter mollified. You told Marigny; he must have searched de Vitry's manuscripts and discovered my true identity. By then it was too late. I was protected by the princess, so they appointed Pelet to her household to watch both her and me.'

'You murdered him?'

'Not I, lord.'

'The princess!' Casales gasped. 'I . . .'

'Her father's true daughter, as Marigny discovered when he tried to question me. If her grace had not been so protective I would have never have left France. As it was, you and Rossaleti attacked me on the steps of the infirmary at St Augustine's Priory.'

'We were—'

'No, it was a winter's night in a gloomy priory. You were two figures dressed in black robes, flitting like bats through the shadows. You used that lay brother, the simpleton. Rossaleti acted the Benedictine and, to confuse matters, grasped the poor man's hands. Why should he do that? Well, such simpletons remember touch; he talked of two hands, of their skin being coarse, which meant it could be neither you nor Rossaleti.'

'And?'

'Why, Sir John, if you could throw a piece of sacking over me, Rossaleti could use something similar to roughen his hands. You carried out that attack. You were there, Sir John. The feasting at the Chequer of Hope was busy, people coming and going, whilst the distance between the tavern and priory is only a short walk. If you had had your way I would have died then; as it was, I was rescued by Demontaigu.' I smiled at his surprise. 'Oh yes, more than one assassin was in the priory that night. During the attack I was pulled and tugged as if two people were forcing me towards the top of those steps. Indeed there were two, you and Rossaleti.'

'It was Rossaleti . . .'

'He cannot answer. He's dead, Sir John, because you murdered him. He didn't take a barge or a boat; he was terrified of the water. You asked to meet him somewhere along that night-shrouded, fogbound Westminster quayside. He'd come down near the water to meet a man he trusted. You acted as swiftly as a plunging hawk or a striking snake, pushing him into the river. The shock alone would have killed him, a short struggle in the freezing water. He lost his life as he had lost his soul.'

'If he was my accomplice, why should I kill him?'

'Because you're an assassin. God knows, Rossaleti may not have had your midnight soul; perhaps he regretted what he'd done. Maybe the dead came back to haunt him. Rossaleti rather liked me. I caught a sadness in his gaze. He may have begun to have scruples. In your eyes, however, he was weak and could not be trusted. He was the only member of the English court who knew the full truth; you judged him and you carried out sentence. Your sinister masters back in Paris would accept that. A few scruples could not be allowed to endanger you or, more importantly, their enterprise.'

Casales rose to his feet, stretched and glanced down the nave. Demontaigu stood, the arbalest primed. From outside came the clash of weapons and a low murmur from the bowmen Ap Ythel was deploying.

'Why should I kill de Vitry?'

'Oh, he knew too much about everything and Philip had good reason not to trust him. De Vitry was a good man, a loyal subject, accustomed to royal intrigue but unable to stomach Philip's wicked attack on the Temple. I suspect he failed to hide that and so he paid the price.'

'And you lay the other deaths at my door.'

Casales showed no contrition, no regret. Nothing nervous except darting eyes, an occasional wetting of the lips. He was a true soldier, coldly calculating the enemy and what might happen.

'Of course I do. Baquelle was easy. The tops of those pavilions were vulnerable, even more so stored in a darkened transept. You, Sir John, cloaked and cowled, could slip into the abbey with sword and dagger. You hacked away at those pegs, what, no more than an inch thick? You would flatter Sir John, giving him the position of honour to the right of the sanctuary. You would ensure that the damaged pavilion would be placed there. If Baquelle survived there'd be other occasions, though the coronation was a unique opportunity. The accidental death of the king's own councillor during such a ceremony! What auguries and omens people could read into that.'

'My pavilion too . . .'

'Nothing but a subtle ploy to include yourself amongst the list of intended victims, as you did in Paris with the help of Marigny. Do you remember? We journeyed back to the city. You'd informed my mistress and myself that you wished to converse with her about England. You always rode beside us, but on that afternoon you moved to the front of the column. This was to help Marigny's hirelings when they launched their mock assault. You killed some of them, acting the role of the brave, chivalrous knight. The rest of the coven escaped. They wouldn't care about the deaths of their comrades;

there'd just be more gold to share out when it was handed over by Marigny's agents.'

Casales bowed his head, shuffling his booted feet.

'Are you a Templar, Demontaigu?' Casales' head came up.

'What I am, sir,' Demontaigu replied, 'is my concern. What you are is being ably proven.'

'I thought as much.' Casales' grim face broke into a smile. 'Yes,' he nodded, 'I thought as much, but,' he leaned forward, 'what about Wenlok's death? I was not at his table.'

'Poisoned!' I replied. 'You gave him the potion shortly after he arrived at the palace and then distanced yourself. It was simply a matter of time. You know a great deal about herbs and potions, don't you, Sir John?'

'And Pourte?'

'Ah well,' I smiled, 'an apparent accident like my death was supposed to be. All we had was the word of Marigny and his creatures that you and Rossaleti were deep in council with them. Well,' I shrugged, 'that's logical. You and Rossaleti were in Marigny's pay so of course he would lie for you, two of his own Secreti, whom he was moving deeper and deeper into the counsels of the English crown. In truth, on the night Pourte died, you and Rossaleti visited him. You struck him from behind and threw him out of that window. I suspect you left by the door, which Rossaleti locked; he then used the ladder brought by Marigny's agents. He climbed down, threw that chain over the wall-bracket, made sure Pourte was dead and rejoined his fellow conspirators.'

'You're sharp, Mathilde!'

'I wish I'd been sharper sooner. You watched me, Sir John, here and in Paris. The other day you knew I'd left the Tower and travelled into the city. How did you know that? I could have gone anywhere. You knew where I went because you were watching and waiting for a fresh opportunity to kill me, just as you nearly did in Paris. You tried to drown me with that barge slipping like a thunderbolt out of the mist. Oh, you may have been with the princess, but you learnt where and when I was going and passed the information on to Marigny's killers. Two good men died that day, Sir John, two more souls who've been crying to God for vengeance.'

Casales glanced sideways as if fearful of Sandewic's coffin.

'Ah yes, my good friend.' I took the knife from my waistband even as Demontaigu came further up the nave. He too had seen Casales move, gather himself as if to attack. My opponent, however, glanced down the nave, sighed deeply and relaxed.

'Old Sandewic,' I continued, 'aching and wound-filled. You sent him potions, nothing serious but enough to disturb his humours. Once the coronation was finished and Baquelle was dead, you decided to clear the board. Rossaleti brought the killing drink, wolfsbane, in a jar similar to those I use. Sandewic wouldn't even suspect.'

'Why should I kill these men?' Casales muttered, his eyes and voice betraying his desperation.

'Why? Well, because of the Enterprise of England.'

Surprise flared in Casales' eyes.

'Oh yes, I know all about that, as does the king. How he would provoke his earls then secretly call on Philip of France for assistance. What *mon seigneur* didn't know, but does now, was that he'd been betrayed. He had invited the foxes into the hen-coop. Philip never intended to assist Edward but aimed to destroy him, weaken England, take Gascony and remove the Plantagenet threat to France once and for all.' I gestured round the chapel. 'Sandewic began to suspect that history was about to repeat itself, that a French fleet would sail up the Thames, occupy the Tower and set up government. No wonder he called this place his Cup of Ghosts. If Philip had his way those ghosts would come back to haunt us all.'

Casales' lips moved as if talking to himself.

'The king now accepts the truth.' I moved the dagger to the other hand and plucked the parchment from the pocket of my robe. 'A *littera plenae potestatis*, Sir John.' I paused to gather my thoughts. 'You killed those men for three reasons: first they were members of the peace party; they counselled Edward, as you well know, to be friends to all and allies to none. They may have seen through Philip's offer and glimpsed the truth. They were restraining voices which had to be silenced for ever. You pretended to be one of them. Second, they were important men. Baquelle and Pourte controlled London, Sandewic the Tower, Wenlok Westminster. Who knows what others might think about such men, and royal councillors, dying in such mysterious circumstances? You hoped Edward would be blamed; that would weaken his cause even further. Baquelle's death particularly was an omen, an augury of what might happen to the king's friends, especially those,' I added, 'who opposed Lord Gaveston.'

Casales bent down, picked up the letter and studied the seal.

'And the third reason?'

'Only you know that. Why an English knight banneret who'd served the English crown so loyally for years should became the canker in the rose. I may suspect the reason. That story you told me about the Battle of Falkirk, where you lost your hand? The old king met you and said, "Better men have lost more."' I paused. 'You could deny all this, but the serjeants of the coif will draw up your indictment, they'll collect the evidence. They are already searching your chambers; that's before the interrogators begin their work. You know the punishment for treason, Casales? To be dragged on a hurdle to Smithfield, to be half hanged, your stomach ripped open, your entrails pulled out, your manhood castrated. To then be cut down and beheaded, your body quartered and pickled and sent to decorate the gates and bridge of London.'

Casales lifted his head, tears brimming. 'The old king,' he replied hoarsely, 'he never really trusted me! Oh, I could see that in his eyes. No, it was worse! He never really liked me. That remark after Falkirk began the rot in my soul. No preferment, not really.'

Casales talked quickly, delivering a litany of grievances nourished over the years, brought to a head by the new king and his attachment to Gaveston.

'I've laboured long and hard.' He glared at me. 'Now I am alone. I was like a priest and the English crown was my God, but for what?' He tossed the letter down. 'Then I was sent to France. Rossaleti drew me in. Marigny and the rest favoured me, promising me fresh years of exalted service once the Enterprise of England was completed, but there was a price to pay.' He swallowed hard. 'Mathilde, you often take a path and realise there is no going back.' He glanced down the nave. 'I'm glad I killed Rossaleti. He drew me in, then, like the coward he was, had his regrets, his scruples.' He blinked. 'Rossaleti could leave whenever he wanted; he was the one person who knew the truth, he had to die. I thought there might be a path back, but . . .' He pulled a face and pointed at me. 'I should have killed you, Mathilde, you are so dangerous. Oh yes,' he grimaced, 'I found out who you really were – de Deyncourt's niece. I remembered you.' He wagged a finger at me. 'A slip of a girl! I told Philip. De Deyncourt was no fool, and the more I discovered about you, the more certain I became that you were a threat. Ah well.' He breathed in noisily. 'I am trapped. I recognise that. I don't want to delight the crowds at the Elms in Smithfield, but I'll not confess, not fully, not in writing.'

I gestured at Sandewic's coffin.

'You'll die here, Sir John.'

I got to my feet, filled Sandewic's cup with claret and added the potion of wolfsbane the royal apothecary had delivered to my chamber the night before. Demontaigu had drawn closer, standing by the coffin, the arbalest cord winched tight. I walked back, waved him away and placed the goblet by Casales' chair.

'Take,' I urged, holding his gaze, 'drink. Death at least will be swift.'

'And if I don't?'

'Demontaigu will wound you so you'll live to die at the Elms. By the way, Casales, he is a Templar priest. He can shrive you. Farewell!'

I walked down the church. Demontaigu stood aside.

'And if he doesn't drink, Mathilde?' he whispered.

'Kill him!'

I walked out into the weak sunlight. Ap Ythel's men were formed in an arc facing the church. I sat down on a wooden bench and looked at Sandewic's Cup of Ghosts. I waited for a while in the cold until the door opened, and Demontaigu came out and handed me the empty goblet.

'He drank.' Demontaigu stared at me strangely. 'He's dead.'

'Then God speed him,' I replied.

Five days later I gathered with my mistress in the central courtyard of Westminster Palace. The French were leaving, but because of the weather, they would not trust themselves to the river but were to ride down to Queenshithe where their war cog was moored. There were farewells and presents, assurances of friendship, kisses of peace; my mistress even made a speech. Marigny, who'd been watching me all the time, pushed his horse closer and leaned down, green eyes bright, red hair peeping out from under his beaver hat.

'Mathilde,' he whispered, taking advantage of the noise in the courtyard.

'Why yes, my lord?'

He pushed his horse a little closer, crossing his arms over the horn of his saddle.

'Very sharp,' he whispered. 'We certainly underestimated you.'

'My lord, you and Sir John Casales are paying me the same compliment!'

'Casales is dead.'

'God's judgement on his crimes.' I gestured at the palace buildings around us. 'My lord the king has decided to call a parliament to treat with his earls.'

'This thing between us, Mathilde.' Marigny fluttered gloved fingers. *'A l'outrance!'*

'My lord.' I blinked prettily and did a mock curtsy. 'I would have it no other way. As you say, *à l'outrance, usque ad mortem.'* I straightened up. 'To the death!'

AUTHORS NOTE

Medieval medicine was not as limited as some of the popular histories would have us believe. Women did play a prominent role as physicians, apothecaries and leeches. (Mathilde is based on a true character, Mathilda of Westminster.) Women's contribution to medieval medicine was only seriously checked when that great misogynist Henry VIII passed an Act of Parliament in 1519. As Kate Campbell Hurd-Mead writes in her *History of Women in Medicine,* 'In the Middle Ages women doctors continued to practise in the midst of wars and epidemics as they always had, for the simple reason that they were needed.'

The events described in this novel are based on the politics of the period. Isabella appears to have had a most unhappy relationship with both her father and her three brothers. She never attended any of their funerals, and as this series will demonstrate, where she could she did terrible damage to her own family. When I studied Isabella for my doctorate at Oxford I received the distinct impression that she was a very beautiful, highly intelligent, strong-willed and manipulative woman. She was one

359

of the few monarchs before 1603 who realised that any war against Scotland was destructive for both countries and of profit to no one.

The events of 1307 are as I have described them. Wenlock, Pourte and Sandewic died within twelve months of Edward II's succession, and their characters, as depicted here, are based on primary sources. Baquelle, according to the *London Chronicle*, was crushed to death during Edward II's coronation which in turn was a disastrous event, poorly organised, the fury of the earls so intense that a clash of arms was only narrowly averted. Edward's II's character, and that of Gaveston, is also based on primary sources. Edward's love for Peter was so deep, that when his favourite was later executed, the Church had to order the king to have his body buried. Gaveston's mother is, in many sources, described as a witch, but that was a common allegation against women whom men feared or resented.

The events of 1307–08 are also faithfully reflected in the primary sources. There is no doubt that Edward II and Philip were involved in some subtle game over the destruction of the Templars (which occurred as I have described it) and the marriage of Isabella. Edward II put up stiff resistance to French demands, then suddenly did a volte-face. My explanation, as contained in this novel, is a strong possibility. Philip entertained the idea of becoming a new Charlemagne. He must have recalled French intervention in English affairs during the minority of

Henry III. He and his coven of ministers, all of whom died violent, mysterious deaths, were certainly a group of sinister men playing for the very highest stakes.

Paul C. Doherty
July 2005
www.paulcdoherty.com